CLASSICAL WHODUNNITS

CLASSICAL WHODUNNITS

Murder and Mystery from Ancient Greece and Rome

Edited by
Mike Ashley

Carroll & Graf Publishers, Inc.
NEW YORK

Carroll & Graf Publishers, Inc.
260 Fifth Avenue
New York
NY 10001

First published in the UK
by Robinson Publishing Ltd 1996

First Carroll & Graf edition 1997

ISBN 0-7867-0418-7

Typeset by Hewer Text Composition Services, Edinburgh
Printed and bound in the United Kingdom

10 9 8 7 6 5 4 3 2 1

CONTENTS

INTRODUCTION
The Ancient Mysteries

This anthology brings together twenty whodunnits set in the great days of ancient Greece and Rome. The stories span over fifteen hundred years from the time of the Trojan War to the aftermath of the fall of the Roman Empire in the West. On our journey through time we will encounter the detective skills of Socrates, Alexander the Great, Archimedes, Brutus, Epictetus, Apollonius of Tyana and, believe it or not, the goddess Aphrodite.

I am delighted that the anthology contains stories by all four leading writers of Roman mysteries – Lindsey Davis, Steven Saylor, John Maddox Roberts and Ron Burns, as well as the man who started it all, Wallace Nichols. Other popular writers of detective and mystery fiction have here turned their minds to the ancient world – Amy Myers, Edward Hoch, Anthony Price, Keith Heller and Theodore Mathieson, whilst others, not normally associated with mystery fiction, have taken up the challenge – Keith Taylor, Brian Stableford, Phyllis Ann Karr and Darrell Schweitzer. Fifteen of the stories are brand new, written especially for this anthology. Only two have appeared in book form before. ·

Some of the authors look behind the curtain of history and present what, for all we know, may be the true story. Perhaps the stories contained here tell us what *really* happened concerning the founding of Rome, the deaths of Alexander the Great and Julius Caesar, and the exile of Ovid. And what happened to Roman law on the day the Roman Empire collapsed?

Here you will find stories set all over the classical world, from Athens to Alexandria, and from Troy to ancient Britain. In all of them you will find ingenious crimes with ingenious solutions. Poisoning was perhaps the most popular means of disposing of an enemy in ancient Rome, so it is not surprising that several of these stories use poison as the weapon, but it is fascinating to see in how many different ways the lethal dose might have been administered and how the crime is solved. One story contains perhaps the most bizarre death of a victim I have ever encountered – in (yes, *in*) a tree.

When I first considered compiling a volume of detective stories set entirely in the ancient world I was a little unsure if there were enough good stories around. I knew there were plenty of good writers, but would they be interested? Maybe they would be too busy? I was staggered at the response. I ended up with more stories than I had ever expected, and this book is far bigger as a result. I must thank all the contributors for their inventiveness, and for meeting such tight deadlines. May I give special thanks to Steven Saylor, who not only wrote a new Gordianus the Finder story but also provided an insightful preface. I'm also delighted to be able to publish the very first story by Claire Griffen. May I also thank my editor, Jan Chamier, for her remarkable patience and help during moments of crisis.

So, with no more ado, let me hand over to Steven Saylor to open the doors on the Golden Age of Crime.

Mike Ashley
April 1996

PREFACE
A Murder, Now and Then . . .

Steven Saylor

---

*Why do you work in passions, lies, devices full
of treachery, love-magics, murder in the home?*
Euripides, *Helen*, 1103–4

Not long ago I wrote a story called 'Murder Myth-Begotten', in
which two modern-day, would-be matricides (any resemblance
to Orestes and Electra being entirely intentional) try to persuade their vulgar, anti-intellectual mother (more like Medea
than Clytaemnestra) to read the Classics. 'They're not dry at
all,' insists the snooty daughter. 'You're always reading those
tawdry murder mysteries and awful true-crime books. Well, the
Greek tragedies are full of murders. That's what they're all about.
Lurid, shocking stuff!'

That may be simplifying things a bit, but it's no coincidence that
the Oxford don who spends his day lecturing about Euripides may
curl up at night with Colin Dexter, or that the insatiable reader of
Agatha Christie may just as avidly devour *I, Claudius*. The inspira-
tional link between the ancient world and the modern mystery story
– the happy circumstance which has produced the stories in this volume – is hardly surprising. Sophocles' *Oedipus the King* can be read
as a stunning whodunnit (in more ways than one!); Cicero's defense
orations tell stories as seamy and gripping as today's courtroom
thrillers; Polyaenus gives us the nuts and bolts of Classical espionage,
revealing how ancient spymasters concealed their secret messages;
and for surefire page-turners, full of sex, murder, politics and poison,
Plutarch and Suetonius set the standards. It seems to me only

reasonable (indeed, irresistible) to draw upon these sources not only for themes and inspiration, but more directly, recasting their stories for modern readers in the form of the modern murder mystery.

Reading Umberto Eco's *The Name of the Rose* first convinced me that the combination of historical and mystery fiction could be sublime; reading Cicero's defense of Sextus Roscius, a man accused of murdering his father, inspired me to try my own hand at the game with my first novel, *Roman Blood*. I originally intended to make Cicero himself the narrator, but the more I got to know him, the less I savored the idea of spending twenty-four hours a day with such a prig – and so my detective-hero, Gordianus the Finder, came into being. Reading between the lines of Cicero's oration, researching the era, placing the trial in its political context, and walking with Gordianus down the mean streets of Rome, circa 80 BC, I stumbled upon an insidious conspiracy that spanned all levels of society and ultimately reached to the highest circles of power. Snooping through the musty stacks of the San Francisco Public Library and rushing home to pound the keys of my Macintosh, I often felt as exhilarated and edgy as a hero in a John Grisham thriller, carrying dangerous (albeit 2,000-year-old) secrets in my head.

And there you have the great pleasure of writing the historical mystery: the detective work. You begin with a crime. You research (investigate) the long-ago scene, interrogate the long-dead witnesses, evaluate the suspects and their motives. One clue leads to another. You backtrack; in a book opened by chance, you come across a name that's vaguely familiar and suddenly realize how it fits in, and with a thrill you discover a whole new set of suspicious circumstances. You start to get so close to the truth that you can almost taste it . . .

All historical researchers know this excitement of discovering the past, but for the researcher with the goal of constructing a murder mystery, the game is especially complex and rewarding. This is because of the built-in Aristotelian closure of the genre: the murder mystery, by definition, must have a beginning, middle, and end. The research – the detective work – is never an end in itself, but a search for the unique resolution that will restore order and meaning to a universe thrown out of kilter by crime.

Such a pursuit would have been understood intuitively, I think, by our old friends, the ancient Greeks and Romans. They knew what hubris was and where it inevitably led. They understood the agency of Nemesis. Yet they realized, too, that guilt and innocence are seldom simple matters, and they doggedly explored, in their laws as in their stories, all the possible, mysterious permutations of justice, retribution and revenge.

APHRODITE'S
TROJAN HORSE
(*or* Murder on Mount Ida)

Amy Myers

Amy Myers should need no introduction to devotees of historical mysteries. Her novels about the Victorian cordon bleu chef and solver of mysteries, Auguste Didier, which began with Murder in Pug's Parlour *(1986), are immensely popular. But her presence in a volume of classical mysteries may seem a little surprising. Amy, however, was keen to bring her special skills to the ancient world, particularly the time when history became legend. She takes us back to the dawn of the ancient Greek world, to the time when men were heroes and heroes were gods (or was it the other way round?) – to the time of the Trojan War. And though our sleuth is none other than the goddess Aphrodite, don't imagine Amy pulls any supernatural punches. She abides by the rules. Though her tongue remains firmly in her cheek throughout.*

$\backsim$

'Murder? *Me*? You accuse me falsely, O Cow-Faced Lady of the Golden Throne.' (Goodness knows why Hera always considers this appellation such a compliment.)

I burst into tears with one of my splendid hyacinth-blue orbs carefully on Father – sorry, Great Zeus the Thunderer, ruler of the heavens. You can never be sure which way Father is going to rumble; he is terrified of Cow-Faced Lady, otherwise known as his wife.

I had been rudely summoned to a full council of the gods in the Hall of the Golden Floor just when I was anointing my golden body with a most delightful oil of violets. There they all were, the happy family: Pallas Athene, Ares, Apollo, Artemis, Hephaestus, Hermes, Dionysus, even Uncle Poseidon had turned up for the occasion, not to mention every nymph and naiad who could scramble into her gauze knick-knacks in time. And I, Aphrodite, goddess of laughter and love, was promptly not only accused but apparently convicted. Father cleared his throat, his sable brows twitching, and decided to thunder a little. Coward. 'Hera has justification, daughter. A dead body had been found and one of my thunderbolts is missing.'

'Hera's always been jealous of me, just because I'm Dione's daughter, not hers.' My mother, the goddess of moisture, was a *bête noire* of Hera's, just like Thetis, Europa, Leda and all the other thousands of ladies whom Zeus had favoured with his own private thunderbolt.

'Is that why you're always weeping, O laughter-loving Aphrodite?' enquired the Poisoned Dart of the Flashing Helmet, otherwise known as Pallas Athene. Like Hera, she thought those dull long-haired Greeks were the sacrificial sheep's whiskers, just because when she, Hera and I paraded our charms for Paris of Troy on Mount Ida, he awarded the Golden Apple Prize for beauty to me. Well, *naturally*. How was I to know when I told him he could have of Helen, the fairest woman in all the world, in exchange, that it would start the Trojan War, which after nearly ten years was still raging? We may be immortal, up here on Olympus, but we're not omniscient, nor omnipotent, not even the Thunderer himself, though he likes to pretend he is. He may be sovereign administrator for Destiny, but he can't decide it, and he does tend to nod off from time to time.

I ignored her. Just wait till she pleaded for my *kestos* next time, my magic girdle in which my immortal aphrodisiac powers reside. She needed it. These Amazonian types couldn't seduce a centaur without it. It all comes of her having leapt out of Zeus' head fully armed instead of being conceived in the usual far more interesting manner which is my domain.

'But why me?' I wailed.

The Mighty Son of Cronos lost patience with me; his nectar must have been off this morning. 'Because the blasted body belongs to Prince Anchises,' Zeus thundered. 'What else can we think?'

I put my hands over my shell-like ears. I was truly shocked. 'But I wouldn't kill *Anchises*.' (Give me half a chance!) 'He is the father of my beloved son.'

'Which one?' enquired my husband Hephaestus, with a rare flash of what passed for wit with him. We have no children, the god of the forge being too hot to handle. I ignored him too. I usually do.

'Aphrodite,' Father said more kindly. 'You've been threatening to punish Anchises ever since you heard he'd been boasting about his relationship with you. Now his body has been found on Mount Ida. Near *my* shrine,' he added crossly.

Mount Ida! The very place where Anchises and I had consecrated our love – he had looked so sweet lying there asleep with that natty little leather apron awry exposing a truly princelike appendage. He was serving the usual shepherd's apprenticeship obligatory for Trojan princes (even the junior line to which he belonged), a year out to see how other folks lived. I just had to swoop on him there and then. Darling pious Aeneas was the result, and Anchises never let anyone forget it.

'But, Mighty Zeus, I didn't touch your thunderbolt.'

'The thunderbolt store in the Chamber of the Golden Bed was rifled.'

'But there is no proof I did it.'

'There is.' The sable brows looked even blacker, and my peerless knees began to tremble. 'All the gods with keys, save you, have sworn that they were all occupied in" – Zeus paused – "amorous nocturnal occupations. I've already decided only you could have stolen the thunderbolt.'

I pleaded with him, but this time all my beauty and winning ways failed to move him. It was just my bad luck that this was the one day in a thousand when he didn't need the help of my girdle to carry out his busy agenda.

Then he delivered his verdict: 'I sentence you to be expelled from Olympus, and thrown down to my brother Hades in the Underworld.'

'You can't do that.' I was horrorstricken. 'They only eat pomegranate seeds down there, and they wear the most *dull* clothes. Who's going to do my hair?' I'd only just got the Graces trained to curl my tresses properly over the shoulders – Thalia, I think (otherwise known as Good Cheer. She's always giggling anyway).

It was then I had my first bright idea. There's always been a rumour flying around that just because I'm beautiful, and loving, and kind, I haven't a brain in my head. What happened now was to disprove all that for ever.

'I claim the right to see the body. I wish to gaze once more upon the body of my love before it is swallowed by the funeral pyre,'

I intoned as dolorously as I could. Even now I can't imagine why this brainwave struck me, but it was to save me from a fate of immortal death.

Zeus coughed, and ostentatiously looked round his 'council', though he takes all the decisions. 'I see no reason why not,' he ventured. There's courage for you!

'She must be guarded,' snapped Hera.

'I'll send Paean with her. A medical man might be useful.'

'He's a fatuous old fool. She'll twist him round her slippery body,' quoth the Queen of the Sour Grapes, Pallas Athene, of the gods' physician. Who'd have sisters – well, half-sisters?

'Ares, you go too,' Zeus barked.

I tried not to look too overjoyed. I'd always fancied the god of war. At least he is a real man, not a Hephaestus, roaring around like an ox in a nectar-cup shop, or mooning over nymphs like sneaky Sun God Apollo.

Ares stepped to my side with alacrity, I was pleased to see.

'Do you wish to chain me?' I asked in a low seductive voice.

He turned red. 'I don't usually, not the first time,' he stuttered.

One-track minds these gods! Really, what could he have thought I meant? I arched my body towards him, aware that my wondrous breasts were shimmering sensuously through my diaphanous gown.

'Can we take the golden chariot, Mighty Zeus?' I asked winningly. No one seems to credit that we goddesses can get tired winging through the air, on our own two feet as it were, and Olympus is some way from Ida.

Zeus hesitated, obviously noticing Queen Hera's glare. Surely it wasn't her day for visiting Grandma Rhea? 'In the interests of speed, yes.'

Splendid. I'd pick up darling Aeneas on the way, and hope Zeus was safely tucked up in bed with Cow-Faced Lady so that he didn't spot this diversion from his orders.

I do dislike dead bodies, particularly of my former lovers. Today, however, my future was at stake. Odd that the body was on Mount Ida, almost exactly in the place where Anchises and I had made love. And ever afterwards he'd had the nerve to boast about bedding a goddess! I summoned up my courage and approached the body where it lay on the ground under an olive tree, blackened to the point of unrecognizability, but indisputably wearing the remains of clothes of the royal house of Sacred Troy. The emblem of the crane was quite unmistakable; what's more, there was only one crane, and

King Priam's brood had two. That meant it was Aeneas or Anchises. And as my beloved son was at my side . . .

Aeneas promptly burst into tears. 'Father,' he wailed.

To tell you the truth, I find Aeneas rather dull. I get quite worried about him; he's plumpish, shortish, not much of a fighter, a little pompous, and he seems to have no interest in women whatsoever, and that includes his wife, Creusa. Why can't he be more like his half-brother, Eros? I have lectured him on it many times, but he talks nothing but politics and the need to found nations. I blame his father. He'd always borne a grudge because he was from the junior branch of the family. I even offered Aeneas the most beautiful – sorry, second most beautiful after Helen – woman in the world, but no.

I felt I had better make a show of sorrow, so I flung myself over Anchises' body and wept in a most convincing manner, while Aeneas sobbed on at my side.

'Darling Paean,' I said tremulously, as soon as I dared recover from my grief, 'are you sure that's a thunderbolt strike? Couldn't he have burned himself some other way?'

Paean rather reluctantly took a closer look at the body. He's past it, but what can you do? He's got a job for immortality.

I averted my eyes from the blackened face and arms – I'm always a leg lady anyway – so I concentrated on the way they peeped out from under the ducky little short apron, and tried to recall the desire I had once felt for him. Instead I recalled my own, very present, plight.

'He's under a tree,' I observed hopefully to Paean. 'Perhaps he was accidentally struck by lightning.'

'Zeus rules all thunder and lightning.'

I glared at him. Silly old fool. Perhaps I'd have to sleep with him. Fortunately I was to be spared this ordeal. A new lease of immortality now seemed to overcome Paean as he developed a morbid interest in the blackened corpse. He took various nasty instruments out of his golden leather case, and carried out investigations which I preferred not to watch. At last, he staggered to his feet: 'There's no evidence of thunderbolt blackening to his air passages, and there are no signs of hyperaemia.'

I didn't want a long lecture – Zeus made me sit through one by Aesculapius once in an attempt to educate me – so I asked hastily: 'And what does that mean?'

'It means Anchises could well have been dead before the thunderbolt struck. Did you notice?' he asked me brightly.

I think I would have done, I was tempted to reply, but refrained. It does not do to be too laughter-loving at the older gods.

At that moment, due no doubt to Paean's investigations, the leather apron, partly burned away, slipped a little further, and the belly I had once admired so intimately was in view. Then I let out a shriek.

'This isn't Anchises!'

'Not now. His soul has left us, Mother.' Aeneas heaved again.

'It isn't his body,' I insisted. 'You can rejoice, my son.' (Even if I had mixed feelings. I could cheerfully have wished Anchises in Hades, but I wasn't going to share this with Aeneas.) 'I remember Anchises' body quite distinctly. It was flawless. Look at that.'

Gods and man stared down at a huge strawberry-shaped birthmark on the side of the belly which the thunderbolt had not affected.

'Aeneas, you must know he has no birthmark. You bathe with him, don't you?'

'Then my father lives,' Aeneas exclaimed joyfully.

'Apparently without his clothes,' I pointed out brightly. 'How typical.'

'My father lives.' So dull, Aeneas. It takes time for things to sink in. 'Thanks be to Zeus.'

'And thanks be to your mother,' I added pointedly.

Then Paean suddenly got the professional bit between his teeth. 'Who is it, if not Anchises?' He seemed to be addressing *me*.

'Paean, I have seen many mortals in the nude, not to mention gods, in the course of my profession, but even I am unable to identify a man by a birthmark.'

Ares decided to weigh in. 'Don't you know there's a war on?' he pointed out reprovingly. 'I've been running it. Of course there are dead bodies lying around. Someone wanted us to think they'd killed Anchises.'

'But why should the Greeks bring the body *here* if they wished to pretend it was my father?' Aeneas asked, having got over his awe at having three gods to chat with.

'To frame me,' I cried indignantly. I don't mind being framed by the likes of Botticelli, but I draw the line at Pallas Athene playing tricks like this.

'With Anchises' assistance?' Paean asked doubtfully. 'How did they get his clothes?'

'You are clever, Paean,' Ares said approvingly. (You could have fooled me.) 'Unless they've killed him too.'

'Ay, me, alack,' was all my son could offer.

No one took any notice, so he said it again somewhat louder. 'When you told me, Gracious Mother, the body of my father had been found, I feared the Greeks had captured and slaughtered him.'

'Thank you, my son.' I was surprised and grateful that at least he had not blamed me.

'Now I suspect it is a dastardly plan by the House of Priam.'

I was startled. Old King Priam of Troy is waging the war so incompetently, he appears to have no plans at all, dastardly or not.

'Mother, Great King Priam dreads a rising against him in Troy, because there is still no end to this war in sight; he believes any such rising would unite under my father Anchises. My father and I, loyal as we are, have feared for our lives. Now I know my father lives, I am happy again.' He cried to prove it.

'Oh, my beloved son.' All my few maternal instincts came to the fore. 'Do you not see? The House of Priam would not dare kill Anchises; they would incur Zeus' wrath.' I was in no doubt of this. Father thinks this war is his own private chessboard and gets very upset if a pawn is removed without his say-so. Ares, god of war, is merely around to roar a little, in Father's view.

'And my wrath also,' Ares put in indignantly. 'It might affect my war.'

'True.' I fluttered my eyelashes at him, but for once my mind was elsewhere. 'But do you not see, if they buried this stranger as Anchises, they would achieve the same object without offending the mighty gods?' Apart from me, I thought crossly.

'Let's bury the body here,' Ares rumbled eagerly. 'Then they'll be thwarted.'

'Hold on, I've been thinking,' I said quickly, as Paean appeared about to agree. 'Zeus will throw me to Hades if I don't come back with some evidence of who this man was.' Blood drained from my rosy-hued cheeks. 'I need that body.'

'I can't take it to Olympus,' Paean decreed, pompous idiot. 'It's dead. It would be against all the rules. I'd have to get a special dispensation from Hades.'

I made an immediate decision. 'Then I shall take the body to Troy myself and demand to know who did this terrible deed.'

'If you're right,' Aeneas said slowly, 'then it must be King Priam himself or more likely one of his sons. Great Hector of the Flashing Armour is the most likely. Or sly Helenus, Seer of the Second Sight. Or, of course, Paris.'

I bristled. '*Paris?*' I asked dangerously.

Belatedly my son remembered I was a goddess, fell to his knees, and paid a few overdue obeisances. 'He is a good and honest prince,' he conceded hastily, 'but much under the influence of Hector, Helenus and Helen.'

I forgave him. I've always been ambivalent about Helen. 'Very well. I will come to Troy, demand to know which of them is responsible, and then make full report to Olympus.'

'You will terrify them into silence with your goddess aura.'

'That's true.' I thought for a moment. Just as I did so, I thought I saw a girl watching us from the shelter of some trees; it was a face that rang a bell with me, but I couldn't place it. Then she was gone. But it put an idea in my mind. 'I'll come in disguise.' One power we immortals do have is the ability to take on any disguise we like, provided it's mortal. 'I'll come as a sixteen-year-old vestal virgin.'

Ares shouted with laughter, and I began to change my mind about his desirability. 'In Troy?'

'Why not come as Hecuba?' my son suggested.

'That old hag?' Priam's consort was as ancient as he was.

'She is the queen as well as wife and mother.'

Reluctantly I saw some sense in this. If anyone could strike fear into my Trojan heroes, it was her.

I left Aeneas to struggle back across the plain with the body slung across his horse's saddle. Ares had obligingly magicked one up from a local farm, since I thought Father might notice if his chariot came back minus one horse. It was a night's journey to Troy from Mount Ida, and apart from ensuring that Aeneas wasn't slaughtered by the Greek army en route, it gave me time to make my report to Zeus. I found him in the Ambrosia Room, it being about time for supper. The sounds of Apollo strumming on that awful lyre drifted in from the Room of the Marble Columns. Only Hebe, the Bearer of the Mighty Cup, was flitting around in the dining chamber pouring nectar and she doesn't count, so I told Zeus my news immediately.

'Not Anchises? Then where the devil is he? I've seen nothing of him.'

'That, Father, is what I propose to find out.'

He gave me a suspicious look. 'Not going to bump him off, are you? I still haven't found that thunderbolt.'

'Of course not. How could I? I loved him once,' I said virtuously. Several times, actually.

'Two days, and then I want a full statement of what happened. *And* proof. I must say, Aphrodite, you're quite a girl,' he added approvingly. 'I never thought you had it in you. Of course, you're my daughter.'

'I have both your brains and beauty, Father,' I oozed.

Ten minutes later I was on my way, having snatched only the merest mouthful of ambrosia from the kitchens en route.

'Great Queen, Wise Hecuba, welcome!'

'Mighty King Priam, honoured husband, greetings.' What a bore, I thought. Suppose he kissed me? I hadn't thought to investigate their marital relations before I shot in.

I had materialized inside the door of his council chamber just in time. Trumpets were sounding in the audience chamber to announce Aeneas' arrival. Hecuba herself, I had observed, was over having a woman's chat with her daughter Cassandra at the temple. She'd be hours; Cassandra is not only a bore when she pontificates about the future, she's a very slow bore.

I swept out in Priam's waddling wake (longing to kick his *chiton*-clad bottom), having already sent slaves to fetch Hector, Helenus and – if he could be prised out of Helen's bed – Paris. Aeneas was right, those were the three of Mighty Priam's mighty large brood who were the obvious suspects. Fortunately they didn't have far to come. Priam had adapted his palace into about fifty rather tasteful apartments for his children, their families, and the lesser royals. The only clever thing he'd ever thought of, keeping everyone under his ageing eye.

We lined ourselves up in the royal pecking order down the raised steps of the chamber; Priam at the front, me slightly behind him, winking at Aeneas, then Mighty Hector of the Solid Muscle Body, Helenus of the Slim Sexy one, and Paris, once my darling boy, now rather going to seed. One of them, I told myself, was a murderer, and I was going to find out who.

'I demand justice, O King.' Aeneas draped the body tastefully at his feet.

Priam did a good imitation of a startled monarch. 'The Prince Anchises!'

'His clothes only. A stranger lies within them.'

'Then why bother us with it?' Helenus piped up.

I always knew he was the intelligent one of the family.

Aeneas turned wounded eyes towards him, as he trotted out the line I'd suggested to him. 'The corpse was found on Mount Ida near to the shrine of Mighty Zeus, Son of Cronos. He will rise up in anger against Troy if he is not appeased and grant his favour to the Achaeans.' (The latter are the Greeks to you and me, but I told you Aeneas was a little pompous.)

Hector began to display more interest. 'Are you sure it's not your father?' he asked rather wistfully.

'I am,' my son replied with some dignity. 'I'm sorry if you're disappointed.'

Hector drew a dagger from his belt. 'Meet me in combat, Prince Aeneas. Now.'

'It's the Greeks you're supposed to meet in combat,' Priam pointed out irritably. You can see why he thinks he's a great king.

Hector's reply was drowned by the trumpets blaring out again, a thing they did with monotonous regularity. Could it be Anchises himself, I wondered, come to my aid? For once I'd be glad to see him. Then I realized. All those oohs and aahs in the corridor outside, together with the heady cloud of perfume already discernible advancing between the marble columns could mean only one thing: the face that launched a thousand ships was on her way, Helen of Troy. Or, strictly speaking, of Sparta, once wife of King Menelaus and one of my biggest mistakes.

In she swept, while we all gave the routine gasp at her beauty; golden tresses shimmered, silver diadems glinted, wondrous breasts poked demurely out under her wrap-around silk gown. She opened her limpid blue, blue eyes upon me and made straight for me. 'Great Mother,' she began.

I tried to listen patiently, but it was hard. In giving Paris the most beautiful woman in the world I had been extremely self-sacrificing, for I fancied him myself, and since Helen came on the scene he has had eyes for no one else. She is beautiful, I have to admit that, and she is also clever, which tends to make her, among the simpler, pleasure-loving Trojans, very short-tempered. Coy shyness is her retail stock-in-trade, but back there in the warehouse she wholesales in sulkiness spiced with shrew's blood. Now the years are passing, sullenness is adding little lines that all the bees' cream in Assyria won't eradicate. I must remember I am immortal, and try to be tolerant, ho-ho!

'This is no place for you, darling,' Paris said solicitously – like an infatuated youth, though he's been bedding her for ten years.

'Who's that?' she asked idly, seeing the burnt corpse on the ground at Priam's feet.

'An unknown stranger, darling.'

'With a huge strawberry birthmark on his belly,' I added helpfully, forgetting Hecuba hadn't had the intimate privileges I had.

There was a scream, and a thud. Helen had fainted.

*   *   *

Why were they all looking at me? Did they think I had suddenly struck her with a thunderbolt? I only wished I had the courage. Then I realized I was not Aphrodite, goddess of love, at the moment; I was Queen Hecuba, the only woman (give or take half a dozen slaves) present. I was therefore in a superb position to learn the truth, and I certainly needed to if I was going to escape having to dress in the dark of the Underworld for ever and ever. I don't know King Hades well, but I am pretty sure he would not allow me out to have fillets of hyacinths and pearls wound into my hair by Mesdames Aglaia, Euphrosyne and Thalia, better known as the Three Graces. Their names roughly translate as Magnificence, Laughter, and Jolly Good Cheer, none of which is highly rated by Hades, I understand. Nor was I at all certain I could continue to practise my profession there. Hades' attendants have the reputation of being rather quiet, sombre young men with pale bodies and the ugliest clothes.

I therefore rushed with great concern to my daughter-in-law. 'Come, my child,' I crooned, bending my craggy face close to hers, and then throwing a beaker of wine over the latter with great satisfaction. Her eyes opened without any great affection for me. 'Come with me to my chamber,' I said invitingly, 'so that I may tend you.'

I might have known Paris would cause trouble. 'I'm coming too,' he announced. 'Anything that affects Helen affects me.'

I looked for support from Beefy Hector, Handsome Helenus, or my own husband. I might have known Priam wouldn't support me. He's a descendant of Zeus too, but the brains and courage were in short supply by the time they reached him. So there was no help for it. I went up very close to Paris and let him sense my aura. Strictly speaking, only Apollo is allowed to do this, but desperate times call for desperate remedies. I grinned with my toothless old woman's smile, and I thought he was going to faint too.

'Leave this to me, Paris,' I cooed.

He was only too happy to do so. For some reason he associates me with trouble, which is most unfair. I didn't force him to leave Oenone, the nymph who was his first love, for Helen. I merely offered him the most beautiful woman in the world; he didn't have to take her. We gods can't take all the blame. Oenone! Now I remembered who that girl was I'd seen on Mount Ida. She still lives there, in a shepherd's hut, so that she can moon over her lost love, and is continually mixing potions designed to make him fall in love with her again. Silly child. I'm the only one who could achieve that with my magic girdle. She doesn't stand a chance beside Helen.

Once in the chamber, Helen pretended to faint again by closing her eyes and drooping herself over a leather couch. I stayed right there, digging my fingernails accidentally into her. 'Tell me sweet child, who he was. I shan't go away.'

No answer.

'Who was that man?' I asked more sharply, digging harder.

She opened her large blue eyes and gazed straight at me, so I knew she was going to lie. 'He's a melon-seller in the market. I see him there from the walls when I take my walk.'

'And can you see his bare belly from the walls, sweet child?'

She decided to faint again, so I decided to come the heavy matriarch.

'Daughter of Zeus,' I began (I suppose that makes her a kind of sister to me, ugh!) 'is it not enough that you have brought this war upon our innocent heads by leaving your husband, Menelaus? Must you now bring shame upon us too?'

This stirring appeal had no effect.

'I shall find out who the man was,' I told her conversationally, 'and then I shall tell Paris. Now Hector, as you know, doesn't like anyone upsetting Paris, especially mere women. There's strong support in Troy for making peace with the Greeks, and so if I could think of a good reason for my husband Mighty Priam to throw you out of Troy, it might be very helpful.'

She paled, and I knew I was home and dry.

I cooed a little. 'Tell me the truth, beauteous Helen, and this shall be kept between ourselves. If you refuse, I shall make a convincing story about your unfaithfulness with a marketman and demand my son's vengeance on you.'

'Very well,' she agreed sullenly. 'But promise by Artemis that you won't tell.'

I've nothing against the goddess of the chase even though, not having caught anyone, she's still a virgin, so I did so, hoping Artemis was having a nap and couldn't check on who I was.

'It's Marmedes.' Helen squinted at me to see how I was taking it.

For a moment it didn't register, but when it did . . .

'He's a *Greek*,' I shrieked. 'And isn't he Chief of Staff to Diomedes?' The immortal goddess nearly exploded out of Hecuba's shape to put in a chit for an authorized thunderbolt straight away.

Diomedes, King of Argos, was the villain who had dared to wound a goddess! *Me!* This is strictly against the rules, but Pallas Athene, bless her welded iron chastity belt, had given him special dispensation. All because I swept into the battle to rescue my darling son Aeneas from death at Diomedes' hands. What mother would do otherwise? And just for that he wounded me in my hand, so that some of the immortal ichor flowed and it *hurt* and I had to run weeping to Paean for a *pharmaka* to cure it.

And here was Helen, who owed me everything, having it off (I was quite sure) with his Chief of Staff. I had to step carefully, however, remembering I was Hecuba.

'And what is a Greek doing in Troy? You, daughter-in-law, were consorting with a spy?'

'Oh, *no*!'

'He had come to steal you back for Menelaus?'

'No. He rather fancies me himself. In fact, we are in love,' she cried recklessly. 'Or were.' She cried anew, making her eyes red, so I knew she meant it.

'*Love?*' I said incredulously. 'Paris is supposed to be your one and only true love – that's what this whole war is about.'

'I've been here for ten years,' she pointed out crossly. 'Surely I can see one of my own countrymen occasionally?'

'How occasionally?'

'Only three times a week,' she told me complacently. 'He disguised himself as a melon-seller and came in at the Scaean Gate at nine o'sundial when it is opened for the marketmen to enter. At noon I went for my walk along the walls, and we met in one of the tower guardhouses.'

'Did the guards notice?' I enquired sarcastically.

'There is only one guard, for the tower looks out on the open plain, not towards the Greek encampment. We bribed him. I left Marmedes at four, and came back to meet Paris after his councils of war with your honoured husband.'

'Husband?' I repeated, thinking for a moment she meant Hephaestus.

'I'm sorry, Great Queen. Mighty Priam, King of Troy.' She mistook my bewilderment for disapproval, luckily. 'Marmedes then returned to the market and left with the other stall-holders at dusk.'

'And when did you last see this magnificent specimen of manhood?'

'Two days ago. I left the tower as usual at four, and was expecting to see him at noon today. And now he's out there, *dead*.'

'And in Anchises' clothes,' I pointed out. 'Marmedes was a Greek and a spy. Possibly a murderer, who killed Anchises and was then killed himself.'

'So it hardly seems worth investigating,' Helen informed me hopefully.

That's my daughter-in-law, or rather Hecuba's. Love flies out
the window when her own rosy-hued skin is threatened. She
wasn't getting off so easily. *My* rosy-hued skin was of far more
importance.

'Daughter, a human life has been taken. And where is Anchises?
Marmedes' murderer may know. We must hunt him down.'

'Marmedes was a dear. He wouldn't even kill a scorpion, let
alone Anchises.'

'Who else knew of your trysts besides the guard?'

'I told no one.'

'Paris never suspected?'

'He would never dream I could look at anyone other than him.'
She wriggled complacently.

I let this pass. 'And if he did?'

'He would kill him, or ask Hector to do it for him – oh!' She
exclaimed at her own words, but I thought she had seen someone
outside. Looking out, I could see, to my horror, the old queen
herself staggering back towards the palace after her session with
Cassandra at the Temple of Athene. Fat lot of use offering good
goats at her shrine. A more dedicated Greek supporter I have yet
to see, and if she found out that the corpse on Ida was not a Trojan
but Marmedes, she'd be after my ichor.

I quickly withdrew from my chamber on the pretext of an old
woman's call of nature – how fortunate we immortals are not to have
to worry about such matters, though I've often wondered where all
that nectar goes – and whisked my bright blue dress away, just as
Hecuba clad in orange swept in. I grinned to myself. Let the ladies
sort it out. I had more important ambrosia to fry.

I removed myself quickly to Aeneas' own house within the palace
complex, where his precocious young son Iulus was marching
around with a *himation* wrapped round his shoulders, and Aeneas'
ceremonial large-brimmed hat, pretending to be Priam. I am not fond
of my grandson and could not have swept in at a more convenient
moment. 'You mock my husband, Iulus?'

'Great Queen.' Aeneas went bright red, clipped Iulus round the
ears, and abased himself.

'Never mind,' I told him graciously, 'I need your help,
Aeneas.'

I saw his face change, as he realized it was still me.

'We are going to interview a guard. The corpse was Helen's
lover, a Greek, Chief of Staff to Diomedes. You remember him?'

He flushed; he is always so ridiculously sensitive about being
rescued from death in battle by his mother.

'He was a spy – here?' he growled.

'He disguised himself as one of the market-sellers, and was in the habit of meeting Helen from noon to four in one of the guardhouses. I am quite sure Helen was betrayed by the guard to someone. Once he tells us who it was, we have our murderer.'

'Why don't you leave this to me, mother? It is my duty as a son to find out what has happened to my honoured father.'

'Because –' I broke off. This was confidential Olympus business. Instead I said, 'It is known that I support Troy in this war. If Troy is not to fall, then this murderer must be found.'

'Troy fall?' He smote his chest. 'Zeus defend us.'

'It's no use asking the impossible,' I replied shortly. 'Hera is browbeating him all the time to help her support the Greeks. This business must be settled quickly, or it's curtains for Troy.'

And for Aphrodite, I thought with a shiver of fear as we walked around the walls. I was nevertheless rather enjoying masquerading as a mortal, as a queen anyway. It's not much fun masquerading as a slave – so difficult to have any choice of lovers.

We reached the guardhouse Helen had described and tried to enter the tower room. It was locked. Aeneas threw himself valiantly against the door, hurting himself needlessly. Goddesses do have their uses. I whisked us both inside, only to find that the guard wasn't going to be telling us anything. He was dead, slumped over the table, the remains of a meal strewn around. I have seldom been more frustrated. I even considered a quick trip down to the River Styx to have a word with Charon before the corpse crossed the river. A glance at the corpse, however, told me he had been dead too long. He was already over the river, past Cerberus and safely in Hades. Somebody had thoughtfully placed his boat fare, two coins, in his mouth, and Charon is such a greedy old so-and-so he doesn't always wait for the body to be buried before he grabs his ill-gotten gains.

'Poisoned,' said Aeneas grimly. 'Henbane or atropine probably. There's a thriving black market in it.'

'It's terrible,' I said indignantly. 'I remember this poor guard.' I did indeed. Only two years ago I decided to requite his love for a young priestess, and Pallas Athene had stomped around in a temper for days.

'Poor man, indeed. I wonder which of them it was?'

'Hector, Paris, Helenus or Priam,' I mused. 'Marmedes was dressed in Anchises' clothes. How could that happen, Aeneas?' I was getting worried, for it was getting on for afternoon nectar time and Zeus would be expecting an interim report from me.

'Only those with houses within the royal complex could get hold
of them. If Father suspected a plan was afoot to kill him, he might well
have escaped and be in hiding. I believe they dressed this stranger in
his clothes, so that the Trojans should think him dead. As I suggested
earlier, Mother,' he said reproachfully, as if I were a birdbrain.

It was then that I had my second brilliant idea.

'Hail, Mighty Zeus, Son of –'

'Where the Hades have you been, Aphrodite? I've had both Iris
and Hermes out looking for you. Found out whose that body is
yet?' Father was stomping angrily around the Hall of the Marble
Columns.

'Helen, your daughter,' I said meaningfully, 'has identified
him as Diomedes' Chief of Staff.' Father chortled, anger suddenly
evaporated. 'And her lover.'

He stopped chortling and roared again instead. 'How can the
Greeks sack Troy to regain Helen if she's just taken a Greek lover?
This is your doing, Aphrodite.'

'*Me?*'

Even he realized he was being unjust and patted me absent-
mindedly. 'There, there, just arrange to lead that Egyptian shepherd-
girl to me with your girdle and we'll say no more about it.'

'Thank you, Great Zeus,' I muttered savagely.

'But you're still going to Hades till you find out exactly what
happened.'

'I have!' I cried hastily, just as my third brainwave blessed me.
'The vital question is why Marmedes should be dressed in Anchises'
clothes. He must have been killed by someone who had easy access
within the palace complex both to them and to Anchises. To have
Anchises thought dead would be very handy for the House of
Priam. What, you will ask,' – I was getting quite carried away
– 'became of the Greek's clothes? I will tell you. *Anchises* is
wearing them – he's been despatched by Priam as a spy into the
Greek camp.'

Unfortunately I had not reckoned on the effect this would have
on Father. The famous sable brows shot up to the Mighty Hairline.
'But he might learn the Greek plans!'

I hastily backtracked. 'Not a chance. Aeneas inherited his lack
of brains from somebody, you know.'

He seemed about to say something, but changed his mind. 'Find
Anchises –'

'But you can do that,' I said indignantly. 'You're all-seeing Zeus
whenever you want to be.'

'I promised Hera an evening in the Golden Bed,' he muttered. 'I deserve *some* free time.'

My heart sank. In my view, chasing every mortal woman who hasn't got a squint and three legs, is not an occupation. 'Very well, I'll do it,' I said bravely.

'And while you're about it, find out which of those blasted Trojans decided they could run the war better than me!'

Was it Paris of the once golden skin, Helenus of the slim sexy body, flashing-armoured Hector, or mighty Priam himself? I sank onto my azure silken-sheeted bed and thought about my plan of action. How was I to proceed? I couldn't keep impersonating Hecuba, and to go as my goddess self would terrify everyone into silence, innocent or guilty. Idly I ran my hand over the sheets – then I knew exactly how to get Helenus' story out of him – through my own charms. So I *could* go as myself.

I quickly had the Graces run me up a nice little number in lilac and then dress my hair with hyacinths to match my eyes with darling little irises in between. I perfumed my body with rose oil, stretched sensuously, and peered down to earth. I concentrated all my powers on Helenus to see what he was doing. (This sort of thing takes it out of us, so we can't do it too often.)

He was in the baths. I had wondered about Helenus' body for some time – and I was right. Delicious. I promptly magicked his slaves away.

'Where are you?' he yelled to them, cross at having to towel his magnificent bronzed body himself.

'Here I am,' I called in a low husky voice, gracefully materializing with my aura circulating round him madly. He was so overwhelmed by my beauty he tried to seek the nearest way out. Silly boy. I led him to a couch and laid him down, sat at his side and finished the towelling for him, gently, slowly, tantalizingly. By the time I had finished we were both more than ready for what was to come, and he had quite forgotten his awe of being clasped in a goddess's arms. He was so good a lover that I almost considered binding him with my girdle so that he would fall in love with me, but decided against it. It might be a hindrance in my investigation. As he lay in my arms afterwards, I cooed gently at him:

'Where do you spend your afternoons, Helenus?'

'My lips are sealed,' he murmured sleepily.

It must be a woman. 'Then unseal them, dearest, and tell me where you were three afternoons ago.'

'Oh, great goddess, thou knowest all without my telling.'

'That is a misconception,' I replied crossly. 'We can't watch everything at once.'

Helenus is an intelligent young man as well as sexy. He raised himself on one elbow, stroked my left breast and grinned. 'It's about that lover of Helen's, isn't it?'

'So you knew about him!' I exclaimed.

'We all did, Hector, Paris – and Father.'

'And which one of you killed him and took the body overnight to Mount Ida to incriminate *me*?' I asked grimly, having explained Helen and Marmedes' timetable.

'Not me. I was with a lady friend that afternoon.'

'By name of –?'

He hesitated. 'You won't be jealous. Or tell . . .?'

I could hardly claim, as his hand seemed to be travelling downwards, that I was here primarily in a professional capacity.

'Never. We gods are above petty mortal emotions.' It was an old line, but it worked.

'It was Creusa.'

'*What*?' I sat up indignantly, forgetting for a second all about that delightful hand. 'But she's my daughter-in-law. I thought you had your eye on Hector's Andromache.'

He grinned. 'I'm saying nothing.'

I tried to shame him by sighing, 'What will become of my beloved Troy if such shenanigans go on within the royal house?'

'Ah, that I can tell you. It will fall.'

I had forgotten Helenus' great gift. Like that little madam, his sister Cassandra, he has second sight. A direct line to Zeus, you might say. Father hadn't even told us yet.

'Why? Because of your philandering?'

'I see only the result, not the reasons or means. Creusa will back up my story.'

'It hardly matters,' I said sulkily, 'if Troy is to fall.'

'Before it does,' he offered enticingly, his hand resuming its delightful movements, 'how about . . .'

My next target was Paris, and once again I decided I didn't need to disguise myself. I debated whether to strip again to remind him of Mount Ida and how much he owed to me, but in the end I went down in my old early morning ambrosia gown. After all, I'm beautiful whatever I wear and he was growing rather portly. No wonder Helen was going off him.

He at least had the decency to be in awe of me. 'Good goddess,' he stuttered, as I swooped through the air into his chamber, just as he was admiring his new calf-length leather boots in the mirror. I made rather too fast a landing and scattered a few jewels from my diadem on the floor. That would give Helen pause for thought.

'Where were you three afternoons ago,' I demanded, 'between four and six?'

'Why?'

I looked at him, intimating that I was not to be trifled with (except in intimate circumstances of my own choosing).

'I was at the bowmakers.'

A menial, who would doubtless back up anything Golden Boy Paris said. If he spoke the truth, though, he could not have killed Marmedes. I decided to get tough. It was Helen or me, and I rather favoured being the survivor myself.

'That corpse was Marmedes of Argos. Did you kill him?'

'A Greek?' He reeled. He did it very well.

'You know he was,' I replied sweetly. 'And you also know Helen was having an affair with him.'

Paris looked sulky. 'Who told you?'

'We goddesses know all,' I lied loftily.

'Then you must know who killed him,' he answered, reasonably enough I suppose.

'Nearly all,' I amended with dignity. 'You can't have been at your bowmakers for two hours. Helen left the trysting place at four o'sundial, and there would be two whole hours in which he could have been killed before the Scaean Gate was closed.'

'I went to the temple to offer a goat to Hera.'

Very suitable, I thought, but mention of the Cow-Faced Lady was not the way to my heart. 'Try again, Paris.'

He glanced at me and his eyes slid away. 'As a matter of fact I was at a place where we men go –'

'A *brothel*, when you've got Helen?' I asked incredulously.

'Good Zeus, no. I wouldn't have the strength. We just sit around and drink, set the world to rights, or go into the gymnasium to practise valiant feats, as Hector is always nagging me to do.'

'One of these days you might pluck up the courage to go and fight,' I said tartly.

The cheeky boy had the nerve to laugh. 'There are ten or more will vouch for me.'

'And you were there until six?'

'Quarter past seven,' he said smugly.

I have always been a little nervous of Hector, so I took Aeneas with me. I do dislike men that roar, and Hector is very good at roaring when he isn't flashing his armour at the Greeks. It must be about all he does flash; I can't see how he ever got time to beget a son. I dislike men who claim to be upright, too. They'd sell their own grandmother for the sake of being upright. I had a flash of inspiration, and cunningly disguised myself as Paris for this interview, but I suspected Helenus tipped him the wink for he looked at me very oddly. He needn't have worried. I was on the warpath, not the lovepath.

I was rather proud of my opening gambit: 'Mighty brother, blessed is the House of Priam that you rid us of this dishonour to our glorious family and ignoble shame to me, and that you had the happy thought of sending Anchises into the ranks of the Greeks as a spy dressed in Greek clothes.'

'What?' He looked completely blank, so I repeated it.

'Hail, Hector, Glorious Warrior of Troy.' (He likes this stuff.) 'You avenged me, and then killed the only witness, the guard in the tower.'

'And then you thought to rid yourself of Anchises, my beloved father,' Aeneas decided to roar, 'so that the House of Priam should not be toppled from the Trojan throne. So you dressed the melon-seller in his clothes and drove my father to certain death in the Greek camp.'

'*What?*'

'Please don't shout.' I cupped my hands over my dainty ears, only to remember Paris didn't have dainty ears but a rather large bronze helmet on at the time.

'I only wish I'd thought of it, Prince Aeneas,' Hector said wistfully.

'Perhaps Helenus did. He's cleverer than you,' I said hopefully.

'Brother, you shall answer for that.' He drew his sword and I began to see distinct disadvantages in my present disguise.

'Keep away from me,' I shrieked, transforming into my own beautiful body only belatedly remembering to transform my clothes as well.

He fell to his knees, and so did Aeneas after a great show of surprise. 'Forgive me, great goddess.'

'Only if you tell me where you were three afternoons ago.'

'I hardly like to confess.' He moaned and groaned and finally did so. 'I was in bed with Andromache.'

'But she's your wife.' I was rather disappointed.

'What's wrong with that?' He looked puzzled.

'It's unusual for a prince of Troy.'

'Well, that's where I was,' he said obstinately.

Several hours later, by dint of disguising myself in turn as my own grandson, the bowmaker's wife and a Nubian slave, I traipsed back to the palace, extremely annoyed. I could not fault any of their stories. Now it was Priam's turn, and I decided I'd enjoy terrifying him out of his royal tunic. I elected to come the heavy goddess, and arrived in all my glory (though clothed) to greet a king – I suppose since he is a grandson of Zeus he is my nephew in a way, the stiff-necked old fool.

'Hail, Mighty Priam!' I materialized on the adjoining throne.

'Goddess!' He began to lever himself unwillingly on to the floor to bend his knee. I let him, then set about charming him. I oozed my aura all about him, and let honey drip from my lips.

'What a *clever* plan of yours, Priam, to pry out the intentions of the Greeks.'

'What was?'

I had to explain it to him very simply. 'You and your sons conspired to rid yourself of the Greek spy, Helen's lover, and rid yourself of Anchises at the same time.'

He positively gawped at me. I had not thought him such a good actor.

'Where were you between four and six three afternoons ago, or was it one of your sons who did the killing?'

'What killing?'

Despite my sweet nature, I almost snarled at him. 'Of Marmedes, Diomedes' captain. Helen's lover.'

'The boys did say something to me about it. I didn't believe them, of course.'

'But it must have been your cunning that devised the scheme,' I cooed.

He grew almost intelligent. 'Kill a Greek inside Trojan walls? If Achilles of the Fragile Heel found out, it would give him all the excuse he needed to have every damned Achaean out of the camp and attacking our walls.'

He had a point. 'But where were you?' I persisted.

'At the temple of Zeus, great goddess.'

My heart sank. If he was speaking the truth, Father was his alibi.

What was I to do? Time was running out and I was still no nearer a solution. I decided to go to a quiet glade where I could do some thinking. It is here that my handsome Adonis and I consummate our love every spring when that horrible Hades graciously allows him to come back to my arms for a while. (I had to get an Olympus court

order to force Hades to surrender my beloved.) Unfortunately it
wasn't spring now, but I still found the grove an inspiration.

My beloved Adonis was thus the means of my fourth brainwave.
*I suddenly realized there was one person whose word I had taken
without question* – heaven knows why. Immediately I rushed with
winged feet back to Aeneas, hardly bothering to over-awe him at
all. Anchises was his father, after all. I was very excited.

'Come with me, my son, while I confront the murderer of
Marmedes!'

'And my beloved father too?' he asked doggedly.

'Yes, yes,' I said impatiently, whisking him through the air for
speed – a thing he hates.

We landed in the chamber just as she was changing her gown. I
could see Aeneas' eyes bulging a bit, so perhaps he isn't quite so
uninterested in women as I thought.

'Helen,' I cried, '*you* killed Marmedes. Was he tired of you,
beauteous Helen? Was he going to leave you? Who else would he
allow so near as to kill him? Who else could so conveniently poison
the guard?'

'Me?' she shrieked.

'What have you done with my father, evil Helen? Temptress,'
Aeneas added confusingly, his eyes on her breast which she was
still struggling to cover.

'Does his body lie in some corner of a foreign field?' I demanded.
It was time for my fifth brainwave. I thought of Oenone, Paris' first
love. 'No. I see it all. You've worked on Paris to persuade Oenone
to imprison Anchises, haven't you?'

She lost colour. 'That snake's venomed piece of monkshood?'

'So that's who you got the poison from!' I shouted in triumph,
just as Helen fainted again.

I returned to the Hall of the Golden Throne in golden glory for
a private meeting with Father.

'And so I have proved it, Mighty Zeus,' I concluded my
exposition triumphantly. 'Helen was plotting to overthrow the
House of Troy from within.'

'Aphrodite –'

'I claim acquittal from my terrible sentence.'

'Aphrodite –'

I swept on. 'I, the goddess of love and laughter –'

'*Aphrodite*!' he shouted. 'Have you actually spoken to
Anchises?'

'Aeneas insisted on going to release him from Oenone's clutches,
but you will find –'

'Aphrodite, look at this.'

'What is it?' I broke off, rather hurt he was still looking so grim.

'It's Paean's autopsy report on the body of Marmedes.'

I scanned it quickly. 'Oh.' Seldom have I been so immortified.

'You see, Aphrodite?'

I did. The man had been strangled.

'Somehow I don't see Helen doing that, do you?' Father sounded almost gentle.

'Aphrodite, how nice to see you again.'

I wished I hadn't left that thunderbolt I stole behind in my closet on Olympus. I could cheerfully have struck Anchises dead. I hadn't bargained on his being ensconced at the family table when I shot in to have a word with Aeneas.

'You boast about my private parts again, Anchises, and you can say goodbye to yours,' I told him briefly. That shut him up. How could I ever have fancied him? The things we women do. I turned to our son. 'Had Oenone imprisoned Anchises as we suspected?'

'She had, Mother.'

'You can forget all that mother stuff,' I replied coldly. 'You're lying. Anchises was an honoured guest there. I now know Oenone hates Paris, Troy and everyone in it. She was in it with the two of you, wasn't she? And you, my beloved son, are the murderer of Marmedes.'

For I had had my sixth, and, for the time, last brainwave.

'It was simple, Mighty Zeus,' I explained modestly. 'I was blinded by a mother's love, until I remembered a conversation in which Aeneas accused Hector of killing the melon-seller. But I had never mentioned melons to him, merely that Marmedes was a trader in the market.

'Aeneas, I fear, Father, was too concerned with politics and not with his mother's profession of love. He and Anchises had ambitions. If they could topple the House of Priam they could make peace with the Greeks, and take the throne themselves. So they killed Helen's Greek lover, for if the Greeks had known of the liaison – unsanctified by *me* –' I pointed out crossly – 'they might have seduced Helen back to them and sailed home, leaving Troy with Priam still in charge. Aeneas wanted to make peace with the Greeks himself at any price, even if it meant Troy falling, and he and Anchises being rewarded as founders of a new city.'

'Make peace with the Greeks?' Zeus thundered. 'How dare Aeneas presume to alter the gods' will?'

'Helenus said Destiny had planned that Troy should fall,' I said miserably. 'Can't you think of some other way, Mighty Zeus, rather than through my son's evil-doing? He's been very naughty, but I'd like him to live.'

He patted my shoulder absentmindedly. 'Do you know, Aphrodite, I've just had this wonderful idea about a wooden horse.'

INVESTIGATING THE SILVIUS BOYS

Lindsey Davis

Lindsey Davis helped establish the Roman detective story as a genre in its own right with her books about Marcus Didius Falco, who lived during the reign of the Emperor Vespasian. There have been eight Falco novels to date: The Silver Pigs *(1989),* Shadows in Bronze *(1990),* Venus in Copper *(1991),* The Iron Hand of Mars *(1992),* Poseidon's Gold *(1993),* Last Act in Palmyra *(1994),* Time to Depart *(1995) and* A Dying Light in Corduba *(1996). The following story, which was Lindsey Davis's first, does not feature Falco. Instead, she takes us back to the founding of Rome in 753* BC *and introduces us to the first Roman private investigator.*

∽

The location of the crime was critical. The scene was a marshy river valley, between low but significant hills. Alongside the river ran an ancient salt road. It came up from the coast, about twenty miles away, then continued into the interior towards a city which at that time ruled the neighbourhood. In a wide curve of the river lay an island which offered the first crossing point inland. This bridgehead made a natural halt, for it was about one day's journey for the beasts bringing salt from the sea. These factors had encouraged settlement. The hills were crying out to be defended – and someone had just begun surrounding them with a rampart wall. In the footings of the new wall the investigator had seen a recent corpse.

There had been no attempt to hide the body. As soon as he

asked, bystanders told him freely that the victim was one of the two Silvius boys. They also admitted quite openly who had battered him to death. One of the oldest crimes in the world: a young man had quarrelled bitterly with his brother and killed him with a building tool.

That was when the investigator should have gone home. He was a visitor who had come merely to sightsee. But he knew something of the family involved and so he found himself intrigued. Being drawn in despite himself was a hazard of his profession. Once his interest had been caught there was no escape.

The purist inquirer likes a date for a murder. That posed a problem. Time had no set limits. The tribes north of the river maintained a rough calendar by banging a nail into a temple door every year. It worked well, unless the temple burned down, as happened fairly frequently. Here the people were more primitive. Even so they were practical, and quite capable of devising their own methods of reckoning. Very soon they would calculate everything from the most important date they had. So if you wanted to be pedantic, you could say that the man who was killed by his brother had died in the year time began.

Well, that was the kind of easy-to-remember fact which helps keep casework archives neat. This was, without any question, Case Number One.

Number One – with no arrest foreseeable. It did not bode well for the future of the profession.

On the driest and highest of the hills above the river's marshy floodplain stood a group of shepherds' huts. They had a venerable, weathered air – and the shepherds who lived in them had a reputation for beating up strangers. As he climbed the hill, which was harder going than it looked, the investigator sighed. He hated shepherds. This collection were known to be formidable. They did not wait to be raided by bandits, like most countrymen who knew their lot was to lead a hard life and suffer. These themselves rode out in armed groups, attacked the bandits vigorously, and shared out their spoils. They were famous for flouting authority. They had found themselves young leaders who encouraged them to plunder the herds of neighbouring landowners, even including the royal estates. The investigator knew this because he worked for the king.

As he climbed towards the hilltop he noticed a flurry of movement. They had seen him coming. They knew exactly who he was. They also knew he was at a disadvantage. As he came up, gasping, he saw only a huddle of hostile people in rough sheepskin dress, who all looked surly and all looked the same. To a city man they had an obtrusive smell of woodsmoke and lanolin. It made him feel his own habits were over-fastidious.

'I need to speak to Faustulus.' He felt a taut knot in his belly. It was always the same at the start of something: dread of the unknown.

'What do you want?'

'Someone is dead.'

'What's it to you?' The man who spoke was being no more obstructive than usual. He just belonged to a group who took pride in being blunt. Like all such groups, outsiders judged them plain rude.

Faustulus himself had come out of a hut. The investigator knew him already because Faustulus was the previous king's herdsman. This had made for complications during the raids on the royal estates – for Faustulus was also foster-father to the ringleaders who organized the raids. Now nearing the end of his working life, he was hardy, skilled and too intelligent for his own good. The stubborn, confident type, the type who breaks the rules. Twenty or thirty years ago he took home two abandoned infants when any sensible man would have left them to die. They grew up to be the Silvius twins.

It was clear from his eyes that Faustulus already knew that one of his rowdy foster sons was now lying alongside the new rampart with his head cracked open, and that the other was responsible. Those eyes said that, like any man who brought up children who came to grief, he was now wondering why he had bothered. But there was a hard defiance in their gaze as well. He would stand by the survivor.

The investigator gave him a courteous nod, then braced himself. 'Where's Romulus?'

A murmur ran through the crowd. 'Go back to your work,' ordered the investigator. 'Disperse. There's nothing to see.'

A woman rushed to the front, tear-stained and shrieking abuse. He ought to have known Larentia would not be far away. 'Get out of here! You're not wanted. Get back to Alba.'

She was younger than Faustulus, but well matched in spirit. She had a reputation for putting herself about too much. Maybe she did, though in a small, and small-minded, community any woman with character risks jealous talk. This one had never cared what others thought.

'Larentia, I'm sorry to find you in this trouble.' She checked herself, seeing that the investigator was a quiet and steady man who would not be swayed from his purpose. 'I have to see Romulus before I leave,' he told her levelly. He could take his time. Romulus belonged right here. He would not flee.

Larentia still looked ready to fly at him. If she appealed to the others the investigator would be lost. He knew this was the most dangerous moment. Walking up the hill alone had been stupid. His mouth dried, as if he had been chewing grapeskins to nothing. If these people decided to tear him apart he had no means of defending himself.

'Let Romulus be. He's grieving for his brother,' Larentia cried.

'I can understand that,' the investigator said.

'You don't understand anything!' Behind the spitting rage of a creature defending her young lay darker feelings. She was standing apart from Faustulus as if pain had erected a barrier between her husband and herself. She also knew that whatever happened she had lost not one, but both her boys.

'I'm trying to understand,' said the man from Alba Longa. 'Maybe the best thing is if Romulus himself stops hiding in the hut behind you and comes out to explain.'

Romulus emerged of his own volition. If he wanted to remain a power in the community there was no alternative. Once he looked like a fugitive he would lose all powers of leadership.

Pushing past his knee as he ducked out of the hut came a large dog, growling fiercely at the stranger. The investigator stood his ground. Presumably a man who had been suckled by a she-wolf was good with animals.

The watchdog sat on its tail and and fell silent. Romulus came further forward. He was strong and fit, past boyhood but still young. His expression was dark, but otherwise unfathomable. People said he made a happy companion exchanging stories around a campfire, but if you met him at market you would not attempt conversation. He was rural and close. That was how he set out to be, even normally, let alone on the day he had killed his twin brother.

Seeing him, the crowd relaxed. No one, including the foster parents, made any move to intervene when suspect and investigator walked to another part of the hilltop where they could talk in privacy. The two men were now looking south, across a deep cleft which divided the hill that would be known as the Palatine, the hill where the twins had been brought up, from the crag called the Aventine.

'I don't have to say anything to you!' declared Romulus. He sounded like anyone caught poaching on the royal estates.

'That's right.'

'You're wasting your time.'

'It goes with the job.'

The investigator surveyed him thoughtfully. Hardened and self-opinionated. A fighter, who could devise a plan and then organize the muscle to carry it out. A young thug. But then what else could he be, with that background?

The Silvius family, now the hereditary kings of Alba, claimed descent from Aeneas, that pragmatic old hero who escaped from Troy then pushed his way to power in Italy without a by-your-leave. His descendants were never renowned for peaceful living. The twins' grandfather had been shoved off the throne by his brother, who methodically killed all his nephews, then ordered his niece to become a vestal virgin. Instead of sticking to her intended life of chastity she let herself be raped – or, according to her, she was deflowered by Mars, the god of war (good story: a quick-thinking girl). The resultant sons had been ordered to be drowned in the Tiber, but the job had been bungled and Faustulus had found them in the flooded fields, being suckled by a she-wolf.

Well, the she-wolf tale was a ludicrous rumour. Romulus and Remus were just one more set of tearaways: a violent background, mother no better than she should be, unknown or absentee father, children pushed around between foster parents, unusual relations with animals. They had been brought up in dirt and poverty, always dreaming of the better life and striving to grab it the fastest way. Now one had come to a sticky end. The other was implicated. How long before he too met some sordid fate?

'What are you thinking about?' asked Romulus.

'I saw you, that night in Alba,' the investigator told him. 'The night the old king was killed.'

'Oh, that night!' exclaimed the old king's nephew in a soft, bitter voice. He seemed much older than he should.

'It looked like a happy ending for you and your brother.'

'Do you believe in happy endings?' Today, with Remus dead, Romulus clearly did not.

'I believe in order,' the investigator said. 'So when people get killed, I believe in calling the perpetrator to account.'

'You'll wear yourself out!' jeered the tearaway prince. 'I'll stick with believing in fate.'

Fate had certainly seemed to be on their side when he and his brother had come to Alba. At that time the twins had been at the height of their success as community heroes attacking bandits. One group, however, had set a trap for them. Remus had been captured

by these robbers and handed over, first to the king of Alba, then to
his deposed brother whose estates had been raided by the twins. So
Remus had come face to face with his grandfather for the first time.
The grandfather started to think.

Faustulus, who had long ago worked out the twins' royal origin,
realized the truth was bound to come out. Back in the shepherd's
hut there was urgent discussion. Romulus knew he had to act.
With typical flair he infiltrated the city, rescued his brother, killed
the usurping king, and saw their grandfather finally reinstated as
monarch.

'So what went wrong?' mused the man from Alba. 'You had been
greeted in triumph. You were princes restored to your heritage.'

'You can never go back,' said Romulus darkly. His expression
cleared a little: 'We wanted space. We were uncomfortable in the
old city that had once rejected us. We wanted our own territory.'
He spoke as if fleeing the nest were some new idea. The investigator
smiled. Alba was sorely overpopulated, all agreed. And the Silvius
boys had always looked as if they were driven by unusual strength
of will.

'So here you are. Back where you were found in the floods and
brought up. About to found a new city that could rival all others
– but now Remus is dead. Do you want to tell me about it?'

'No.'

The eyes of Romulus seemed to glitter as he stared out across the
river. Was this simply the madness of a born killer? Or was it the set
face of a man who had committed a horrific act by accident against
the person he had always been closest to, a man who knew he now
had to live with that for the rest of his life?

'It would be better if you told me,' repeated the investigator
quietly. The forces of right and wrong fought their old battle in
silence.

Despite his previous refusal, the surviving twin began speaking.
His voice was controlled but tense. 'The situation was impossible.
No city can have two founders.' Why not? Well, any idea of
partnership had always been lost on the Silvius family. Suggesting
notions of brotherhood was just asking for a black eye. 'Because
my brother and I were twins there was no seniority. We decided
to ask the gods of the countryside to say which of us should govern
the new city, and give his name to it.'

'So you chose to use augury?'

'One has to be civilized.'

'Of course.'

Augury was a rural art. In theory it was scrupulously impartial.

To the sceptic from Alba it was open to misinterpretation, otherwise called fraud. The diviner foretold the future by looking at flight patterns of birds. That was random enough. The trickery entered when the diviner gave his opinion of what the patterns meant. At this point human error was inclined to creep in.

'I stood upon this hill here; Remus was on that one.' Romulus gestured to the Aventine. 'My brother spoke first. He had seen six vultures.'

He fell silent. The investigator had already heard what happened next. Immediately after Remus had made his pronouncement, Romulus doubled the tally and saw twelve birds. Well, that was what he said. Presumably Remus soon realized he had walked right into that one.

'Your brother's followers claimed priority for him, on the grounds that he had seen his sign first?'

'Yes. While mine did the same on grounds of number.'

'So nothing was solved!'

'Fighting broke out,' Romulus confirmed wryly.

'And is that when you killed him?'

'No.' Had the rediscovered prince not been so heavily sunburnt after his life as a shepherd, he might have looked as if he were blushing. An admission of the stupidity of it found its way into his voice: 'The majority seemed to agree that I should be the city's founder. I harnessed an ox and ploughed a furrow to set out a boundary. Then I set to, building a rampart. That was when Remus came over and jeered at my work. He jumped over the half-built wall, scoffing. I lost my temper and went for him.' Dangerous places, building sites. Not a sensible playground for such a pair of squabbling brothers.

To his credit, Romulus was not the type to inaugurate his city by sitting on a stool in a clean tunic giving orders from a chart. He would have been right in there with a hod or a mattock, stretching his muscles and getting his knuckles grazed. When his brother came and kicked at the newly mortared stonework with a maddening laugh, Romulus would have been hot, sweat-stained and covered with dust. After their tussle over the augury, his temper must have been stretched to breaking point. Remus never stood a chance. Still, he should have known that.

'So Remus is dead. What's your plan now?' asked the investigator cautiously. He thought he knew the plan. It could be unwise annoying a man who had just put a shovel through his own twin brother's skull for interfering.

'The plan,' stated Romulus, who also realized the fine points of the situation, 'is the same as before: I am founding a city. I mean it to rival all other cities. I shall fortify the hill on which we are standing, enclose ground, and attract manpower.'

'Mould the rabble into a body politic?' suggested the man from Alba.

'Your terms are a bit Etruscan,' said Romulus drily. He was referring to the tribesmen from north of the river, who traded with Greeks and had absorbed some exotic practices.

'Founding a city's more complex than herding sheep.'

'I realize that.' The prince was grim.

'For instance,' said his companion, 'you will have to address the issue of social order. Cities need rules. One rule which you may want to suggest to the community is "Don't murder each other." '

'I shall insist on it,' said Romulus calmly.

'Oh I see: "Don't do what I do, do what I say"?'

'That seems a nice definition of civic authority.'

'Now we're getting somewhere!' scoffed the investigator, who was after all a city man. He had a highly developed sense of irony, and was wary of people in charge.

Romulus had caught him gazing across the unwelcoming landscape. 'I'm going to make something of this place,' he declared. His tone was that of a visionary, as if he dreamed of ineffable empire. But since he came from rural stock, out loud he made only cautious claims: 'All you see now is wild country peopled by lawless tribes, but it will become far greater.'

'I wish you every success.'

'Why have you come to challenge me, then?'

'If whatever you're planning is meant to improve standards, maybe a murder is a bad way to start!'

'Prevent me founding my city, and there never will be anything here but the wilderness,' warned Romulus. 'You'll be interfering with history.'

'As special pleading, that's certainly different!' The investigator smiled. 'Normally when I tackle a suspect he says, "Put me away, and one dark night my pals will get you!" I have to admit, I wasn't expecting anything subtle from one of the Silvius boys . . . but it still leaves me as the high-minded idiot who has to allow you your second chance.'

There was a theory that if you gave hoodlums from a deprived background something to care about, they would come good. The man from Alba doubted it. On the other hand, not many roughnecks from difficult families were offered the chance to establish an empire as their sweetener to reform themselves.

'Think of it as an investment in the future,' said Romulus. Adding, 'As for me, I shall atone for Remus by devoting my life to the new city.'

'Ah – community service!' replied the investigator, inventing a dubious concept without intending to.

There was a short silence, which was not unfriendly.

Romulus stirred. As a man with a nation to found, he rarely stayed still for long. 'So is that all you wanted to ask me?'

'Yes.' The investigator's tone had a decisive note. 'Well, there's just one more thing –'

Romulus stared at him, unfamiliar with the concept of an investigator suddenly turning back with the unexpected question that overturns the alibi. Even so, he had a feeling he was about to be tricked. 'What's that?'

'Only –' For the first time a slight note of bashfulness entered the investigator's voice. 'If you're founding a city, you're going to need law enforcement –'

'So?'

'So I wondered if there might be a job for me.'

Decades later two investigators were comparing notes. The elder, retired now but still an expert in his own eyes, tried to cheer up his colleague by relating his own worst experience.

'Believe me, I know the nightmare: the witnesses clam up and the prime suspect is boasting that you can't touch him. There's unavoidable publicity; the whole population is watching and waiting for your big mistake. Mine had a royal connection – in fact, even the gods were taking an interest, according to some.'

'So what was this – a family case? Gang warfare? Or a business partnership that went wrong?'

'Oh, all those! I'm talking about the Silvius brothers.' The name meant nothing. Time had moved on. There were new villains now. 'I knew who did the killing. There had been plenty of onlookers. He admitted the crime. The problem was, I couldn't touch him.'

'They all say that,' the young man disagreed. 'It's standard: "You've nothing on me! You'll never make it stick!" Normally once you've got as far as accusing them, you know you'll take them all the way to court.'

'Mine,' smiled the old expert, 'was never a normal case.'

'No case is normal,' snapped the rookie impatiently, as they turned down an alley (looking twice in case of muggers) then peeled off into a favourite bar. Immediately they both wondered

*why it had become such a favourite. The frosty girl who took their
order growled with irritation at their greeting. She hated men in
their line of business; well, she hated men in any line. She was
suffering from an appalling cold. Her bar-room etiquette was to
cough all over any drinks she was serving, then she coughed all
over the customers. When they paid up, she fiddled the money.*

Some things never change.

'No case is normal,' agreed the retired agent with a smile.
'Especially if you try and arrest Romulus!'

His young companion was choking on his drink. 'Romulus!'
Now, sitting in Rome, which was already a leading city amongst
its neighbours, with Romulus the great leader after a lifetime of
wise public service, the idea of anyone taking him to task seemed
unbelievable.

'He killed his brother. I thought he should account for it.'

'You set about him like a suspect – and then he gave you
a job?'

The old expert looked diffident. When he had risked the question,
Romulus had suddenly smiled – the calm, confident smile of a man
who knows he will fulfil his destiny. 'He said I had the right
attitude.'

The young one spluttered again, but subsided in awe. 'Well, it
all worked out.'

'Letting him off? Well, he wasn't going to offend again. We agreed
what happened to Remus was all in the family – the fighting Silvius
brothers doing what their ancestors did best. Unless their mother,
the vestal virgin, had secretly borne triplets to the so-called god of
war, Romulus had run out of brothers. I had two options: I could
arrest him – if I wanted to be thrown off a crag by the mob. Or I
could give him his chance.'

'So why do you call the case a problem?'

'I hate loose ends. Even when Romulus gave the city laws and
made the populace respect them, when his own reputation had
become impeccable, I could never forget that Remus was dead
and nobody had answered for it.'

The younger man laughed. 'You're obsessed!'

'That's why it's a problem,' agreed the other quietly.

'Madness! He's built the greatest city in Italy. You're vindicated.'

The rookie's friend felt obliged to be fair: 'There was the business
of the gang rape. I was never happy with our result on that.'

'The Sabine girls?' Surprised at first, the younger colleague forced
himself to take the professional view. 'Well, yes; I can see there

was a case – against Romulus as the ringleader, and every male in the city.'

'There had been a prior conspiracy; and the women were abducted and held against their will.'

'But when their fathers made a complaint, surely the victims all refused to testify?'

The retired officer shrugged. 'Marital rape is always tricky to prove in court.'

'They knew when they were well off,' said the young man, taking the robust Roman view. 'Husbands who were not bad, and life in a bright modern city.'

'Oh I'm sure that's how they saw it,' agreed the old expert gravely. For a moment his young friend felt disconcerted. He sympathized with Romulus all those years before, standing on the edge of the Palatine and hearing this stubborn maverick suggest that the dead Remus should perhaps not be lightly passed off as a mere hitch on the road to destiny.

'Don't tell me you're still hoping to get him one day?'

Without comment, the retired investigator smiled and made ready to leave. In the doorway he paused for a moment. An old habit. Rome was a city, so it was full of thieves and fraudsters and people knocking each other on the head; sometimes there was a reason, but sometimes they did it just because they felt like it. Anyone who knew what he was doing stopped to sniff the air and look down the street before he stepped outside. That's what cities are like.

After he had gone, the younger man sat on, finishing the wine. When he rose, fumbling reluctantly for money, the miserable barmaid spoke: 'Your friend left a tip. He's not in the same line as you, is he?'

'He was once.' The rookie chortled, still amused by the story. 'That's the investigator who once tried to arrest Romulus!' The girl appeared impressed for a moment so the man added, 'Just think; if Romulus hadn't bashed his twin brother, we could be living in a city called Reme.'

'Get away!' said the girl.

'My pal would still arrest him, if he had a chance.'

'Too late.'

The rookie paid the waitress more attention. Rome's law-enforcement men had already learned the fine principle of picking up information from bored girls in tawdry bars. 'Why's that?'

'Romulus has gone.'

'What do you mean?'

'He vanished. Did you notice that nasty storm this morning?

Romulus was out reviewing some troops on the Plain of Mars. A thick cloud of mist enveloped him, so nobody else could see him. When it cleared, he had disappeared. They reckon he was taken up to heaven in the whirlwind, and that that's the last we shall ever see of him.'

'Carried off by a whirlwind, eh?' The rookie sighed. 'You're right, it's too bad.'

He stood at the counter, staring into his own thoughts. The barmaid pretended to wipe down a table.

People don't just disappear. Being carried off by a whirlwind was about as likely as being suckled by a she-wolf.

Romulus had been a popular ruler, but only among the common people to whom he gave his own loyalty. The young man knew that Romulus had attracted jealousy from some of the city senators. Could it be that the senators had set upon Romulus and despatched him secretly? There would be a body somewhere; someone just had to hunt for it . . . The insistent voice of his profession suggested that the Plain of Mars incident should be looked into.

Another voice told him not to be a fool. Law and order men are not required to involve themselves in politics. This was one case for which he would never get civic funding. And if he was right, even if he discovered the truth, he would never be allowed to make it public or take any credit.

He knew what a sensible man ought to do. But when he walked from the bar, his feet were taking him towards the low plain alongside the river where Romulus was supposed to have vanished. His head was full of unanswered questions, and in his eyes was the haunted expression of a man obsessed.

THE GATEWAY TO DEATH

Brèni James

Long before the Roman world established its power throughout the Mediterranean, the culture, language and authority of the Greeks held sway. Unlike the Romans the Greeks never sought world domination – they were too busy squabbling with each other to achieve it, but it never interested them. Their culture held art and philosophy almost as precious as power. One of their most famous philosophers was Socrates, who lived in Athens from 469–399 BC. Brèni James wrote two stories about Socrates. The first, 'Socrates Solves a Murder', I reprinted in The Mammoth Book of Historical Whodunnits. Here's the second.

∾

Socrates paused at the foot of the Acropolis and looked up at the marble façade of the outer gates. He stood with the grace of a soldier, though his military career was some ten years behind him and a certain roundness at his waistline belied his graceful carriage.

The setting sun dipped beneath the overcast that had darkened the afternoon sky, and flashed its final splendor across Athens like a retreating hoplite tossing a flambeau over his shoulder. The fire-red beams fell on the columns and the great bronze doors of the Propylaea, the outer gates, that rose above the western brink of the hill.

'It is truly the jewel in the forehead of Athens,' said the philosopher, his eyes still on the marble gateway. Despite the pug nose and protruding eyes, his face showed a great and serene beauty. He turned and smiled at his companion of the moment, Mnesicles, who was the architect of the great outer gates.

Mnesicles, a man in his late forties, blushed like a youth at this compliment from the man who, though almost ten years younger than himself, was acclaimed by many as the greatest thinker of their time.

At length he ventured, 'Socrates, if the Propylaea is indeed a jewel, it is complete only in its setting.'

'I know,' Socrates said quietly. The great dream of the architect had been cut short by the new government. Four hundred talents had already gone into the construction of the great gates, but war and the whim of the city had cut off appropriations. The south wing of the edifice had scarcely been begun, and now it hung like an undeveloped limb on an otherwise perfect body.

'Perhaps when Athenians tire of seeing so splendid a work left in such imbalance, they will find money enough for you to finish it, Mnesicles.'

'I've always thought they would,' shrugged the architect. 'The money was withdrawn while we were still working on the north wing. I could have modified my plans, but I kept hoping that at the last minute, perhaps . . .'

His voice trailed off. Socrates looked at him closely. Mnesicles was a pale, unobtrusive little man; today he looked as though a great sickness had come upon him. Even his bald head had a certain unhealthy pallor about it, and his fine eyes were glazed.

'After we get a permanent peace,' Socrates began helpfully, but the architect cut him off.

'No, no,' he said dismally. 'There is money enough now, but there are other plans for it.' He looked at his friend. 'Have you noticed the two murals being painted in the west portico?' he asked.

'I've not seen them yet, but I understand they are the works of Parrhasius and Zeuxis.'

'And not just in the west portico, my dear Socrates. They have commissions for every bare wall in the place.'

'I should think they would first let you build them more walls. Well, I'm glad I found you in the market; a few peaceful moments in the Acropolis together will cheer you.'

The philosopher took the other's arm, and led Mnesicles up the winding slope, past the random votive offerings and pieces of statuary that lined the path. One of the architect's slaves, a young boy of perhaps sixteen, fell in silently behind them as they walked up to the Propylaea.

The huge bronze doors in the center of the gateway were closed this late in the day, but one of the smaller ones on their right was still open. They walked through it and found their way to the large west portico of the structure. Their destination was to have been a sanctuary beyond, in the Acropolis, but they were halted by a strange sight: next to the south wall, beneath a flamboyant mural, lay the naked body of a youth not much older than the slave who attended them.

The two men bent over the lifeless form, Socrates hitching his untidy mantle out of the way of a pool of blood that had seeped from the underside of the naked youth's head.

'Who do you think it is?' asked Mnesicles in a whisper.

Socrates passed his hands over the heavy muscles of the back and turned one of the limp hands over, touching the calluses there with a gentle finger. 'A slave, wouldn't you say? One that carried heavy loads. Perhaps a stonemason's or statuary's helper.'

The architect remained silent. Socrates looked troubled for a moment, eyeing the peculiar position of the graceful body. It was spread out, face down, limbs apart, as though the boy had been beaten and had been thrashing about on the ground before his death. But there were no marks on the body, save for what was obviously a fatal blow on the head.

One glance at the mural before which the body lay, however, explained the discrepancy. 'Compare them,' said Socrates, indicating the corpse and the central figure of the painting. They were exactly alike, save for the fact that the boy's face showed nothing but death, and the face of the figure in the mural showed an ecstasy of pain. They could almost hear screams of insult and indignant agony from the lifelike mouth of the painted creature.

Mnesicles sucked in his breath as the horror of the sight brought a flush to his sallow cheeks.

'Which of the two painters would you say did this scene?' Socrates asked.

'Parrhasius.' The architect spat out the word as though it had blood on it.

'I have heard that Parrhasius will go to great lengths to get realism in his paintings. Do you think that is true?'

'He is said to . . . to torture slaves to get the look of pain he wishes to copy, Socrates.'

'Perhaps you had better send your attendant to fetch Parrhasius. And Zeuxis, too. But no word of this death to either of them.'

The philosopher had risen from the body and turned to look

at the mural on the wall across the portico – the one that, to judge from its style, was being done by Zeuxis. It was a portrait of the young Endymion, a beautiful youth reclining in an attitude of undisturbed sleep.

At Socrates' suggestion the architect and he waited for the painters outside the bronze gates, and at length they spied the pair walking up the slope followed by Mnesicles' servant.

Zeuxis was more readily discernible in the twilight, not only by reason of his six-foot-four stature, but because he wore a mantle of remarkable fashion: it was checkered red and green. Once along the path he paused to speak to his companion, turning his back to the men above, and they could easily distinguish in the dusk the great gold-embroidered letters on the back of the mantle which spelled out ZEUXIS. He swaggered, gesturing freely, apparently deep in a one-sided conversation.

His listener and fellow artist, Parrhasius, was robed in purple; and as the pair reached the marble stairs of the Propylaea, the fading sun caught the golden crown that Parrhasius wore atop his dark curls, and by which, as everyone knew, he proclaimed himself 'The Prince of Painters.'

Physically Parrhasius was somewhat less prepossessing than his competitor. He was nearly as tall, but a thickness of indolent fat encased what might otherwise have been a well-proportioned figure. His features were gross, his beard a tight-curled fur that clung to his round face like a small frightened animal.

'Socrates!' exclaimed Zeuxis in a high voice, pushing the other artist arrogantly aside. 'My dear friend, my fellow art-lover, how good of you to come to see my work! I regret it is not yet finished.'

Parrhasius nodded to the two older men, but only slightly, as though his crown might topple. 'Are we to have another contest?' he smiled faintly.

It had been the talk of Athens, not too long before, that the rivals had agreed to a public showing of their best works. Zeuxis had displayed a portrait of a boy holding a bunch of grapes, and it was so realistic – or so gossip said – that it deceived birds which swept down to peck at the luscious fruit. But when Parrhasius was asked to unveil his panel, it was discovered – to Zeuxis' dismay – that the heavy drapery that had seemed only a covering was, in fact, the painting. It was after this triumph that Parrhasius crowned himself and took to wearing the purple.

Socrates looked at the two intently. 'We shall indeed have a contest,' he said.

'Then I take it,' said Parrhasius in a deep baritone, 'that you have seen my mural of Apollo beating the flute player?'

'I have seen both that and Zeuxis' Endymion. And I should like to know more about both. If Zeuxis will give us leave, let us, Parrhasius, speak first of yours.'

Zeuxis' restless eyes glanced over the other three men and the slave who had returned with them. He pressed his lips into a trembling, moist smile and nodded, adjusting the checkered mantle with fastidious hands.

Socrates: Parrhasius, we two have spoken of art before. I recall that we agreed that whereas men copy the gods, artists copy men, did we not?

Parrhasius: Yes, I recall that we did.

Socrates: And it was your feeling that art should mimic faithfully the actions of men?

Parrhasius: And their states of mind, too, Socrates.

Socrates: By state of mind do you mean their character, Parrhasius? Or what they are thinking at a particular moment?

Parrhasius: Their thoughts.

Socrates: Perhaps we should qualify it even further. Not their thoughts so much, would you say, as their feelings, their reactions to what is inflicted upon them?

Parrhasius: That would be more correct, Socrates.

Socrates: Do you feel you convey this in the portrait of Marsyas you have painted inside?

Parrhasius: I shall have, when it is completed.

Socrates: And what is left to be done?

Parrhasius: I wish to add a few refinements to the face and hair.

Socrates: The body is finished?

Parrhasius: As finished as bodies ever are for me.

Socrates: You don't feel the limbs still need more work?

Parrhasius: It is Zeuxis who prides himself on knowing bone structure and such things.

Socrates: Then, Parrhasius, you were working on the face today?

Parrhasius: I would have, but it was too cloudy to get the proper light.

Socrates: And what do you do when you cannot paint?

Parrhasius: Today I took a walk on the banks of the Ilissus. But what of that?

Socrates: A charming place to walk. You were alone?

Parrhasius: Yes, alone.

Socrates turned now to the other artist, who was fidgeting with his checkered mantle and pushing the blond curls off his forehead with slender, nervous fingers.

Socrates: Now, Zeuxis, perhaps you will tell us in what fashion you disagree with Parrhasius in matters of art, for I know you are lively opponents.

Zeuxis: I can achieve greatness without resorting to his cruel . . .

Parrhasius interrupted him with a snort. 'You would do anything for what you call beauty!' he snapped.

Zeuxis: For beauty one does not have to resort to violence!

Parrhasius: And for truth, Zeuxis, one can crush beauty underfoot!

Socrates: Gentlemen, please! A few more questions, Zeuxis, and then we can talk more about truth. You say you seek beauty in art. Is this beauty as the gods have conceived it, or as an artist perceives it in man?

Zeuxis: The latter, Socrates.

Socrates: And do you, as Parrhasius does, strive to capture in your work the beauty of a man's emotions?

Zeuxis: I do not think emotions are beautiful, Socrates. I prefer to copy beauty in perfect repose, so long as it makes for a true picture.

Socrates: True to life, you mean?

Zeuxis: If that is my subject, yes.

Socrates: And I take it that on this cloudy day, you also were unable to paint?

Zeuxis: Parrhasius paints in the afternoons, but I in the morning. There was sunlight before noon.

Socrates: And in the afternoon?

Zeuxis: I was weary after the morning's work. I slept this afternoon, as I often do.

Socrates: Now then, my friends, let us go within the gates and see what truths we can discover.

The quartet walked to the west portico where Socrates stood aside to watch the two artists make their macabre discovery. Zeuxis paled and bade the slave of Mnesicles to support him. Parrhasius reddened with anger. He turned to glare at Zeuxis.

'If this is your trick,' he menaced the artist, 'I'll thrash you till Apollo takes the whip!'

'Do you know the boy?' Socrates asked coolly. Both artists protested they had never seen the young man before. They glowered at each other, but there was a deep perplexity in their faces and silently they turned to Socrates.

Mnesicles, looking from one to the other of the artists, at length muttered to the philosopher: 'Could either of them use a corpse for a model, Socrates, without attracting unwelcome attention?'

Socrates: We happened on the body just after the gates were closed and neither of them was here. But do you think we would have shown unseemly curiosity if an artist pretended to paint from so still, so apparently obedient a model?

Mnesicles: Someone would surely have seen the blood.

Parrhasius: And do you think I would leave a dead body here until morning, for Zeuxis to come upon?

Socrates: If you wished to paint from such a model, I think you would have decided yourself that the morning sun is sufficient.

Zeuxis: And you're cold-blooded enough to do such a thing, Parrhasius! You'd torture to get that look on the face of Marsyas!

Parrhasius: I . . . I will admit that, but . . .

Socrates: That is precisely why I fail to see any possibility that Parrhasius is guilty of this crime.

Mnesicles: I'm afraid I don't see that at all!

Socrates: It was a quick death, we are agreed?

Mnesicles: Yes, certainly – a vicious blow on the head.

Socrates: And do you think, then, that he would use a *dead* man from which to copy Marsyas' living agony?

Mnesicles: But, Socrates, how else would you account for the extraordinary similarity of the pose?

Socrates: I think the body was placed thus to lead us to your error, Mnesicles.

Mnesicles: Then . . . Where is Zeuxis?

For the first time they noticed that Zeuxis had slipped away. Parrhasius flushed with indignation, and Mnesicles began to wring his hands. Then he suddenly clapped his hands and blurted out: 'Of course, of course! The sleeping Endymion! I'll send my boy to fetch him!'

Socrates: It is not necessary, Mnesicles. I rather think he was too ill to stay. He's probably outside the gates, waiting for us. It is not Zeuxis who is the murderer.

Mnesicles: How can you say that, Socrates?

Socrates: You will recall, Mnesicles, that when I first questioned them they both agreed they strive for true copies of men. If Parrhasius used a model for the tortured Marsyas, you may be sure the model was tortured. And likewise, if Zeuxis used a model for the sleeping Endymion, you may be equally sure the model would be sleeping. Neither of them needed a model for death.

Mnesicles: Then we are left with an unidentified slave killed for an unknown reason.

Socrates: Perhaps not. If we assume that neither artist gained by the death, may we not also say that they suffered from it?

Mnesicles: What do you mean, Socrates?

Socrates: Should either artist have been blamed for the murder, would the city punish the one and retain the other? Or, since they are working as a team, wouldn't the entire project be discontinued?

Mnesicles: I suppose the scandal would cause the latter.

Socrates: And, with money left unspent that would have gone into the decoration of the unfinished Propylaea, do you suppose the city might authorize the completing of the structure itself? Indeed, Mnesicles, was that not your supposition when you killed your slave this evening?

Mnesicles backed toward the wall. Parrhasius moved toward him, fists clenched. 'Confess!' said the artist.

Mnesicles: Certainly not! It is all the slimmest of conjecture. None of you recognized the body as that of my slave!

Socrates: But a gentleman of your position does not enter the market place with only one attendant, Mnesicles. You ought to have sent this lad to fetch another.

Parrhasius: Yes, the boy here! I've no doubt you will need his help in this. Wait until he testifies!

Socrates glanced at the slave and then at Mnesicles. He touched his beard with a speculative gesture. 'It is a pity,' he said, 'that our laws require that slaves be tortured to get their testimony – a pity we cannot confirm the truth without such means.'

Mnesicles looked affectionately at the sixteen-year-old who served him. The slave hunched his shoulders almost imperceptibly and pulled in his chin like a stubborn child awaiting a disciplinary blow. His eyes were frightened. He smiled crookedly at his master.

'I will say nothing,' he whispered bravely.

'Will they make the boy testify,' Mnesicles asked softly then, 'if I confess?'

DEATH OF THE KING

Theodore Mathieson

Alexander the Great (356–323 BC) was the first Greek (or more properly Macedonian) leader who was interested in world domination, and he created the first major Mediterranean empire, stretching as far as the borders with India. Theodore Mathieson wrote a series of stories featuring famous historical characters as detectives. Called The Great Detectives *it was published in 1960. In the opening story, which is reprinted here, Alexander the Great investigates his own death!*

❦

I, Jolas of Philippi, returned to Babylon on the first day of the month of Hecatombaeon bearing a heavy heart and fearing lest the word I carried from our homeland, Macedonia – whereunto I had gone at the express wish of my dearest friend Alexander – should make my king turn against me. I left the caravan, with which I had traveled so many weary stadia through the steppes of Asia, in the western part of the city, and crossing the Euphrates by means of the ferry, went at once to my house by the edge of the palace gardens.

From my servant Bessus, who was exeedingly glad to see me, I learned that the city had the previous day held a great festival to celebrate Alexander's planned campaign against the coasts of Arabia. He was to leave Babylon in five days with the fleet under the command of Nearchus, and I knew I had come barely in time to tell the king my news.

With many sighs for what lay before me, I bathed briefly and put on clean garments and sandals, for the opportunities for bathing upon my journey had been few, and I knew that no matter how glad Alexander would be to see me again, except when he was upon the battlefield, he was most fastidious about the cleanliness of those about him.

I went then to the palace, passing the guards at Ishtar Gate who gave me familiar greeting, and ascended the steep stairway to the great terrace. There I learned the king was preparing for his bath, so upon the decision to surprise him I went at once to the lavacre, which was as yet deserted, although the warm water in the deep pool steamed invitingly in the evening air.

Sitting upon a bench beside the bath, surrounded by the paraphernalia for vigorous exercise, I played musingly with a ball until I heard footsteps, and then considering my activity unseemly in view of the portentous news I had to impart, I threw the ball aside.

Shortly thereafter Alexander himself entered with his attendants, and when he saw me, his joy was great.

'My thoughts have been with you constantly, Jolas,' said he, embracing me. 'Since dear Hephaestion died, I have been quite lonely, and I waited eagerly for your return.'

Indeed, although Alexander was a big man, compared with myself who am slight but agile in the games, he was so well proportioned and carried himself with such grace that one felt not overwhelmed by his proximity. His features were strong and proud, with a fresh pink color to his skin that Apelles, who painted Alexander holding lightning in his hand, did not accurately reproduce, making him somewhat black and swarter than his face indeed was.

Alexander disrobed and descended the tile steps into the pool, where he swam as we talked casually and I told him of the rigors of the journey and its adventures, but did not touch upon the burden of my intelligence, which he seemed unwilling to hear knowledge of. Whenever our talk verged upon the serious he would start cavorting like an aquatic mammal, disappearing beneath the surface, and rising again to cough with the access of water into his mouth.

When he had done this thrice, I rose concerned and said, 'Will you hear now what news I bear, Alexander?'

He looked reproachfully at me, but left the pool and, motioning away the attendants who came to anoint him with oil, put on his gown. Then he signaled me to follow him and we went to his chambers. There he dismissed his servants and stood looking at me with a frown.

'Have you ill news for me about Antipater?' he asked at last, with a flicker of suspicion in his eye. I knew Alexander feared the

growing power of his regent in Macedonia; that was why he had
sent me to discover how affairs went in the home country.

'Not about Antipater,' said I, 'but from him. Antipater is loyal
to you, Alexander, and governs as you would. But he sends this
news: Leanarchus, governor of Phrygia, has engaged mercenaries
and is occupied in plundering Thrace, and boasts of descending
upon Macedonia itself!'

'Cannot Antipater deal with this traitor as he deserves?' Alexander demanded.

'He has already put soldiers into the field against Leanarchus, and
no doubt will be successful. But that is not the worst. Leanarchus,
as you know is uncle of Medius, captain of your forces here in
Babylon. It is upon Medius' strategic skill that you will depend
for conquest of Arabia. And yet, Antipater wishes to inform you
that Leanarchus has spoken of his nephew's desire to rule all Asia
in your place. Leanarchus has hinted that Medius heads a plot to
assassinate you. I prayed I would return in time to bear you this
news.'

Alexander's face and chest grew red, as they always do when
he falls into a rage, and he turned upon me as if I were his
adversary.

'By the divine fury of Bacchus! I do not believe Antipater. *I trust
Medius!* Together we have fought five years from the Hindu Kush
to the Great Ocean. 'Twas he who saved me from death at the siege
of Multan when I received this!' Alexander touched the scar upon
his breast. 'With the help of Medius' ingenuity we have rebuilt
the phalanx, which we shall use with crushing effect against the
Arabians. We have planned our victory side by side – he is like a
very brother to me. I love him not less than I have loved you, Jolas
– until you came to me with such impossible news!'

It was as I had feared. Alexander, my dearest friend, had turned
against me at my words. I shrugged and made obeisance and turned
to leave the chamber, but Alexander stopped me by smiting his hand
into his palm.

'Stay, Jolas,' he said, less wildly. 'You must give me time to
think.' But even as I turned there came a knock upon the door
and Medius himself entered. He is a heavy-set plethoric man, with
a weighty chin and a forehead that bulges aggressively over deep
and canny eyes. Because Alexander favors me, Medius also shows
a liking which I am sure he does not feel.

'Welcome back to Babylon, Jolas,' said he, touching me. 'I come
to fetch Alexander to a private drinking bout, but if he is willing,
you must join us as well.'

'Yes, dear Jolas,' Alexander said with his customary affection. 'Do join us. We drink again to the health of the gods but talk of the exaltation of mortals through the conquest of Arabia!'

'Thank you, Alexander,' I said, 'but I am weary with many days of travel. With your permission I shall return home.'

'Of course, you must be tired,' Alexander said. 'Come tomorrow at noonday, and we shall talk further of – Antipater.'

I bowed and left the chamber, and at my last look at Alexander he was frowning at Medius.

But Alexander did not wait until midday for my visit. Next morning as I stood upon my balcony watching the shadows vanish upon the terracotta bosom of the Euphrates, a messenger brought me a letter from him, telling me to put aside all business and hasten to his side at once, as he had urgent need of me.

I returned to the palace, and within the vast reception chamber – from whose windows one can see past the fertile greenery that lines the Euphrates into the blank desert beyond – I found Alexander lying upon a couch.

At once he arose and spake to his attendants, telling them to leave him, and when we were alone he sat upright upon the couch and with a sigh covered his face with his hands. When he drew them away I was shocked to see how ravaged was his visage, and wondered at his great will power that hid what must be intense suffering from the eyes of his court.

Then he stepped down from the dais and clapped his hands upon my shoulder.

'Oh, thou bosom friend of Hephaestion, who once quarreled with him how much you loved me more than he, I need now your help in my extreme moment!'

His hand upon my shoulder burned with fever, and his words came in unsteady gusts, as if he drew breath with painful difficulty. I could see the gleam of fever behind the swart steadiness of his eye, and smell the good savor of his body which always clung like incense about him.

'I am ever your faithful servant, dear Alexander,' I said.

'Yes, I trust you. And therefore you must know, and no one else – *that I have been poisoned, and am dying.*'

The fervent words that sprang to my lips he stemmed by upraised hand, while with the other he withdrew his ring with which he sealed his letters, and pressed it firmly against my lips.

'Thus you must swear to keep silent,' he said.

'I swear,' I said, when Alexander removed the seal.

'Listen then, Jolas,' spake my king, sinking in sudden lassitude upon the couch. 'Last night, as you know, Medius came to carry me off to a drinking bout in Nearchus' chambers in the palace. There were only four of us – Medius, Nearchus, Susa the Persian treasurer, and myself. The chamber was guarded without, and no one entered nor left the whole time; we poured wine for one another as we listed, and we quaffed greatly, for the wine was sweet. If I had not dulled my palate I would have complained sooner of the sudden bitter cup that was poured me, but it was near daybreak and my senses were lulled; as it was, I drained it all but a third, and then remembering with a sudden stab what you had said, I demanded to know why I was served bitter vintage, and cried treason in my cup. Nearchus said he had served me, and that I did but taste the dregs of the flagon. Medius, whom I accused, picked up the very cup and himself drained the remainder. That calmed me, and I forgot my accusations until this morning. But while I knelt at the sacrifice within the temple, I felt a flush come over me, and later when I tried to write in my journal, I felt weak and faint. I knew then that I had been poisoned.'

'Perhaps it is some passing ague that you feel,' I said, but Alexander shook his head.

'Nay, Jolas, because I know this poison well. When Calisthenes languished in his prison at my command, I had him given it myself and watched the progress thereof. It waits from six to eight hours to make itself felt, and then one is taken with fever, which grows day by day for six days, until the life has been burned away. See, it is a poison I myself carry ever with me should I be taken captive!'

He seized his sword and pressed a spot upon the silver hilt close to the haft, and I beheld a lid suddenly spring open, revealing tiny white crystals within.

'It is gathered as liquid, and is formed into crystals which are cold to the touch. Do you know of this poison, Jolas?'

'No, Alexander,' said I.

'It is that which was put into my cup last night,' said he. 'And if Medius had not drained the remainder I would have had him quartered at the first flush in my cheek!'

'But perhaps you drank with him earlier in the day, Alexander,' I said. 'It would not be unusual.'

'True. But for two days I have fasted to the gods for a successful expedition to Arabia. *Neither food nor drink has passed my lips in all that time until I went to drink with Medius last night*. No, Jolas, as certain am I of the time of my poisoning as that I am Alexander.'

He closed the little receptacle, and held his sword over his knee, his hand gripping the hilt. Then with an access of violent energy he rose and swept down from his dais, swinging his sword as if at an imaginary enemy, and I withdrew for safety to an alcove while he raved.

'Would that I could kill them, all three!' he shouted. 'Then I would be sure of punishing my assassin! There was a time I would have done it! But not now. I must at the last use stealth, and pusillanimous *investigation* to discover the culprit, for the power of Macedonia must not be weakened, and each one of those men is part of the keystone in the arch of that power!'

'But Medius,' I insisted, 'has he shown signs of poisoning also?'

Alexander straightened and breathed deeply, and when he spake his voice was calm, and I knew his mind had gained control. 'He was here just now. I had a servant feel of his forehead and his body. He has no fever. The poison has not touched him.'

He turned to me and smiled, and the sight of his implacability chilled me.

'That is my problem, you see. The poison was in that cup. Until I find how I could be poisoned and Medius not, I cannot act. For not only had Medius reason to kill me, if your report from Antipater be accurate, but Nearchus, the admiral of my fleet also, as you shall see. And it was Nearchus, remember, who admittedly poured my drink.'

'And Susa the Persian?'

'He too, and for the best reason of all: that I have conquered his homeland.'

Somewhere a gong sounded. Alexander pulled a cord, and presently the doors to the reception chamber opened. Two Persian slaves entered and prostrated themselves upon their knees, and a Macedonian servant in exquisite tunic bowed low and announced Nearchus and Susa the Persian.

The admiral of the fleet entered with regal stride and stood at attention before the dais as Alexander returned to his couch. The Persian stood behind Nearchus and a little to his right.

'We have come, Susa and I, at thy command,' said Nearchus, his face showing the strain of the occasion; at the same time he gave me a sidelong glance that told me he cared not much for my presence. He was a stern-faced man with hollow cheeks and the pale-blue eyes of an anchorite, and was perhaps the most powerful man among the Macedonians, for Alexander trusted and honored him highly.

'Yes, Nearchus, be seated,' Alexander said, and Nearchus sat upon a stool below the king and watched with wary eyes as Alexander, showing now no signs of his illness, picked up several scrolls from a cushion beside him.

'These have been found among your possessions, Nearchus,' said Alexander. 'Letters from my stepbrother Arideus in Lydia, arguing the futility of further conquest in Arabia. He urges you to return to Macedonia, where Olympias, my mother, will heap honors undreamed of upon you.'

'I have told Alexander of these letters,' Nearchus said quietly.

'Yes, but you did not tell me your decision. Should you have decided to go, I would first have to be dead. Because alive I would not permit it!'

'Have our plans for the Arabian campaign ever suffered the slightest reservation of my enthusiasm, or diminution of my efforts on their behalf?'

Alexander's eyes fell before the cool inquiry of the other, and he shook his head. Then Nearchus turned to me and pointed an unwavering finger.

'There stands one whom you should suspect, Alexander. Jolas is the troublemaker, the one who pours false assertions into thine ear.'

'I think Alexander does not doubt my love for him,' said I.

'Nor do I,' said Alexander. 'My welfare has ever been uppermost in Jolas' mind.'

'Unless Antipater has corrupted him,' said Nearchus.

'Is it likely,' I said, 'when my life has been spent at Alexander's side, and I was in the company of Antipater only a few days?'

'Antipater is subtle at corrupting,' Nearchus persisted. 'Perhaps you would not know it.'

'I would know it,' said I.

'Enough!' Alexander cried, dismissing Nearchus, and the latter went out stiffly. The king then pointed his finger at Susa the Persian, who approached with a low obeisance.

'Last night, Susa, you told of great treasure buried beneath the ground by your emperor Darius at Opia, a day's journey to the north. You say that your love for me bade you tell me of it so our campaign to Arabia might prosper with such wealth to sustain it.'

'It is true, O King,' the Persian said. He was an elderly man, clad in the garishly dyed Persian garments, wearing a high headgear which rose as far above his face as his white beard fell below it.

'Now you will have a chance to prove your fealty. You will assemble porters and carriages and soldiers, and go to Opia to fetch the treasure here to me. At once. I will give you three days – one to go, one to load the treasure, and one to return. If you are not here three days hence, I shall send swift messengers to kill you. When I see the treasure, my doubt concerning you shall be cleared.'

'I understand, O King,' said Susa, bowing low.

'And you, Jolas, will accompany him to see that all goes well.'

I stood stiffly with surprise at the sudden appointment, and Alexander smiled gently.

'You have often complained of the boredom of litigating among the Macedonians, dear Jolas,' he said. 'Now I give you opportunity for treasure hunting and adventure.'

With a wave of his hand he dismissed the Persian, who backed out of the chamber, and then Alexander descended from the dais and took my hand.

'I am relying upon you, Jolas, to get the treasure safely to Babylon. While you are gone I shall continue probing the matter here. And take no longer than three days, dear friend, *for I shall be dead in six!*'

On the outward journey to Opia I shall not dwell, except to mention that we left Babylon with fifty foot soldiers and ten carts, and twenty mounted horsemen, including Susa and myself, and all went well. Since Opia lies, like most other Persian towns, along the river, we did not digress into the desert, and never lost sight of trees and greenery.

There was the matter of digging for the treasure, which lay in a cemetery to the east of Opia; and among the bones of departed natives, Susa indeed did reveal great wealth, and thus establish his fealty to Alexander – amphorae of gold, masks of silver, heavy bronze chests filled with darics – gold coins with the figure of an archer impressed upon one side – as well as urns filled with tiny golden siglos, and much other wealth besides.

By sunset of the second day, the whole of the treasure, well worth an emperor's ransom, lay battened down securely within the carts, and I had to promulgate the warning that any soldier found with treasure upon his person would instantly be put to death.

Planning to return to Babylon early the following morning, we retired early – I to my tent, Susa to his. But in the middle of the night I was awakened by a sound outside, and rose to investigate. I had but stepped out into the moonlight when an arrow whirred by my cheek, penetrating the fabric of my tent, and turning, I saw the archer behind a tall dark cypress and set out after him. He fled at once among the graves and I followed as best I could; but so busy was I watching lest I tumble into the great holes we had dug and thus keep their ancient occupants company, I soon lost sight of him and stopped and stood in the quiet moonlight, smelling the odor of decay and trembling in the cool breeze that blew from the river.

On sudden thought I returned at once to the camp and looked in upon Susa in his tent, and found the Persian sleeping soundly there.

But that proved nothing. Susa could have hired an assassin to kill me. As well as could Nearchus – or Medius.

I returned thoughtfully to my tent, but did not sleep the remainder of the night.

On our return to Babylon I found that Alexander had quit the palace for a garden villa across the river, and thence Susa and I repaired upon the ferry.

While crossing, Susa praised Alexander exceedingly for his policy of integrating the conquered peoples of Asia into the governmental fabric of the new empire, which stretched from the Aegean to the borders of India, and said how fortunate a man was he, Susa, a Persian, to have Alexander's trust in being appointed treasurer to the royal coffers. I replied that Susa's predecessor, Harpalus, a Macedonian, had proved himself faithless by stealing from the treasury, and Alexander had thought it fair and wise to entrust it thereafter to a native.

'But there are many, especially in Macedonia,' I added, 'who do not favor Alexander's policy of racial equality, and would like to reverse it.'

Whereupon Susa fingered his beard and fell silent.

At the villa, which lay in lush gardens close to the edge of the river where it was cooler, we were shown into Alexander's presence by an elderly doctor, who, when I questioned him as to our king's condition, murmured, 'It is truly a strange disease which works in him. I cannot mark the end of it.'

And when I saw Alexander I knew why the doctor shook his head so doubtfully. The king sat upon his bed on a terrace overlooking the river, playing at dice with Medius, and his face looked white and strained, like a mask stretched into place by the fingers of Death himself. My heart smote me with pity as I knelt by Alexander and told him of the treasure we had brought from Opia.

'Good, Jolas,' he said, laying aside the dice and smiling upon Susa. 'You have proved my trust, Susa. Nevertheless, you will lodge here in this villa with me, as do Medius and Nearchus.'

Thereupon Alexander dismissed the Persian and turned to Medius who sat opposite him and who was flushing redly and scowling at me the while.

'Why do you glower at Jolas, Medius?' Alexander asked. And when Medius did not answer, I spake up thus, 'Perhaps Medius is surprised that I am here, dear Alexander. My life was set upon while at Opia, and if the archer had not aimed poorly, perhaps Medius would be smiling now.'

With an oath Medius leaped to his feet, his hand upon his sword.

'Go, Medius!' Alexander cried, rising, and with an obeisance and a final black look at me, Medius left the terrace. Alexander sighed and walked unsteadily to the balcony, saying, 'A furnace rages within me, Jolas, and consumes me steadily. In three days hence I will be dead.'

'No, dear Alexander,' said I, stung with anguish. 'The gods will not permit your passing.'

Alexander stooped to the edge of a small fish pond set into the floor of the terrace and picked up a cup of greenish glaze and held it before my eyes.

'This cup poisoned me,' said he, 'and will help me to discover who my murderer is. I have not been idle these three days. Come, I will show you what I have done.'

In one room of the villa the king pointed out several near-naked men lying chained upon the floor. Two looked at us with fever-clouded eyes, and one was unconscious with great beads of sweat standing upon his forehead.

'I had several condemned criminals brought to me and gave them a choice: they could drink the poison I gave them, and let me watch the results, or be put at once to the sword, which was their just punishment. On the other hand, if they recovered from the poison, they would be free. Several volunteered gladly. Unfortunately, two have already died from the heavy dosage I gave them.'

'But what did you seek to determine?' I asked as we returned to the terrace.

'How little of the poison is required in a third of a cup before it brings no fever. I think I quaffed the major lethal portion from the top, for the crystals are instantly soluble. Doubtless there was *some* mingling below, and if I can find a minimum dose that will leave the drinker unaffected . . .'

'Then it would explain how Medius could drink without being poisoned?'

'Yes,' said Alexander, his lips turning cruel.

'But, dear Alexander, has not another thought occurred to you? A man bitten by an asp, who lives, may be bitten again with less effect, and yet again. Could not Medius have accustomed himself to small doses of the poison by taking first a grain and then a larger quantity?'

Alexander breathed heavily in sudden anger, and, unusually, spoke sharply to me.

'Of course I did think of it,' he said. 'But I do not have time to determine whether this could be done!'

He rang a bell and when the attendants arrived he ordered that Nearchus should bring him the final prisoner.

'You shall watch the end of my experiment, Jolas,' said he, equable once again. 'This poison is most powerful. Five crystals are lethal – but so are four; three bring fever and so do two, and both are probably lethal in the long run. Now if a *single* crystal brings fever by tomorrow, I shall know at least that Medius is in all probability innocent, for it means one is not immune from the smallest possible dosage.'

Thereupon Alexander filled the green-glaze cup a third full of wine, and from the receptacle in his sword picked out a single crystal of the poison with a fine tweezers, his hand shaking in sudden weakness, and dropped the crystal into the liquid.

By then Nearchus had entered with a bearded, half-naked prisoner of tremendous proportions and the yellowish skin of a Paphlagonian. The man had a truculent expression and Nearchus watched him carefully as Alexander stepped forward, holding the cup out to him.

'Drink,' he commanded. 'I think perhaps freedom lies ahead for you, who are the last.'

The dull eyes of the Paphlagonian looked first at Alexander and next at the cup. Then I beheld a spark rise in his orbs, and the following moment he raised his hand and dashed the cup out of the king's hand so that it crashed against the edge of the fish pond, the contents spilling into the water.

Almost at the sound of the shattering of the cup, Nearchus stepped forward, swung his sword aloft, and swept it down with tremendous force at the point where the prisoner's neck met his shoulder. The Paphlagonian fell with his head half severed and lay athwart the coping of the fish pool, covering the shards of the poison cup, while his heart, still beating, pumped blood into the clear water.

Meanwhile I saw Alexander back unsteadily toward his couch, his face flushing scarlet, beads of sweat forming upon his upper lip.

'I am aflame,' he murmured, and I took him by the arm and helped him to his couch.

'You must cover your feet for they are cold,' I said as the sight of my weakened king made my own heart bleed, 'and support your back for the sharp pain that is in it.' And I put a cushion gently behind him.

By the time Alexander lay resting easily, with his eyes closed, Nearchus had ordered the body of the Paphlagonian removed and I stood alone with the admiral in an antechamber.

'You are a troublemaker,' Nearchus said, looking at me with loathing. 'With your talk of conspiracy, you have caused many deaths, and will bring ruin upon us all! Could it not be that Alexander has caught a mere disease and will recover? Must you call us all assassins?'

'It is no disease,' I said simply.

'Liar!' Nearchus cried, and left the chamber.

I returned at once to the terrace.

'Will you have me at your side?' I asked softly. But Alexander watched me not, so absorbed was he gazing upon the shards of the green glaze and the blood mingled with the wine that still spread, staining the limpid waters of the pool, and now making invisible the fish within it.

For the remainder of the day, every time I sought admittance to Alexander's chambers, the doctor turned me away, saying the king was too ill to grant an audience. At the evening meal Alexander was absent, and Susa and Nearchus and Medius and I sat together without a word, and I could feel the united force of their dislike directed against me. I could not finish my supper, and rose to walk along the river bank until sundown, returning to my quarters at the villa and retiring early, for I was greatly fatigued.

I was awakened in the middle of the night by the doctor, who told me to come at once, that Alexander had expressed a wish to see me.

At the sight of him I knew death was not far away. He put out a dry hand as I sat beside him, and I felt the heat of it burn my wrist.

'Dear Jolas,' he said weakly. 'Again I have cut the Gordian knot. I know now who has poisoned me, and you must help me to see justice done. Call Nearchus and Susa and Medius here at once. We shall make the final judgment!'

I went at once and awakened the others, and when they all stood before the king he spoke again.

'Nearchus – Medius – you have known me long, have stood beside me in battle, abided by my decisions and rarely found me wanting in wisdom. Susa, you know me for a fair sovereign, and one who governs wisely. I tell you now. You *must trust me*. I have discovered my assassin, but I wish to reveal my knowledge in my own way. Jolas –' he extended a hand in my direction. 'Upon the table is a tray with three cups, filled with wine. Give one to each of them.'

I handed a glazed cup, much like the one the Paphlagonian had recently shattered, to the two Macedonians and the Persian.

'Now believe me when I say this: *that the ones who are innocent of poisoning me need fear nothing*. But the one who is my murderer will himself be poisoned tonight! Now then, I command you to drink, Susa!'

Susa blinked at Alexander and I thought his lip trembled, but he seized the cup with both hands and drank the contents in three great draughts. Then he put down the cup, rubbling his beard with the back of his hand.

'Drink, Nearchus,' said Alexander.

Nearchus did not hesitate, but drained the cup as quickly as Susa had done.

'And now you, Medius,' said Alexander.

Medius raised the cup to his lips and then lowered it.

'But suppose you are wrong, Alexander?' he asked quietly.

'I asked you to trust me. I am not wrong.'

Thereupon Medius raised the cup and drank, having trouble halfway through, as if his throat had closed against the liquid; but finally he managed to drain the cup and looked at Alexander defiantly.

Nearchus spake then. 'We have all three drunk, trusting thee, Alexander, but you have raised Jolas of Philippi above us, as if he alone were free of thy suspicion. Why not have him drink as well?'

'But I have not forgotten him,' Alexander said. 'Jolas, there stands a cup of water upon the table for you to drink. If you, too, participate in this test, perhaps the anger of the others against you will be diminished. I say to you as I said to the others; if you are innocent, you have nothing to fear. Drink the water.'

I raised the glass to my lips and as I did Alexander spake again. '*It is as pure as the water of my bath, Jolas.*'

At that I hesitated and looked at Alexander with staring eyes and beating heart – and put the cup down upon the table.

'You are my murderer, Jolas,' said Alexander, his eyes burning. 'You were sitting beside the pool when I arrived there four nights ago. How did you poison it?'

'With some of the poison, which I tossed into it,' said I, almost crying now that my perfidy was so inevitably disclosed. 'But I did not mean to kill you, Alexander,' I pleaded. 'Antipater assured me

that he had tested the poison upon others and that taken through
the pores the poison merely induces a fever that will pass away. But
I saw you *swallow* some of the water!'

'Antipater knew you for a fool! He meant Alexander should die!'
Nearchus cried, stepping toward me, but he stopped as Alexander
raised his hand.

'And what reason did Antipater give you?' he asked.

'He wished Medius dead and disgraced, so members of Medius'
family in Macedonia, who have been troublesome to Antipater,
could be removed from authority. He knew Medius was your
great drinking companion. I was to poison you harmlessly, plant
the knowledge of Medius' desire to assassinate you, then when the
effects of the poison became manifest, to indicate their origin, and
accuse Medius of administering it in your drink.'

Alexander nodded with satisfaction.

'And what was to be your reward, Jolas?'

'Antipater would beg you to release me from duty here in Babylonia, and once in Macedonia he would give me the governorship
of Sestos, a position, Alexander, you would never give me, since you
would have me litigate in Babylonia until the end of my days.'

'Not now, Jolas, not now!' Alexander said. Then rising unsteadily
he pointed at Medius.

'You were to be the victim, Medius,' he said. '*Make Jolas drink
the water*!'

With Medius' all-too-ready sword at my throat, I had no
alternative and I drained the water to the last drop.

In the silence that followed I asked, 'How did you know that it
was I, Alexander?'

'The other day I asked you if you knew this poison, and you
denied any knowledge of it. Yet when the Paphlagonian was killed
I was stricken with a sudden seizure and you helped me to my couch.
'Warmth for your feet,' you said, 'and a pillow for the great pain
in your back!' *But how could you know my back hurt, feeling as if
someone thrust a sword between my shoulder blades, if you did not
already know the effects of the poison?* I had not told it to anyone.
That began a train of thought, and when I saw the poisoned wine
spreading within the pool and wondered how soon the fishes would
die, I remembered the bathing water, and realized why Medius had
not been poisoned by the third of the bitter cup, and why all my
investigation had been fruitless. *There was no poison in the cup!*
I had been poisoned *before* the drinking bout, not during it! . . .'

Alexander was too weak to go on, so Nearchus had me sent under
guard to my house at the edge of the palace gardens and confined

there. Medius wished to kill me at once, which was but natural, since it was he who had sent the archer after me, but Alexander and Nearchus were against it. It would be better for the ruling officers if it were thought Alexander died of disease, and so it will be told that I, too, died of the same, from my contact in the service of the king.

It is two days now since the great Alexander died. There is the sound of weeping and mourning in the streets of Babylon, and a hush in the palace gardens. The fever that burns me makes my pen cold to the touch, but I must finish this so the world will know that I did not mean that my dearest friend Alexander should die.

I have no use for men who would kill merely to satisfy their ambition.

THE FAVOUR OF A TYRANT

Keith Taylor

*Keith Taylor is an Australian writer who has an avid interest in early
British history. He has written a series of historical fantasy novels set
at the time of the downfall of the Roman Empire in Britain which
began with* Bard *(1981). Here, though, he travels back further in
time to explore scientific intrigue and treachery at the time of the
Greek mathematician and inventor, Archimedes, who lived from
around 287 to 212 BC.*

∽

The master had been at court the night before. He entered the
workshop with such careful steadiness, it was clear he had done
his share of drinking. Not that I'm one to raise an eyebrow if a
man punishes the wine bowl. Still, this one was moderate as a rule,
so I guessed there had been something out of the ordinary in last
night's feast.

He held up a hand. The saws and mallets stopped at once. I swept
shavings off his favourite chair and offered him a hair of the dog,
some watered Chian wine. He accepted it, taking three measured
swallows.

'*Chaire*, my good Phanes,' says he. 'How my head aches!'

And still he was here, a scant hour past dawn. Something was
up besides the sun, no question.

'I drank like a fool of a boy last night,' he confessed. 'The
excitement of proving at last, *by pure mathematics*, my laws of
leverage and mechanical advantage. I fear I claimed that if I had a
place to stand and a lever long enough, I could move the world!'

I reckoned he could. He was the greatest man I ever knew. Mind, I'd been using his principles to make levers and windlasses for over a year. He'd also devised a compound pulley block that I'd worked with until I understood it better than he. I didn't care if they lacked rigorous proof on paper, so long as they were useful. I'm not a mathematician.

'Was that bad, sir?' I asked.

'Several men laughed, and the Roman ambassador tapped his head, I believe. The licence of wine. My royal cousin's pride was offended. He challenged me to prove my words by launching the *Syrakosia* single-handed.' He sighed. 'Well, I agreed, to shorten the tale. Else the king had looked foolish before dignitaries from Athens, Rome and Carthage.'

No, that wouldn't do. Archimedes wasn't rich, you see. He depended on his cousin's favour.

The *Syrakosia*? She was the hugest ship ever built, a whim of King Heiron's. I'd seen her take shape; light of the Sun, I'd worked on her! If Archimedes was worried about launching that marine monster single-handed and losing Heiron's favour, it seemed to me he was worried for nothing.

'Sir, I've been working with your ideas for months. We can contrive a tackle that'll launch the *Syrakosia* at the touch of a lever. Simple.'

It was simple, too. Once you knew how. Believe me, friends, except that it was a morning after for him, he would not have worried for a minute. We're talking about the man who discovered how much silver a cheating goldsmith had mixed into a golden crown – without melting it down or cutting off the smallest bit, it's true. He could have done *anything*.

'It must be begun now,' Archimedes said.

'It's as good as done, sir. The ambassador from Rome will not be tapping his head when we've finished.'

I watched him leave the harbour-side warehouse we had fitted out as our marine workshop. You know, most great men I've seen, kings and lords and such, don't *look* great. Archimedes did. He was only a finger's length shorter than I, strong and straight at fifty, with a bearded face that made me think of statues of Zeus. Being a gentleman, he had to pretend he thought all useful, down-to-earth knowledge sordid and vile, fit only for slaves, and it's true he had an endless passion for things like the movement of stars or the exact proportions of a circle, but I can tell you he loved engineering, too. He was delighted when the king ordered him to devise war machines to defend the city. It gave him a perfect excuse to spend time in the workshop.

I handed over to my foremen, and went to walk along the ramparts of the harbour-wall. Soldiers let me pass freely; I was known to them all as Archimedes' master-carpenter, and easy to recognize, a towhead six-and-a-quarter feet tall, muscled like a bull, with moustaches down to my collar-bones.

There on the ramparts, I looked over a couple of the war engines Archimedes had designed. These were massive timber cranes meant to sink attacking ships. The long arms were made to swing out over the water, holding huge lead weights that could then be released, to drop through the enemy hulls and smash them. I'd tested the idea, using worthless old tubs with reinforced decks. It had worked. The cranes were certainly strong enough for what I had in mind now.

I stood there rubbing my chin and thinking for a while. Then I visited the construction docks, down by the Great Harbour. Complete now, the *Syrakosia* lay there, ready for launching. Splendid she appeared, indeed, with her immense size, lead-sheathed hull and three masts, each tall as a tree – if you weren't a sailor or craftsman.

For one thing, she was just *too* huge. A 'twentier' galley has so many oars that their best arrangement will still be clumsy. Worse, it had been Heiron's whim to make her a grain transport, war galley and royal pleasure ship all in one. I ask you! If you want a grain bottom, you build a grain bottom. If you want a warship, you build a warship. Try to combine both in the same hull, and the result won't be much good for either function. Then she had other useless adjuncts, like a suite of sybaritic cabins and an immense fish-tank.

Still, you don't say to a king that his pet project cannot work, even if you are Archimedes, much less if you are a slave. Our concern was to launch her. I felt certain those two cranes would serve the purpose. Control them together from a single windlass, through a couple of Archimedes' compound pulley-blocks, and they could lift and pull her forward so that she glided down the slipway at the movement of one man's hand. Let's see the Roman ambassador smirk then!

You know the cold feeling that goes over your skin when you're being ill-wished, or a ghost is walking nearby? I suddenly felt it. Glancing around, I saw nothing out of the way, just a dark Punic sailor who'd also stopped to gawk at the *Syrakosia*, scratching his head. Thanking his gods he would never have to row in her, I supposed. But the chill on my skin remained.

I forgot the misgiving with the hour. I'd work to do. After

discussing things with the master, I had the cranes unclamped, mounted on wheels, and dragged down to the quayside. My workmen braced and blocked the wheels under my direction, so that an earthquake would hardly move them, and left the machines there until next morning.

With the dawn I was down by the construction dock. The cranes needed placing in exact positions. I'll ask you, friends, what could go wrong? I am not careless, and my workmen were picked experts in siege work and leverage.

Well, something went wrong. We had barely touched the first crane when its whole ponderous height lurched to one side. One of the big wooden wheels came off and rolled into the sea. I grabbed a lever and sprang to jam it under the carriage. It made cracking noises; so did my muscles. Sweat popped out of my skin.

'Help me, you Persian-sired bastards!' I yelled. 'Take the strain on those dexter ropes or she'll fall! Right. Now pull for your rascal lives! Charicles – uh! – chocks under the wheels, *now*!'

If the men hadn't hauled strongly on those ropes at once, I'd have been a red smear on the quayside. Charicles was quick with the wedges, and other men slid baulks under the axle until the wobbling crane held steady. I stared at its top-heavy, ungainly height with relief. Had it fallen, it would have smashed like kindling, and probably killed men.

Well, the sweating and swearing was over now, with no broken backs. I went looking for the cause. It wasn't far to seek, and it hadn't been mischance. Some dirty maggot had cut through the linch-pin, sticking it back together with wax to make it look sound! The other wheel on that side had been treated the same way. Luckily, it hadn't come adrift with the other, as it had surely been meant to. I tested them all before we went further, and examined both cranes from base to tip, climbing them myself.

Nothing else was wrong.

It seemed too purposeful for idle mischief. Did someone want Archimedes to fall from his cousin's favour? That could be anybody from Rome, Carthage, or – closer to home – Zancle. Yes, and there were plenty of possible culprits in Syracuse itself, and they needn't be acting for political reasons. Some courtier might want Archimedes removed so that he could advance himself. It occurred to me, too, when I thought a bit further, that this might not be meant to discredit Archimedes, blazing sun to my mechanical planet though he was. Hades. Someone might dislike *me*.

I wondered if he was persistent or a quitter.

When I told the master what had happened, and what I suspected, he turned out to be having one of his high-flown moods; poring in ecstasy over a letter from some astronomer in Egypt. He barely listened to me. After warning me absently to have an eye to my safety at work, he was lost again in this Alexandrian's notions of the harmonic movements of the planets, or some such.

I took care, right enough! From that moment, the machinery we worked on was guarded night and day. I looked it over for effects of sabotage each morning and afternoon. Then I heard a piece of gossip from Calluella, a servant in Archimedes' house who sometimes shared my bed. Fine girl, Calluella. Freed and married long ago, I believe.

She told me the master had nearly been killed at the theatre.

Once she ran out of excited chatter, it turned out to have been less fearful by far. The master had been watching a tragedy by Lysander, a local talent, in company with Heiron's court. The huge awning that was supposed to unfurl, neatly and obediently, to shade them all from the sun, had come away from its fastenings all together in a massive roll. It crashed down less than an arm's length from Archimedes. It also broke someone's shoulder and knocked five or six folk flat. Even though it hadn't come near the king, he'd been highly displeased. The slaves whose duty it was to roll and release the shade-cloth were still screaming.

'That'll be me,' I said, 'if anything bad happens at the launching. I wonder . . . Calluella, if you hear of any other accidents like that happening near the master, be sure to tell me – quickly.'

'If you desire me to take all that trouble,' she said, 'you had better love me again – slowly.'

Tarnus the All-Competent, but she drove a hard bargain.

The next morning, Archimedes sent for me again. There was nothing of the dreamy savant about him this time, and the movement of planets was far from his mind. He told me about the falling shade-cloth, and I listened like a schoolboy, pretending it was news to me. You don't let your master guess how much slaves hear, or how much we talk among ourselves. Funny that masters rarely think of it; perhaps they don't want to. For certain, *we* don't want them to. Not even a master as good as Archimedes.

'You recall the event of the wheels on the siege crane, good Phanes?' he asked, looking more like Zeus in the dignity of judgement than ever. 'The linch-pins were deliberately broken, you said.'

'They were, sir.'

'Interesting.' He stroked his beard. 'Something very like it was done to the sun-awning at the theatre. The lacings that held it to the base had been cut, *and on the inner side*, so that it looked in perfect working order. Until it was untied to roll down over the framework. It almost struck me down. It may have been intended to do so.'

Noises of astounded horror from the awed Phanes. I felt glad the master had become aware he might be in danger, mind you.

'I should like you to attend the king's banquet with me tonight,' he said. 'My royal cousin demands it. He's greatly preoccupied with the launching of the *Syrakosia*. Our good names are at stake, to be sure. We had a part in building her.'

Right. Archimedes had devised, according to the king's enthusiastic whims, and I had built. The king had foisted a Corinthian named Archias upon us, in the belief that he was a shipwright, but I'd found him about as much use as the giant fish-tank I'd had to instal amidships. Naturally he took all the credit and complained about the idle mischief of his subordinates.

He was present at the king's banquet. Even if he'd been missing, I'd not have liked it, for I'd been summoned to Heiron's board before. This time, as previously, I was welcomed in the way of a performing dog or valued chariot-horse, and questioned with great condescension about the siege engines and the ship. Well, there was one who didn't condescend, and he was the Roman ambassador, Tetricus. Haughty as Priam and cold as stone, that one, and didn't even condescend, just addressed me as though I was not even alive, showing in every gesture and word how Romans think of slaves. *Instrumentum vocale*, they call us – the tool that talks.

The Carthaginian, Hartho, was more hearty, but I didn't take to him, either. I reckoned there was treachery under the bluff surface. It didn't seem to fit that any of them would be behind the mishaps we'd suffered, though. Our king was firmly on the Roman side, and they had broken the Carthaginians' fleet years ago; they had nothing to worry about in naval matters. Carthage? Right enough, they would like to remove Archimedes from the king's favour and gain his services themselves, but then it wasn't likely they would try to injure him. Even if they did, Romans or Carthaginians, they'd take more effective measures than dropping a rolled awning on the man, surely?

Archias? A little man, jealous of Archimedes, might try to injure him. I could believe that. I could also believe he'd try such a half-baked method. He wouldn't try to spoil the *Syrakosia's* launching, though. That would redound to his own discredit.

I looked over that noble gathering. Lysander the playwright was talking to Tetricus about the ceremony to honour Poseidon that would be held at the ship-launching – and holding forth about some sculptures he'd made for the occasion. Hartho was ogling a flute girl, while Archias flattered the king until he nearly yawned with boredom. All much as usual, and I couldn't say which of them, if any, was guilty. I only knew that I'd paid for eating the rich viands prepared by the king's Persian cook. In full.

Archimedes asked my opinion later, and I'll say this, he listened with care, as one man to another. I hadn't a thing to give him but speculation, though, not even sharp suspicions. It would have pleased me to think Archias the one, but only because I did not like him.

'You do well to have our launching mechanism guarded day and night,' Archimedes told me. 'Let that continue. For the *Syrakosia* herself, assign two dozen, Phanes, between sunset and dawn, and let them patrol her in four watches, six men to a watch; one of your trusty workmen and five soldiers. The ordinary quayside guards will do by day.'

I protested. I had to. 'Master, I can think of a dozen places in that ship that need watching all hours! The incendiary missiles for the catapults – all that sulphur and naphtha – it shouldn't be left aboard if we think someone means harm!'

'Excellent, Phanes.' He sounded happy, on my oath. 'Have it removed, and take any other precautions you think are required. But my express command is that the guards' numbers be as I've stated.'

He knew something, or had divined something I couldn't perceive. I had worked for him long enough to know the signs.

You'll conceive the care I took and the sleep I lost, sweating. I understood Archimedes' order to leave the ship all but unguarded by day. Nobles of the city and visiting dignitaries were all over her, making comments and wagers, and we couldn't bar them, or question them. We knew pretty well which ones were out-and-out spies, but that wasn't a matter for concern. A spy couldn't learn much aboard the *Syrakosia*, except that as a fighting ship she'd be useless. He was welcome to that intelligence for me. I was perturbed for Archimedes' honour and my precious skin.

He himself was often aboard, talking to the men who came to see around the curious vessel. I wished I knew what he was up to. Did he suspect someone? If so, whom? And why?

He arrived at dawn on the day of the launching. First he wandered the length of the upper deck, then moved around below the vast, lead-sheathed hull, peering and frowning. I had plenty to occupy me, or I'd have joined him to learn what he was about, but the next time

I saw him he was walking the deck with Lysander. The playwright looked worn out but cheerful. Taking leave of Archimedes with a laugh, he set out – I supposed – towards his home. I noticed him stumble as he went.

'He's about early, sir.'

'He confessed he spent the night in revelling and has not yet been to bed.' The master shrugged. 'He assures me he has made large wagers on the complete success of the launching. It would appear he found no dearth of men to accept. So much for the power of Archimedes' name.'

There were plenty of brothels among the harbour area. The noble Lysander was known to be active among them, too.

'Well, he's at the right end of those bets, sir.'

'He will be if we make haste!' Archimedes' eyes were bright and intent. 'Phanes, bring caulkers with mallets, wood and oakum, this minute, and join me beneath the hull. I have things to show you. *Run*!'

I ran as ordered, and had three caulkers on the spot a little later. Archimedes' face was pink, but he'd found his stately manners again, and only by a clipped, curt way of speaking did he show any part of his colossal anger.

'Observe, my Phanes.' He pointed to the ground below the great launching-cradle. 'Wood shavings and scraps of lead, both spiriform – the castings of a drill or large awl. Here, here, and again here. What does this suggest to you?'

It didn't suggest anything at first. One finds all kinds of refuse underneath the hull of a ship that has just been built. Then I looked closely, and saw how the wood and lead shavings were entwined together.

'Hades, master! Someone has been drilling holes in the bottom of the twentier – since her hull was covered in lead!'

That meant long after any honest drilling could have been necessary, for the lead covering had been the final stage, a thin hammered sheath to repel barnacles and worms.

'Just so.' Archimedes bent low and pointed. His finger quivered with passion. 'See here, and here as well! Those specks of white powder are salt. Someone has drilled those mischievous holes, plugged them with hard salt, and then smeared paint on the outside, paint grey as lead, to hide his work.'

I didn't know if the paint had been necessary, but I saw the purpose of the rest. 'Once the twentier is launched and takes the water, the salt will start to dissolve –'

'And the harbour will enter by half a hundred jets. Yes. Find the holes and plug them, my invaluable Phanes; no time is to be lost. The launching takes place in a few hours.'

I asked no more questions. We worked like desperate ants, first finding those holes, then ramming dowel wadded around with oakum into them, until it fitted tightly. Jerry-work, yes, but it would save the launching from disaster. Once it was over – this I swore by Tarnus and the Earth-Mother – the master was going to explain to me how he had known.

Well, the ceremony went off finely, with the king and his priests making sacrifice to Poseidon, and the whole city gasping in awe as Archimedes turned his windlass – alone – and the immense bulk of the *Syrakosia* obediently took to the water. Then she lumbered about the harbour, moved by her multiple banks of oars, hurling six-talent balls and smoking masses of sulphur from her catapults, with the Tyrant of Syracuse beaming on the quayside. The city looked upon Archimedes more than ever as a wonder-working magician, and I stopped sweating for the first time in days.

Back in the workshop, I asked, 'How did you know?'

He was beaming more broadly than King Heiron had done. He had immortal qualities and a mighty mind, but for all that, he enjoyed being right as much as the next vulgar clod – and I was the only one he could really tell.

'Partly, it was knowing the king's court, and those who frequent it, but chiefly logic and ratiocination. Pure, strict reason clarifies all things, Phanes, in life as in mathematics. It all proceeded from the first two events.'

'The crane and the awning, sir?'

'Yes. Both partook of the banal and petty, yet both showed a knowledge of mechanics. Agents of another nation who wished to disgrace me would try to make me appear guilty of treason; who wished me merely slain, would use a dagger. I therefore posited that the culprit was one individual man, with some of an artisan's or engineer's cast of mind. It was at any rate a strong working hypothesis.'

I nodded.

'I hypothesized further. His acts with the crane and the awning amounted to little more than schoolboy malice.' Not to me they didn't, by all the gods! That crane had almost killed me. 'Poorly conceived acts. Yet it appeared both were aimed at me. Again I took this for my working hypothesis.'

'Then you were on the lookout for one man, sir, acting for himself, just for his own gain?'

'Until further knowledge contradicted the idea. And someone in court circles. Nothing certain was likely to emerge unless he went further. Therefore, I had the ship lightly guarded. No guard at all would make him suspicious, while, if he could not evade the slight precautions I did take, he was not worth troubling about.'

'But how did he drill so many holes in the *Syrakosia* without being seen?'

'How do you suppose?' Archimedes asked, a bit shortly. 'I have tried to teach you to think with your mind like a civilized man, not with your hands like a Celtic barbarian. Did I waste my time?'

I thought about it, talking as I reasoned my way through. 'He couldn't have stolen aboard at night. The guards would have seen him. All right, then. He must have come aboard openly, during the day, and that means he's a noble or courtier whom nobody would question. He could hide the salt, and a drill or big awl, under his clothes. Then he could conceal himself in any of fifty places until nightfall. Six men patrolling that whole vast ship wouldn't be likely to catch him!'

'They did not catch him. They heard him, however, more than once. The scoundrel crawled under the floor-timbers of the bilge and went to work. Obviously, it held no water because the ship had yet to be launched. He had easy access to the hull and was out of sight. He could cease working whenever he heard the tramp of feet approach.'

'Yes!' I grew enthusiastic. 'I see it, sir! He'd need strong, tough hands to work all night drilling so many holes in ship's timber. Very strong. The thin layer of soft lead on the outside would be nothing. To go aboard unquestioned he'd have to be a noble or functionary. Noble rank, but artisan's hands. There'd be few men with both.'

'So it seemed to me. By then I had suspicions of one particular man, but they were still no more than speculation. I questioned your guards by the first light of dawn this morning. Most of them believed the ship to be haunted, but when they described the sounds they had heard (and the parts of the ship from which they emanated) I believed I knew the name of the ghost, and the generality of what he had been doing. When I examined the area beneath the hull, it became certain.'

'I admire your thinking, sir,' I said, truthfully. 'My own wits must still be in my hands, though. I'm no closer to knowing who did this.'

Archimedes stroked his beard. 'You do not know all, yet. How do you imagine he left the ship?'

'Wriggled out through one of the oar-ports and climbed down?' I hazarded. And there was another clue. To leave thus unobtrusively, and to hide and work under the floor-planks, too, he'd have to be a lean man.

'I believe he did. Afterwards, he rushed home, hid his tools, washed and donned fresh garments. Then it was that he did something utterly foolish, and confirmed his guilt to me. He literally placed the proof in my hands, Phanes. See.'

Archimedes showed me his right palm. It carried a smear of grey paint.

'Dark care sits behind the horseman, does it not? He hadn't yet seen, *from the outside*, the holes he drilled in our ship. The morning was still too grey and he in too much of a hurry when he escaped. He fretted that a casual glance would discover them if they were not concealed in time. That risk – slight, I think – preyed on his mind. He could not endure it. So he performed the astonishingly silly act of coming back to the *Syrakosis* at dawn, this time with a small pot of paint which he smeared on the holes as camouflage. He did this while pretending to examine the steering-paddles and keel.'

'Indeed, that was stupid,' I said feelingly. 'A few dozen holes over that immense ship's bottom? As you say, matter, they'd likely have gone unnoticed, except that you were already on to the fellow.' I shook my head. 'I wonder at him, whoever he is. His first large, bold, well-conceived stroke of villainy, and he doesn't know to leave well enough alone.'

'*Whoever he is*? Do you say you do not know even yet? Think!'

His voice cracked like a whip. It was an order. I stopped and thought.

'You said he was there at dawn, examining the ship. Only one man – *Lysander*?' I said, unbelievingly. 'He didn't spend the night among the whorehouses? He was tired, because –'

'I am afraid so. You grow less than coherent, Phanes. Discipline, if you please. It's good for the mind.'

'Sir, I've never looked closely at his hands, but he's a playwright, not a workman! Isn't he? If he hadn't the strength for that job, then he couldn't have done it, no matter how guilty he looks. *Lysander*?'

'Who is familiar with machinery. The machinery of the stage. Who was present at the theatre when the awning fell, because a play of his was being performed. Who, besides being a playwright, is an architect and sculptor, *used to cutting stone*. Who evidently fancies he could take my place as the king's master of ordnance.'

Archimedes sighed again.

It fitted, it all fitted. Even Lysander's lean figure and the wagers he had placed on the success of the launching, in order to make himself seem innocent. Huh! And he'd won them, too, now! Not that it would compensate a man of his conceit for failure.

'This morning I became certain. He allowed me to understand that he had caroused all night and not yet returned home. Yet his clothes were too fresh for that. More damning still, his knuckles were skinned, his hands, tough as they are, were so sore that he winced when I clasped them – and left a trace of grey paint on mine. When I looked into his eyes and told him I knew all . . . his face changed. He might as well have confessed.'

'But you have proof, sir!' I burst out. 'You can tell the king!'

'No. I think we may leave it to his own mind. Dark care sits behind the horseman.'

I wouldn't have been so lenient. Well, I'm not Archimedes, and he proved right about Lysander's mind. The dramatist came less and less often to court, pleading ill health. Within a month he fled Syracuse altogether. He ended up in Rhodes, I think, or was it Epirus? I never heard of any more plays by him, but he seemed to prosper well as a builder – as the artisan he didn't wish to be. And maybe that's justice.

THE WHITE FAWN

Steven Saylor

Starting with Roman Blood *(1991), Steven Saylor introduced the delightful character of Gordianus the Finder, a Roman who, by his own wit and cunning, has established himself as the city's premier investigator. He lived at the time of Cicero, in the eighth decade* BC. *Saylor has written a further four novels about Gordianus,* Arms of Nemesis *(1992),* Catilina's Riddle *(1993),* The Venus Throw *(1995) and* A Murder on the Appian Way *(1996), and a collection of his short stories will be issued in 1997. In this story the setting is Rome and eastern Spain, 76* BC.

The old senator was a distant cousin of my friend Lucius Claudius, and the two had once been close. That was the only reason I agreed to see the man, as a favor to Lucius. When Lucius let it slip, on the way to the senator's house, that the affair had something to do with Sertorius, I clucked my tongue and almost turned back. I had a feeling even then that it would lead to no good. Call it a premonition, if you will; if you believe that such things as premonitions exist.

Senator Gaius Claudius' house was on the Aventine Hill, not the most fashionable district in Rome. Still, there are plenty of old patrician households tucked amid the cramped little shops and ugly new tenements that sprawl over the hill. The façade of the senator's house was humble, but that meant nothing; the houses of the Roman nobility are often unassuming, at least on the outside.

The doddering doorkeeper recognized Lucius (could there be two men in Rome with his beaming round face, untidy red hair and dancing green eyes?) and escorted us at once to the atrium, where a fountain gurgled and splashed but did little to relieve the heat of a cloudless midsummer day. While we waited for our host to appear, Lucius and I strolled from corner to corner of the little square garden. On such a warm day, the various rooms facing the atrium all had their shutters thrown open.

'I take it that your cousin has fallen on hard times,' I said to Lucius.

He pursed his lips. 'Why do you assume that, Gordianus? I don't recall mentioning it.'

'Observe the state of his house.'

'It's a fine house. Gaius had it built when he was a young man and has lived here ever since.'

'It seems rather sparsely decorated.'

'You saw the busts of his noble ancestors lined up in their niches in the foyer,' said Lucius, his nose tilting up. 'What more ornamentation does the house of a patrician require?' Despite his genial temperament, Lucius sometimes could not help being a bit of a snob.

'But I think your cousin is a great lover of art, or used to be.'

'Now why do you say that?'

'Observe the mosaic floor beneath our feet, with its intricate acanthus leaf pattern. The workmanship is very fine. And note the wall paintings in some of the rooms around us. The various scenes are from the *Iliad*, I believe. Even from here I can see that they're works of very high quality.'

Lucius raised an eyebrow. 'Cousin Gaius does have good taste, I'll grant you that. But why do you assume he's fallen on hard times?'

'Because of the things that I don't see.'

'Now, Gordianus, really! How can you walk into a house you've never entered before and declare that things are missing? I can see into the surrounding rooms as well as you, and they all look adequately furnished.'

'Precisely; the furnishings are adequate. I should expect something more than that from the man who built this house and commissioned those wall paintings and mosaics. Where is the finely wrought furniture? Everything I see looks like the common stuff that anyone can buy ready-made down in the Street of the Woodworkers. Where are the paintings, the portable ones in frames, the portraits and bucolic scenes that are so fashionable nowadays?'

'What makes you think that cousin Gaius ever collected such works?'

'Because I can see the discolored rectangles on the wall where they used to hang! And surely a rather substantial statue once filled that empty spot atop the pedestal in the middle of the fountain. Let me guess: Diana with her bow, or perhaps a discus-thrower?'

'A rather good drunken Hercules, actually.'

'Such valuables don't vanish from a patrician household without good reason. This house is like a bare cupboard, or a fine Roman matron without her jewelry. Where are the urns, the vases, the precious little things one expects to see in the house of a wealthy old senator? Auctioned off to pay the bill-collector, I presume. When did your cousin sell them?'

'Over the last few years,' admitted Lucius with a sigh, 'bit by bit. I suppose the mosaics and wall paintings would be gone by now as well, except that they're part of the house and can't be disposed of piecemeal. The Civil War was very hard on cousin Gaius.'

'He backed the wrong side?'

'Quite the opposite! Gaius was a staunch supporter of Sulla. But his only son, who was my age, had married into a family that sided with Marius, and was contaminated by his wife's connections; he was beheaded when Sulla became dictator. He did leave an heir, however – Gaius' grandson, a boy name Mamercus, who is now not quite twenty. Gaius took custody of his grandson, but also had to assume his dead son's debts, which were crushing. Poor cousin Gaius! The Civil War tore his family apart, took his only son, and left him virtually bankrupt.'

I looked around. 'The house itself looks valuable enough.'

'I'm sure it is, but it's all that Gaius has left. The wealth has all fled. And so has young Mamercus, I fear.'

'The grandson?'

'Gone to Spain! It's broken his grandfather's heart.'

'Spain? Ah, so that's why you mentioned Sertorius on the walk here . . .'

The Civil War had been over for six years. Marius had lost. Sulla had won, and had made himself dictator. He disposed of his enemies, reordered the state, and then retired, leaving his chosen successors in firm control of the senate and the magistracies. The Marians – those who had survived the proscriptions and still had their heads – were lying low. But in Spain, the last embers of resistance still smoldered in the person of Quintus Sertorius. The renegade general not only refused to surrender, but had declared himself to be the head of the legitimate Roman state. Disgruntled Marian military men and desperate anti-Sullan senators had fled from Rome to join Sertorius' government-in-exile. In addition to his own legions, Sertorius had succeeded in rallying the native population to his side. Altogether, Sertorius and his forces in Spain constituted a considerable power that the Roman Senate could not ignore and had not yet been able to stamp out.

'Are you saying that young Mamercus has run off to join Sertorius?'

'So it appears,' said Lucius, shaking his head. He leaned over to sniff a rose. 'This smells very sweet!'

'So young Mamercus rejected his grandfather's Sullan politics and remained loyal to his mother's side of the family?'

'So it appears. Gaius is quite distraught. The folly of youth! There's no future for anyone who sides with Sertorius.'

'But what future would the young man have if he'd stayed here in Rome with his grandfather? You say that Gaius is bankrupt.'

'It's a question of loyalty, Gordianus, and family dignity.' Lucius spoke carefully. I could see he was doing his patrician best not to sound condescending.

I shrugged. 'Perhaps the boy feels he's being loyal to his dead father, by joining the last resistance to Sulla's faction. But I take your point, Lucius; it's a family tragedy, of a sort all too common these days. But what can your cousin want of me?'

'I should think that was obvious. He wants someone to – ah, but here is Gaius himself . . .'

'Cousin Lucius! Embrace me!' A frail-looking old man in a senatorial toga stepped into the atrium with wide-open arms. 'Let me feel another of my own flesh and blood pressed against me!'

The two men could hardly have been more different. Gaius was older, of course, but also tall and narrow, where Lucius was short and round. And where Lucius was florid and flushed, there was a grayness about the old senator, not only in his hair and wrinkled hands, but also in his expression and manner, a kind of drawn, sere, stoic austerity. Like his house, the man seemed to have been stripped bare of all vain adornments and winnowed to his essence.

After a moment the two drew apart. 'I knew you wouldn't disappoint me, Lucius. Is this the fellow?'

'Yes, this is Gordianus, called the Finder.'

'Let us hope he lives up to his name.' Gaius Claudius regarded me not with the patronizing gaze I was used to receiving from patricians, but steadily and deeply, as if to judge whether I should be a cause of hope to him or not. 'He looks reliable enough,' he finally pronounced. 'Ah, but what judge of character am I, who let my only son marry into a Marian family, and then could not foresee my grandson's intentions to follow the same course to disaster?'

'Yes, I was just informing Gordianus of your situation,' said Lucius.

'And is he willing?'

'Actually, we were just coming to that . . .'

There must indeed have been a last, thin veil of vanity over the old senator's demeanor, for now I saw it fall away. He looked at me imploringly. 'The boy is all I have left! I must at least know for certain what's become of him, and why he's done this mad thing, and if he can't be persuaded to see reason! Will you do this for me, Gordianus?'

'Do what, Gaius Claudius?' I said, though I was beginning to see all too clearly.

'Find him! Go to Spain for me. Take my message. Bring him back to me!'

I cleared my throat. 'Let me understand you, Gaius Claudius. You wish for me to venture into Sertorius' territory? You must realize that the whole of the Spanish peninsula is racked with warfare. The danger –'

'You will demand a large fee, I suppose . . .' Gaius averted his eyes and wrung his hands.

'The fee is not an issue,' said Lucius.

'I'm afraid that it most certainly is,' I said, not following his meaning. Then I saw the look that passed between Lucius and his cousin, and understood. Gaius Claudius had no money; it was Lucius who would be paying my fee, and Lucius, as I well knew, could afford to be generous. The commission would be coming just as much from my dear friend as from his cousin, then. That made me feel all the more obliged to accept it.

Thus I came to find myself, some days later, on the eastern coast of Spain, near the village of Sucro, which is situated not far from the mouth of the river of the same name.

I was not alone. After a great deal of internal debate and hesitation, I had decided to bring Eco with me. On the one hand, I was likely to encounter danger, quite possibly a great deal of danger; who knows what may happen in a foreign land torn by warfare? On the other hand, a nimble, quick-witted fourteen-year-old boy who had survived the harsh streets of Rome from his earliest years (despite the handicap of his muteness) is not a bad companion to have around in unpredictable surroundings. And for his own benefit, I thought it a good thing that Eco should learn the lessons of travel while he was still young, especially since Lucius Claudius was paying the expenses.

First had come the sea voyage, on a trading ship out of Puteoli bound for Mauretania. For a reasonable sum, the captain agreed to put us ashore at New Carthage, in Spain. That had gone well enough. Pirates had pursued us only once, and our experienced captain had managed to outrun them easily; and Eco had suffered from seasickness only for the first day or two. Once ashore, we sought for news of Sertorius' whereabouts, and made our way north until we caught up with him at Sucro, where we arrived only two days after a tremendous battle on the banks of the river.

According to the locals, Sertorius had suffered heavy casualties, perhaps as many as ten thousand men; but so had the opposing Roman general, the Sullan boy-wonder Pompey (not quite such a boy any longer at thirty), who had been wounded himself, though not gravely. The two sides appeared to be regrouping their forces, and a fresh rumor had it that Pompey's colleague Metellus was soon to arrive with reinforcements from the north. The townspeople of Sucro were bracing themselves for another great battle.

Getting into Sertorius' camp proved to be easier than I anticipated. The traditional rigid discipline of a Roman army camp was missing; perhaps, given Sertorius' mix of Spanish tribesmen and rag-tag Romans, such discipline was impossible. In its place there seemed to be a great sense of camaraderie, and of welcome to the local camp followers who came to offer food and wares (and in not a few cases, themselves) for sale to the soldiers. The air of the camp was open and almost festive, despite the great slaughter of two days before. Morale, clearly, was very high.

I inquired after the whereabouts of Mamercus Claudius, using the description his grandfather had given me – a young patrician of nineteen, tall, slender, with a pleasant face and a shock of jet-black hair, a newcomer to the ranks. Among the grizzled Roman veterans and their Spanish allies, such a fellow was likely to stand out, I thought, and sure enough, it took only a little asking (and a pittance of bribes) before Eco and I were pointed to his tent.

The location surprised me, for it was very near the heart of the camp, and thus not far, I presumed, from Sertorius' own quarters. Despite his youth and inexperience, Mamercus Claudius was probably quite a catch for Sertorius, evidence to his fellow Romans that the renegade general could still attract a youth from one of Rome's best families, that his cause looked toward the future, not just the past.

This presumption turned out to be more astute than I realized. When I asked the centurion outside the tent to inform Mamercus that he had a visitor, I was told that Mamercus was elsewhere.

When I asked where he might be, the centurion suggested that I try the commander's tent.

So Eco and I made out way to the tent of Quintus Sertorius himself, which was quite conspicuous thanks to the phalanx of guards around it. There was also a great crowd of petitioners of the usual sort, lined up to seek audience – locals who hoped to sell provisions to the army, or had suffered property damage and wanted restitution, or had other pressing business with the commander and his staff.

Eco tapped the edge of one hand against the flattened palm of the other, to suggest that we had run into a solid wall: *We shall never get inside that tent*, he seemed to say.

'Ah, but we don't need to get inside,' I said to him. 'We want someone who's already in there to come out, and that's a different matter.'

I walked to the head of the long line. Some in the queue glared at us, but I ignored them. I came to the man who was next to be admitted and cleared my throat to get his attention. He turned and gave me, a nasty look and said something in his native tongue. When he saw that I didn't understand, he repeated himself in passable Latin. 'What do you think you're doing? I'm next. Get away!'

'You're here to see Quintus Sertorius?' I said.

'Like everyone else. Wait your turn.'

'Ah, but I don't want to see the general himself. I only want someone to give a message to a young fellow who's probably in there with him. Could you do me the favor?' I patted my hand against the coin purse inside my tunic, which clinked suggestively. 'Ask after a young Roman named Mamercus Claudius. Tell him that someone has come a very long way to talk to him.'

'I suppose.' The man seemed dubious, but then his face abruptly brightened, as if reflecting the glitter of sunlight on the coins I dropped into his hand.

Just then a guard approached, searched the fellow for weapons, and told him to step into the tent.

We did not have long to wait. Soon a lanky young man stepped out of the tent. His armored leather fittings seemed to have been tailored for a shorter, stockier man; I had noticed that many of Sertorius' junior officers were outfitted in similarly haphazard fashion. The young man pulled uncomfortably at the armholes of his leather shirt and peered into the crowd, looking rather put out. I caught his eye and beckoned for him to meet me at one side of the tent.

'Mamercus Claudius?' I said. 'I come with a message from –'

'What do you think you're doing, you idiot, summoning me

from the commander's tent like that?' He was angry but kept his voice low.

'I suppose I could have lined up with the rest for an audience with the general —'

'What!' He looked at me dubiously. 'Who are you?'

'My name is Gordianus, called the Finder. This is my son, Eco. We've come all the way from Rome. Your grandfather sent me.'

Mamercus seemed taken aback at first, then smiled ruefully. 'I see. Poor grandfather!'

'Poor indeed,' I said, 'and poorer still for lack of your company.'

'Is he well?'

'In body, yes. But his spirit is eaten away by fear for you. I've brought a message from him.'

I produced the little folded tablet that I had faithfully brought all the way from Rome. The two thin plates of wood were bound together with a ribbon and sealed with a daub of red wax, upon which Gaius Claudius had pressed his signet ring. Mamercus broke the seal, pulled the tablets apart and gazed at the wax surfaces inside, upon which his grandfather had scratched his plea by his own hand, no longer having even a secretary to write his letters for him.

Had Mamercus' reaction been callous and uncaring, I would not have been surprised. Many an impatient, bitter, dispossessed young man in his situation might have scorned a doting grandparent's concern, especially if that grandparent had always supported the very establishment against which he was rebelling. But Mamercus' response was quite different. I watched the swift movement of his eyes as they perused the words and saw them glisten with tears. He clamped his jaw tightly to stop his lips from quivering. His evident distress made him look almost as boyish as Eco.

Gaius Claudius had not kept the contents of his letter secret from me. On the contrary, he had insisted that I read it:

My dearest grandson, blood of my blood, what has induced you to take this foolish course? Do you think to please the shade of your father by joining a hopeless struggle against those who destroyed him? If this were the only course open to you — if your own name and future had been ruined along with your father's and mother's — then honor might demand such a desperate course. But in Rome you still have my protection, despite your father's downfall, and you can still make a career for yourself. We are woefully impoverished, to be sure, but together we will find a way out of our misfortune! Surely the best

*revenge for your father would be for you to restore our
family's fortunes and to make a place for yourself in the
state, so that when you are my age you can look back
upon a long career and a world you have had a hand
in shaping to your liking. Do not throw your life away!
Please, I beg you, calm your passions and let reason guide
you. Come back to me! The man who bears this message
has funds sufficient for your passage home. Mamercus,
son of my son, I pray to the gods that I shall see you soon!*

After a while Mamercus pressed the tablets together and retied
the ribbon. He averted his eyes in a way that reminded me of his
grandfather. 'Thank you for bringing the letter. Is that all?'

'*Is* it all?' I said. 'I know what's in the letter. Will you honor
his request?'

'No. Leave me now.'

'Are you sure, Mamercus? Will you think on it? Shall I come
back later?'

'No!'

My commission from Gaius Claudius was specific: I was to locate
Mamercus, to deliver the message, and to help Mamercus, if he chose,
to escape unscathed from Sertorius' service. It was not incumbent on
me to persuade him to leave. But I had come a long way, and now I
had seen both the old senator's distress and his grandson's response
to it. If Mamercus had reacted with derision, if he had betrayed no
love for his grandfather, that would have been the end of it. But
his reaction had been quite the opposite. Even now, from the way
he gently held the tablets, almost caressing them, and reached up
to wipe his eyes, I could see that he was feeling a great flood of
affection for the old man, and consequently, perhaps, considerable
confusion over the choice he had made.

I thought it wise to change the subject for a moment. 'You seem
to have done well for yourself, here in Sertorius' army,' I said.

'Better than I expected, in so short a time,' admitted Mamercus.
He tucked the tablets under his arm and smiled crookedly. 'The
commander was very glad to take me in. He gave me a position on
his staff at once, despite my lack of experience. "Look," he said to
everyone, "a young Claudius, come all the way from Rome to join
us! But don't worry, son, we'll be back in Rome before you know it,
and it's the blasted Sullans who'll be searching for their heads!" '

'And do you believe that? Is that why you choose to stay?'

Mamercus bristled. 'The question is, what's keeping *you* here,
Gordianus? I've given you my answer. Now, go!'

At that moment, the crowd before the commander's tent broke into a cheer. I heard the name Sertorius shouted aloud in acclamation, and saw that the great man himself had emerged from the tent. He was a tall, robust-looking man with a strong jaw and a smile that radiated confidence. Some mortals possess a charismatic allure that is almost divine, that anyone can see at a glance, and Quintus Sertorius was such a mortal. This was a man whom other men would trust implicitly and follow without question, to glory or death. The cheers that greeted his appearance, from both his own soldiers and from the local petitioners, were absolutely genuine and spontaneous.

Then the cries died away to a whispered hush. Eco and I looked at one another, puzzled. The cheering was understandable, but what was this? It was the hush of religious awe such as one hears in Rome at certain ancient rites performed in the temples in the Forum, a barely audible welter of whispers and murmurs and muttered prayers.

Then I saw the remarkable creature that had followed Sertorius out of the tent.

It was a young fawn. Her soft pelt was utterly white, without a single spot of color. She gamboled after Sertorius like a loyal hound, and when he paused she nuzzled against his thigh and lifted her nose for him to stroke. I had never seen anything like it.

The hush grew louder, and amid the strange dialects I heard snatches of Latin:

'The white fawn! The white fawn!'

'They both look happy – that must mean good news!'

'Diana! Bless us, goddess! Bless Quintus Sertorius!'

Sertorius smiled and laughed and bent down to take the fawn's head in his hands. He kissed her right on the snout.

This evoked an even louder murmur from the crowd – and from one onlooker, a loud, barking laugh. My dear mute son has a very strange laugh, alas, rather like the braying of a mule. The fawn's ears shot straight up and she cowered behind Sertorius, tripping awkwardly over her spindly legs. Heads turned toward us, casting suspicious looks. Eco clamped his hands over his mouth. Sertorius peered in our direction, frowning. He saw Mamercus, then appraised me with a curious eye.

'Mamercus Claudius!' he called. 'I wondered where you'd got to. Come!'

Sertorius pressed on through the worshipful crowd, with the white fawn and a cordon of guards following behind. Included in the retinue, I was surprised to see, was a girl who could hardly have been older than Eco. She was a beautiful child, with dark eyes and cheeks like white rose petals. Dressed all in white, with her black hair bound up in a scarf, she looked and carried herself like a priestess, keeping her eyes straight ahead and striding between the soldiers with a grace and self-assurance beyond her years.

'A white fawn!' I said. 'And that girl! Who is she, Mamercus?'

But Mamercus only glowered at me and went to join Sertorius. I ran after him and clutched his arm.

'Mamercus, I shall try to find lodgings in Sucro tonight. If you should change your mind –'

He yanked his arm from my grasp and strode off without looking back.

Lodgings were not hard to find in Sucro. There was only one tavern with accommodations, and the place was deserted. The battle between Pompey and Sertorius had driven travelers far away, and the likelihood of another battle was keeping them away.

The tavern keeper was a strong-looking Celt with a shaggy black beard, named Lacro. He seemed to be in high spirits despite the hardships of war, and was glad to have two paying guests to share wine and conversation in the common room that night. Lacro's family had lived on the banks of the Sucro for generations. He boasted proudly of the bounty of the river and the beauty of the coast. His favorite recreation was to go trapping and hunting in the marshes near the river's mouth, where birds flocked in great numbers and crustacean delicacies could be plucked from the mud. Lacro had apparently been spending a lot of time in the marshes lately, if only to stay clear of the fighting.

But he did not complain about the war, except to excoriate Pompey and Metellus. Lacro was very much a partisan of Sertorius, and praised him for unifying the various Celtic and Iberian tribes of Spain. He had no quarrel with Romans, he said, so long as they were like Sertorius; if it took a Roman to give his people leadership, then so be it. When I told him that Eco and I had come that very day from the great commander's camp, and indeed had caught a glimpse of Sertorius himself, Lacro was quite impressed.

'And did you see the white fawn?' he asked.

'Yes, we did. A strange creature to keep as a pet.'

'The white fawn is not a pet!' Lacro was appalled at the idea. 'The white fawn was sent to Sertorius as a gift, by Diana. The goddess speaks to him through the fawn. The fawn tells Sertorius the future.'

'Really?'

'How else do you think he's gone undefeated for so long, no

matter how many armies Rome sends against him? Did you think that Sertorius was merely lucky? No, he has divine protection! The white fawn is a holy creature.'

'I see,' I said, but apparently without sufficient conviction.

'Bah! You Romans, you've conquered the world but you've lost sight of the gods. You saw the white fawn with your own eyes, and thought it was a mere pet! But not Sertorius; that's what makes him different.'

'How did Sertorius acquire this amazing creature?'

'They say some hunters came upon the fawn in a wood. She walked right up to them, and told them to take her to the great leader. The hunters brought her to Sertorius. When he bent down to nuzzle the fawn's face, she spoke to him, in his own tongue, and he recognized the voice of Diana. The two have never parted since. The fawn follows Sertorius everywhere, or strictly speaking, he follows the fawn, since it's she who tells him where his enemies are and what routes to take. Ah, so you saw her with your own eyes. I envy you! I've never seen her, only heard of her.'

'This white fawn is quite famous, then?'

'Everyone knows of her. I keep a tavern, don't I? I know what people talk about, and every man from the Pyrenees to the Pillars of Hercules loves the white fawn!'

Since there was only one tavern in Sucro, Mamercus Claudius had no trouble finding us the next morning. He stepped into the common room just as Eco and I were finishing our breakfast of bread and dates. So, I thought, the young man has decided to return to his grandfather after all. I smiled at him. He did not smile back.

I realized that he was still in his military garb, and that he was not alone. A small band of soldiers entered the room behind him, all wearing the same grim look.

His visit was official, then. My breakfast turned heavy in my stomach. My mouth went dry. I remembered the evil premonition I had felt about this mission from the very first, even before I met Gaius Claudius . . .

Mamercus marched up to us. His manner was soldierly and impersonal. 'Gordianus! Quintus Sertorius has sent me to fetch you.'

Then it *was* the worst, I thought. Mamercus had betrayed me to Sertorius, and now Sertorius was having me arrested for trying to engineer the defection of an officer. I had known the mission would be dangerous; I should have been more cautious. Mamercus had made it clear the previous day that he had no intention of returning to Rome with me; why I had lingered in Sucro? I had tarried too long, a victim of my own sentimental sympathy for the old senator. And I had made Eco a victim, as well. He was only a boy – surely Sertorius would not lop his head off along with mine. But what would become of him after I was gone? Sertorius would probably conscript him as a foot soldier, I thought. Was that to be Eco's fate, to end his days on a battlefield, fighting for a lost cause in a foreign land? If only I had left him behind in Rome!

I stood as bravely as I could and gestured for Eco to do the same. Mamercus and his men escorted us out of the tavern and marched us up the river road, back to the camp. The men's faces looked even grimmer under the bright morning sun. Not one of them said a word.

The same grimness presided in the camp. Every face we saw was glum and silent. Where were the high spirits of the day before?

We came to Sertorius' tent. Mamercus pulled back the flap and announced my name. He gestured for Eco and me to enter. He himself remained outside, as did the other soldiers.

The commander was alone; more alone, in fact, than I realized at first. He rose from his chair eagerly, as if he had been waiting impatiently, and strode toward us. This was not the reception I had expected.

'Gordianus the Finder!' he said, grasping my hand. 'What good fortune that you should happen to be here, on such a day! Do you know why I've summoned you?'

'I'm beginning to think that I don't.' The look on Sertorius' face was grim but not hostile. My head started to feel noticeably more secure on my shoulders.

'Then you haven't heard the news yet?'

'What news?'

'Excellent! That means that word hasn't yet spread to the town. One tries to keep down the gossip and rumors when something like this happens, but it's like putting out fires in a hayfield –'

I looked about the crowded tent, at the general's sleeping cot, the portable cabinets with maps and scrolls stacked on top, the little lamps on tripods. Something was missing . . .

'Where is the white fawn?' I said.

The color drained from his face. 'Then you *have* heard the news?'

'No. But if there is some crisis at hand, shouldn't your divine counselor be with you?'

Sertorius swallowed hard. 'Someone has stolen her, in the night. Someone has kidnapped the white fawn!'

'I see. But why have you sent for me, Quintus Sertorius?'

'Don't be coy, Finder. I know your reputation.'

'You've heard of me?'

Sertorius managed a wry smile. 'I do have some idea of what goes on in Rome, even if I haven't been there in years. I have my spies and informants there – just as Pompey and the Senate no doubt have their spies in my camp. I try to keep abreast of who's taking whom to court, who's up and who's down. You might be surprised how often your name comes up. Yes, I know who you are.'

'And do you know what brought me here?' I wanted to be absolutely certain that we understood each other.

'Yes, yes. I asked Mamercus about you yesterday. He showed me the letter. What a silly hen his grandfather is! The Sullans can have the old fellow – I have the grandson, and he's turned out to be worth any three of Pompey's officers, I'll wager! Bright, curious, clever, and wholly committed to the cause. If the powers-that-be in Rome had any sense, they'd have restored his family's estates and tried to win Mamercus over to their side, once his father was out of the way. But the Sullans always were a greedy lot of short-sighted bastards. They've driven all the best young men to Spain; all the better for me!' For just a moment he flashed the dazzling smile which had no doubt won the hearts of those bright young men. Then the smile faded. 'But back to the business at hand. They call you the Finder, don't they? Well, I am a man who has lost something, and I must find it again!'

At night, Sertorius explained, the fawn was kept in a little tent of its own, near the general's quarters. For religious reasons, the opening of the fawn's tent was situated to face the rising moon; it had so happened, in this particular camp, that the front of the fawn's tent faced away from most of the others, and so was not visible to Sertorius' own night watch. The tent had its own guards, however, a pair of Celts who had vied for the religious honor of protecting Diana's emissary. These two had apparently been given a powerful drug and had slept the night through. Sertorius was convinced of their tearful remorse at having failed the white fawn, but otherwise had not been able to get any useful information from them.

I asked to see the tent. Sertorius led me there himself. Before we entered, he glanced at Eco.

'The boy has seen death before?' he said.

'Yes. Why do you ask?'

'It's not a gory sight – believe me, I've seen gore! Still, it's not pretty to look at.'

He gave no further explanation, but led us into the tent. A little pen had been erected inside, with straw scattered on the ground along with pails of water and fresh grass. There was also, outside the pen, a little sleeping cot, upon which lay the girl we had seen in the general's entourage the previous day. She was dressed in the same white gown, but the white scarf was no longer around her head, so that her hair lay in a shimmering black pool around her white face. Her legs were straight and her hands were folded on his chest. She might almost have been sleeping, except for the unnatural, waxy paleness of her flesh, and the circle of bruised, chafed skin around her throat.

'Is this how you found her?' I asked.

'No,' said Sertorius. 'She was there in front of the pen, lying crumpled on the ground.'

'Who was she?'

'Just a girl from one of the Celtic tribes. Their priests said that only a virgin should be allowed to feed and groom the white fawn. This girl volunteered. It brought great honor to her family. Her name was Liria.'

'Where is her white scarf, the one she wore around her hair?'

'You *are* observant, Finder. The scarf is missing.'

'Do you think . . .?' I reached toward the marks on her throat. 'A scarf would be one way of strangling someone.'

Sertorius nodded gravely. 'She must have tried to stop them. The guards were drugged, which means that Liria should have been drugged as well; she always ate the same food. But last night she may have fasted. She did that sometimes; she claimed that the white fawn would order her to fast, to keep herself pure. When they came to take the fawn, she must have woken up, and they strangled her to keep her from crying out.'

'But why didn't they simply kill the fawn, instead of kidnapping it?'

Sertorius sighed. 'This land is crawling with superstition, Gordianus. Omens and portents are in every breath, and a man can't take a piss without some god or other looking over his shoulder. I suspect that whoever did this had no intention of murdering anyone. What they wanted, what they intended, was that the fawn should simply disappear, don't you see? As if it had fled on its own. As if Diana had abruptly abandoned me to my fate. What would my Spanish soldiers make of that? Can you understand what a disaster that would be for me, Gordianus?'

He stared at the dead girl, then tore his eyes away and paced back and forth in the small space before the pen. 'The kidnappers added murder to their crime; that was sacrilege enough, though Liria wasn't really a priestess, just a girl from a humble family who happened still to be a virgin. But they would never have killed the fawn. That would have defeated their purpose. To kill the emissary of Diana would be an unforgivable atrocity. That would only strengthen the resolve of the tribes to fend off such an impious enemy. That's why I'm certain the fawn is still alive and unharmed.

'I've tried to keep this quiet, Gordianus, but I think the rumor has already begun to spread among the men that the fawn is missing. The Roman soldiers will suspect the truth, I imagine, that she was kidnapped for political reasons. But the natives – the natives will think that the gods have turned against me.'

'Is their faith in the white fawn really so great?'

'Oh, yes! That's why I've used it, as a powerful tool to bind them to me. Powerful, but dangerous; superstition can be turned against the man who uses it, you see. I should have guarded her better!'

'Do you believe in the white fawn yourself, Sertorius? Does she speak to you?'

He looked at me shrewdly. 'I'm surprised that you even ask such a question, Gordianus. I'm a Roman general, not a credulous Spaniard. The white fawn is nothing more than a device of statecraft. Must I explain? One day my spies inform me of Pompey's movements; the next day I announce that the white fawn whispered in my ear that Pompey will be seen in a certain place at a certain time, and sure enough, he is. Whenever I learn a secret or see into the future, the knowledge comes to me from the white fawn – officially. Whenever I have to give an order that the natives find hard to stomach – such as burning one of their own villages, or putting a popular man to death – I tell them it must be done because the white fawn says so. It makes things much, much easier. And whenever things look uncertain, and the natives are on the verge of losing heart, I tell them that the white fawn has promised me a victory. They find their courage, then; they rally, and they make the victory happen.

'Do you think me blasphemous for resorting to such a device? The best generals have always done such things to shore up their men's morale. Look at Sulla! Before a battle, he always made sure his troops would catch him mumbling to a little image he stole from the oracle at Delphi; the deity invariably promised him victory. And Marius, too – he kept a Syrian wisewoman in his entourage, who could always be counted on to foresee disaster for his enemies. Too bad she failed him in the end.

'Even Alexander pulled such tricks. Do you know the story? Once when things looked bleak before a battle, his priests called for a blood sacrifice. While the sheep was being prepared at the altar, Alexander painted the letters N I backwards on the palms of one hand, and K E on the other. The priest cut open the sheep, pulled out the steaming liver and placed it in Alexander's hands. Alexander turned it over to show his men, and sure enough, there it was, written on the liver in letters no one could mistake – the word for victory!'

'And your device was the white fawn?'

Sertorius stopped his pacing and looked me in the eye. 'Here in Spain, the local tribes, especially the Celts, have a special belief in the mystical power of white animals. A good general makes note of such beliefs. When the hunters brought Dianara to me that day –'

'Dianara?'

Did he look slightly embarrassed? 'I call the white fawn Dianara, after the goddess. Why not? When they brought her to me, I saw at once what could be done with her. I made her my divine counselor! And the strategy has paid off handsomely. But now –'

Sertorius began to pace again. 'My scouts tell me that Metellus has joined Pompey on the other side of the Sucro. If my Spaniards find out that the fawn is missing, and I'm forced into another battle – the result could be an utter disaster. What man will fight for a general whom the gods have deserted? My only chance now is to withdraw west into the highlands, as quickly as I can. But in the meantime, the fawn must be found!' He gave me a look that was at once desperate and demanding.

'I'm a Finder, Quintus Sertorius, not a hunter.'

'This is a kidnapping, Gordianus, not a chase. I'll pay you well. Bring Dianara back to me, and I shall reward you handsomely.'

I considered. My commission from Gaius Claudius was completed. I had verified young Mamercus' whereabouts, delivered the letter, and given him every chance to accompany me back to Rome. I was a free agent again, in a foreign land, and a powerful man was seeking my help.

On the other hand, to aid a renegade general in the field would surely, in the view of the Roman Senate, constitute an act of treason . . .

I liked Sertorius, because he was honest, and brave, and in the long run, the underdog. I liked him even better when he named an actual figure as a reward.

I agreed. If I could not return an errant young man to his grandfather, perhaps I could return a missing fawn to her master.

Sertorius allowed me to question the two guards who had been drugged. I could only agree with his own assessment, that the men were truly remorseful for what had happened and that they had nothing useful to tell. Neither did any of the other watchmen; no one had seen or heard a thing. It was as if the moon herself had reached down to fetch the white fawn home.

By the time that Eco and I arrived back in Sucro that afternoon, the tavern was full of locals, all thirsty for wine and hungry for any news they could get of the missing white fawn. The secret was out, and rumors were flying wild. I listened attentively; one never knows when a bit of gossip may be helpful. Some said that the fawn had actually deserted Sertorius long ago (this was patently false, since I had seen the creature myself). Others claimed that the fawn had died, and that Sertorius had buried it and was only pretending that it had disappeared. A few said that the fawn had been stolen, but no one reported the death of the virgin. Perhaps the wildest rumor (and the most ominous) asserted that the fawn had showed up in Pompey's camp, and was now his confidant.

None of this very helpful. After the local crowd dispersed to their homes for the night, I asked our host what he made of it all.

'Not a one of them knows a blasted thing! All a bunch of windbags.' Lacro said this cheerily enough, and why not? He must have turned a nice profit on the sale of wine that day, and quite a few of the crowd had stayed on for dinner. 'The only story that rang true to my ears was the one about the fawn being seen in the marshes.'

'What's this? I missed that one.'

'That's because the fellow who told it wasn't shouting his head off like the fools who had nothing to say. He was here behind the counter, talking to me. An old friend of mine; we sometimes go trapping in the marshes together. He was there early this morning. Says he caught a glimpse of something white off in the distance, in a stand of swamp trees.'

'Perhaps he saw a bird.'

'Too big for a bird, he said, and it moved like a beast, from here to there along the ground.'

'Did he get a closer look?'

'He tried. But by the time he reached the trees, there was nothing to be seen – nothing except fresh hoof prints in the mud. The prints of a young deer, of that he was certain. And footprints, as well.'

'Footprints?'

'Two men, he said. One on each side of the fawn.'

Eco gripped my arms and shook it. I agreed; this was very interesting. 'Did your friend follow these tracks?'

'No, he turned back and went about his business, checking his traps.' Lacro raised an eyebrow. 'He didn't say as much, but from the look on his face, I think he felt afraid when he saw those tracks. This is a fellow who knows the marshes like his own mother's face; knows what belongs there and what doesn't, and if something's not right. He saw those tracks and felt a kind of awe, standing where Diana's gift had passed. Mark my words, that white fawn is in the marshes.'

Eco nudged me and put his hands to his throat, miming strangulation. Lacro looked puzzled.

I translated. 'If your friend was afraid to follow those tracks, then his instincts probably *are* good.' At least one person had already been murdered by the fawn's abductors.

'I don't quite follow you.'

I looked at him steadily. 'Yesterday, you spoke well of Sertorius . . .'

'I did.'

'And you spoke with reverence about the white fawn . . .'

'Diana's gift.'

'Lacro, I want to tell you a secret. Something very important.'

'So, what are you waiting for? Who can keep secrets better than an innkeeper?' He hooked his thumb and gestured to the sleeping quarters upstairs, as if alluding to all the trysts which had taken place under his roof that would never be revealed by his telling.

'And do you think this friend of yours could keep a secret, as well?' I said. 'And more importantly, do you think he might agree to guide a couple of strangers into the marshes? There's likely to be some danger – but there'll be a fee in it, too. A fee for you both . . .'

Before daybreak the next morning, we set out for the marshes.

Lacro and his friend, who was called Stilensis, led the way. Eco and I followed behind.

We came to the stand of trees where Stilensis had seen the tracks. They were still visible in the mud, picked out sharply by the first slanting rays of sunlight. We followed them. In places where the ground was too hard or too soft, the trail seemed to vanish, at least to my eyes, but our experienced guides were able to discern even the faintest traces. Occasionally even they lost the trail, and when that happened they would patiently circle about until they found it again. Sometimes I could see how they did it, by spotting a broken twig or a crumpled leaf; at other times it seemed to me that they were guided by some hidden instinct, or simple luck. Perhaps Lacro would say that Diana showed them the way.

They also seemed to sense, by some unknown faculty, the moment that we came within earshot of our prey. At the same moment, Lacro and Stilensis both turned and gestured for us to be utterly silent.

As for the enemy, there were only two of them, as the tracks had indicated; but the tracks had also indicated, by their size and deepness, that the men making them were large fellows, with large shoes and heavy bodies. Fortunately for us, they were still asleep when we came upon them. They had no tent, and had made no fire. They slept on a bed of leaves, with light blankets to cover them.

Lacro and Stilensis had brought their hunting bows. While they notched arrows and took aim, Eco and I yanked away the men's blankets. They woke at once, scrambled to their feet, then froze when they saw the arrows aimed at them. They cursed in some native tongue.

Lacro asked them what they had done with the white fawn. The men grumbled and pointed toward a thick patch of bushes.

With, in a little clearing, Eco and I came upon the creature. She was tied to a small tree, asleep with her legs folded beneath her. At our approach she stirred and lifted her head. I expected her to scramble up and try to bolt away. Instead, she stared at us sleepily and blinked several times, then threw back her head and seemed to yawn. She slowly and methodically unfolded her limbs and got to her feet, then sauntered toward us and lifted her face to be nuzzled. Eco let out a gasp of delight as he stroked the back of his hand against the shimmering white fur beneath her eyes.

We marched our prisoners through the marsh and then along the river road, with Eco leading the fawn by her leash, or as often as not being led by her. We stopped short of Sertorius' camp, and while the others waited in a secluded spot by the river, I went to give the general the news.

I arrived just in time. Only a single tent – the general's – was still standing. The troops had already begun the westward march toward the highlands. Sertorius and his staff were busily packing wagons and seeing to the final details of disbanding the camp.

Sertorius was the first to see me. He froze for an instant, then strode toward me. His face seemed to glow in the morning light. 'It's good news, isn't it?'

I nodded.

'Is she well?'

'Yes.'

'And the scoundrels who took her – did you capture them as well?'

'Two men, both native Spaniards.'

'I knew it! I woke up this morning with a feeling that something wonderful would happen. Where is she? Take me to her at once! No, wait.' He turned and called to his staff. 'Come along, all of you. Wonderful news! Come and see!'

Among the officers I saw Mamercus, carrying a cabinet out of the general's tent. 'Put that down, Mamercus, and come see what the Finder has caught for us!' shouted Sertorius. 'Something white! And two black-hearted Spaniards with her!'

Mamercus looked confused for a moment, then put down the cabinet. He nodded and stepped back into the tent.

'Come, Gordianus. Take me to her at once!' said Sertorius, pulling at my arm.

On the banks of the Sucro, the general and his fawn were reunited. I don't think I had ever seen a Roman general weep before. I certainly know that I had never seen one pick up a fawn and carry it about in his arms like a baby. For all his protestations that the white fawn was only a tool of statecraft, a cynical means of exploiting superstitions he did not share, I think that the creature meant much more than that to Sertorius. While she might not have whispered to him in the voice of Diana, or foretold the future, the white fawn was the visible sign of the gods' favor, without which every man is naked before his enemies. What I saw on the banks of the Sucro was the exultation of a man whose luck had deserted him, and then had returned in the blink of an eye.

But Sertorius was a Roman general, and not given to undue sentimentality, even about his own destiny. After a while he put down the fawn and turned to the two Spaniards we had captured. He spoke to them in their own dialect. Lacro whispered a translation in my ear.

They had treated the fawn well, Sertorius said, and had not harmed her; that was wise, and showed a modicum of respect for the goddess. But they had flouted the dignity of a Roman general and had interfered with the will of the goddess; and a young virgin had been murdered. For that they would be punished.

The two men comported themselves with considerable dignity, considering that they were likely to be slain on the spot. They conferred with each other for a moment, then one of them spoke. They were only hirelings, they explained. They knew nothing of a murdered girl. They had merely agreed to meet a man at the edge of the camp two nights ago. He had brought the fawn to them, wrapped in a blanket. They were to hide with the fawn in the marsh until Sertorius and his army were gone. They would never have harmed the creature, nor would they have harmed the girl who kept her.

Sertorius told them that he had suspected as much, that one of his own men – indeed, someone on his own staff, with adequate knowledge of the general's routine and the workings of the camp – must have been behind the kidnapping. If the two Spaniards were willing to point out this man, the severity of their own punishment might be considerably mitigated.

The two men conferred again. They agreed.

Sertorius stepped back and gestured to the members of his assembled staff. The two Spaniards looked from face to face, then shook their heads. The man was not among them.

Sertorius frowned and surveyed his staff. He stiffened. I saw a flash of pain in his eyes. He sighed and turned to me. 'One of my men isn't here, Finder.'

'Yes, I see. He must have stayed behind.'

Sertorius ordered some of his men to stay and guard the fawn. The rest of us hurried back with him to the camp.

'Look there! His horse is still here,' said Sertorius.

'Then he hasn't fled,' I said. 'Perhaps he had no reason to flee. Perhaps he had nothing to do with the kidnapping –'

But I knew this could not be the case, even as Eco and I followed Sertorius into his tent. Amid the clutter of folded cots and chairs, Mamercus lay quivering on the ground, transfixed on his own sword. His right hand still gripped the pommel. In his left hand, he clutched the virgin's white scarf.

He was still alive. We knelt beside him. He began to whisper. We bent our heads close. 'I never meant to kill the girl,' he said. 'She was asleep, and should have stayed that way ... from the drug ... but she woke. I couldn't let her scream. I meant to pull the scarf across her mouth ... but then it was around her throat ... and she wouldn't stop struggling. She was stronger than you might think ...'

Sertorius shook his head. 'But why, Mamercus? Why kidnap the fawn? You were my man!'

'No, never,' said Mamercus. 'I was Pompey's man! One of his agents in Rome hired me, to be Pompey's spy. They said you would trust me ... take me into your confidence ... because of my father. They wanted someone to steal the white fawn from you. Not to kill it, just to steal it. You see, Gordianus, I never betrayed my grandfather. Tell him that.'

'But why did you take up with Pompey?' I said.

He grimaced. 'For money, of course! We were ruined. How could

I ever have a career in Rome, without money? Pompey offered me more than enough.'

I shook my head. 'You should have come back to Rome with me.'

Mamercus managed a rueful smile. 'At first, I thought you were a messenger from Pompey. I couldn't believe he could be so stupid, to send a messenger for me into the camp, in broad daylight! Then you said you came from my grandfather . . . dear, beloved grandfather. I suppose the gods were trying to tell me something, but it was too late. My plan was set for that very night. I couldn't turn back.' He coughed. A trickle of blood ran from the corner of his mouth. 'But I turned your visit to my advantage! I showed Sertorius the letter . . . vowed that I had no intention of leaving him . . . not even to please my grandfather! How could he not trust me after that? Sertorius, forgive me! But Gordianus –'

He released his sword and blindly gripped my arm. With his other hand he still clutched the scarf. 'Don't tell grandfather about the girl! Tell him I was a spy, if you want. Tell him I died, doing my duty. Tell him I had the courage to fall on my own sword. But not about the girl . . .'

His grip loosened. The light went out of his eyes. The scarf slipped from his fingers.

I looked at Sertorius. On his face I saw anger, disappointment, grief, confusion. I realized that Mamercus Claudius, like the white fawn, had meant more to him than he would say. Mamercus had been a sort of talisman for him, in the way that a son is a talisman – a sign of the gods' love, a pointer to a brighter future. But Mamercus had been none of those things, and the truth was hard for Sertorius to bear. How had he described Mamercus to me? 'Bright, curious, clever, wholly committed to the cause.' How painfully ironic those words seemed now!

I think that in that moment, Sertorius saw that the white fawn counted for nothing after all; that his days were numbered; that the might of Rome would never cease hounding him until he was destroyed and all traces of his rival state were obliterated from the earth. He picked up the scarf and pressed it to his face, covering his eyes, and for that I was thankful.

The voyage back to Rome seemed long and tedious, yet not nearly long enough; I was not looking forward to meeting with Gaius Claudius and giving him the news.

I had done exactly as he asked: I had found his grandson, delivered the letter, invited Mamercus to flee. I had accepted the task and completed it. When Sertorius asked me to find the white fawn, how could I have known the end?

None of us could have known the outcome of my trip to Spain, least of all Gaius Claudius. And yet, if Gaius had not sent me to find his grandson, Mamercus might still have been alive. Would the old man be able to bear the bitterness of it, that seeking only to bring the boy safely home, he himself had instigated the events that led to the boy's destruction?

And yet, surely Mamercus alone was responsible for his downfall. He had deceived his grandfather, no matter that he loved him; had been a spy for a man and a cause he did not love; had murdered an innocent girl. And for what? All for money; nothing but that.

I should not waste a single tear on the boy, I told myself, leaning over the rail of the ship that carried me back to Rome. It was night. The sky was black and the moon was full, her face spread upon the dark waters like a great pool of white light. Perhaps I did shed a tear for Mamercus Claudius; but the cold breeze plucked it at once from my cheek and dropped it into the vastness of the salty sea. There it was lost in an instant, and surely never counted for anything in the scales of justice, either as reckoned by mortals or by the gods.

THE STATUETTE
OF RHODES

John Maddox Roberts

Starting with SPQR *(1990), John Maddox Roberts introduced us to the character of Decius Metellus, a Roman administrator who lived throughout the last days of the Roman Republic. His investigations have been further chronicled in* SPQR II: The Catiline Conspiracy *(1991),* The Sacrilege *(1992) and* The Temple of the Muses *(1992).*

∽

Rhodes is the most beautiful place in the world. Above its gemlike harbor the houses and public buildings ascend the encircling hills in blinding whiteness and the flowers bloom the year round. The whole city is adorned with the most fabulous works of art, for, unlike mainland Greece and the other islands, Rhodes has remained unplundered by foreigners since the days of its greatest glory, and the citizens have made every effort to prevent great works of art from leaving the island, no matter how high the bids and bribes of collectors.

The populace are as civilized as the island is beautiful, the Rhodians having cultivated good manners the way others cultivate war, and their legal and governmental institutions are models for others to follow, the laws extending even to the protection of slaves and foreigners. For centuries artists, authors, philosophers and rhetoricians have chosen Rhodes as their home and the noble youth from the whole world are sent there for the final polish on their education.

It is, in short, an unutterably boring place. When a nation, however small and insignificant, has no better claim to prominence than beauty, scholarship, education, art and culture, it is in the terminal stages of decadence. Where would we Romans be if we'd sat around making pretty pictures and being polite to one another? We'd all be hauling plows for Gauls and polishing chamberpots for Carthaginians, that's where.

Actually, I was about ready for a little boredom the day I was thrown off the ship onto the mole at Rhodes. My last port of call, Alexandria, had furnished an overabundance of excitement, culminating in my being carried, bound and gagged, from the palace of Ptolemy and hurled aboard the first departing Roman warship. Thus, when the immense, spike-bristling harbor chain was lowered to let the galleys *Swan, Neptune* and *Triton* pass, I was not entirely displeased to see the place, even if it wasn't Rome.

The captain of the *Swan*, one Lichas, directed his men to toss my chests and bags ashore. Last of all came my slave, Hermes. The boy dropped to all fours and dry-heaved, an activity he had been pursuing nonstop since we had struck open water upon passing Pharos.

'You are a sore loser, Captain,' I said, standing and gathering up the shreds of my dignity. I had whiled away the voyage winning most of the money on the ship at dice.

A little delegation of town dignitaries had hurried down to the harbor to greet the three-ship flotilla. They seemed puzzled upon beholding my convict treatment. Rogues, persons of bad character and those who draw bad luck are often cast unceremoniously ashore by mariners, but such persons rarely wear the red-striped tunic of a Roman senator. An important-looking fellow stepped forward, looking back and forth between me and the captain, his expression more than a little bemused.

'Welcome, Captain Lichas. How comes it about that you thus manhandle a Roman senator?' The man spoke beautifully cultured Greek.

Lichas hopped ashore and handed the man a scroll. 'King Ptolemy and Metellus Creticus, Roman ambassador to his court, would esteem it a great favor if you will keep this troublemaker confined to the island until he is sent for.'

The man scanned the scroll and raised his eyebrows. 'My, my. Senator, you do seem to have earned yourself some enemies.'

'I saved the Republic *and* Egypt from a disastrous war and this is the thanks I get.'

Lichas snorted. 'Alexandria was in a state of riot when we left.

You could see the smoke for miles out at sea.' Like most mariners in the Roman service, Lichas was actually a Greek. We don't take to the water naturally.

'Then, Senator,' said an older fellow, 'I extend to you the hospitality of our island. I am Dionysus, president of the city council. This,' he gestured gracefully toward the one who had spoken first, 'is Cleomenes, the harbormaster.' That worthy bowed, and the others were introduced. These Greeks knew how to treat a senator, however irregular his arrival. They also knew that today's rebel, exile or reprobate could well be tomorrow's proconsul.

For a while they chattered on and on about the city's many cultural attractions. Having just come from Alexandria, whose Museum held the greatest collection of books and scholars in the world, my interest in such matters was less than minimal. I was nonetheless extravagant in my praise of their beautiful city and their distinguished selves. If I was to be stuck here for a while, I wanted as much local good will as possible.

After accepting a number of invitations to dinner, Hermes and I made our way up the slope into the city in search of an inn. Until I could find a congenial resident Roman bound to me by *hospitium*, I preferred public lodgings. Many of the local Greeks would have readily extended me hospitality, thrilled to entertain a genuine senator, but then I would run the risk of having to listen to a lot of talk about philosophy.

'This could turn out to be a pleasant stay, Hermes,' I said, fondling the merrily clicking purse tucked into my tunic.

'Anything's better than a ship,' he said, already much recovered from having his feet on dry land. 'Still, we're in exile among foreigners.'

'But the natives are civilized, the city is famous, we're flush with money and, for the first time in years, I've no official duties. It's vacation time, Hermes. From now until I'm summoned to Rome, we can take it easy and live as we please.'

It is with such statements as these that we furnish the gods with endless amusement.

The first days passed exactly as I had anticipated. I dined with local dignitaries, attended some athletic contests, saw the sights and generally lived a life of pleasant dissipation. My hosts were attentive, but when they weren't talking about cultural matters the subject was always the petty politics of their little republic. In Rome, men of my station lived and breathed genuine power politics, played on a world stage. Compared to the life-and-death stakes of games played for rule of provinces and command of armies, the little political feuds of Rhodes seemed piddling affairs. Nonetheless, these were matters of import to the locals and I paid diligent attention. After all, I might someday be given the task of conquering Rhodes, and a knowledge of regional affairs could come in handy.

'It's the Populars behind all this, no doubt of it,' said Eudemus, whose hospitality I was enjoying that afternoon. Some seven or eight of us reclined upon the spacious terrace of his beautiful villa overlooking the harbor.

'Populars, eh?' I said, listening with only half an ear while I held out my cup for more wine. Greek drinking cups are almost as shallow as saucers, and it takes a steady hand to avoid spillage. I was most accomplished at this art. 'We've had them in Rome for generations. I didn't know they were expanding their operations.' This was an alarming prospect. Leave it to Clodius to export Roman street politics to the foreigners.

Dionysus set my fears at ease. 'This is not your party, Senator. They've been here for centuries, too: malcontents and rogues always demanding privileges to which they are not entitled by birth. I suppose they are an inevitable consequence of a republican form of government.' I had learned that, like Rome, Rhodes had a severely limited democracy, in which real power was restricted to a handful of noble families.

'No doubt,' I mumbled around a mouthful of olives. I spat the pits over my shoulder. 'What are they up to here?'

'In the old wars between the Greek states,' said Gylippus, a prominent shipping magnate, 'the Populars were always trying to set one or another of the allies or visiting navies against the best people. Fortunately, Sparta had a wise policy of intervening in such cases.'

My admittedly spotty reading of history told me that the Spartans had made a practice of installing vicious tyrannies wherever they had influence, but I long ago learned the futility of arguing over other people's version of their own history.

'They're up to the same old tricks again,' said Dionysus.

'How?' I asked. 'Old Mithridates is finally gone and the power of the pirates is smashed for good. This part of the world is finally at peace, thanks to Rome.'

'For which our gratitude is immense,' Gylippus said dryly. 'But, that being the case, the common scum have switched their intriguing to Rome itself.'

'Passing a few bribes in the Senate, are they?' I said, looking around for yet another refill. 'No harm in that. The Senate's full of men who'll promise to send out an army, slaughter the lot of you and put the beggars in power. They'll just pocket the money and do nothing. It's done all the time.'

'A few years ago,' said a landowner named Aristander, 'your Julius Caesar was here and the Populars made much of him, entertained him lavishly.'

'They did the same last year when Pompey was here,' said Dionysus.

This, for me, cast a pall over the convivial gathering. I had hoped that here, at last, I could be free of those two names. 'They'll have accomplished nothing with Pompey,' I said. 'He's far too conservative to take the popular side in anything. Caesar is famous for his popular sympathies at home, despite his patrician birth, but that's no more than practical politics. He's been elected one of next year's consuls. Once he's back in Rome after his time as a proconsul, he'll forget it was the mob that put him in power.'

Needless to say, I knew little about Caesar at that time.

'I fear that our Populars believe otherwise,' said Cleomenes, the harbormaster. 'They're agitating for the right to put some of their own on the city council. They claim it's so that the common people will have representation, but we know that they intend to betray our ancient independence and sell Rhodes to the highest bidder.'

'And who might that be?' I asked. 'Mithridates is gone. Egypt amounts to nothing. Pompey destroyed the pirates. Parthia has no ships, and therefore no use for an island. Only Rome is left, and we just conquer what we want.'

'Very true,' Gylippus acknowledged. 'But baseborn traitors practice treachery out of pure habit.'

'Maybe,' I said. 'But I suppose they can't be blamed for sucking up to Pompey. Everybody does, these days.'

'Speaking of outsized persons,' said Dionysus, 'have you visited our Colossus, Senator?'

'I thought it toppled ages ago,' I said.

'So it did, during an earthquake almost two hundred years ago. It stood only fifty-six years.' He sighed for the loss of the island's most famous attraction. 'But even the shattered fragments are a wonder. The head alone is larger by far than most other sculptures.'

'I must have a look at it,' I murmured, not terribly excited. My stay in Egypt had likewise inured me to huge monuments. With all its immense pyramids, temples and statues, there were places in Egypt where you could stand in one spot and just glancing around see more masonry and statuary than was possessed by the rest of the world combined. The prospect of a heap of scrap bronze failed to stir my interest.

Nonetheless, a day or two later, my steps led me to the spacious plaza where once the towering statue of Helios stood in splendor. Hermes accompanied me as usual, packing along a satchel that held my bath items, some snacks I'd purchased at a market, and a skin of decent local wine, all basic supplies for a day of idling and sightseeing.

'Are those *feet* up there?' Hermes exclaimed, gawking.

'I believe so.' The pedestal, itself as large as a good-sized temple, was still tolerably intact. Atop it stood a pair of bronze feet the size of triremes, the nail of the smallest toe larger than a legionary's shield. Having beheld this odd spectacle, it took a few moments to realize that the green hillocks strewn all over the plaza were actually the rest of the statue.

The torso was almost shapeless, collapsed from its own weight, but the lesser members were quite recognizable once the eye and mind adjusted to their size and whimsical juxtapositions. Here the extended finger of a vast hand pointed portentously toward the shop of an oil merchant. There, a well-shaped knee seemed to grow from the crook of an elbow. The long points of the god's solar crown had once been highly polished, their gleam visible to ships far out at sea. Now, the laundry of local housewives dried on lines stretched between them.

Abruptly, the quiet of the day was shattered by an unearthly howl. I imagined that Cerberus might make such a noise to greet a particularly distinguished visitor to the underworld. Then, on second thought, it occurred to me that Cerberus would howl with three voices. Whatever, it was a most impressive noise.

'It's a ghost!' Hermes cried. He had picked up a good many local superstitions during our stay in Egypt.

'They shun daylight,' I told him. 'Come along. I think it came from the god's laundry rack.'

'Are you sure about this?' he asked, taking a surreptitious pull at the wineskin.

'No, but this is the closest thing to excitement that's happened since we got here.'

The head of Helios, bigger than my house in the Subura, lay tilted so that the right cheek and jaw lay against the pavement, the spikes of the crown on that side bent at odd angles. The sound, which had diminished to a series of low moans, seemed to emanate from the neck.

We found a woman standing before the cavernous opening, hands clasped to her mouth, a basket of damp tunics forgotten at her feet. It had been her scream, echoing about within the god's cranium, that had made the unearthly sound.

'I knew it had to be something like that,' Hermes muttered. Next to the basket, a small, brown dog was placidly lapping from a dark pool. Flies buzzed busily around the dog's head. A crowd gathered rapidly, attracted by the singular shriek.

'What's happened?' I asked the woman. Wordlessly, she pointed into the god's hollow head. Hermes and I stepped inside. A dark trickle led from the pool within. Holes and cracks in the bronze skin admitted a dim light, enough to see that a body lay about five paces within, head toward the opening, which was now crowded with gawkers. Hermes crouched by the corpse.

'Looks like someone smashed this one's head in,' he reported. 'Blood and brains all over.'

Outside, a wail went up, from the men as well as the women. 'Murder! Murder!' and so forth.

Hermes looked up in annoyance. 'What's all the fuss about? It's just a body.'

'Perhaps this is an uncommon occurrence here,' I hazarded. In Rome, the corpse of a murder victim scarcely rated a glance from passersby. I'd known less uproar to be raised over a murdered praetor than these Greeks were showing for someone whose identity they couldn't yet know.

Careful not to touch the body, I took a fold of the man's tunic between thumb and fingers and rubbed it back and forth. 'First-class material,' I commented.

'He's wearing a silk diadem with spangles on it,' Hermes reported. Then, a moment later: 'The spangles are real gold, not gilded tin.' Trust the little thief to discern that in the dimness, by touch alone.

I went to the neck opening and beckoned toward a broom-wielding municipal slave. 'Go to the home of Dionysus, president of the city council. Inform him that someone of importance has been murdered.' The man dashed off and I summoned another. 'Get a priest qualified to purify the body. I want a look at him in the light.'

I was just a visitor, but I was accustomed to taking charge in situations like this and no one else seemed to know what to do. I turned to an idler. 'Is there such a thing as a city watch here?' Unlike Rome, many Greek cities have police forces.

He shrugged. 'Only at night. They're usually down by the docks, where the sailors stay.'

Dionysus arrived shortly, bustling up with a few other town notables in tow. A very sizable crowd had gathered by this time, of all ages, sexes and conditions. There was much babbling, the gist of it being that extraordinary bad luck had to be in the offing, what with a murder taking place *inside* the head of the island's tutelary deity. I was wondering about that myself. But then, if the locals used his crown to support clotheslines, he couldn't be all that sacrosanct.

'Senator,' Dionysus puffed, 'what has happened here?'

'I think we're about to find out,' I said, nodding toward a priest whose slaves cleared him a way through the crowd. One slave carried a box that doubtless contained religious paraphernalia. Another shouldered a litter of poles and woven leather straps.

While the priest and his staff went within, I pointed to the dark-brown, congealed puddle. Someone had taken the dog away but the flies still swarmed merrily.

'That's been here several hours, at least. I've investigated enough murders and gathered up enough Roman dead from battlefields to know.'

'I believe you are correct,' said the president, 'but this seems a strange place to commit murder. A person of importance, you say?'

'Well-dressed, at any rate.' The crowd roundabout seemed to be turning ugly. I had seen the phenomenon before. All it takes is a rumor, an omen, some unexpected happening like an eclipse of the sun, and a happy crowd can become a murderous mob in minutes. But these people had no target upon whom to vent their unease. Or did they?

After a brief purification, far less complex than the Roman variety, the slaves loaded the body onto the litter and carried it into the daylight. There came a gasp from the watchers, including Dionysus and the other officials.

'It's Telemachus, the high priest of Helios!' Dionysus said. Now the women of the crowd set up a lamentation worthy of a chorus from Euripides.

'Was he such a popular man?' I asked, astonished at the display.

'Not just popular,' said Dionysus, 'but a Popular.' This made a very neat word play in Greek, but I could tell that he wasn't just coining a witticism for our mutual amusement.

'Your high priest was a Popular?' I said, amazed. 'I might expect that in Rome. Most of our high priesthoods are held as a part of public office. I thought yours were hereditary.'

'They are. But even priests are not immune from the degrading attractions of politics.' I had heard that sort of talk before. All my life, in fact. Any place where power has through long tradition been wielded by a handful of families, anyone else who tries to enter the charmed circle is doing something improper if not downright depraved.

'Here's the murder weapon,' said Hermes, emerging from inside the giant's head. He had been my servant long enough to fancy himself an expert investigator. He held up his trophy with pride. It was a bronze statuette about as long as a man's forearm, its base covered with a ghastly mess of blood, brains and hair. I took it from him and examined it. It depicted a nude, standing man wearing a solar crown and had a decidedly familiar look.

'Is this a miniature of the Colossus?' I asked Dionysus.

'Why, yes, it is. The local artisans make them by the hundreds. Visitors buy them as keepsakes. People here send them as gifts to friends, as pledge-tokens and so forth.'

I looked the thing over. 'It's an odd choice of weapon. If I were planning to kill someone, I think I'd choose something better designed for the task.'

'Perhaps in Rome you are more conversant with these activities,' he sniffed.

'It goes without saying. Is there any way to determine who made this?'

'I've no idea. Why do you ask?'

'It could be significant.'

'Significant in what sense? Our respect for Rome is very great, Senator, but you are not an official here,' he reminded me.

'Just curious,' I said, not wishing to tell him that I was already bored half out of my mind and eager for something to engage my faculties.

'Please, Senator,' he said, 'leave this to us. And now, if I may take my leave, I must see to the arrangements for Telemachus' funeral.' He and some other dignitaries bowed politely and followed the train of wailing mourners toward the temple of Helios where, presumably, Telemachus would be cremated.

I detained the priest for a moment. 'Does murder in this spot constitute a sacrilege?' I asked him.

'No. This is not a *temenos*; a place set aside as sacred to a deity or to the shades of the dead. There are no priests, and sacrifices were never performed here. The Colossus was an image of the god, but even when it was whole it was just a statue.' With a bow he rejoined the procession.

I handed the statuette back to Hermes. 'Wash this off.' He ambled off toward one of the city's many fine public fountains and returned a few minutes later, our trophy now free of the sticky evidence of its misuse.

'Why brain him with a statue?' I mused, examining the base.

'It certainly got the job done,' Hermes pointed out.

'But, if I was planning to kill someone, looking about my lodgings for the proper tool, I can hardly imagine thinking, "My sword? No, too cumbersome. My dagger? No, too common. Aha! The miniature copy of the Colossus of Rhodes! Just the thing!" '

'We've seen people murdered by roof-tiles,' Hermes said. 'I knew a slave once, was killed with a kitchen pestle. Bricks, candlesticks, anything handy will do.'

'Yes,' I said, waxing philosophical. Philosophical for me, anyway. 'Yes, when passions flare abruptly, anything that comes readily to hand may serve. Had Telemachus been found murdered in a house, with this lying close by, I would think no more of it. But he was killed in a lonely spot late at night.'

'Someone might have debrained him at home, then lugged him over there to hide the body.'

'I think not. That sort of head wound bleeds very freely. There should have been a huge trail of blood leading to the hiding place. And why carry along the murder weapon? No, it looks to me as if he was killed on the spot. Moreover, I think it unlikely that the killer had homicide in mind.'

He shrugged. 'What's one more dead Greek, anyway?'

'Relief, Hermes. Relief. Come along.'

As he walked, I examined the extempore weapon more closely. It was finely cast, the figure of the god being made in one piece with the pedestal. I could find no name, initial, or other maker's mark. The bottom of the pedestal was sealed with a nicely cut and polished piece of green marble, also unmarked.

Asking directions as we went, we soon came to the Sculptor's Market, a spacious forum where the musical chime of chisel against stone went on nonstop. The sculptors worked outdoors, with no more than an awning to protect them from the sun, inclement weather being a rarity on idyllic Rhodes.

'Now,' I said, 'all we need to do is locate the artist who made this statue.'

'It could be a sizable job,' Hermes said, looking round.

Everywhere in the market we could see copies of the Colossus. There were images done in fine marble, in cheap terracotta, in fired ceramic, in wood, in bronze like the murder weapon and in mixed media. Some were miniatures six inches high, others more substantial, and a few were man-sized. Some were painted, others left in the natural color of the medium.

I walked over to a life-sized specimen. He was of bronze, standing upon a base of Parian marble, and he had been given the full Greek treatment. Most of the flesh part was left in the mellow sheen of polished bronze. The hair and crown were brilliantly gilded. The lips and nipples were sheathed in slightly darker copper and the teeth, barely visible behind the lips, were silver-gilt. The eyes were inlaid with white shell and lapis lazuli. The thing had to cost as much as a good estate in Campania.

'May I help you, ah, Senator?' The dealer knew how to spot the insignia. I knew he wasn't the sculptor, with his fine tunic and his soft hands. 'I can make you a very favorable price for this sculpture. It was made by the sculptor Archelaus more than two hundred years ago, while the Colossus still stood, a very faithful copy.'

'Actually, I was interested in something more recent.'

'Oh?' he said, disappointed, 'what might that be?'

I held up my statuette. 'I need to find out who made this.' Just my luck if it was two hundred years old, too.

He pursed his lips. 'A common piece. I can think of more than two or three dozen artisans who might have made it. The founder might know.'

'The founder?'

'Yes. The bronze sculptors make their images in wax, then all of them take the wax images to the bronze foundry to be cast. There is only one on the island.'

I thanked him and made a mental vow that, should I ever get a chance to conquer Rhodes, I was going to claim that statue as my first piece of loot.

Like all the smokier businesses, the bronze foundry was located on a spit of land downwind of the city, where the whoosh of bellows vied with the clamor of the smiths' hammers and the roar of the fires to determine what could make the most noise. The foreman of the foundry was a sooty Greek with singed eyebrows. He turned the statuette over in hands so covered with burns that they shone like glazed ceramic.

'This is Myron's work. I cast it for him no more than a month ago. I can tell by the color. We'd just got in a shipment of Spanish copper. It's a little darker than the Syrian metal we'd been using.'

Now I was getting someplace. 'Did he say if it was a special commission?'

He shook his head and cinders sprinkled his shoulders. 'No, it was one of maybe ten pieces he brought in. He comes by three or four times a year, and it's almost always the Helios images.'

'Do you supply this base plug?' I tapped the marble on the bottom.

'No, it's all specialist work. The sculptor makes the wax image. We do the casting. A polisher does the polishing and if the base is marble it's cut by a lapidary.'

'Why isn't the base just cast in place?' I asked.

'Sculpture is always cast hollow. It saves weight and it saves bronze, which is an expensive metal.'

I thanked him and we headed back into the city proper. 'Now we find Myron?' Hermes asked.

'No, now we look for a lapidary.'

The quarter of the lapidaries was somewhat quieter than those of the sculptors and metal workers. The tools are much smaller. A little asking around brought us to a stall where five or six slaves worked industriously at a bench, overseen by an elderly craftsman.

'Yes, this is my shop's work,' he acknowledged with a glance at the statuette's base. 'I have the only stock of green Italian marble on the island just now.' He nodded toward a big block of greenish stone which a pair of slaves were patiently sawing into inch-thick slabs, the saw moving slowly back and forth while a small boy trickled water into the cut.

'When was this?'

He scratched his head. 'Myron came to pick them up about ten days ago.'

'Did he say who had commissioned them?'

'Copies like this are seldom made to commission. I do remember that he wanted special treatment for one.'

'How so?'

'Ordinarily, the bases are glued in with pitch. He wanted one base left unglued.'

'Did he say why?' The Greek just shrugged.

'Now we return to the Sculptor's Market to look for Myron?' Hermes asked wearily.

'No,' I told him. 'Now we find a nice, shady spot and have lunch. Then we go find Myron.'

Back in the Sculptor's Market, after a little side trip to the harbor mole, we found Myron before his shop, molding wax. Everyone has heard of the famous Myron, the sculptor who created the Discus-Thrower. This, needless to say, was another Myron. The original has been dead for about four hundred years. Like charioteers, sculptors like to use the names of old champions.

'That's mine, all right,' he said, not interrupting the rhythm of his hands on the wax.

'Who bought it?' I asked.

'I've made and sold hundreds of those. Most of the buyers are foreign travelers like you.'

'Who asked for one with the base left unattached?'

Now the busy hands paused. 'Oh, that one. It was Cleomenes, the harbormaster.'

'I see. Did he say why he desired this eccentric treatment?'

Again, that Greek shrug. 'No. Why should he?'

As we walked back toward our digs, I said to Hermes, 'I don't understand how the Greeks got their reputation as a curious, inquiring people. Most of them are utter dullards.'

'Maybe,' he opined, 'they know some questions are better left unasked.'

When we got to the temple of Helios, things were in full swing. In the balmy climate of Rhodes, they waste no time in getting the dead disposed of. Telemachus lay on a bier atop a great heap of timber that reeked of oil. The mourners had quieted down so that the eulogies could be delivered. Rhodes had the world's most illustrious teachers of rhetoric, and I think it was the famous Molon, teacher of Cicero, who was speaking as we arrived. A whole crowd of students from many lands stood around while the old man showed them how a real expert dispatches a dead nonentity to the netherworld.

'The heavens weep,' intoned the orator, 'and the sun hides its face in mourning for the peerless Telemachus, priest of Helios.' Actually, it had been perfectly clear all day, and the sun was merely getting ready to go down the way it does every day. I suppose it's the sentiment that counts. 'Surely, the god cannot permit this perfect servant to descend, a mere bodiless shade, to the Stygian shore. Rather, he now attends his deity with his own hands, perhaps grooming the fiery steeds of the sun, or pouring the nectar to soothe the god's thirst after his daily ride in the solar chariot . . .' and so forth in this vein for some time. I've heard the same sort of eulogy for innumerable dead priests. If they were all true, every god would have more servants than Crassus and there wouldn't be enough work for most of them to do.

'Do you see Cleomenes among the mob?' I asked Hermes. 'He must be here. Everyone of importance is.'

'Over there, with all the men in gilded wreaths. I guess that's the rest of the city council.'

'Right. They're looking a little uncomfortable.' The council members, dressed in their best robes, were trying to maintain their dignity. The surrounding crowd were clearly in a dark mood, muttering and glowering. A Roman mob would have been in full riot by now, but as I have said, the Rhodians are rather more easy-going.

'Well,' I said, 'time to liven things up.'

'Maybe you'd better wait until tomorrow,' Hermes cautioned. He held up the wineskin and examined it. The thing had gone flat during the course of the day.

'Nonsense. No time like the present. We have an audience now.' I pushed my way through the mob of mourners, into the cleared zone just before the temple steps, where the pyre had been erected. 'May I have your attention, please!' I shouted in my best Forum voice, which had considerable volume.

The speaker, Molon or whoever it was, broke off in mid-praise. 'Sir, do you wish to deliver a eulogy for the departed? If so, you shall have your turn.' The fellow had tremendous, almost Roman *dignitas*, for a Greek.

'Not a bit of it,' I said. 'I've come to make an accusation of murder.' At this there was an uproar from the crowd.

'Senator!' cried Dionysus, outraged. 'This is not the place for such an action! You have no right to . . .'

'Nonsense!' I interrupted grandly. 'I'm a Roman senator and I can do anything I want to.' I really had been hitting the wine too hard that day. 'I accuse the harbormaster, Cleomenes, of braining the late Telemachus, high priest of Helios, with this statuette of his own deity!' I held up the bronze figure for everyone's edification.

'Death to the Aristocrats!' shouted some idiot, safely anonymous within the midst of the crowd.

'Oh, pipe down, moron! That fool,' I jerked a thumb over my shoulder, indicating the body on the pyre, 'and Cleomenes were conspiring to sell out your republic.'

'Be silent, you interloping barbarian!' Cleomenes shouted, gone quite red in the face. 'Not only is your charge absurd, but Rome has no business meddling in the affairs of the ancient Republic of Rhodes!'

'Hah!' I said, wittily. 'That's not what you said when you entertained Pompey last year, was it?' Actually, I wasn't certain that it had been Pompey the traitors had been conspiring with, but in those years he was certainly the best candidate. His red face whitened and I knew my dart had struck home.

'Senator,' Dionysus said, this time in a lower voice and casting nervous glances in the direction of the restive crowd, 'are you telling us that General Pompey, that glorious conqueror, while enjoying our hospitality, was plotting against us?'

'Not directly and with no immediate designs upon your republic,' I assured him. 'But Pompey, like any good general, no sooner wraps up a successful war than he makes preparations for the next. His recent campaign against the pirates taught him the importance of naval power, a thing long neglected by Rome. He knew that a big eastern war would necessitate a strong base with a good harbor, and what finer harbor, what stronger island than Rhodes exists in the eastern part of the sea? Was it not in celebration of your defeat of Demetrius, that theretofore unconquered besieger, that you erected your Colossus?' I just thought I would show these Greeks that they were not the only ones who knew how to give a rousing public speech. This even roused a mild cheer from the mob, remembering their island's greatest moment of military glory.

'You, yourself,' Cleomenes protested, 'have said that Rome has no enemies left!'

'I mentioned Parthia and Egypt. Alone, either is a negligible quantity. But together, remembering that Cyprus, too, belongs to Egypt, they could prove troublesome.' I did not think it wise to point out the greatest danger: that a future war in the east would most likely be a civil war, between Pompey and one of our other successful, trouble-making generals, someone like Lucullus, Crassus, Gabinius, or even Caesar, whose star was ascendant at the time.

'Pompey wanted assurances of cooperation from both camps, the Aristocrats and the Populars, so he suborned promises of aid from two prominent members of those parties. You recall, noble Dionysus, how you told me just this morning that these statues of Helios are often given as pledge-tokens?'

'So I did,' he admitted.

'This statuette,' I waved the thing aloft, really warming up to my denunciation, 'was to symbolize their pledge to Pompey. As good conspirators always do, they divided the incriminating activity between them. Cleomenes bought the token. Telemachus, high priest of Helios, was to send it to Pompey, supposedly in fond remembrance of his visit here. The two, political rivals that they publicly were, could not meet publicly so that the statuette could be handed over, nor could they trust a go-between. So they met late at night, in a conveniently deserted spot, the Place of the Colossus.' I had their rapt attention now. Even the muttering had stopped.

'But,' I cried, pausing dramatically for effect, 'the two had a falling out. Perhaps one of them wanted a bigger slice of the spoils to be divided when Pompey should take the island, perhaps Telemachus, with a last-minute attack of conscience or cowardice, wanted out of the arrangement entirely. Whichever it was, Cleomenes, in a thwarted rage, bashed him over the head with the only weapon available – this statuette!' I brandished it like a sword and everyone gasped.

'And just how did you come up with this fabrication of blatant lies?' Cleomenes said with contemptuous indignation, his shifting eyes betraying him.

'I admit,' I said, preening, 'that when I learned from Myron the sculptor that Cleomenes had requested a statuette with its hollow base left unsealed, I expected to find incriminating documents within. Naturally, even an amateur conspirator and assassin like Cleomenes would never leave anything so incriminating right next to the corpse of his victim. The token contained nothing so blatant.'

'What, then?' Dionysus urged, torn between indignation at the plot, resentment of me and fear of the crowd.

'Something he thought no one in on the plot would ever notice. But, Cleomenes was not expecting the arrival on the scene of Decius Caecilius Metellus the Younger.' Here I popped loose the marble base, something I had done earlier, while Hermes and I had been enjoying lunch in one of the many delightful little parks that dot the city. 'Here,' I held up the nicely crafted piece of green marble, 'scratched into the base, are words not in Greek but in Latin. They say, simply, 'It is cut.'

'And what does this mean?' Dionysus asked.

'It would mean nothing to anyone who did not know exactly who had made the inscription. But, knowing that it was Cleomenes the harbormaster, I took a little walk down to the mole to examine the one thing in his charge that might be of interest to Pompey: the great chain that blocks the entrance to the harbor. If you will send officers to examine it you will find that some of the links have been cleverly sawn halfway through. The tampering is well disguised, and it does not affect the regular raising and lowering of the chain. But one Roman trireme would snap it like a string and Pompey's troops would be quartered in your houses before you knew he had arrived.'

'Cleomenes,' Dionysus shouted, white-faced, 'you are under arrest pending investigation of the Senator's charges.' The guilty man opened his mouth to speak, but a traitor's death was already upon his face and no sound emerged.

As the crowd broke up in disappointment and confusion I congratulated myself. Personally, I didn't care who controlled Rhodes, but our warmongering generals had already come near to destroying the Republic, and in those days I considered Pompey the most dangerous of the lot. I was pleased to have done him a bad turn.

'Shall we go ahead and burn him?' asked a torch-bearing slave, nodding toward the heap of oily wood. At the president's nod he tossed his torch into the pile which began to crackle merrily.

'It seems, Senator,' said Dionysus as if the words left a foul taste in his mouth, 'that Rhodes owes you thanks. Not that Pompey or any other general would have found us so easy to take, with or without our harbor chain. How may we express our gratitude?' He was used to Roman envoys, a greedy lot back then.

'I care only for justice,' I told him. Then I draped an arm over his shoulders. 'My father, however, is a great fancier of Greek sculpture. Down in the Sculptor's Market there is a statue of Helios that would be perfect for his country estate . . .'

These things happened in Rhodes in the year 692 of the City of Rome, the consulship of Metellus Celer and Lucius Afranius.

THE THINGS
THAT ARE CAESAR'S

Edward D. Hoch

Edward Hoch is a most prolific writer of mystery short stories, having produced around eight hundred since he sold his first in 1955, and he shows no signs of drying up. Although a number of these are historical mysteries, such as his Ben Snow and Sam Hawthorne series, it isn't often that he ventures into ancient history. He isn't one to duck a challenge either, and in the following story he creates a new mystery out of the death of Julius Caesar.

∽

In Rome, early in the year that would someday be known as 44 BC, the prostitute Cybele had moved out of the brothel on the second floor of the Romulus Tavern and taken two rooms of her own. She had come to the city from the countryside to the north, choosing to be known by the name of the earth goddess. It was a name that suited her, and it brought her at once to the attention of those men high in the government who often sought out the pleasures of the forbidden.

Now, with the gold coins paid by her protector, she was able to afford these rooms on the Street of the Sandal Makers. One served as both living and dining room, where she prepared food over a charcoal brazier and ate it at a nearby table. The other was the bedroom, furnished only with a bed, table, washstand and chamber pot. Olive oil lamps furnished necessary light. It was here each day that Cybele cleansed herself by rubbing oil on her body and then scraping it off. It was here that she applied cosmetics to her face, eyebrows and eyelashes in preparation for a visit from her lover. He came in the evening, if the affairs of state allowed, though she never knew when this would be. She was always ready and loving, believing herself to be his particular favorite despite the presence of the Egyptian queen in the city.

On this night, when a light rain had begun to fall on the city, the Street of the Sandal Makers was all but deserted. He came at last, some hours after sundown, and she lit all of her lamps to bring some cheer to the little rooms. 'You have made this into a place of beauty,' he remarked. 'Oh that Calpurnia could make my home quite so lovely.' He rarely mentioned his wife's name and never that of his mistress, Cleopatra, though she now lived in Rome with his bastard son. He shed the cloak which served to protect him from both the rain and prying eyes. Underneath he wore a tunic designed for street wear, and his sandals. As always there was the dagger at his waist.

'Are you hungry, my lord?' Cybele asked.

'Perhaps a little wine would be nice.'

A short time later he removed his tunic and stood before her clad only in a loincloth. At fifty-six he still had the body of a general, with the demeanor of a statesman. She had admired that body many times, feasting her eyes on the wounds of battle as he told the stories again and again. 'Lovely Cybele, this sword stroke came as I led my troops across the Rubicon and defied the Roman Senate with its armies. Let me tell you of it.'

'I have heard the story of your bravery, mighty Caesar,' she remarked with just a trace of mockery. They had known each other for many seasons.

'Very well,' he said with a sigh. 'Let us retire to the bed.' From his lips it was always a command, not an invitation.

'In the marketplace I hear talk of corruption in your government,' she told him later, toward dawn, when the night's shadows were still deep in the room. It was a remark meant as conversation and nothing more, and as she spoke she toyed with the golden cord from his tunic.

'It is always so,' he answered dismissively.

'Members of Rome's ancient families are said to be involved. They say even the noble Brutus has loaned money to a community of Greeks at interest rates approaching fifty per cent.'

'Why bother your head with such harmful gossip?'

But she persisted, pouring out the words she had meant to save for another time. 'They say that Crassus when he lived used scouts to report on fires in the city. He then hastened to the scene and offered a low price to purchase the ruin from its agonized owner. Thus he was able to buy up much valuable property.'

Caesar was growing uncomfortable. 'Enough of this, woman! You speak of things you do not know. Crassus was a good and true friend whose fortune helped finance my political career. With the late Pompey we formed a powerful triumvirate.'

'You betrayed them both and caused their deaths.'

She saw that her words had truly angered him. 'I have paid you well for your services, woman. Why do you now turn against me?' He stormed about the tiny room. 'Crassus died in battle in Syria and Pompey in Egypt, as you must know.'

'Pompey was murdered, probably on your orders.'

'Pompey was my own son-in-law!'

'Not after Julia died. Then he was an enemy who had driven your daughter to an early grave.'

'How do you know these things?' he whispered. 'How do you know of my daughter Julia? Are you a sorceress or soothsayer?'

'Neither. As a young girl I worked in your daughter's household, before her death. Have you forgotten that she died just ten years ago, not yet thirty years of age?' She had not planned it this way, but she'd known from the first that someday it would happen. 'Look into my eyes, O Caesar, and tell me what you see. Do you see the lovely daughter you forced into an unhappy marriage with Pompey for your own political ends, simply to win his backing?'

'You are a demon!'

'I am your conscience.'

'How do you know these things?'

'Julia confided her heartbreak to me. I never dreamed then that I would become her father's whore.'

Caesar fell back as if physically struck by her words. She watched him grapple for the dagger on his mound of discarded clothes but still she saw no reason to fear him. Even when he lunged at her and she felt the blade slip easily between her ribs, she could not quite believe what was happening.

Marcus Junius Brutus had never considered himself a friend of Julius Caesar. He could never forget the fact that his mother had once been Caesar's mistress, or that his love for Caesar's daughter Julia had been shattered by her marriage to Pompey. He was fifteen years younger than Caesar, who had ruled Rome as a virtual dictator since the end of the Triumvirate. Crassus and Pompey were both dead, and Brutus himself was lucky to be alive. At a crucial point in the political maneuvering, during the civil war between Pompey and Caesar, he had allied himself with the losing side. Julia was long dead by that time, and Pompey seemed the lesser of two evils. But Pompey was defeated and fled to Egypt where the assassins found him. Caesar showed mercy and pardoned Brutus, even appointing him governor of Cisalpine Gaul for two years.

Now he was back, as praetor of Rome, an elected magistrate charged chiefly with the administration of civil justice. It was not unusual for his duties to take him among the criminal classes, but it was mere chance that brought him to the rooms in the Street of the Sandal Makers where a prostitute named Cybele had been killed.

Her body had been found on the morning of her death by a slave who cleaned the rooms once a week for the building's owner. That owner, a man named Maximus, sent a runner to fetch the praetor because he feared legal entanglements from the killing in his building.

Brutus, at forty-one, was a grim-faced man with hard eyes and an acne-scarred skin. Like many wealthy government officials he had learned the trick of using money to make more money. If one accused him of charging interest rates approaching fifty per cent, he was not one to deny it, only to ask how much the accuser desired to borrow. Someday, he knew, it would all catch up with him. Perhaps then he would follow the wily Pompey's flight into Egypt, and pray he was better at dodging the assassins' knives.

'Who is this woman?' he asked Maximus, staring down at the body sprawled over the edge of the bed. In life she had been quite lovely. Now her loincloth, which she would have worn to bed, was crusted with dried blood from a stab wound. There were more spots of blood on the bed and floor.

'Her name is Cybele. She has been here only a few months, since the beginning of winter.' Maximus was a squat bearded man in his fifties, owner of several abodes in the neighborhood. There were many like him in Rome.

The stench of death was strong in the room and Brutus opened the shutters, allowing the cool outside air to circulate. 'Only a whore would call herself by the name of a goddess,' he said.

'She paid me three hundred sesterces each month and I asked no questions,' Maximus replied.

'What do you want of me?'

'I am an honest man, my lord. A slain woman in my building will surely bring trouble.'

'Not if you are truthful. Was she a prostitute?'

The bearded man shrugged. 'She moved here from the bordello

over the Romulus Tavern. Some knew her there, but I have only seen one man visit her in this building.'

'What did he look like?'

'He wore a cloak that concealed his face and body.'

Brutus saw something glisten in the light from the open window. He knelt and removed a gold cord from the dead woman's right hand. 'Have you ever seen this before?'

'No.'

'Was it hers?'

'I do not know.'

Brutus pulled it around his waist. 'It is long, more for a man than a woman.'

'She might have pulled it from the killer as he stabbed her.'

'I was thinking exactly that.' He wound the gold cord into a coil and slid it under the belt of his tunic. 'Something like this implies a gentleman wearing a tunic. I have seen Caesar himself wearing such a belt.' He continued studying the floor, especially where the woman's blood had stained it. 'Look here! This could be the imprint of a sandal's heel in the dried blood. See how the stain curves around?'

'But there is no blood underneath,' the landlord noted. 'Where is the rest of it?'

'On the sandal, I imagine.'

'If you find that sandal you would have your killer.'

Brutus smiled at the idea. 'I am certain it has been scrubbed clean by now.' He began searching the two rooms, first examining the bed itself. It was an expensive one made of wood with legs of bone, perhaps a gift from the man in the cloak. There were glass inlays along the sides, serving as mirrors for the light. It was covered with a wool mattress as protection against the winter chill.

Next he moved on to a lamp stand which held a cluster of oil lamps. The oil had burned out in all of them and he wondered if that indicated the killer had spent the night. He would likely have blown out the lamps when he departed, rather than allow their glow to illuminate the body of his victim. If the lamps had burned out and the shutters were closed, he might not have noticed the drop of blood on his sandal.

Brutus moved on to the charcoal brazier, used for cooking and the room's only source of heat. Even at this hour, close to noon, he could still detect a bit of warmth when he held his hands near the ashes. 'Who paid you for the room?' he asked.

'She did. I came for it each month and she always had the silver sesterces ready.'

Brutus continued his search but could find nothing of interest. 'I will report this to the authorities,' he said at last. 'They will try to locate her family so the body may be claimed for burial.'

'I hope so. I have no money for an undertaker.'

'One will come to remove the body. I will see to it.'

'Thank you, my lord.'

Brutus had expected it to be a simple task, but by day's end he realized that the dead woman's true identity was hidden behind that name of Cybele. He knew he should turn the task over to a clerk, but something about the killing intrigued him. Perhaps it was the beauty of the victim. Maximus had said she'd lived in the brothel above the Romulus Tavern before moving to his building. That seemed a likely place to begin.

Like other Romans, Brutus usually dined at home around three in the afternoon. After a tasty meal of pheasant and turbot prepared by the household slaves, his wife Portia suggested they ride over to visit some friends, but he pleaded the pressure of his civil cases and went off alone. By late afternoon he was on the street where the Romulus Tavern was located. He kept the cloak wrapped tightly around him, hiding his expensive tunic, and entered the place as any customer would.

'Is the brothel open upstairs?' he asked the man dispensing wine behind the counter.

'They never close. The stairs are over there.'

At the top he was met by an aging madam who asked his preferences and explained the rules. He interrupted to say he was looking for a particular girl named Cybele. 'I was here once last year and I remember her striking beauty.'

'Cybele is no longer with us,' the woman explained. 'But I can offer beauties even more luscious to behold.'

'I must find Cybele.' He offered a silver coin. 'Surely there must be someone here who knows her whereabouts.'

The woman seemed dubious. When he added a second coin she said, 'Her best friend was Athena.'

'Of course! Athena and Cybele! An opportunity to sleep with the gods, or goddesses!'

'Second room on the left. You have an hour.'

'More than I'll need, good lady.'

Athena was dark and brooding, with a bruise on her face she had tried to cover with cosmetics. She got up off the bed as he entered and opened her arms to him. 'This is the place, my lord.'

'I come seeking Cybele.'

'I am the new Cybele, born again to enchant you.'

He handed her some coins. 'You were her friend, I am told.'

'I still am.'

'She was killed early this morning.'

The color drained from Athena's face. She sat down on the bed. 'I saw her only two days ago.'

'She had a regular customer who paid for her apartment.' He made it a statement, not a question.

The woman on the bed nodded. 'He wanted her for himself, not to share with others.'

'What is his name?'

'She could not utter it. She told me once he was at the highest rank of the government.'

The highest rank? If taken literally that would mean Caesar himself. It hardly seemed likely he would be dallying with a prostitute when Calpurnia was at home and Cleopatra was in Rome with his three-year-old son Caesarion.

'Did she tell you anything else about him?'

'Just that he came when he could and sometimes spent the night, leaving as the shops were opening around seven. He had to cover his face then, so as not to be recognized.'

'Thank you,' Brutus said, slipping her another small silver coin. 'You have helped me.'

'That is all you want?' she asked, not quite believing it.

'That is all.' He left her and went back downstairs, through the tavern to the street.

The killing of the prostitute Cybele caused no great stir within the city, and was little noted outside the immediate neighborhood of the crime. It was two days after the discovery of the body that Brutus happened to call at Caesar's home at a time he knew the ruler would be at the Forum. A slave showed him to Calpurnia's inner chamber. She was a pleasant, bland woman, whom some thought Caesar had married for political reasons following the death of his first wife and a divorce from his second.

'My husband is at the Forum,' she told Brutus, interrupting the slave girl who was preparing her hair and makeup. She sent the girl from the room and continued, 'I thought you would have known that.'

'I am concerned lately about your husband's schedule. He was to have met me two nights ago but he never appeared.'

Calpurnia pondered this for a moment and finally said, 'That would have been the night he visited the fortuneteller, Mother Sysius. He returned late.'

'After dark?'

'Much after dark.' She smiled calmly. 'Toward morning, I believe. Since we have separate bed chambers I cannot be certain of the time.'

Brutus smiled. 'There is no need to tell Caesar I called. I will see him at the Forum.'

'Very well, Brutus.'

Mother Sysius was an elderly woman who lived in a small room behind her shop near the Senate House in the Forum. That building was one of the accomplishments of Julius Caesar's reign, and even Brutus admired the long, high-ceilinged room where the legislative body met. Though he had no time for fortunetellers himself, he had often watched as the Roman senators made their way from the Forum to Mother Sysius's tiny shop.

Now as he entered he saw the woman in her odd pointed hat, seated on a sort of table or altar. A small dog ran about the room as she peered at this new arrival through clouded eyes. He suspected she was almost blind, and was surprised when she greeted him by name. 'Ah, fair Brutus! This is the first time you have ventured into my dwelling place.'

'It is,' he agreed.

'Do you wish to know what the gods hold for you?'

'Not really. I come about our leader, the great Caesar.'

She nodded. 'I have often given him words of advice.'

'Was he here two nights ago?' Brutus asked.

Mother Sysius wrinkled her brow. 'Not for a fortnight have I seen him.'

'You're certain of that?'

'Yes. Perhaps he visited his astrologer, Sosigenes, instead.'

He laid out some coins on the table before her. 'Tell me about Caesar.'

Her eyes closed and she seemed to sway a bit. 'He consults the oracles. He believes in signs and wonders. The letter C and women's names starting with that letter are considered lucky by him, and he listens to the words of the soothsayers in the streets.'

'What else?'

'He fears assassination, but who among you does not?'

Brutus nodded. 'We wear our daggers and our short swords everywhere. Sometimes the person we assassinate is ourselves.' He hesitated and then asked, 'Will Caesar die by his own hand?'

'I cannot say. The future is clouded. Tell him to come here himself if he needs a clearer answer.'

'I will do that. Thank you, Mother Sysius.'

On the following day, which was the fourteenth of March, Brutus arranged to meet with a number of others in the orchard at his home. First Cassius and then Casca arrived, followed by Decius, Metellus, Trebonius and Cinna. Once they were assembled, strolling out of earshot of the slaves, Brutus came to the point.

'I believe Julius Caesar to be guilty of the murder of a young prostitute named Cybele, three nights ago.'

A few of them gasped, but it was Cassius who spoke first. 'He is a colossus among us, but even such a figure is not without his flaws. What proof do you offer for this accusation?'

Brutus told them quickly of being summoned by the landlord Maximus. He described the scene of the crime, and the gold belt such as Caesar wore. He told of his visit to Cybele's friend Athena. It was Casca who protested. 'But the highest rank of government does not mean Caesar alone, dear Brutus. More likely this little whore attracted someone other than the mighty Caesar. Or even if Caesar was the woman's lover, someone else might have killed her.'

'Let us take your first point, Casca. The fortune teller, Mother Sysius, tells me that Caesar believes women with names beginning with a C bring good luck for him. Now is there any evidence of this odd fact in his life? Yes, there is. Caesar's first wife, you will remember, was the doomed Cornelia. He loved her deeply. For a second wife he took Pompeia and realized his mistake too late when she was accused of violating the mysteries of the fertility cult and forced to resign as its leader. As he said when he divorced her, Caesar's wife must be above suspicion. Since that time he has remained safely with the C names. Calpurnia became his third wife and Cleopatra became his mistress. The Egyptian queen bore him a son, whom he cannot publicly acknowledge, though the child has another C name – Caesarion. Calpurnia is barren, as we all know. Is it any wonder that he would turn to a prostitute named Cybele? Not only does her name begin with the proper letter but it is that of the ancient goddess who is a deification of the female generative principle. Caesar was hoping to father a daughter to replace the one lost ten years ago.'

Cassius laughed at that. 'Your ideas are far-fetched, Brutus. Do you have any evidence of this? An eye-witness?'

'Of course not. I only say to you that we must take action against this murderer.'

'We support you, of course,' Decius assured him. 'But you must bring us proof of such a charge.'

And he knew they were right. Julius Caesar was the Father of Rome. Who could accuse him of killing a prostitute on the basis of some foolishness about names? 'Give me until tomorrow,' he said finally. 'There is someone I must speak with.'

'Who would that be?'

'Sosigenes, Caesar's astrologer.'

The astrologer was a wise man who devoted his days and nights to a study of the heavens. Only two years earlier, after determining that the calendar was no longer in keeping with the seasons, he had persuaded Caesar to adopt a new calendar of 365 days each year, with 366 days every fourth year. Eighty days had been added that year, to compensate for past inaccuracies.

Brutus found him alone in his observatory, surrounded by representations of the sun and moon. 'A cloudy day after our recent rain, Sosigenes,' he said. 'What do you find to study on such a day?'

'The sky is always with us. There are signs and portents if we are wise enough to read them correctly. What can I do for you, dear Brutus?' He was a slender man, dressed in a long robe of colorful design. When he moved, his body seemed to flow.

'I am arranging a surprise for Caesar, to be presented on the ides. I know of his liking for certain numbers and letters of the alphabet, and I wish to be certain that the gift is appropriate. Could you advise me as to his favorites?'

The astrologer took a seat and motioned Brutus into an opposite chair. Touching the fingers of his hands together like a high priest in prayer, he answered, 'Of course there is the letter C. He favors men and women whose names begin with that letter, because it is his own. Thus the senator named Cicero, and others named Cassius, Casca and Cimber are all known to him, as is Cinna the poet.'

'And Caesar's wife Calpurnia.'

'Of course,' Sosigenes agreed.

'I thought as much.'

'With numbers it is different, depending upon my readings of the stars. Is that any help?'

'I think so. Tell me, did mighty Caesar visit you three nights ago?'

'Not in a fortnight have I seen him.'

Brutus nodded. 'Thank you for your time.'

Sosigenes waved a hand at the sky. 'As you observed, it is a cloudy day. And even the clouds are shapeless.'

All his visit to the astrologer had accomplished was to confirm Caesar's affinity for the letter C. Brutus still had no proof against him, nothing linking him directly with the murder. He needed an eye-witness, and there was none.

As he rode back from Sosigenes' observatory, he remembered the print of a sandal in the blood on Cybele's floor. If he could find that sandal, and show that its outline matched the bloody print . . .

Certainly Caesar had many pairs of sandals at home. A slave could have scrubbed away the blood within minutes, while he wore another pair.

But would he entrust that task to a slave? Might he try to do it himself and risk questioning by Calpurnia? Better to throw the bloodstained sandal away, not at home where it might be found but somewhere on the way home.

Brutus was thinking more clearly now. Disposing of the sandal would have been most important to Caesar. He would have been alone at Cybele's apartment, with no slave to go off for another pair. Where, in those early morning hours, could he find fresh sandals to wear home?

That was when it hit him, as clearly as one of Sosigenes' signs from heaven.

The murdered Cybele had lived on the Street of the Sandal Makers!

The street had been well named. Brutus counted five shops along the way, all devoted to sandal making. Like most of Rome's shops they opened at seven in the morning, though Brutus sought one which might have been open even earlier on the day in question. Starting with the shop closest to the murder scene, he worked his way down the block.

The second shop he tried had opened early three mornings ago. Unable to sleep because of an aching tooth, the tradesman had come into the shop from his living quarters just after first light. 'And did you have an early customer?' Brutus inquired.

The tradesman, whose sour face hinted at continuing discomfort from his tooth, nodded and said, 'An older gentleman, well dressed in a fine tunic. He said he'd broken a sandal strap but when I offered to fix it he told me he had no time. He laid out some coins for a new pair, and took the first ones he tried on.'

'Did he wear them out?'

'He did just that, carrying the old ones under his arm.'

'Did you recognize him?'

The man looked puzzled. 'No.'

'Could he have been Julius Caesar?'

'I have never seen the great Caesar.'

'But you would recognize your customer if you saw him again?'

'I think so, yes.'

'Then come with me,' Brutus urged.

'I cannot leave the shop.'

He gave the man some coins. 'Close it for two hours. I will need you no longer than that.'

When the shopkeeper agreed, Brutus took him to the public market near the Forum, knowing Caesar would be passing that way. He dressed him in the black cloak of a sooth-sayer and told him, 'When Caesar comes I will point him out. Go up to him and say something while you study his face.'

'Should I ask him how the sandals fit?'

'No, no! You are a soothsayer! Warn him to beware the ides of March.'

Brutus hurried to join Caesar's party, which was approaching from the Forum. Then he signaled the disguised tradesman as they were passing some street musicians. The sandal-maker came forward and shouted, 'Beware the ides of March!'

Caesar paused, hearing the shout but not understanding it. 'What man is that?'

As the black-cloaked figure came forward, Brutus said, 'A soothsayer bids you beware the ides of March.'

'He is a dreamer. Let us leave him.'

As the group moved on, Brutus fell back and asked the man, 'Did you recognize him?'

'I did. It was my morning customer who bought the sandals. See, he wears them even now!'

'Come with me. There are others who must hear your words.'

Within an hour Cassius and the others had heard the charges against Caesar. It was Trebonius who asked, 'What good is this? What can be done now?'

Brutus had an answer. 'Tomorrow, I will bring this good tradesman to the Capitol. We will arrest Caesar as he enters the building, and remove him from office.'

'Tomorrow,' the sandal maker said. 'The ides of March.'

*   *   *

As Caesar's party entered the Capitol the following day, he saw the black-garbed soothsayer in the crowd. 'The ides of March are come,' he told the man.

'Ay, Caesar, but not gone.'

Caesar turned to Brutus, a look of puzzlement on his face. 'Who is that man in black? Why does he seem familiar to me?'

Brutus, at his side, spoke up as they walked. 'He is the ghost of your past sins, O Caesar. He is the sandal maker you visited after killing the whore Cybele.'

Caesar turned on him in a fury. 'What say you? Have you betrayed me, Brutus?'

'Your crimes betray you. We are removing you from office.'

Caesar stared into their faces as they moved to form a circle around him. 'I will have you put to death for treason!'

'Your day is over, great Caesar. You stabbed Cybele to death.'

Caesar's hand went for his dagger, lunging out at Brutus. *Et tu, Brute?* 'You too, Brutus?'

Then Casca struck with his own dagger, catching Caesar in the chest. The others followed, and Brutus struck the final blow. Caesar died at their feet.

'It is finished,' Cassius said.

'Finished.'

Brutus stared down at the body. 'My only hope is that the historians remember it the way it happened.'

MURDERER, FAREWELL

Ron Burns

Ron Burns has written two mystery novels set in ancient Rome,
Roman Nights (1991) and Roman Shadows (1992). The first is set
toward the end of the tyrannical reign of the Emperor Commodus,
whilst Roman Shadows is set earlier, at the start of the Roman
Empire. It is toward those earlier days that we go. Ron Burns was
interested in the reason behind the banishment of the poet Publius
Ovidius Naso by Augustus in the year AD 8. The public view was
that it was because the Emperor Augustus had taken offence at one
of Ovid's poems. But Ovid hinted at a darker, more sinister motive.
How much of the following story is true?

∾

Little book – no, I don't begrudge it you – you're
    off to the city without me, going where your only
begetter is banned!
On your way, then – but penny-plain, as befits an
    exile's sad offering, and my present life.
For you no purple slip-case (that's a color goes ill with
    grief), no title-line picked out in vermilion, no cedar-
    oiled backing . . .
Leave luckier books to be dressed with such trimmings:
    never forget my sad estate.

Publius Ovidius Naso – Ovid to you – was a poet, and as everyone
knows poets recollect everything. It is their curse.
So it wasn't a matter of what could he remember. It was more

along the lines of was there anything he could forget. And the shock of a macabre new crime brought it back easily enough. Brought it back in torrents:

Ovid the prodigy. Ovid the little freak. Ovid the squawking pubescent, aged twelve, being brought before the new ruler Octavian, still young himself: stern and erect, yet smiling – though somewhat snidely.

It was a time when Octavian's image needed touching up. Actually a full-blown cover-up was more like what was required. It was back in 719* coming after a dozen or so years of joint rule with Mark Anthony, who had just taken part in a ritual double suicide with that Egyptian woman. Octavian, though victorious, had had immense problems – which was no surprise all things considered. Such as his signature at the bottom of hundreds of death warrants. Warrants for the murders of Roman citizens. Some of them illustrious, the glorious Cicero being one.

So Octavian needed help, and when word reached him of this boy who wrote beautiful poems and spouted aphorisms of pithy advice as well, he summoned him to the Imperial court.

'You must first of all change your name,' the child unblinkingly told the king of the world – which prompted a mixture of sniggers and gasps from the attendant ministers and hangers-on.

'Octavian is a boy's name; I suggest Augustus,' little Ovid continued, 'as a new signal of greatness for you and for all Rome.

'And never call yourself Emperor,' he went on. 'Use "Princeps" – first citizen. Also, restore the rituals of the Senate. Not the power, nor the substance. Just the form.

'And finally, needless to say, *no more murders*. A *justice* of substance must rule in Rome.'

As is widely known, Augustus adopted all these caveats, and within a year or so Octavian the bloodthirsty was known far and wide as Augustus the great and the good. And the prodigy Ovid moved into apartments of his own inside the palace, where he grew to manhood and flourished as poet and sage.

Until, thirty-eight years later, there came a time when Augustus once again was threatened by a 'perception problem.' It involved this new crime – a murder, and once again he was rumored to be the murderer. And this time (it was said) no trumped-up warrant nor writ lent even a semblance of legality.

Once again he called upon the poet to fix it, and Ovid quickly

---

* 31 BC by our calendar, 719 according to the old Romans (counting from the founding of ancient Rome).

concluded that this time to save Augustus' image he would have to solve the murder itself. Remarkably, he realized very soon how easy that would be.

And how impossible.

And for those very reasons he shook with a terror that only Rome could inspire.

The victim was Marcellus Gaius, a much loved young man, quite dashing in that Roman way, definitely appealing to men (though of doubtful accessibility) and women alike. And a fighting general to boot – just back from a triumph at the German front. He was also a favorite of Augustus' and was believed more and more to be his likely successor. Thus, the rumors flew. Marcellus had grown too overtly ambitious. Augustus felt threatened. They had had a falling out. Also, he *was* murdered in the palace, after all, in a chamber not far from the Emperor's own rooms.

'The people are saying I did it,' Augustus snarled. 'I don't like it, so find out who did. And be quick about it.'

Ovid, unhappy but knowing his master's moods, backed silently, obediently, into the nearest corridor.

The murder room, still under heavy guard, had been sealed and nothing touched. In a way it was disgusting – the crime was already two days old – but Ovid was pleased. Perhaps he would find something . . . helpful. Or at least not harmful.

Marcellus' body had been cut in three places: there was a clumsy slashing wound to the stomach, a powerful thrust to the chest, in the area of the heart, and finally a cleanly-made slit across the throat, ear (it might be said) to ear. There was blood around the body. Some, though not, he thought, as much as there might have been. There was also blood in . . . places where (one might think) it shouldn't have been at all. He examined the spots, followed a trail that, mercifully, petered out, returned to the death scene and bent close to the corpse.

'Tragic, tragic,' he heard himself muttering. A moment of low melodrama. Then: high alarm. Did anyone hear me? Did I sound sarcastic? When there was no reaction, he relaxed a little. Keep your mouth shut! he told himself.

Poking through the folds of Marcellus' toga he felt something weighty around his waist. His purse! Undisturbed! Filled with gold sesterces! 'Well, this was no robbery,' he announced earnestly, then wondered: Why am I heralding the obvious? And again reminded himself of the virtues of silence.

There was also a potentially powerful piece of evidence beside the body: a distinctive dagger with a handle of intricately carved ivory and studded with gorgeously colored rubies and sapphires. That, it should be noted, was covered with blood. So whose is this? he wondered. Should be easy enough to find out, then actually went, 'Hah!' Laughing at himself out loud.

'Bodies, I have in mind, and how they can change to assume new shapes,' the poet had written a few years before, meaning something quite different. But it came back to him now as he circled the remains. 'I ask the help of the gods, who know the trick: inspire me now, change me, let me glimpse the secret and sing.'

He smiled.

And looked up to see a Praetorian guardsman watching him. Scowling.

'Harumph.' He cleared his throat haughtily. 'You there. Yes, and you. And you, also. Let's get this mess cleaned up. And careful how you handle him. This was Marcellus Gaius, nobleman and patrician.'

What followed was amazing. The guardsmen carried away the body. A platoon of maids swept in, scrubbing and dusting. And after five minutes the room, a waiting area and occasional private dining room, was restored. There was no sign that trouble of any sort had taken place, let alone a brutal murder – save one old woman who scoured away for a long time after the others had gone, working with a tiny brush where the blood had seeped deeply into the cement between the tiles.

Again, his own words came back to him. '*Nature,*' he had written

> *was all the same: what men imagine as 'chaos,'*
> *that jumble of elemental stuff, a lifeless heap,*
> *with neither Sun to shed its light, nor Moon to wax*
> *and wane, nor earth poised in its atmosphere of air.*
> *If there was land and sea, there was no discernible*
>   *shoreline.*
> *no way to walk on the one, or swim or sail in the other.*
> *In the gloom and murk, vague shapes appeared for a*
>   *moment, loomed*
> *and then gave way, unsaying themselves and the world*
>   *as well.*

It was, of course, a tricky matter in the Emperor's palace to find the true owner of the ivory-handled dagger – the presumed murder weapon. Ovid sat in the murder room for an hour thinking of nothing but that. And finally determined that was the thing to do.

Nothing.

For the time being, at least.

He hid the knife away in his own quarters, but took the only other article he had seized – the victim's overflowing purse – and dropped it almost too casually in front of Augustus as he sat at his work table dashing off letters to officials halfway across the world.

'No robbery, this, my lord,' Ovid said.

Augustus was not unimpressed as he fondled the purse. But then: 'Chancellor's office for safekeeping, my boy,' he said with dismissive ingratitude (or so the suffering poet believed). 'And I knew that much all along,' he chided just before Ovid could safely reach the door.

He now began a different phase of his investigation. He would trace Marcellus' every move for the final three days of his life. Everyone he spoke to, everyone who saw him. Everything he ate. Or drank. Everywhere he went. Everything he did.

All this, Ovid expected, would lead to nothing. And everything. Some would just get annoyed. Or enraged at his prodding questions. But someone somewhere along the line would get nervous. And make a mistake. Hopefully a big one.

Marcellus had been killed on Friday, so Ovid used the previous Tuesday for his starting point. The hard part was beginning at the logical place, with the grieving widow, Camilla. She was a small, dark woman – nondescript at first glance. But her intense manner, the sound of her voice, the way she moved when she spoke, unmasked a raw, compelling beauty.

'You're really looking for the killer?' she said. 'So you don't have so far to look.'

Ovid shook his head. 'My Lady, I assure you –'

'So what's a poet doing investigating a murder anyway?' She snorted and tossed back a glass of wine with the aplomb of a teamster. 'Ah, wait a minute. That's right. You're *that* poet. So . . . I see. You're just . . . going through the motions, as they say.'

She downed another glass and offered Ovid a refill, but he waved her away. Actually, he hadn't touched his first round, though not from any abstemious sentiments. He was simply afraid this widow might do . . . anything.

'My Lady, I need your help badly. We have little enough evidence now. So I'm hoping, sincerely, that by tracing your husband's movements in those last days we can uncover something that will solve the case.'

She studied him a long moment, then slowly finished her wine and poured another. Mercifully, she gave up offering the poet any more.

'They were hectic days for him,' she began last. 'Just back from the front. I saw little of him, actually. We had breakfast together Tuesday – he had oysters and boiled asparagus, in case you're interested. Then he was off to the Forum. He returned so late that night and left so early Wednesday I hardly saw him. We finally had late supper Wednesday night . . .'

She trailed off, staring wistfully.

'Did he say anything that might give some clue to . . . any trouble he was having?'

She ignored him, evidently basking in her reverie. He tried to imagine what she saw: the great times of a blazing life with a famous man. Or, more likely, some tender moment. Some gesture she loved, some little thing he did that he himself was hardly aware of. The poet waited patiently, then started, gently, to repeat the question, but she cut him off, replying at last: 'We talked of friends and family. The private conversation of a private man – a contented man and his devoted wife. He explained, as always, what was keeping him so busy, and it was predictable. A crush of ceremonial duties and personal tributes. His triumphal march and the games in his honor were to be on Sunday. Then we were going to his father's estate at Tivoli for time together. I didn't mind. He'd been away three months, so I could wait a few more days. The dutiful wife, you know. Of course I didn't expect him to be murdered . . .'

The muscles in her neck throbbed. She was plainly distraught, and Ovid waited for the tears. But her eyes stayed as cool and dry as a desert in December. He studied her: the graceful arch in her neck, the happy dimples in her cheeks, the slightly pouty lips. And those dark, unfathomable eyes: fiery but without anger, pitiless but not bitter. Cold but not cruel. Not surprisingly, he swiftly decided she was quite wonderful. And, as well the gods knew, Ovid knew women. But more about that later.

Despite protestations of being merely a compliant wife, Camilla had no trouble providing him (albeit after some prodding) a detailed guide to her late husband's closest friends and associates. And with that Ovid was off to the Forum himself in search of one Gallius Novo, influential senator and, save the Emperor, Marcellus' most important mentor and benefactor. After just missing him several times, he finally caught up with him in the late afternoon at one of the rowdy new taverns on the fringes of the Campus Martius. Novo was with another friend, Avitus Lollianus.

'You've come to the right place, poet; to know us is to know Marcellus Gaius.' Novo was a great, red-faced bear of a man who boomed out his reassurance with a robust invitation to join them in a glass of wine. 'We were with him every minute of those last days,' Novo declared.

With that Ovid was of a mind to dismiss his claims. But then with a horrible wink and uproarious laughter Novo put in, 'Well, not every minute,' so the poet joined them anyway. And though both men were drunk and loud and prone to digress, they seemed to grasp the details of the business in hand and managed on the whole to tell their story with reasonable clarity.

Starting on Tuesday morning, Novo had escorted Marcellus to the Senate, where they listened for hours to syrupy praise from scores of windy senators. It was quite an ordeal, for though the speeches were sincere enough, the sheer extravagance of their praise, not to mention their length and repetitive detail, were based more on politics than merit.

'. . . the greatest triumph since the inimitable Julius . . .' '. . . a victory worthy of the gods . . .' '. . . your name linked forever to the greatness of Rome . . .' '. . . Marcellus, savior of the empire . . .'

Of course each time Marcellus' name was mentioned, it was in conjunction with Augustus – as if he owed his very existence, as well as all measure of success, to the Emperor himself. The trick, the hope, was that each man's words would be repeated for the ruler's facile ear, thus gaining favor at court. Truth be told, their hopes were futile, for it was an old game by now and a tired one – a game which Augustus, now sixty-eight, had stopped playing long ago.

There followed an award ceremony on the Campus, then a bestowal of Jupiter's blessing at the temple that ruled his house. That evening came a formal dinner at the palace, then a ribald gathering at one of the more fashionable bath houses – 'Not for your official report, I trust,' Novo interjected.

On Wednesday Novo hosted a luncheon for his friend at his Palatine town house, and that evening Lollianus had Marcellus join two dozen key senators and ministers for an informal gathering at his house just across the hill.

'He left early to join his wife,' Lollianus said. 'I know because I rode in the carriage with him, dropped him at home.'

Thursday came another Senate ceremony – the formal announce-ment of the triumphal march and games on Sunday. Then a variety of informal get-togethers, some of them involving serious discussions of affairs of state. Late that night, as Marcellus was about to go home, a summons arrived from the Imperial palace.

'What time was this?'

'A good six hours after dark, about midnight I'd say,' Novo answered.

'Who was it from, could you tell?'

'Well, that was the oddest part. It wasn't clear. It didn't seem like it was from Augustus. It certainly didn't bear his seal; I know that mark, believe me. But he can't be ruled out, either.'

'And . . . Marcellus went, I presume.'

Both men squinted at him as if he had to be from someplace very far away to pose such a question.

'And do you know, did he go home at all that night?' He somehow hadn't gotten a clear answer from Camilla, and now both men claimed they simply didn't know.

By their accounts of the festivities and fun one could easily believe that Rome was an idyllic place of ambitious but fair-minded men who craved wealth and power but nonetheless lived primarily by a code of mutual trust and honor. It was hardly the truth, of course. Double-dealing and betrayal were often as not the order of the day. Even the admirable and popular Marcellus Gaius had known men he distrusted and who in turn conspired against him. It was, it seemed, the way of the world, especially in public life. Even poets knew that. Ovid surely did.

Thus as dusk fell and Gallius Novo in particular became very drunk, he decided to stay with these men, to laugh at their jokes, even to tell a few himself (if he could remember any). And with gentle urging to take them through it all again – through the formal bombast of those three days and the (arguably unmentionable) vulgarities of the nights. To pry loose something that would point to someone that would lead somewhere which would begin somehow to identify . . . who again? Oh, you know who, Ovid told himself with an inner smirk. And then he drank more wine.

> *I'm an exile's book. He sent me. I'm tired. I feel
> trepidation approaching his city – kind reader, lend
> a hand!*
>> *Have no fear, I won't turn out an embarrassment
>> to you: no instructions on love, not one page, not
>> a syllable . . .*
>> *See what I bring: you'll find nothing here but
>> lamentation . . .*

Ovid was vulnerable. Which is to say a case could be made against him. If one wanted to because one was his enemy. Or as a threat because one wanted something from him.

'*When she saw the mark of a body on the flattened grass,*' he had written just the other month,

> *her leaping heart beat within her fearful bosom. And now midday had drawn short the unsubstantial shadows, and evening and morning were equally removed. Lo, he returns from the woods and scatters spring water on his glowing cheeks. Anxiously, she lies hid; he rests on the wonted grass and cries, 'Come breeze, come tender Zephyrs!' When the name's pleasing error was manifest to the hapless woman, her reason returned and the true color to her face. She rises, and speeding to her lover's embrace stirred with her hurrying frame the leaves that were in her way.*

So went but a tiny portion of a book the poet called *The Art of Love*, and there were blushing faces and some outraged lips as it began to circulate in the weeks before the murder. It was one thing, some said, to write that earthy tome of years ago. What was it again? Oh, yes, the . . . *Metamorphoses*. But this . . . This was different. This was so . . . blatant. So . . . well, filthy, they said.

Besides, it wasn't just what he wrote. It was how he lived – that man and all those . . . women. By the dozens, so the rumors proclaimed. Thus his reputation was unsavory, to say the least – though only among those who didn't know him. Those who did found him a gentle man – bright, pleasant, interesting. Clear of mind and fair of heart.

All those women (and over the years there had indeed been more than a few) adored him, evidently, because he was that rarity: a man who truly liked them, truly enjoyed their company. Loved having them around, loved listening to them talk. About some kitchen mishap. Or a dazzling new outfit. Or some entrancing new shade of lip rouge or style of silk just off an elephant train from India. All the things that most men found so silly, even loathsome, kept our poet amused by the hour.

Ovid of course had been a favorite of the Emperor's for many years, and partly because of that he was acquainted with a host of distinguished Roman men. But he frankly found it something of a chore to be in their company for long. Whiling away the hours talking and drinking with them held little appeal. He simply didn't see the point, unlike the majority of men who apart from sex cannot wait to escape their wives or mistresses in search of masculine companionship.

Thus, Ovid was in the truest sense a ladies' man. He was also, sad to say, a scandal of what might be called the chronically nascent sort: which is to say, a scandal-in-waiting. It was a lingering sore that had been lanced at long last a few weeks before – and at the worst possible time: just days after the first copies of his 'love book' (as everybody was calling it) had gone into circulation.

A woman of especially noble birth and connection had been seen leaving his rooms in the black predawn hours. 'Relax. Stay awhile. Wait till after breakfast, no one will notice you then,' he had implored her. But feeling sudden pangs of remorse she felt compelled to return at once to her twit of a husband.

The shock waves were mighty indeed from that transgression. The sniping took an ugly turn, with vicious new remarks reaching his ears daily. He was accosted and threatened by a friend of the cuckold in the highly public confines of a bath house, and, horror of horrors, someone even offered a thinly-veiled innuendo on the Senate floor.

'Are Rome's morals not in shambles enough without our most scholarly denizens, ostensibly dedicated to the beautification of the world, sinking to the low behavior of some freedman or ponce?' inquired one Decius Curio, scion of one of Rome's most ancient families and another friend of the aggrieved husband.

It was then that Ovid, becoming seriously alarmed, sought the personal protection of Augustus.

'Fix it all up for you; nothing to worry about. Don't give it another thought,' the Emperor had told him in his most reassuring manner (a manner, it should be pointed out, that was known to have sent defeated and trembling generals out of his presence and back into battle aglow with renewed fervor and confidence).

Well, he'd fixed it, all right. The sniping stopped, well enough. But the next thing he knew he was neck-deep in this murder thing. As the 'detective,' no less, and with all the pitfalls inevitable to the case. And he honestly didn't know where it might lead. Or end. As he had recently written (though in another context):

> *What a fire was in thy maddened heart! Soon, she would come, that Aura, whoe'er she might be, and thine own eyes would see the shame. Now dost thou regret thy coming (for thou could'st not wish to find him guilty). To commend belief there is the name and the place and*

*the informer, and because the mind ever thinks its fears
are true.*

Indeed, Ovid's fears – and his belief in them – grew by
the hour.

A starless, moonless night. Ovid in his unlit rooms. Alone. He has
listened to the stories of the drunken men, the senator Gallius
Novo and his friend Avitus Lollianus. They have laughed about
the bombast and boredom of the days, and cried over a touching
night-time episode or two.

'No one had any reason to take his life, I'm sure of that much,'
said Gallius Novo, and his friend nodded in solemn agreement.

But as poor Ovid, sitting in the pitch blackness, thought it all
through he realized that without even knowing it they had implicated
someone. Not once but again and again this man's name had come
up. Not in any terribly dramatic way. But in his glum, standoffish,
even scowling manner, the man in question seemingly posed a stark
contrast to everyone else who had seen Marcellus Gaius in the final
hours of his life.

Unluckily, the man was a formidable figure in his own right, so
the question of the moment was what would the poet do about
that. He continued to sit and think.

'Platter and loincloth' was the ancient rule for searching a man's
home. That is to say, if a man stood under a cloud and you wished
to search his quarters, you could enter wearing only a loincloth and
carrying only a tray – to ensure that you couldn't plant evidence in
an attempt to impeach him falsely.

It is a harsh rule, Ovid thought glumly, glancing at himself in
the mirror. At twenty, possessing a kind of sylphic comeliness, he
wouldn't have minded. Now, at fifty, he cringed a little at his own
reflection. He would do it, nonetheless. He had decided: he would
search the palace apartments of no less than Tiberius Drusus, son
of the Emperor's wife by a previous marriage. And, by the way, the
other heir apparent.

And even though the ancient law technically required Tiberius
to admit him, once he agreed to abide by the platter-and-loincloth
rule, he felt it best to seek more palpable authority for an action
that many would consider thoroughly outlandish.

'Tiberius!' Augustus exploded when Ovid saw him shortly past
daybreak. 'You suspect Tiberius?'

'Well . . .'

'It makes sense, of course. They were rivals, always have been. Never liked each other. Oil and water, they were. Together, but never mixing. Always disagreeing.' The king of the world paced off the room, shaking his head, muttering. 'But . . . murder?'

'It's horrible, I know, My Lord. But there are indications . . .'

Augustus whirled on him, his face dangerously set. 'Indications? For a search? But what about evidence?' At least that was what Ovid expected him to say – and by rights those should have been just the words he chose. Instead, as if abruptly remembering something important, he eased the look on his face and said: 'Well, fine, then. I'll swear you in as *delator*, investigator, loan you a few guardsmen and you'll search the place in your skimpies, eh?'

Augustus laughed and Ovid smiled thinly.

'Oh come now, it's not that bad, my boy.'

'Oh no, sir, not at all. I was just . . . admiring your –'

'Ah, I see. You thought I would have forgotten the ancient rank. But no, it was drilled into me as a boy, that one and all those long-ago titles and forms.'

Augustus stared off a moment, seemingly deep in thought. Quickly enough he was misty-eyed, which was not unusual for him. He cried more easily than most men, often for no apparent reason.

'You and I seem to have grown old together, my friend,' he began somewhat suddenly. 'I mean, I'm facing imminent decrepitude, I know that. But I called you "my boy" a minute ago, and it suddenly dawns on me that you're no spring chicken yourself anymore, and that it's been a very long time indeed that we've been friends. Which is why I chose you for this nasty little job. Because I know you, know I can trust you. Know you'll handle it . . . properly.'

Augustus put his hand on Ovid's not-so-young shoulder and stared into his eyes – and as always the poet found himself enveloped within the magical folds of his mentor's overpowering charisma. Small comfort though it was, he knew he was hardly alone in his inability to overcome it. For throughout his long life, Augustus had been virtually irresistible to nearly everyone he'd met.

'I'll take care of everything, My Lord,' Ovid heard himself saying. He looked back at Augustus, struggling to meet his gaze on equal terms. But it was no use.

'I know,' the king of the world replied in his sweetest voice. And when Ovid finally left him he was both amazed and angry to find his own eyes wet with tears.

'Tiberius Drusus, I have been empowered as Delator of Rome to search your quarters, and I inform you in the presence of these men' – he gestured at the five Praetorian guardsmen beside and behind him – 'that I will do so now and that, in accordance with Roman law, I will carry out the search wearing only a loincloth and carrying only a simple wooden platter.'

Tiberius, a not-widely-liked, frequently grimacing man, often joked about as Rome's 'town grouch,' scowled in his usual sourpuss way. 'What? You can't! By what right . . .?!'

Ovid displayed the scroll with Augustus' seal, and Tiberius shut up at once – didn't even bother to open it, let alone read it.

His apartments were large and lavish, with their own entrance and atrium, seven bedrooms, a moderate-sized banquet hall and a small private kitchen. Ovid suddenly felt exhausted at just the thought of the hours of work ahead. But, having stripped to the required minimum, he plunged right in, starting logically enough, he thought, with Tiberius' private rooms – a study and connecting bedroom. They were sizeable and well-furnished, and after nearly two hours of going through several large desks, cabinets and closets, he was about to give up when he noticed a few loose tiles in the bedroom floor.

The tiles formed a mosaic of some idyllic country scene, and the loose fit was in the foot of a sheep farmer guiding his flock. Ovid bent down, and picked at it till it came out. With a little pressure, several more fell away, then several dozen, exposing a hole about a foot in diameter. He called for the guards to come up and to bring Tiberius. When they arrived, he pushed aside the jumble of tiles and pulled out what lay beneath: a tunic, a purple sash and a pair of sandals. Blood, now dried and flaking in some places, covered large parts of all the garments.

'Step forward please,' Ovid told Tiberius, who did so at once, his mouth and eyes wide open with surprise.

'Do these articles of clothing belong to you?' Ovid inquired, though of course he knew they did. The sash in particular was unmistakably his.

Tiberius looked at them closely, held them in his hands and nodded slowly. 'But . . . what does this mean?'

'And this?' Ovid demanded, holding out his hand to the nearby sergeant of the guard, who in turn pulled out the ornate dagger which Ovid had found beside Marcellus' body. His energetic inquiries around the palace had already given him the answer to that question as well.

'Yes, of course,' Tiberius said. 'But that was stolen . . .'

'Oh, that's bloody likely,' Ovid said, though his tone lacked the sarcastic bite to make his point convincingly.

'But it was, I tell you. Stolen over a week ago. Look here, this is outrageous. I know Marcellus and I were hardly the best of friends. Everyone knew that. But if anyone thinks I murdered him . . . Well, that's nonsense. As for these clothes, I don't know how they got here. And as for that argument we had, well it was nothing, I can assure you.'

'What argument?' Ovid blurted out. Or almost did. Luckily, he kept his head and instead said, 'Nothing, eh. That's not the way I heard it.' And, recalling Novo and Lollianus, thought, Those drunken fools! 'I heard you almost came to blows,' Ovid plunged on. 'And that you had damn good motive for killing him!'

Tiberius paced a small, nervous circle. 'All right! So we almost did. So I told him to stay the hell away from my wife or I'd . . .'

Ovid struggled to keep too much astonishment from showing on his face. Astonishment that his ploy had worked so well. Astonishment that Tiberius would blather out so much that was so incriminating. (Even though he'd trailed off at the end it was probably enough.) Most of all, astonishment that he thought it was Marcellus that his wife was seeing – Tiberius was known for being remarkably out of touch!

And now came the oddest moment yet in this case. Ovid, though managing to look determined, nonetheless just stood there. The guards were waiting. Tiberius was waiting. His next words were supposed to be: 'Tiberius Drusus, in the name of the Emperor and on behalf of the people of Rome I hereby place you under arrest for the murder of Marcellus Gaius.'

But for whatever reason the words did not come. Instead, he said: 'I don't have to tell you, Tiberius Drusus, that you appear to be incriminated in a serious crime. The investigation is continuing, and I strongly advise you not to leave the palace and to remain available for later questioning.'

With that he scooped up the clothing and motioned for the guards to follow. A twit indeed is what you are, Tiberius, he thought, as he dressed and left those apartments with all possible speed.

Dark nights. Darker days.

Ovid drunk and in hiding. Ovid confused. Giddy with laughter one minute. Weeping miserably the next. Alternately outraged and acquiescent. Determined and defeated. Contumacious and cowardly.

He stayed in the home – the hovel, really – of a prostitute named Livilla whom he'd known for about ten years and who was madly in love with him.

'Why leave? Stay as long as you like. They'll never look here.'

Each night, as he cradled her face softly in his hands, she would tell him such things. He never argued the point; it was no use. But he knew how untrue it was, knew they were looking for him even now. Knew that eventually they would dig enough, question enough to learn his whereabouts. And all that would do would add her death to the carnage that was so surely on its way.

Each morning he would try to summon his courage and leave, but instead would reach for the wine and by noon be too drunk to go anywhere. Eventually he would pass out, then awaken at dusk in her arms.

'You would do anything for me, wouldn't you?' he said one evening in a wide-eyed, wistful tone.

'You know that's true,' she said, and he replied with a solemn nod. 'Then why ask?' she asked him.

'I don't know. I'm . . . sorry. A stupid question. A . . . man's question.'

She laughed. 'That's true enough,' she said, but even then couldn't help adding: 'But please . . . there's no need to apologize.'

On the evening of the third day, after darkness had fallen, when she had stepped out for a few minutes to fetch water, he simply got up and left. Without a word. Without even a note left behind. In his favor, it was an act that was entirely out of character for him, but in this case he simply lacked the energy for the inevitable goodbye scene; he was even afraid if she saw a note that she might chase after him. And he knew that by now he had already stayed too long and that every extra minute she spent in his company increased her danger exponentially.

He made his way through the streets to the palace and bribed a porter at a side gate to let him slip in unseen. He reached his apartments and went straight to bed. He slept the restless, shallow sleep of the doomed.

It came much more softly than he'd supposed it would, and not even all that early. Just a lone secretary knocking gently around breakfast time, wondering if he might join the Emperor for a few minutes.

Ovid shambled the thousand feet or so of hallways that separated his own quarters from Augustus' lavish domain, still not sure what to expect.

'Where've you been!' the Emperor growled the instant Ovid walked in, and he knew his trouble was every bit as serious as he'd figured in the first place.

'Investigating, My Lord,' he said. His tone was unflinching, even a bit needling, as was his manner. He helped himself to eggs and oysters and stretched out on a sofa.

The Emperor looked up slowly at his favorite poet, his eyes fiery with the ancient anger. With a quick, violent motion he sent his plate crashing across the room in Ovid's general direction. A guard rushed in but Augustus waved him off.

'You being smart with me! Hmm, Ooovid.' He stretched out the first syllable of his name as if he'd just as soon be stretching him out instead. The poet's jaunty demeanor deserted him outright, and it was all he could do to keep from trembling.

'Investigating what, may I ask? You have all the evidence. Hell, I hear you practically have his goddamn confession. Enough to boil the son of a bitch in broccoli. And that was three days ago! So what's going on! Why haven't you arrested him? Would you mind too terribly explaining that to your decrepit old Emperor. Eh, Ooovid?'

Ovid gulped. 'My investigation is . . . continuing, Your Majesty. There are certain . . . questions I feel remain unresolved. And frankly, sir, I would have thought you might have appreciated my caution when it came to arresting one so highly-placed and so closely connected to the Imperial house.'

Augustus slowly swung his legs over the side of his own sofa. Then he stood and casually walked – ambled, really – to the food table and made himself a new plate. The one he'd thrown to the floor had long since been cleaned up. Then he eased his way back to the couch, stretched out and resumed eating. All the while Ovid watched him as one might watch a wild cat – a jaguar, say – that seemed ready to spring, either in direct assault or to set some deadly trap.

'Like what?' Augustus said over a mouthful of food.

'Pardon me?'

'Like what? What questions? What questions, um, "remain unresolved"?'

Though he tried hard not to, Ovid gulped again. 'Well . . . uh, for one thing I felt Tiberius' surprise at the discovery of the bloody clothes in his bedroom might be sincere. And notice, please, I said *might*. For another, I was able to check in a roundabout way, admittedly not a hundred per cent reliable – but it appears his claim that the dagger was stolen several days before the murder *might* be valid.'

Augustus, still eating, nodded with seeming interest at these disclosures. 'Anything else?'

Ovid shook his head. 'I'm sorry, sir, what did you . . .?'

Augustus pointed at his mouth and shook his head apologetically. Then he swallowed, cleared his throat and said, 'Anything else?'

'Uh, no. No, My Lord. That's all for now.'

The Emperor smiled, put his plate aside, stood, walked over to where Ovid was stretched out and sat down beside him. The poet who had just spooned a heaping bite of eggs into his mouth swallowed as best he could and stared at Augustus in rapt attention.

'Listen, I understand now. You're intimidated by my family, afraid of being caught in the middle of some Imperial row. But don't worry about that. I'm the only one in my family that counts. The only one that matters. It's been that way nearly forty years now, and will be a good while longer, I suspect. So I want you to grab a few of those guards outside, go over to Tiberius' apartments and arrest him.

'No, no,' he said, gently pulling Ovid's plate away as he tried to spoon another nervous bite. 'Eat later. Arrest him now.'

Ovid smiled obligingly as he always did when Augustus asked him for something, got to his feet and made his way to the door. He was halfway through it and almost out when, as if literally stuck, he could go no farther. In a way he wanted to. Very much. And he made another halfhearted try. But it was no use. It was the same trouble he'd had the other day with Tiberius when the words of arrest just wouldn't come.

Slowly, poor Ovid turned around and walked a few reluctant steps back into the private quarters of the king of the world.

'My Lord –' He wanted to say so many things now, wanted to pay tribute, really. Tell him what a great friend he'd been and what a great man he was. The greatest in all history. He wanted to say this because he believed it – he'd feared him, yes, but loved him too. And understood the debt he owed him. It was the reason he'd pursued the charade, gone on with his 'investigation' as if it were real, despite everything that had happened. Despite everything else he had to tell him; the words that even now were stuck in his throat. And in his heart.

'My Lord, I'm afraid I can't do that,' Ovid said. 'I can't arrest Tiberius. Because I know he didn't do it. Because I know who did.'

Augustus stood and walked toward him and their eyes met. And for once Ovid felt on equal terms. Or even as if he might have a slight advantage. Should he tell the truth, or bluff? Ovid did not avert his eyes as he spoke:

'My Lord, I was . . . in the next room. I heard everything. And saw ... enough. More than enough. You're ... not used to not getting your own way, Your Majesty. You wanted Marcellus as a lover, but he wouldn't have it. And after a long, terrible argument, your rage –'

Ovid stopped and shook his head. He was crying now at the thought of what had happened.

'I've never seen anyone so ... angry. You ... were like a mad dog, sir, and I think your rage overcame you. And you pulled out a knife and started slashing with it. And then you stabbed him. And then you killed him.'

For one brief moment, Augustus' kingly mask deserted him and his old friend could glimpse the confused and tormented man who had committed a senseless murder. And then just like that it was over, the mask was back and Ovid once again was facing the man who ruled the world.

'I'll have to send you away, of course,' Augustus said with stunning matter-of-factness.

Ovid flinched. He hadn't expected that. To be executed, yes. Or even murdered on the spot. But exile? He wasn't sure that was better. In fact, after a minute or so he was certain it wasn't.

Augustus ordered him placed in house arrest pending his departure. As the guards escorted him back to his rooms he had a realization that nearly knocked him down:

He'd been ready to overlook that Augustus was the murderer! And why not? He'd known of his murders in the past. But only now did he understand what had finally turned him against his mentor – what had really horrified him at last: that Augustus would actually plant the evidence – the dagger, the bloody clothes – to convict an innocent man. Had Ovid been willing to go along with the ruse? Or had he expected some miracle to come along and save Tiberius from the executioner – and himself from a looming fate of doom and dishonor? A lightheadedness almost overcame him as the guards helped him to his rooms. He had no answers. He never would, save in the end he had done the right thing. For the sake of justice – and himself.

The homicide investigation was quietly dropped, and the murder of Marcellus Gaius remained unsolved. Ovid left Rome ten days later for his assigned destination, a desolate place called Tomis at the mouth of the River Danube on the Black Sea, where he would spend the final eleven years of his life. The official reason for his banishment was the supposed pornographic nature of his poems.

Though his subject matter changed, he never stopped writing

poetry, never stopped bombarding official Rome with anguished pleadings to come home. When Augustus died seven years later, he briefly had hopes. But his successor, Tiberius, also refused to bring him back. Evidently, he'd found out who his wife had really been romancing in those long-ago glory days: when a sophisticate named Publius Ovidius Naso ruled Roman society with a gentle wit and his beautiful way with words.

> *If it's seemly to say so, my talent was distinguished, and among all that competition I was fit to be read. So, Malice, sheathe your bloody claws, spare this poor exile, don't scatter my ashes after death!*
> *I have lost all: only bare life remains to quicken the awareness and substance of my pain.*
> *What pleasure do you get from stabbing this dead body?*
> *There is no space in me now for another wound.*

[**Author's Note:** This story was inspired by Augustus' true-life exile of Ovid in AD 8. The real reason for the banishment has been lost to history.]

A POMEGRANATE
FOR PLUTO

Claire Griffen

Claire Griffen is an Australian writer, secretary and actress, who has also won prizes for her stage plays, including the pre-Trojan War comedy Hawk Among the Doves. *She has only recently turned to 'straight writing', as she calls it, and apart from the short story 'Catalyst' in the experimental science-fiction magazine,* Boggle, *this is her first professional appearance. It is set during the horrific reign of the Emperor Caligula.*

~

Hengist, the ex-gladiator and proprietor of the best wineshop in Pompeii had a simple philosophy. Life was made up of sensations, some to be indulged in, others to be avoided.

He had escaped death in the arena not only by his strength and his skill as a *retiarius* (net-and-trident fighter), but by a shrewd ability to read human nature. Pain was a sensation that could be avoided by accurately reading the fighting stance of an antagonist.

Hengist knew men. And some women. Of all ranks, from slave to patrician. After capture as an infant in Cisalpine Gaul, Hengist had been raised in the home of a Senator, taught to read and write Latin and Greek and how to calculate. When the unfortunate Senator had incurred Imperial wrath and found himself flung down the Weeping Stairs with a hook through his noble neck, it might have been thought that the Imperial favourite who inherited his estate would have recognized Hengist's skills as a scribe or lictor.

Instead, Marcus Valerius saw only a tall, muscular young man with the corn-coloured hair of his race, the type to draw a Circus crowd. So Hengist had been despatched to the Ludus Magnus, the gladiators' barracks, to begin his training for the arena.

He not only survived, but coming through game after game virtually unscathed gave him celebrity status. Marcus delighted in trotting him out at banquets, showing him off like a prize Arab stallion. It became fashionable for other patricians to invite him into their homes and to court his favour.

Hengist accepted this patronage placidly. Popularity, he knew, led to freedom. When, in the Taurine Amphitheatre, he was awarded the *rudus* or wooden sword of liberty the crowd went wild. He disappointed many of his admirers by refusing to free-lance, choosing instead to retire to a wineshop in Campania with a woman whose freedom he had purchased from the Ludus Magnus.

Hengist was not surprised to see the magistrate Aulus Piso coming through his portal. Those who had wagered on him and cheered at his victories still thronged to his shop to discuss his exploits and past triumphs and to eat the best food to be had in Campania. Even Claudius, the Emperor's uncle, had said he only visited Pompeii to eat at Hengist's wineshop. Aulus was cousin to Marcus Valerius, but of all patricians he alone treated the ex-gladiator as equal and friend.

Piso blinked as his eyes adjusted to the gloom after the glare of the noonday sun. His glance swept over the wall murals of rustic gods, Ops in the fields, Ceres blessing the corn, Liber Pater making the grapes ripen.

'How refreshing after the austerity of the courtroom.'

'The illustrious Piso brings honour to my humble shop,' murmured Hengist.

'Don't use that tone with me, you rogue. I've seen you slice a man to his second beard, remember.' The magistrate was a plumpish man with a balding head and a fiery complexion. 'Anyway, I'm the bearer of an invitation. From my cousin, the illustrious Senator Caius Marcus Valerius. To the banquet he gives tonight.'

Hengist frowned. 'Am I still in favour? I'm hardly the hero of the hour.'

'No, that fame belongs to Basso,' replied Piso, bluntly.

'Will *he* be there?'

'Naturally.'

Hengist's frown deepened. 'Marcus isn't planning a contest between us for the entertainment of his guests, is he?'

'My friend! What do you take me for?' Piso lifted his hands in mock indignation.

Hengist noticed he had left the cumbersome toga, symbol of his rank and profession, on the floor of his chariot, and was at ease in his white, maroon-bordered tunic.

'So you *have* come to share *prandium* with me,' he observed with a bland smile.

Piso hesitated, savouring the aromas of the wineshop with dinted nostrils. On a long wooden table the cook prepared all meals in the sight of the patrons and then baked them in his charcoal stove.

'Oysters and mussels while we're waiting, then native thrushes with asparagus, cooked in sweet wine, honey and spices with an excellent garum from Cades,' Hengist tempted, adding '*Pro gratis*, of course.'

The magistrate relaxed. 'How can I refuse such generosity?'

Hengist bowed and led his guest to his own table. 'Wine, Tassia.'

Piso glanced up as Tassia crossed the shop with a pitcher of wine. As she caught Hengist's eye she swung her hips ever so subtly. His lips shaped a kiss. Tassia was a sensation to be indulged in.

'Truly, you are blessed with the comforts of life. I envy you.' The magistrate mopped his florid face with the hem of his sleeve. 'You may think me a wealthy man, but I'm not. No one in Rome's a wealthy man these days, not with Caligula fleecing us.'

'Speaking of invitations,' Hengist turned the subject deftly.

'Oh, yes.' Piso looked slightly embarrassed. 'Actually, your invitation comes from a different source than my illustrious cousin. He was *persuaded* to include you in tonight's company.'

Hengist watched him and waited, his craggy face expressionless.

'By a lady.'

'Not by his wife, Valeria Julia. She was scarce of an age when I was in the arena.'

'By his sister, Valeria Claudia.'

'The Vestal?'

'You do remember her.'

'Only as a remote and regal figure in white sitting in a privileged loggia in the midst of her sister Virgins. Of course I knew of her through Marcus.'

'She's finished her thirty-year tenure at the House of Vestals and emerged into the world. She expressed a wish to see you again.'

'I can't think why. I've never exchanged a word with her.'

Piso greedily devoured the shellfish. On his bench the cook

chopped lovage, the wild celery of Campania, the staccato sound
an undercurrent to their confidential conversation.

'Why not come? You would be relieving me of boredom. I'll find
the rest of the company deadly dull.'

'Even Basso?'

'That oaf! He'll spend the evening flexing his muscles and
boasting of his latest bit of slaughter. He's been awarded his
wooden sword, you know, but decided to free-lance. He likes the
adulation of the crowd and the lusting after him of silly women.
Most of all, he likes to kill. In the bloodiest way possible.'

'*Who is the brute, friend? He who kills or he who watches?*'
quoted Hengist, softly.

'Don't throw Seneca up at me. I like a good show as well as any
man. And don't let Basso stop you from coming tonight. You'll enjoy
the food, maybe even steal a recipe or two.' Piso let another oyster
slide down his throat, following it with a gulp of wine.

'What's the occasion?'

'Marcus is betrothing his daughter Paulina to Lucius Maro.'

Hengist opened his grey eyes wide. 'Rumour had it she was
destined for the House of Vestals.'

'Marcus says her health won't permit it.' The magistrate gave
an undignified snigger. 'We both know what that means. She's
no longer a virgin. And possibly with child. Healthy enough for
marriage, indeed. And to one of equestrian status, when Marcus
prides himself on his Valerian ancestors. Who'd want to boast of
lineage from Mark Antony, a man who deserted wife and country
for that whore of a queen, Cleopatra? Families!'

'I wouldn't know. In fact, I wouldn't recognize my own parents
if they came into my shop. Or vice versa. But this affair of which
you speak sounds less of family than of pride.'

'Injured pride. Of course, Claudia's disappointed. The girl was
her protégée. Just as once Claudia was the protégée of the Empress
Livia. Now *there* was a harridan.'

'I think I shall go to your cousin's banquet,' interrupted Hengist.
'Caution forbids me, but curiosity compels me. You have assembled
the cast for me. Now I shall go and watch the play.'

On the peninsula of Misenum not far from the city of Pompeii stood
the villa of the Valerii, which the artistry of man had created in
perfect symmetry as a defiance against the rugged architecture of
nature. A portico of pillars enclosed the house on three sides. The
villa was built so far out on the edge of the promontory that the
view from two sides of the *tablinum* showed a sheer drop to the

sea crawling in on the rocks below. On wintry days the sea made thunder below the windows, pounding and throwing up a torrent of foam.

But this was the time of summer when the warmth of the sun pleased the skin and gilded the cold marble and made the fruit ripen on the boughs.

Fresh from an afternoon at the baths and wearing his finest linen tunic under a brown woollen *pallium*, Hengist arrived at the portal. He was simply dressed, his sandals new but of plain leather not gilt, the *fibula* fastening his pallium at the shoulder a plain bronze pin unembellished with jewel or filigree. His only ornaments were bracelets of bronze and silver stretching from wrist to elbow. They had been an anonymous gift after his first fight and it had been a whim to keep them when he had sold off so much else to buy his wineshop.

The doorkeeper who admitted him was an elderly man who had probably served at the villa before the time of Augustus. He was too well-trained to blink in recognition or evince surprise that the guest had arrived on horseback and without slaves, but behind his imperturbable façade he was ruminating, *It's getting as bad as the Palatium. All kinds of riff-raff admitted. Charioteers, gladiators, actors. They'll be welcoming tax-collectors next.*

'You are the first guest to arrive.' There was the merest hint of reproach in the doorkeeper's voice. 'Will you wait for the *domine* in the atrium?'

The vestibule led into the pillared courtyard with its water-lily pool reflecting between flat leaves the shifting moods of the sky. The mosaic of tiles on the floor depicted Neptune in his sea-chariot, surrounded by a bevy of green-haired nymphs and all manner of creatures from starfish to octopi. From wall niches, the busts of Valerian ancestors gazed out in marble supremacy.

The atrium led out to the peristyle with its *aluvium* and potted shrubs. The steps from the peristyle lured the visitor into the sunken garden, where peacocks uttered their haunting, melancholy cries and spread their tails to capture glints from the sun on their rich hues.

All that would grow so close to the sea bloomed in profusion here, but designed by a gardener's hand into an idyllic landscape. Grottoes and rock-gardens, fountains and statuary, arbours and fish-pools, freshwater canals overhung by bridges and pergolas.

Valeria Julia wandered along the path; the earth was so soft and yielding she had cast off her sandals and walked barefoot in comfort. Curling around the pergola above her head were red and green vines which cast fleeting patterns of colour on her sunlit face.

She seemed fashioned of gold in the radiance of the sunset, dressed in a *palla* of gold Cos gauze over a saffron *stola*. Her hair, washed all week in Gaul soap to heighten its blonde sheen, was braided and coiled under a gold diadem. The light yet vivid blue of her eyes was enhanced with kohl and her lips subtly ripened with carmine.

Her eyes flickered with initial disappointment as she recognized him. He was quick to make an exaggerated gesture of deference and admiration. Her glance flicked over him, then lingered on his body as if she could penetrate his tunic to the scars of the arena. Her lips parted slightly, a pulse throbbed in her throat and her eyes glistened with an almost-greed, not-quite-hunger.

Hengist recognized the look. He had seen it many times and experienced more than a look from the matrons who had bribed *lanistae* to be smuggled into his cell. It was a fascination, a lust to touch the flesh of a man who had spilled the blood of other men and who offered his own body to the sword.

Julia was a seeker of the exotic, he had heard, a devotee of the goddess Isis. Both cousin and wife to Marcus, though many years younger, she too claimed descent from the passionate and wayward Mark Antony.

'Isis pales before such beauty,' he said, greatly daring. 'I behold Julia and no longer worship at the shrine of Egypt.'

Her nostrils flared, but she was not offended, merely offered him a hint of hauteur.

'I'm sure you were an amusing fellow once, but your hour has passed. Beyond the hedge you'll find one more of an age to be flattered by your tributes. I leave you to my sister-in-law, Valeria Claudia.'

His bland smile betrayed no sense of rebuff. He stood aside to allow her to enter the peristyle and then obediently made his way along the path to the break in the hedge.

He found Claudia sitting on a travertine bench under an apricot tree, watching the multi-coloured fish darting about in the *euripus*, one of the miniature canals criss-crossing the garden. She had reached middle age and her hair was grey under the silver diadem, but her expression was serene, almost sweet. She was, he saw, celebrating her release from the House of Vestals, laying aside her virginal white for a *stola* of the rarest colour of all – blue – in cross-weave linen and silk. She greeted him with restrained warmth and made room for him to sit beside her.

'Does such apparel become me?' she asked, noticing his look. 'Or am I too old for such bedizenments?'

He gave the only answer he could. 'You're still a very handsome woman.'

A dimple appeared unexpectedly in her cheek. 'How tactful! Handsome is a word used for women who no longer attract men.'

'Vestals have been known to wed when their tenure is over. You have many years left to enjoy such pursuits.'

'I'll be content to sit in the sunset and watch the fish. I've had a privileged life as a Keeper of the Flame. No women are as well-protected as Vestals.'

'I believe I owe my presence at this banquet to your kind request.'

She slid him a sidelong glance. Her eyes were like bitter lemons or the rim of the sky just before twilight, a greenish-yellow.

'I wondered what had become of you, if the years had drawn your teeth or if you still bite. I remember your first fight in the arena. The Ides of September. The Great Roman Games.

'I remember too the scandal of the murdered *pugile*. The *lanista* tried to insist he died of his wounds, but you proved him guilty.'

Hengist shrugged. 'It was an easy deduction to make. The men were enemies. The *lanista* was too fond of the whip and the *pugile* was proud. And a sword makes a deeper wound than a *cestus*.'

'Still, your accusation and its outcome – the arrest of the *lanista* – was much talked about.'

Hengist shrugged again. 'It was years ago. Talk to me of this evening's banquet. Is it a happy occasion for your little Paulina?'

Claudia raised expressive eyebrows. 'He's presentable enough, this Lucius Maro. An equite, but wealthy. And Marcus needs wealth. Not too much, just enough to appease Caligula from time to time, not enough to make him jealous.'

'Is the Emperor so impoverished? I thought the Treasury was full.'

'So it was. But what Tiberius hoarded away during his reign, Caligula squandered in a year. He's always thinking up new taxes to fleece his friends.'

'Wealthy or not, is Paulina happy with the match?'

The first breeze of the evening shook the apricot tree, casting shadows over Claudia's face.

'She would much have preferred the House of Vestals. She was one born to be a Virgin. And I would have been happy to sponsor her.'

'Yes, I heard you had made a favourite of her. As Livia made a favourite of you.'

'My mother died too soon.'

'Why did you ask me to come tonight?'

She leaned towards him in a touching way, resting her hand not on his arm but on the striped bronze and silver bracelet. He looked at her hand; delicate and blue-veined, it seemed weighed down by her many rings.

'Basso will be here tonight. I wish Marcus hadn't invited him. He's noisy and quarrelsome and he always gets drunk. Lucius is quite a prig, despite his equite status. I don't want him upset. You have a way with you. You know the nature of patricians and you certainly know gladiators. I trust in you to pour oil on any troubled waters.'

'Do you fear the betrothal will be broken?'

'Yes. Basso and Lucius . . .' She spread her hands wide apart, searching for a smile.

'Would it be such a tragedy if Paulina's heart's not in it?'

'She must marry. It's the only course open to my little Proserpine.'

Hengist was silent, thinking of Piso's suspicion. Claudia glanced over her shoulder at the house.

'The slaves are lighting the lamps. It's time we went in.'

'How many dine tonight?'

'Eight. By tradition no fewer than the three Graces . . .'

'And no more than the nine Muses. I have attended Roman *cenas* before.'

As they rose, he reached for an apricot hanging low on the bough. Claudia gave his hand a sharp rap, her rings clashing against his bracelet.

'You'll spoil your appetite.'

The *triclinium* where the guests were invited to dine was hung with garlands to absorb the intoxicating elements of the wine. The door had been rolled back to invite the cool night air and for visitors to admire the vista of cold, pale statues rising against the dark foliage of fig and mulberry branches. In a semi-circle about a single table were the three couches that gave the room its name, each one large enough to accommodate three reclining guests.

Hengist observed the solid silver legs of the table and the rare wood of the couches with its undulating grain and colours that shifted in the play of light like the unfolding of a peacock's tail. If Marcus was crying poverty now, he had possessed money once and lavished it. Like many patricians he owned two residences, a *domus* in Rome and this villa by the sea, where he could escape the malaria and summer heat of the capital.

Caius Marcus Valerius had the aura of a man dissatisfied with life. His once-handsome face was marred by deep grooves about his nose and mouth and his dark hair was coarsely threaded with grey.

He greeted his former slave in an off-hand manner to veil a latent hostility. Hengist was puzzled. He could appreciate the Senator's reluctance to include him in the gathering. His fame had faded, he was only a common shopkeeper and lacked humility.

But Hengist read something else in his demeanour. A disquietude in the ex-gladiator's presence, a something that almost smelt like the fear of a man who knew before the fight he would lose.

A likely cause for Marcus' discontent was the indifference of his beautiful wife. Julia pulsed with a passion for life, she seemed on the brink of some about-to-be-realized expectation and it was patently obvious it was not to be shared with her husband.

His prospective son-in-law Lucius Maro was a small, flaxen-haired man with a prim, lack-lustre personality. Not even the arrival of his betrothed evoked a smile. He surveyed the extravagant festivities with mingled bewilderment and disapproval.

As for Paulina, she looked more like a girl being led to execution than to her wedding. She was the daughter of one of Marcus' previous wives, a dark-eyed delicate creature, demurely dressed in white. Hengist noted how she clung to Claudia's side as if still under the protection of Vesta.

Aulus Piso with his bluff manner and gravelly voice more than made up for the dismal demeanour of the bridal pair. He was delighted to see Hengist and made him his partner on one of the couches.

The Family Valeria had assembled with one outsider and one absent guest.

The majordomo arrived and struck his staff three times on the floor as signal that the *cena* was about to begin.

'But, my dear,' demurred Julia. 'Our number's not yet complete.'

'Basso knew the hour,' growled her husband. 'It's past.' He signalled to the majordomo. 'Bring on the *gustus*.'

Julia, sulking, flung herself down on the central couch. Marcus drew Paulina out from Claudia's wing and led her to the third couch where Lucius stood.

'Come, children, lie with each other in happy prelude to the nuptial couch,' he said, paternally.

Paulina obeyed reluctantly, but shrank away as Lucius lay down beside her. At her imploring glance, her aunt hurried across the room to join her.

'I hope you don't intend to lie between them on their wedding night,' guffawed Piso. 'You're bound to blight Maro's marital bliss.'

'She might learn a thing or two,' muttered Julia, sourly.

Somewhere, a cithara began to play. Slaves entered bearing on salvers the *gustus* or appetizers, salted sea-urchins, jelly-fish in egg sauce, a salad of tree-fungi in *allec*, black and green olives, dormice seasoned with honey and poppy seeds, spiced peacock eggs, prunes and pomegranate seeds. Honey-wine was poured into chased silver drinking horns.

'My cousin must have staked all he has on this little spread' whispered Piso, setting to with gusto. 'I hope the quarry's taking the bait. They want him hooked without delay.'

Hengist glanced at the young equite who was dipping his fingers into the silver-gilt dishes with a fastidious self-restraint. If Marcus had hoped to impress his guest-of-honour with the lavish scale of his entertaining he had missed his mark.

'He looks like one who'd be happier on bread soaked in mother's milk,' Piso added. He offered a ribald opinion on Paulina's wedding night, but his words were lost as he munched on a dormouse and spat out the delicate bones.

Behind each couch stood the diners' personal slaves to attend their owners with finger-bowls and napkins between courses. Having no slave of his own, Hengist was obliged to accept the services available to him from Piso's slave.

Conversation was desultory, the gaiety forced. Julia still sulked, Claudia looked anxious. To Marcus' courteous enquiries about his journey and Piso's good-natured jibes, Lucius returned the same monosyllabic answers.

A change of atmosphere suddenly rippled through the room, the ruffle of a breeze on a sullen sea. Like a statue touched to life by Pygmalion, Basso the gladiator materialized out of the night and stood in the doorway.

'Basso! I didn't hear my doorkeeper announce you,' said Marcus in surprise.

'I invaded your sanctum in my own style,' returned the gladiator. 'Over the wall.'

He was beyond doubt the most potently beautiful male animal that had ever stalked the mica-strewn sands of the circus. His tunic barely covered the proof of his virility, being worn short to show the play of muscles under the copper sheen of his lightly-oiled thighs. The skin of a wildcat he had speared in the arena swung from his shoulders. His hair was long and curling, his eyes needed no kohl to enhance them, his mouth was full and sensual. He was the ideal of splendid manhood allied with an arrogance and savagery that made him the idol and envy of many.

Julia sat up eagerly. 'Welcome, Basso. We were afraid you'd forgotten us. My impatient husband's started *cena*. Come, join us.' She patted the empty space beside her on the couch.

'No,' protested Piso. 'Take your place with us, Basso. Here's Hengist who once rivalled you for reputation.'

Hengist had risen at the gladiator's arrival, the better to take his measure. At the recognition of his name, Basso approached and circled him like a great cat sniffing out the potential of an antagonist.

'Who would consider himself Basso's rival?' murmured the Gaul.

'Not Hengist,' returned the gladiator. He glanced from the space beside Piso to that beside Julia. 'Enticing offers. But here . . .' he swung towards the third couch, 'is the place I'd like to take if someone will oblige me.'

Paulina had also sat up. Her eyes had an unnatural glitter and her little pink mouth had fallen open.

Lucius flushed with indignation as Basso eyed his puny frame with overt ridicule.

'What's this?' He pulled an *ampulla* from under the equite's *pallium*. 'Your own wine! What an insult to your host. But, of course, you intended to share it.' He took out the stopper and gulped down several mouthfuls.

'That's hundred-year-old Falemian,' protested Lucius.

'Then I'll savour every second of it.'

Marcus was scowling in annoyance. In some circles the inclusion of the gladiator would have been an unparalleled coup; on closer acquaintance with his future son-in-law he realized it was a dire mistake. The prim little equite was not the sort to appreciate the glamour of the professional killer.

'I'm afraid my daughter can't be torn from the side of her betrothed nor from the protection of her aunt,' he said, with forced geniality.

'Ah, yes, greetings Valeria Claudia.' Basso made a mock bow. 'The ex-Vestal. Everyone here seems to be an ex-something.'

'Even you, Basso, will run your race,' observed Piso, 'unless you've discovered the Cup of Eternal Youth.'

'I'll live to spit on your tomb,' retorted the gladiator, insolently.

'Ah, the impudence of ex-slaves these days,' murmured the

magistrate, 'particularly when they turn gladiator. They know they can dare anything. After all, what worse can I do to him than will probably befall him tomorrow in the arena?' Aloud, he said, 'Come, Basso, allow us to worship you, our transient god. Take my cup. I haven't touched it.'

Basso downed the honey-wine in a single gulp and sauntered back to the couch where Julia lay.

'Let me entice you further,' she murmured, huskily.

She took a prune from a dish and held it between her lips. With a laugh, Basso knelt on the couch and put his lips to hers. With her tongue she pushed the prune into his mouth.

'Circe turning men into swine,' muttered Piso. Hengist was surprised at the rancour in the eyes that watched the pair.

With a deeper scowl, Marcus took the vacant place beside his Piso.

The next course arrived. Red mullet, sea-perch, dolphin, mackerel, sole and eel, and a dish made from embryo octopi. The centrepiece was an enormous *catinus* with four silver figures of Triton at each corner pouring from their conch-horns a rich sauce over tiny fish which were so stirred by the flowing liquid that they seemed to swim about in its depths. It was a feast, Hengist thought ruefully, that would keep a fleet of galley-slaves alive for a month.

Basso remained on Julia's couch. They fed each other titbits and drank from the same cup, kissing and caressing each other between mouthfuls. They seemed oblivious to the rest of the company. Piso tried vainly to divert Marcus' attention, but the Senator's eyes kept straying to the amorous couple on the neighbouring couch.

The time came for the *commissatio* when the King of the Feast was selected. Marcus over-rode Julia's insistence on Basso to choose Piso. The magistrate cheerfully donned the chaplet of roses and supervised the mixing of the wine in the *crater*, determining its strength and how many cups could be drunk by each guest. He was bending over the bowl, savouring its bouquet, when at Julia's whispered urging Basso sprang off the couch and seized Piso by the neck, forcing his head to submerge. The magistrate spluttered and kicked and struggled, but was unable to free himself from the brutal grip.

'A noble death for a drunken sot,' shouted Basso. 'Drowned in his own brew.'

Hengist rested his hand on the gladiator's shoulder. 'Let him up,' he said, quietly.

'What's it to you?' demanded the gladiator.

'I call him my friend.'

'And who do you call your enemy?'

'No man.'

Basso released his captive, who fell back on the tiles, choking and retching. Crimson rivulets ran from his scanty hair and lashes, swam in his eyes and flowed from his nose and mouth onto his garments. Julia was laughing uncontrollably, Marcus stood clenching his fists in impotent fury, Claudia and Lucius looked on in disbelief while Paulina ate pomegranate seeds like some detached Proserpine watching while the souls of the dead were weighed.

Basso tore the *fibula* from Hengist's *pallium*. The garment fell about his feet, revealing the Gaul's long, lean frame.

'You look hungry for a shopkeeper,' he jeered.

'It's the nature of the beast,' replied Hengist, softly.

Basso studied the fibula. 'This could be a formidable weapon in the hands of a man who knows how to use it.' He glared pugnaciously at Hengist. 'We want better entertainment than the twanging of some instrument. Shall we match?'

The shopkeeper shook his head. 'Basso would win scant honour in besting one past his prime.'

'Scared?'

'No, just bored.'

'You're right. The whole evening's a bore. Maybe it's the company. They need livening up, a tickle or two from my sword. They love the sight of other men's blood while they're sitting safe in the *cavea*, let's see how *they* like to bleed.'

'Why not go back to your couch,' suggested Hengist, mildly, 'and bid our host send for more wine.' He judged that Basso had been more than a little drunk when he arrived at the villa and nursed a fragile hope that he might be coaxed to drink himself into a stupor.

But the gladiator was only warming up. 'I'm bored with Julia's whorish tricks, though the sluts of Subura would be hard pushed to best her. Rich, spoilt women, jaded with every other excitement to be had have paid for my body since I was a slave. Women with noble names and long pedigrees bribing their way into my cell and into my bed. Wives of men who cheer me when I win and whose boos would be the last sound I heard if I lost. But no one quite knows how to play the whore like your virtuous wife, illustrious Senator. Notice any new tricks lately? All learnt from me. Or does she refuse you?'

Julia's laugh had stuck in her throat. Her cosmetics stood out like a theatrical mask on a face suddenly drained of colour. Marcus stood like one who had seen a Gorgon. Claudia, kneeling beside Piso, looked up imploringly at Hengist.

'I think we've had enough blood drawn for one night.' The Gaul's voice was low, but it had an edge to it that made the gladiator look at him.

'Do you think so? Maro doesn't think so. He'd like to see more.'

Paulina shrank back on her couch, concealing her trembling mouth with both hands. Her dark eyes gazed at Basso eloquently.

'Do you imagine, Lucius Maro, that it's your prestige and wealth that made Valerius negotiate a marriage contract. No, it's to conceal his shame that Paulina, the would-be Vestal Virgin, came crawling to me with the same lust of all her kind. I opened the petals of this little rosebud here in this very garden.'

'I feel sick,' said Piso. He staggered to his feet and went out through the doorway. No one moved to help him.

Paulina burst into a paroxysm of crying and ran from the room.

Claudia rose to confront the gladiator. 'I would advise you not to say anymore,' she said, coldly.

'Or what?' he grinned. 'You'll deny me. It's too late. I already know.' He smirked at the rest of the company. 'Even Vestals have their secrets.'

'Get out!' said Julia. Her tone was as pale and deathly as her face. 'Go, before I have my slaves beat you from our door.' She turned on her husband. 'Do you say nothing while we are slandered before your face?'

'He doesn't dare,' said Basso, brutally. 'He knows I have the Emperor's favour. One whisper in Caligula's ear and life and estates are forfeit.'

With that Parthian shot he sauntered out the way he had come, into the night.

Bestowing a glance of withering contempt on his would-be in-laws, Lucius Maro also took his departure.

'I should see to Paulina,' Julia said in a smothered voice. Moments later, Marcus followed her into the atrium.

Hengist and Claudia were left alone. Even the cithara had fallen silent.

'I'm afraid I wasn't much help to you,' he said, ruefully.

'Nothing's so difficult to combat as pure malice,' she replied. 'I was hoping . . .'

'Perhaps I should leave,' he suggested when she did not go on. 'Or at least see how Aulus fares.'

'No, don't leave me.' Again, she rested her hand on his braceleted arm. 'Forgive me. I feel suddenly alone and a little frightened.'

'Frightened?'

'Of Basso. Of his threats.'

'I'm sure he exaggerates his influence with Caligula.'

'I'm not so sure. The Emperor's taken up his summer residence at Baiae with his uncle Claudius. Basso can be there tomorrow.' She gave a quivering sigh. 'Talk to me of pleasant things. What did you last see at the theatre?'

'*The Frogs*.'

'Aristophanes. I prefer tragedy. Someone like Euripides.'

He stayed at her side, chatting on various subjects and avoiding the ugly incidents they had just witnessed. Hengist was beginning to think of the long ride home, of his comfortable bed and Tassia's welcoming arms when he heard a stifled shriek from somewhere inside the villa.

'What was that?'

Claudia rose, suddenly restless. 'Perhaps we should go in search of Aulus. A man of his size may have suffered apoplexy after such an assault. Bid one of the slaves bring a torch.'

The flood of flames made the light within its radius as bright as day. They wandered along the paths they had taken earlier in the evening, occasionally calling Piso's name. Hengist stopped suddenly and pointed to a pool of red-stained vomit close to the hedge.

'Look there, too. It's Maro's amphora. Basso's been this way.'

'Oh, poor Aulus!' cried Claudia. 'I should have let you come out earlier.'

'What lies to the left?' They had come to a break in the hedge, one path leading left, the other to the *euripus* and the apricot tree.

'A circular path leading back to the dormitory of the slaves,' she said in answer to his question.

Hengist hesitated, then decided to check the travertine bench to see if Piso had fallen asleep there. The bench was unoccupied but for two dead birds and a scattering of apricot stones. Instinct drew him onto the miniature bridge. The water below sparkled darkly, but something other than fish lay in its depths.

'Bring the torch,' he ordered tersely.

'What is it?' Claudia's voice quavered. 'Is it Aulus? Not drowned?'

Hengist thrust the torch down to illuminate the object below. Water rippled gently, distorting the features. An inquisitive fish darted close to nibble the corner of a staring eye.

'It's not Aulus,' he said, grimly.

At the moment he spoke, a flushed and dishevelled Piso stumbled through the break in the hedge.

'It's Basso.' Unconsciously, Hengist uttered the traditional '*Hoc habet*. He's had it now.'

'It's as well I happened along when I did,' observed Piso. 'If it had been my cousin who stumbled across your discovery, you wouldn't be alive to tell of it. This is one disaster too many for Marcus.'

It was the eerie stretch of hours between midnight and dawn when the world and mankind were at lowest ebb. The dead man had been dredged up and now lay naked in one of the cubicles. The Valerii had been gathered together in the *tablinum* and searchers sent out to locate Lucius Maro.

'As it is, he's disgruntled,' continued Piso, 'that I've turned this into an investigation instead of hushing it up. He thinks I'm questioning you, not confiding in you or seeking your advice.'

'How can I be of service?' enquired Hengist, modestly.

'Help to convince me that Basso got drunk, fell into the *euripus* and drowned.'

Hengist took the lamp from Piso and studied the dead man's face. 'He doesn't look like any drowned man I've seen after a *naumachia*.'

'I forgot you've seen gladiators drown in those mock sea-battles. But isn't it possible for a man to drown in water as shallow as a *euripus*? If he bumped his head?'

Hengist scanned the body from head to toe. 'Help me turn him over.'

Piso complied, with a shudder. 'What are you looking for?' he asked, nervously.

'Fresh wounds,' grunted Hengist. 'There are plenty of old scars, but no death wound. Turn him back. I want to look into his mouth.'

'Ugh!'

'Bring the lamp closer.' The ex-gladiator deftly prised open the jaw. 'The water will have washed out anything in his teeth or on his tongue. There's something in the back of his mouth though. Have tweezers brought from the bathhouse. I want to see what it is.'

Piso swallowed before he put the next question. 'Do you suspect murder?'

'Don't you? Why else are you holding this investigation?'

'To discover the truth.'

'Or divert suspicion.' His glance wandered over the corpulent figure of his friend. 'I see you've changed your robe.'

'My dear fellow, I simply had to borrow one from Marcus. My own was in a *disgusting* state.'

'Where did you go after you left the *triclinium*? Claudia and I searched for you.'

'Am I really under suspicion?' Piso was astonished.

'You did leave the *triclinium* before Basso . . .'

'To be sick after all that wine he'd forced me to imbibe. I then staggered off to the slaves' dormitory where I lay down until the nausea passed.'

'Did you see anyone else in the garden?'

'I saw no one and no one saw me. Not even a slave. Of course a slave can't give evidence unless he's been tortured first.'

'Which is unlikely under the present circumstances.'

'I assure you I was in no fit state to lie in wait for Basso and avenge my humiliation.' Piso drew together the tattered shreds of his dignity. 'It occurs to me you got your own taste of humiliation from Basso. I bet you learnt a trick or two in the Ludus Magnus. How to kill a man without leaving a mark.'

Hengist smiled sunnily. 'I have the perfect alibi. I was chatting in the *triclinium* with a former Vestal Virgin.'

'Claudia!' grunted Piso. 'Damn you, Hengist. You're always smiling. It's a wonder you didn't get your front teeth knocked out in the arena.'

Hengist continued to examine the gladiator's face. 'Have you ever seen a dead man's features as contorted as this? He looks as if he's seen a horror too terrible to be endured and died of the shock of it.'

'I've seen victims of heart attacks who looked like this.'

'Or victims of poison. It's possible Basso was murdered before he left the *triclinium*.'

'What? How?' spluttered Piso.

'*You* hated Basso even before he humiliated you.'

'Of course I did. I told you that at *prandium*. He was young and handsome and tumbled more girls in a week than I have in my lifetime. I envied him and I detested him.'

'Yet you gave him your drink.'

Piso gave a faint gurgle. 'Didn't you notice? After he'd made that jibe about my tomb I spat in the honey-wine. *Then* I offered it to Basso. It amused me to see him toss it off in a single gulp.' He opened his little eyes as wide as they would go. 'You don't think he died of my spit.'

'It probably held enough venom.'

'Hengist!' Piso gazed at him, reproachfully. 'What a lawyer you would have made. I thought you were my friend.'

'Even murderers have friends. Will you allow me to be present when you conduct your interrogations? Since I read and write I can act as your scribe.'

'Allow you?' echoed the magistrate, eyeing him with new respect. 'I insist on it.'

The *tablinum* was a large room lined with shelves containing furled scrolls, clay tablets and another collection of ancestral busts.

When Hengist entered, a ferocious argument between Piso and Valerius was in progress. Marcus abruptly broke off as he recognized his ex-slave.

'What impudence!'

'He's here at my invitation,' interjected Piso. 'To transcribe for me.'

'I have a secretary who can do that for you.'

'Marcus!' Piso threw up his hands. 'Are you asking me to trust *your* slaves? Hengist is at least impartial.'

'Why do you insist on carrying on with this enquiry?' Marcus was not drunk, but the night's events had whipped him into a state of belligerence.

'Would you prefer me to report the matter to a higher authority, perhaps someone recommended by Caesar himself?'

'That's extortion!' snarled Marcus.

'Of course I might meet with an unfortunate accident on the way home, but two unfortunate accidents involving two notables leaving your banquet might be difficult for the public to swallow.'

'What do you want from me?' Marcus acquiesced, sullenly.

'Just a few answers. For example, where did you go after Basso left the *triclinium*?'

'Great Jove, you're treating this thing as if it were murder.'

'Answer.'

'I was with my wife until I was summoned to view Basso's body.'

'Will Julia verify this?'

'She'd better if she wants to live.' He shot the magistrate an ill-tempered look. 'I didn't mean that as it sounds. Knowing the law, you realize that a man has the right to have an adulterous wife condemned to death.'

'Trust you to think of that, Marcus,' returned Piso, with just the slightest edge to his voice. 'Make yourself available for further questions.

'No one had a stronger motive than Marcus. An outraged father and cuckolded husband,' mused Hengist, 'but the time factor's wrong. If Basso had been set upon by assassins while coming out of a brothel one week hence I'd have suspected Marcus. This was premeditated'

'Unless Marcus already knew Basso was the cause of his trouble.'

'And invited him to a banquet in order to poison him. I doubt it.'

The magistrate sighed. 'Shall we call the virtuous Julia?'

The woman reputed to be the most beautiful in Pompeii was a mess, her hair tumbled and her cosmetics smeared across her face.

'Don't imagine I've been struggling with Basso.' She met Piso's startled look defiantly. 'My husband's been exercising his conjugal rights. A prelude to my execution.'

'I'm sorry,' said the magistrate, lamely.

'Why?' she retorted. 'You've never liked me.'

'Beauty sometimes makes ill choices,' he said, wryly.

'Not as ill as love. Ask your questions.'

'Were you surprised at Basso's death?'

'No, only at how quickly Marcus acted. He must have given the order before he came into my cubicle,' she halted briefly and then hurried on. 'Of course, my erstwhile lover was beaten to death. Just as I promised. Except that I didn't give the order.'

'We . . . I,' Piso amended, swiftly, 'suspect he was poisoned.'

'*Poisoned*!' Her face blazed. 'At Marcus' banquet? How delicious!'

'*You* fed him titbits . . .'

'And he fed me. From the same plate. And we drank from the same cup. No, magistrate, you can't lay that at my door. If you'll excuse me, I want to go to the bath-house to wash off the night's events.'

'Did you know about Paulina and Basso?' Hengist flung the question after her.

She paused, more bemused than offended by his intrusion. 'No, that was a surprise.'

'She could be lying,' muttered Piso. 'There was the prune she pushed into his mouth.'

'He ate and drank a great deal after that.'

'It depends on how fast-acting the poison was.'

'Yes.' Hengist gazed at him as if seeing something else.

Paulina crept into the *tablinum* and sat on the edge of her chair, her hands clasped nervously in her lap.

'I won't keep you longer than is necessary,' said the magistrate, kindly. 'Was it true? Was Basso your lover?'

She gave him a scorching glance from under her swollen lids, but said nothing.

'Where did you go after you left the *triclinium*?'

'Surely it's obvious,' she said, sulkily. 'I've been in my cubicle – crying.'

'Are you sure you didn't meet Basso in the garden?'

She flinched as if she'd been struck. 'No!'

'Did you hate Basso for betraying you and spoiling your marriage plans?'

She stood up. 'I really can't help you. May I go?'

'Were you glad when you learned that Basso was dead?' Hengist asked her, suddenly.

'Yes, yes!' She startled them by the vehemence of her tone. 'I wish *I*'d been the one to kill him.'

'Do you know who did?'

She closed her little pink mouth and went away.

Piso whistled through his teeth. 'What did you make of that?'

'She didn't kill him. It would have been quick, unpremeditated, *personal*, a dagger to the heart. She has a dark core, that little flower.'

The magistrate looked sober. 'Do you think she knows who murdered Basso?'

'Perhaps. I hear they've apprehended the bridegroom and dragged him back to the villa. Shall we have him in?'

Lucius Maro's indignation was obvious. 'I was hardly some fugitive to be hauled in under arrest.'

'My apologies. We've had a tragedy here.'

'What's that to me? I'm not a member of the household.'

'You almost were, but your hopes were blighted tonight by Basso's revelations.'

'I was angrier with Marcus Valerius for deceiving me. He'd assured me the girl was a virgin.'

'Are you one?' asked Hengist.

Lucius coloured furiously and blustered, 'Naturally . . .'

'. . . Not. And just as naturally you were upset when you left the villa. Where did you go?'

'For a walk along the cliff. The breeze cooled my temper and gave me a chance to think.'

'And what did you think when you heard Basso was dead?'

'That Valerius had killed him. Though he could have chosen a subtler *modus operandi. He* obviously didn't give himself a chance to cool down.'

'Or like you he would have chosen a *modus operandi* so subtle he'd have left no trace of suspicion.' Piso took over the interrogation.

'What do you mean by that?'

'A poisoner doesn't require great physical strength. Before you took your stroll, did you meet Basso in the garden for one last drink?'

'He'd scarcely have shared a drink with *me*.'

'He might have thought it amusing.'

'I was on my way back to the villa when the slaves found me, not running away.'

'Why return? Was it to retrieve your amphora with its hundred-year-old Falemian?' asked Hengist, silkily.

'I'd changed my mind about the betrothal. I could see how Basso's accusation might be of profit.'

'Explain.' The magistrate glared at him.

'If I deliver Valerius from a potentially embarrassing situation and protect his daughter's honour, shouldn't I expect gratitude, introduction into the first families, the granting of patrician status, maybe even access to the Palatium and Caesar himself.'

Piso cocked an eyebrow. 'Brave man. The rest of us prefer to keep a healthy distance.'

'And what gratitude would you expect from Paulina?' asked Hengist, quietly.

'A docile wife, something I've always wanted,' Lucius smiled, smugly.

'Hasn't Basso's death put a spoke in your ambition?'

'I hope not,' said Lucius, cautiously. 'I'll have to see how the matter unfolds.'

Hengist drew an *ampulla* from under his *pallium*. 'Do you recognize this?'

Some of the complacency went out of Lucius. 'Yes, it's mine.'

'I found it on the path not far from Basso's body.'

'Why not? You all saw him take it from me.'

'There's still some wine in it.' Hengist drew out the stopper. 'Care to finish it off?'

'Not really.'

'I'm afraid I have to insist you drink the wine,' interposed Piso. 'As magistrate of this enquiry.'

'Unofficial enquiry,' corrected Lucius. He made no move to accept the ampulla from Hengist.

'Are you afraid to drink the wine?'

Lucius smirked. 'Disinclined.'

'*Drink it!*'

Lucius jumped at the stentorian roar and grabbed at the *ampulla*.

He looked at each face in turn for a heart-beat's space before he sniffed at the contents.

'This isn't hundred-year-old Falemian. It's the coarse brew Valerius serves to his guests.' He tipped it up and let the crimson stream run out across the tiles. 'Will there be anything else?'

'What a baboon's behind!' exploded Piso. 'I'd give my oath he's guilty.'

'Would you? He could well have done without any compromise to the Valerian name. As for compromising his own ambition? Never!'

'But the *ampulla* . . . his refusal to drink..'

'Fastidiousness.'

'After Basso had slobbered over it you mean. Anyway, he soon caught on to our trick.' Piso groaned in despair. 'What am I to think? What do *you* think, Hengist?'

'I'm going for a walk to put my thoughts in order.'

Hengist went down the steps of the *tablinum* into the *crypto-porticus*.

Dawn was breaking, pale and thin, the virgin day. A peacock uttered its haunting, melancholy cry. Hengist was drawn irresistibly to the sanctum of the travertine bench and the apricot tree. The gardeners had not yet been abroad to sweep up the dead birds and the apricot stones.

Claudia looked up as he approached. 'Have you discovered your murderer?'

'Yes.'

She made room for him to sit beside her. As he sat down, she touched one of the bracelets. 'You kept them.'

Enlightenment broke upon him. 'You sent them to me.'

'You never guessed? You were my idol. But only from afar. You in the arena – I on the podium. If a Vestal breaks her vows her punishment is to be buried alive.'

'There must be more than one way to be buried alive.'

She stirred a dead bird with the toe of her sandal. 'It's a pity they have to die. Such fleeting lives.'

He reached up and took an apricot from the tree. She watched the fish lurking in a *euripus* made shallow and murky by the dredging up of Basso's body.

'Why did you invite me to the banquet?'

'I told you . . .'

'You wanted me to solve the enigma of Basso's death. I kept hoping there was an alternative, that I'd discover an opportunity or a means that would prove me wrong.'

'There were motives enough.'

'But the time factor, the *modus operandi*, didn't always match the persona of that particular enemy. I needed premeditation.'

He threw the apricot into Claudia's lap. It rolled onto the ground and into the *euripus*, floating for an instant before it sank.

'Are you familiar with the legend of Proserpine, the maiden of the sun carried off by Pluto, King of the Underworld? The classic name for abduction is rape, though now we give it a different meaning. Proserpine ate four pomegranate seeds while held captive by Pluto, so she is constrained each year to spend four months in the gloom of the Underworld as his wife. It's how we Romans explain winter.

'In this garden another Proserpine was raped by a Pluto who invaded her sanctum *in his own style, over the wall,* coming and going as he pleased. It was the hour of twilight; she was alone. It must have appealed to a cruel sense of humour to make her ineligible for Vesta, a different triumph from the arena.'

'And of course she was too shocked and debased to report the outrage to Marcus or Julia, but she did confide in you.'

She nodded. 'Even when it became obvious she'd had congress with a man she refused, despite all Marcus' bullying, to reveal his name. She was dismayed it was someone she considered an inhuman brute.'

He reached up and picked another apricot. 'You stopped me before. Will you stop me again from eating your fruit?'

She slid him a sidelong glance. Her eyes were the same colour as the rim of the sky.

'I might have missed it altogether and gone away unsatisfied if Aulus hadn't reminded me today of Livia. Aulus called her a harridan, but she was worse, a conniving, ruthless woman who was determined that her own son Tiberius would follow Augustus to the Imperial throne. An army of Augustus' grandsons and nephews died to pave the way for Tiberius. Augustus was naïve enough to believe that all these lingering deaths were from natural causes. He grieved, but he didn't suspect. Until the end . . .'

'You speak as if you were an intimate of the Imperial circle, with privileged information.'

'Claudius is a close friend of mine. Uncle of Caligula. Grandson to Livia. When she lay dying she sent for him and confessed. Claudius has always been believed by his family to be something of a half-wit. I think she felt there was no harm to her pride confiding in a fool. And Claudius confided in me, because I respect him and he trusts me and couldn't bear the weight of such terrible knowledge.'

'What have Livia's confessions to do with Basso's murder?'

'It was the *modus operandi* she employed in murdering Augustus. He'd become distrustful and refused to eat at her table, drinking only water and eating fruit off the trees. Yet she achieved her end. Livia was an expert poisoner, slow poisons to ape lingering illnesses, fast poisons to instantly stop the heart. She must have taught her protégée some of her secrets. Aren't you going to tell me how you injected the poison in the apricots while they still hung on the bough?'

'That secret dies with me.'

'How did you induce Basso . . .?'

'Fool!' She curled her lip, spoiling the sweetness of its curve. 'He was easy to deceive. Vanity and stupidity are so often synonomous. I told him the fruit was an aphrodisiac, I promised him all manner of delights and powers, and the fool believed me. He thought as Keeper of the Flame I was privy to the Mystery of Mysteries.'

'Didn't he think it strange you offered the gift to *him*.'

'I think he believed I lusted after him in the last flush of my womanhood. After all, he wasn't the first young man to capture my admiration.'

'And it was sweet irony to kill him where he committed the rape.'

'Yes, to give Pluto the pomegranate and see him carried down to the Underworld forever, yes, that was sweet revenge. When he was late, I hoped it was because he had eaten the fruit first.' She slid him another look. 'You're wise in the ways of wild beasts. No wonder you hung onto life in the arena. What made me capable of murder?'

'You made a strange remark yesterday. *My mother died too soon.*'

'Ah, yes, I wouldn't have been sent to the House of Vestals had she lived. Marcus became my guardian. Even as a youth he was ambitious. He wanted the prestige of a Vestal Virgin in the family. Livia tried to intervene, but Augustus denied her.'

'And you were born for the love of men and to have children. Paulina satisfied your mother-hunger. You were the female of the species fiercely avenging her young.'

'So what will you do now, my own wild beast? Report me to Aulus?'

'I leave that to you.'

'Then I shall say nothing. Justice will be served. Slow poisons. Fast poisons. Perhaps I shan't outlive the year.'

He left her serenely admiring the flamingo colours of the sunrise and returned to the *tablinum*.

Valerius and Piso were in profound discussion which they broke off as he entered. Hengist bowed deferentially before he addressed his former master.

'I've been examining the site of the tragedy and I think I've discovered how Basso died.'

They stared at him in desperate expectation. He fumbled in the pouch at his belt and brought out a small object.

'I found this lodged at the back of Basso's throat.'

'An apricot stone!'

'After Basso left the *triclinium* he must have helped himself to some fruit, devouring it somewhat greedily, I would judge, two or three in his mouth at a time and spitting out the stones. This became lodged, cutting off air to the windpipe. He choked and fell into the *euripus*. There is a precedent of course. It's exactly the way the son of Claudius died.'

'So it wasn't murder after all,' Marcus dealt the Gaul a vindictive look. 'You've been making fools of us. I've always known you had an amused contempt for anything Roman, particularly me. I asked you once what you thought when you stood in the arena and looked up at us, we who are masters of the world. You replied, *I think only of my opponent's next move.*'

'I probably meant it. I'm sorry if I gave some offence. That was not my intention.'

'You did not own me, Gaul. I owned you.'

'How could it have been otherwise?' Hengist spread his hands in a self-deprecating manner.

'I think that now we may safely leave this matter in the illustrious Senator's hands,' Piso interrupted, hastily.

'And a word to the wise,' Marcus' look carried a patent threat. 'Indiscretion is injurious to health.'

'I like my life as it is,' responded Hengist. 'Why should I wish to complicate it? I thank you for a delightful evening. I apologize for the fact that I became so drunk I've forgotten most of its events.'

'May I offer you a lift in my *carruca*,' said Piso as they crossed the atrium. 'We can tie your horse to the back.'

'Are you sure there's room in that bed on wheels for two?'

'If I'm corpulent it's your fine fare.'

Hengist dropped his voice. 'You were ready enough to accept my explanation. You must have guessed it was a lie.'

'I don't want to know the truth. I've reached an understanding with Marcus. A cover-up in return for Julia's life. He'll divorce her and I'll marry her myself. She'll be so grateful.' He chuckled, happily.

'Brave man. And what will become of Basso's body?'

'Carried out to sea and dumped. If it washes up, well, he was drowned on his way to Baiae. The populace will howl for a bit, but the girls will soon be writing another name on the walls of the baths.'

Lucius Maro came into sight, mincing towards the peristyle. 'I presume you won't object if I take a stroll in the garden,' he said, smugly.

'Don't touch the apricots,' Hengist called after him.

Lucius threw a pale sneer over his shoulder and walked on.

'Some people can't be warned,' mourned the ex-gladiator.

'I know,' agreed Piso, solemnly. 'It's the nature of the beast.'

THE GARDENS OF TANTALUS

Brian Stableford

Brian Stableford will be better known to most as a writer of science fiction and supernatural fantasy, with such books as The Empire of Fear *(1988) and the David Lydyard trilogy* The Werewolves of London *(1999),* The Angel of Pain *(1991) and* The Carnival of Destruction *(1994). But his interests are far wider. He has a degree in biology, a doctorate in sociology, and has written books on subjects as far afield as futurology and the Wandering Jew. For the following story he turned his attention to the mysterious Apollonius of Tyana who became famed as a miracle-worker throughout the Mediterranean in the first century* AD.

∽

We live, it seems, in an Age of Miracles – or *lived* in one, at any rate, for the miracles about which the young men always seem to be talking all took place in their grandfathers' time, when Claudius, Nero or Vespasian was Emperor in Rome. Strange to relate, I – who am certainly a grandfather, born in the seventh year of Nero's rule – heard little or no talk of miracles at the time, when the word on all men's lips, in Corinth at least, was *philosophy*.

One rarely hears that word nowadays; it seems that men have a greater appetite for miracles.

My ignorance of the Age of Miracles through which I lived seems all the more remarkable when I recall (as clearly as if it were yesterday, although fifty years and more have passed) that I was present when one of the most widely rumoured miracles took place, and am named in all accounts as the one who benefited from that miracle.

Lest any Christian should read this – although that seems unlikely, given that a literate Christian is almost a contradiction in terms – let me hasten to say that it is not one of the miracles of their beloved Jesus to which I refer. His crucifixion must have taken place near thirty years before I was born. The miracle-worker I was privileged to meet was a very different man: Apollonius of Tyana, whose associate Damis of Nineveh produced the memoir of his life which proclaimed him a great magician. What Damis sought to prove by this I do not know, but I do know that Apollonius would have despised him for it, for Apollonius was a true philosopher, who had no truck with magic, omens or gods.

So far as I can tell, the principal effect of Damis' fantasies has been to call forth hymns of hate from the followers of Jesus, whose instinct is to damn all miracle-workers save their own as black magicians and addicts of the sinister. Apollonius has already been attacked in this wise by one Moeragenes, who never knew him at all. But I am only a white-beard philosopher, in a world where age and wisdom count for nothing. For all I know, the lies which Damis tells might secure the memory of Apollonius until the end of time, so that in a thousand years men will know nothing of his life except that he once wrought miracles, and saved a fool named Menippus from the wiles of a *lamia*.

Perhaps he did; perhaps it is I, Menippus, who am deluded into thinking the world a humdrum place, which might be *understood* if only men would put aside their silly obsessions with the naming of imaginary gods and the everpresent threat of demons.

I will admit that there is much in the memoir of Damis with which I can pick no quarrel. It may be revealing, however, that most of what seems to me to be true relates to matters of which neither Damis nor I had any direct knowledge, merely repeating the account which Apollonius gave of his own history.

Apollonius was born during the long reign of Augustus, at Tyana in Cappadocia. He was well-schooled and showed great precocity in the art of rhetoric. He became a philosopher of the school of Pythagoras and soon became notorious for preaching, according to the creed of that school, that animal sacrifice was a useless evil. He refused to eat meat, never wore any sandals save those made of bark, and wore no clothing save for that made of linen. He renounced his patrimony, refused all use of money, and once took a five-year vow of silence while he travelled the world.

This vow of silence added greatly to his reputation for holiness, which was responsible in its turn for the fact that so many people sought him out as a healer – but he told me that the reason for the vow was to make of himself a distanced observer, that he might use his eyes and ears all the better as he travelled east through Persia to India, then south through Phoenicia and Palestine to Egypt.

'I suppose it was a foolish notion,' he said to me once, 'but I was young then, and young men are always ready to think in absolutes. I would never have kept the vow had I gone to Egypt before I went to India and there encountered the Gymnosophists – the naked philosophers of the Thebaid. Contemplation of their state cured me of any further wish to take the business of living to its imaginable extremes.'

'But you did not begin eating meat,' I pointed out to him, 'nor wearing animal relics upon your body.'

'You could not think that an extreme,' he chided me, 'were you not a young man, and one who has never known poverty.'

As to the reputation which Apollonius had as a healer and an exorcist, I believe that he was as clever as any man of his time – which is to say that the advice he gave to all men who were sick in body was to avoid meat and medicines, and the advice he gave to all men who believed themselves possessed was to avoid meat and magicians. I have offered the same advice throughout my own long life, and by my reckoning it leads to the recovery of three suffers in every five, which is at least one more in five than regain their health after consulting doctors or wizards. Damis, of course, gives a different account – but doubtless he has his reasons.

Which brings us to my own sad case – which Damis calls bewitchment, although I remember it, at worst, as lovesickness.

Apollonius visited Corinth in his sixtieth year, or shortly thereafter. He was welcomed into the household of the Cynic philosopher Demetrius, an avid follower of his doctrines, among whose pupils I was to be counted. I was twenty-five years old, and even Damis concedes that I was handsome and athletic.

Damis misstates the case when he says that I was betrothed to a foreign woman who represented herself as a wealthy Phoenician. I was certainly enamoured of a foreign woman, but she was an Egyptian servant named Nauma, a minor adjunct of the household of a Phoenician widow called Galanthis.

Galanthis had been some months a guest in the house of a

rich merchant named Aradus, who had known her for many years through her husband, with whom he had had commercial connections. Aradus was the father of Bassus, a man of my own age with whom I had grown up, although some strain had been placed on our friendship by virtue of the fact that he too was inclined to think of himself as a philosopher although he was an unrepentant hedonist. I used to think of our arguments as a kind of sport but Demetrius took a dimmer view of them and regarded Bassus as a malign influence who threatened his authority over all his pupils.

I must confess that I was by no means the best or most faithful pupil of Demetrius. I had found, while under his tutelage, that I had little heart for the ascetic life towards which Demetrius was continually urging me. Although I recognized that they were mostly excuses for conscienceless self-indulgence, I was not unattracted by the rival doctrines of Bassus. I was firmly committed to the ideals of philosophy, but I was at that time quite uncertain as to *which* set of ideals was to be preferred. Should it not be possible, I wondered, for a man of wisdom to enjoy life to the full? Should it not be permissible to eat good meat, drink good wine, wear good shoes and love women – marry, even – while still cultivating the art and authority of the mind? Demetrius said that it was not, but Bassus said otherwise.

Such was the antipathy which grew up between Demetrius and Bassus that Bassus became increasingly determined to steal me for his own fledgeling school. He might have succeeded in doing so before Apollonius arrived in Corinth, had it not been for the fact that when I visited the house of Aradus in the month before the fateful visit time spent with Bassus always seemed to be time that ought to have been spent with Nauma. Paradoxically, it was not until I was well away from the house that the words of Bassus began to exert their grip upon me – by which time Demetrius was usually on hand to refute the arguments in the strongest possible terms.

Quite without meaning to, I became the most significant prize that had ever been put at stake in the war of ideas waged between the two men – and Nauma became involved, in spite of the fact that she had not the slightest interest in philosophy. Her one and only vocation was dancing; Galanthis had acquired her on account of her skill in that art – and, I hasten to add, for her skill in that art alone. Even Damis of Nineveh does not dare to allege – as my master Demetrius sometimes did – that my beloved was no more than a common whore.

'She may be a servant,' I told my master, aggrievedly, 'but Nauma is far too precious to be sold in that manner.'

'Only because Galanthis intends to wed Aradus herself,' Demetrius insisted. 'She dangles her serving-maids before him as a cunning fisherman displays the lure, but you may be sure that he shall not touch them – yet.'

'Bassus says that his father is perfectly content as a widower,' I told Demetrius. 'He has slave-girls of his own.'

'If Bassus says that, it is hope speaking,' Demetrius retorted. 'He fears for his father's fortune should the Phoenician ever get her greedy hands upon it, and he has extended his debts to the limit with every moneylender in Corinth. Aradus may be a prince of fools, too long retired from the marketplace, but even he knows better than to pay his son's debts. You may not see what Bassus is, but Aradus does – he knows that an appetite such as that, once unleashed, is likely to devour wealth as a plague of locusts devours a field of green wheat.'

It was, indeed, hope rather than faith that determined Bassus' opinion. On the same day that Demetrius was told to expect Apollonius in Corinth, Aradus announced that his betrothal to Galanthis would be marked by a sumptuous feast. This was the 'wedding-feast' to which Damis refers in his memoir; it was not mine, although I and my beloved were certainly there – and so was Apollonius.

Damis claims that Apollonius used magic to unmask my beloved and expose her as a *lamia* – a serpentine demon whose intention was to drink my blood and feed on my flesh. He also claims that Apollonius proved that all the gold and silver at the wedding-feast was mere illusion. He did neither of these things, and I am certain in my own mind that he never told Damis exactly what did happen, although Damis seems to have learned more about the matter than he perceived at the time. He did recognize a serpent which the other diners could not see, and he did unravel a strange web of illusion in order to assist in the awkward business of my education – but the 'magic' he used was no more than memory and philosophy.

My first meeting with Apollonius was not a happy one, for Demetrius was in a very sarcastic mood when he introduced me. 'This,' he said, 'is Menippus. I do not know whether he will be a member of my school much longer, for he dwells in the gardens of Tantalus, fascinated by the luxury of his dear friend Bassus and mesmerized by the allure of an Egyptian temptress who dances – so I am told – like a snake bewitched by a charmer's pipe.'

I remember that Damis of Nineveh laughed aloud at this. Perhaps that is why he records in his memoir that his master advised me there and then that I was 'cherishing a serpent'. In fact, Apollonius said no such thing, and looked at me with a certain sympathy when he saw how hurt and embarrassed I was by my master's unkind words.

'It is good that a man should pass through the gardens of Tantalus,' Apollonius said. 'How else is he to learn that their promise is false, their reward an illusion? There will be time enough to judge Menippus when he has made his own judgement as to the worth of what is dangled before him.'

I had a speech of my own prepared. 'I met the merchant Aradus yesterday,' I told the great sage. 'He asked me if the world-renowned Apollonius of Tyana were indeed expected to arrive in Corinth today. When I said that you were, he told me that his dearest wish was that the enmity between his son Bassus and the Cynic Demetrius might be set aside for the day of his betrothal. Aradus would be greatly honoured if you and Demetrius would come together to the feast and give your blessing to the union between himself and Galanthis. He knows that you will not eat meat and do not like finery but he says that there would be fruit and bread a-plenty, and that such finery as he intends to display is not intended as an insult to the poor, but merely as a celebration of his own good fortune. He would dearly like Bassus and Demetrius to be friends again, and he hopes that your benign influence might serve to ease the bitterness between them.'

Demetrius scowled, but he dared not make any response until the great man had spoken.

'You may tell Aradus that I will come,' Apollonius said, 'but you must warn him that I cannot settle other people's quarrels with honeyed words. I am a philosopher, not an envoy of Rome. The purpose of my arguments is to arrive at the truth, not to negotiate settlements.'

'I will tell him that,' I promised. 'He will be very glad that your presence will dignify his betrothal feast.'

'So he should be,' said Damis of Nineveh – although Apollonius frowned at his impoliteness.

'There is no possibility of any reconciliation between the ideas of Bassus and those of better men,' Demetrius said, pointedly. 'His answer to the question of how men should live is that they should feed their appetites without restraint; the better answer is that men should become masters of their appetites. Luxury is the greatest barrier to the path of enlightenment.'

Demetrius looked to Apollonius for support, and I could see that he expected it; he saw the invitation to the feast of Aradus as one more phase in his battle with Bassus for the prize of my allegiance, and he trusted Apollonius to win the battle for him – but all Apollonius said in reply was: 'There is more than one path to enlightenment – and there are many barriers that might blind a man to the truth.'

Damis of Nineveh was enthusiastic to lend his support to these words, but I am sure now that he never understood their meaning.

The day of the betrothal-feast was beautiful and clear; the most superstitious of men would have searched in vain for any omen of what was to come.

I had never seen such a repast as that which Aradus laid out for his guests, for he had gone to extraordinary lengths to make sure that the day would not be forgotten. Although he was no longer the busy man he had been fifteen years before, he remembered with great fondness the days when he had built up his petty empire. His ships brought abundant cargoes from Antioch, Caesarea and Alexandria, and carried the best of Corinth's produce to Ancona and to Rome. He had been a man of great influence in his time, and he was still an example to the younger men who followed in his footsteps.

The governor himself, Marcellus Cato, had come to sit at Aradus' right hand. He had his doctor and his astrologer in close attendance, and a dozen men-at-arms under the immediate command of a centurion named Calidius. Arrayed below the governor's party were the wealthiest men in Corinth, landowners and merchants alike. They were men whose names were known to everyone: the men who determined the commerce of Corinth. Almost without exception they were accompanied by the sons and nephews who would one day inherit their wealth and their concerns. They were so many that the position left to mere philosophers – even to philosophers as famous as Apollonius of Tyana – was a long way down the line, but Apollonius made no objection to his placing and Demetrius swallowed his pride.

When we sat down Damis of Nineveh made as if to take the place at his master's left, but the sage asked him to sit to the right of Demetrius, and gave me the place Damis had tried to claim. He asked me to put names to the people in the crowd, and I did so, adding further information when I thought it relevant – which compelled me to whisper in his ear, for some of the things I said were best not overheard.

'The governor is a bitter man,' I told him, 'but not unreasonable. I know that Corinth does not rank as high in Roman estimation as its citizens think it should, and Marcellus Cato considers it a place of exile – far better, no doubt, than some tiny island in the Aegean, but no fit place for a nobleman. He was a friend of Nero but fell from favour when Nero died and was sent here by Vespasian. He has been awaiting his recall ever since Vespasian's death, but that was seven years ago and it seems that the time may never come.'

'Such is the fate of most of Nero's friends,' Apollonius observed. 'He was emperor when I was in Rome, but he did not like me and I did not stay long. My tastes were too austere for him, my philosophy too sparse. He might have preferred your friend Bassus.'

'Bassus affects to despise Rome,' I told him, in a diplomatic whisper. 'Even a man as fond of Greek ways as Nero would not meet his approval. Aradus is always lavish in his praise for the empire, but I think he conceals his real opinion.'

'There is still a tendency in Greece to think of the Romans as barbarians,' Apollonius agreed. 'It is true that they have followed where Alexander led – but it is also true that they have held what Alexander's successors lost.'

Having been seated at his right hand I could not help but try to see the feast as I imagined Apollonius saw it, through austere and forbidding eyes. The luxury of it might have seemed an unalloyed marvel had he not been there beside me, but in his presence I felt a creeping unease about its extravagance.

Galanthis was magnificently dressed in silks and golden threads, but with Apollonius beside me I could not help but see that the powders and paints with which she made up her face were masking wrinkles and flesh made soft by an indulgent life. She smiled a great deal, but my impression was that her smiles were forced, and that some dire anxiety was lurking beneath her good humour. Poor Bassus did not even bother to smile. Everyone knew that he did not want the wedding to take place, for fear that Aradus would alter his will, diverting a too-substantial part of his wealth to his new bride. Perhaps there was nothing to be gained by his pretending to enjoy himself, but I could not help but think that he was being unnecessarily churlish.

Even the food which I tasted was a little spoiled, by virtue of the fact that Apollonius hardly ate at all. The plate that had been set before him remained empty and his knife lay idle. He took what he needed between his fingers, one patient morsel at a time. I was not so deeply entranced by him that I neglected to try the dishes I had never seen before, but every time I filled my mouth I felt disappointed; it was, after all, only food – and even the best of the taste-sensations I had not previously experienced were not unusually pleasant. There was an astonishing profusion of sweetmeats, decked out in many colours and formed into many shapes – but their sweetness was, after all, only honey or beet-sugar, and the ones most cunningly wrought had been so hardened in the cooking as to endanger the teeth of anyone trying to bite into one.

'You might try one of these,' I said to Apollonius, who had finished eating long before I had sampled everything that intrigued me and had begun to make me feel uncomfortable. 'The sticky centre is like the essence of an orange – but you must suck the outer part patiently until it dissolves; there is no short cut.'

'Thank you, Menippus,' said the sage, 'but I find all such confections overly sickly. Is that the dancing girl of whom your master disapproves so strongly?'

It was indeed my beloved Nauma, decked out in all *her* finery as I had never seen her before, ready to play her part in the evening's entertainment. She jangled as she danced, for her silks were sown with hundreds of little silver coins.

The tables set out for the feast were arranged in the form of an inverted U, so Nauma danced at first in the space between the twin ends of the base, but she slowly made her way up the ranks, crossing the distance between the two limbs again and again. I had seen her dance a dozen times before, in public and in private, but this was an occasion like no other and this was a dance like no other. One still hears people speak of the Judaean Salome, who beguiled her stepfather Herod and asked for the head of some petty prophet as a tribute, but I cannot imagine that she danced more delicately or more entrancingly than Nauma danced at the betrothal-feast of Aradus and Galanthis. I had not realized how noisy the room had been until she stilled the noise, claiming a pause for the sound of the lyres and tabors which played for her, and for the magic of her movements.

I do not hesitate, in this instance, to use the word 'magic'. If there was any magic at the feast, it was certainly hers and hers alone. If there was any spell cast, it was she who cast it – but she cast it with the suppleness of her young limbs and the sinuousness of her lovely body, and the discipline of arduous training. When I saw her dance, I knew exactly why I loved her so dearly – and why every man in that great pavilion had cause to envy me.

A snake bewitched by a charmer's pipe, Demetrius had said – but she was not that. Perhaps there was something in her swaying reminiscent of the flow of a serpent's body, and something in her silks and silver trimmings that recalled the sparkle of sunlight on a serpent's scales, but there was so much more. Nauma had arms and legs, hands and feet, full lips and glorious eyes. She was a human being, through and through. Even looking at her, as I was forced to do, in the knowledge that the ascetic Apollonius was sitting beside me, I lost myself in rapt contemplation of her beauty. I am sure that others did likewise, although I saw that some few of the merchants were distracted by the coins which she now began to release from her costume and scatter about the top of the table.

I might have found an unalloyed joy in Nauma's performance had it not been that when she finally reached the climax of her dance she threw herself across the table, planting her painted lips upon the mouth of the astonished Aradus in evident tribute. I could not suppress a horrid shock of jealous rage as I saw him overcome his surprise in time to take full advantage of the kiss, pressing his lips avidly to hers. It was, I suppose, the kind of lascivious act that a man might be forgiven at his betrothal feast, but I could not help but remember what Demetrius had said to me about the cunning fisherman, and how Galanthis was using her delectable slave-girls as bait to entrap her groom.

For a moment, I did indeed see the wedding feast as the gardens of Tantalus, promising so much but without any real substance – but then I remembered that that was exactly how Demetrius wanted me to see it, in order that I might remain a Cynic like himself forever, and I wondered whether that was what I really wanted to be. I looked along the length of the tables, towards the high place where Bassus sat, but I could not catch his eye. He too was absorbed in watching Nauma, who had withdrawn from the embrace of Aradus to take her bow.

The noise returned explosively as the company burst out clapping and cheering. I looked back at Aradus, and saw that he was beating the table with his huge right hand. His mouth was closed, but there was an expression on his face that seemed close to bliss. I could not bear it, and turned to face Apollonius.

'No doubt you have seen such dances before, in the course of your travels,' I said to him, taking care to keep my voice level.

'In Egypt,' he said, 'and in India too – but not in Rome. Nero had little more taste for pretty dancing girls than your master has.' I could not judge the exact quality of his tone, but it seemed to have mellowed just a little. I studied his face, wondering whether a man of his great age could still be stirred in the loins, or whether he merely remembered a time when he might have reacted more passionately – but then the noise about the table changed again, transformed in an instant from wild applause into horror.

It was not until the centurion raced forward to take control that I realized what had happened. Calidius had to draw his sword in order to clear a space, so that his men might come forward and take up the still-writhing body of the stricken Aradus. They carried him away into the house, with Marcellus Cato's doctor in hot pursuit.

Had the death of Aradus happened on any other day I would have been cast adrift on the sea of rumour, with no more opportunity to discover what had happened than any gossiping slave. I might never have discovered the truth. But this was the day that Apollonius of Tyana had come to Corinth, and Apollonius had the reputation of being a healer without equal. Within a quarter of an hour Marcellus Cato had sent a messenger to the sage imploring him to render what assistance he could to his own doctor; because I was still at Apollonius' side, I went with him, along with Demetrius and Damis.

Damis and I were not allowed to go to the crowded bedside, so I had no opportunity to see what condition Aradus was in, but when Demetrius came out again into the antechamber I knew that the matter was very grave.

'He is dying,' Demetrius said. 'No healer in the world could save him.'

'Do not underestimate my master,' Damis said. 'I have seen him work wonders.'

Demetrius shook his head. 'The man has suffered some kind of fit,' he said. 'He was overexcited by the sight of that accursed girl, inflamed by her lewd dancing. You saw how avidly he returned her kiss. There is a lesson in this, Menippus!'

I was hurt that he should try to make argumentative capital out of such a misfortune, but I had no time to reply. Bassus came hurtling from the room then, his face contorted with fury. He stopped as soon as he saw me – but I think he would have stopped for anyone who might give him a hearing.

'Sorcery!' he said. 'Vile sorcery has killed him! That enchantress is behind it, I swear. She has killed my father! Menippus, you must help me drive her out of Corinth.'

I took this speech as an expression of grief. Bassus had never seemed overly fond of his surviving parent but a father is, after all, a father. I could not imagine that Galanthis had any reason for wanting to slay the man she had been on the point of marrying, nor was I prepared to entertain the possibility that she was a sorceress who could strike a man down with a curse, but my first impulse was to soothe my friend's distress. I went to embrace him, hoping to calm his wrath, but Demetrius caught me by the shoulder.

'Stay!' my master said. 'Clearly, the man is mad.'

'Mad he is!' The new voice came from the doorway of the

bedroom, and I knew it was Galanthis before I turned to look. She waited until we were all staring at her before she continued. 'There is only one man here who had motive for murder,' she declared, 'and *there* he stands.' She was pointing a long-nailed finger at Bassus. 'He feared the loss of all his expectations, and he made haste to strike – to deny the father who patiently bore the burden of his every excess a few lost years of happiness. Murderer! Patricide!'

What Bassus had said had astonished me, but this tirade left me thunderstruck. I could not believe that the Phoenician meant her accusations seriously, and imagined that they had been provoked by an ugly combination of grief and wrath – grief at the death of her intended spouse and wrath occasioned by his wild talk of sorcery.

Just as I had moved towards Bassus, Demetrius and Damis moved towards Galanthis. They did not embrace her but she took their movement for approval. 'See!' she said to Bassus. 'They know what you are! Everyone shall know it!'

In his memoir – which separates the incident from the wrongly attributed betrothal-feast – Damis says that Apollonius argued with Bassus and called him patricide, but it was Damis and Demetrius who stood with the angry Phoenician and supported her words with their stares, while I clung hard to Bassus, making sure that he could not react violently to the slander. Demetrius met my eyes, and I could tell that he was instructing me to consider carefully what company I was keeping, but it was Damis who opened his mouth to speak and his manner suggested that he was not about to play the peacemaker.

What Damis would have said only Damis knows, and I suspect that the accusations he now credits to Apollonius were the product of a later fancy. At the time, he was silenced by the entry of Marcellus Cato, who pushed past Galanthis to take a stand between the two accusers. 'Be silent!' he commanded them both. 'It is *my* place to discover whether any murder has been done, and *my* place to determine the responsibility. Are you mad, both of you? Whatever you think or feel, at least be quiet while the poor man lies upon his bed, fighting for his life.'

Bassus' reaction to this instruction was to throw up his hands and turn on his heel. He marched off, not bothering to look at me again, let alone invite me to follow. I could not help thinking that it was not the behaviour expected of a philosopher, nor even of a man of common sense.

'A man should be master of his feelings,' murmured Demetrius, unable to resist the temptation, 'not their slave.' His eyes were still fixed on me, and for once I had no reply. I looked at the ground between my feet.

Galanthis hesitated for a moment, but then she went back into the bedchamber, presumably to wait by the bedside of her husband-to-be. The governor followed her. I heard no more voices raised in anger within the chamber – merely a low hum of whispered discussion.

'My master will know the truth,' Damis said, loftily. 'Nothing escapes him, though lesser men are oft deluded.' He named no 'lesser men' but it was obvious that distaste for Roman upstarts was not confined to Greece. I considered the possibility that the men of Nineveh and Babylon – whose empire had fallen to Alexander as Alexander's had fallen to Rome – might see Greeks and Romans in much the same harsh light.

Eventually, Apollonius came out, accompanied by the governor's doctor and astrologer. Marcellus Cato and Calidius followed two or three paces behind, with the steward of the household.

'It was a natural fit,' the doctor opined, 'brought on by age and excitement.'

'I am not so sure,' the astrologer said. 'There might indeed be sorcery at work here. I can sense its presence.'

The governor, who seemed to be well used to such disagreements, sighed in exasperation. 'What do you say, Cappadocian?' he asked Apollonius.

'I have seen the symptoms before,' Apollonius replied, equably. 'When a man has a reputation as a healer, he is forever being summoned to the sick and dying, and he learns to read the signs. This is a puzzling case, in that I have never seen the signs so dire, but I can say with certainty that no sorcery was involved.'

'Nor was any poison,' said the steward, quickly. He was so anxious to avoid questions being asked regarding his own areas of responsibility that he did not wait to see whether anyone would raise the question.

'Certainly not,' Marcellus Cato was quick to say. He had been sitting beside the stricken man, taking his food from the same plates and pouring his wine from the same flasks.

'The food was tasted,' Calidius growled. 'Wherever a Roman governor comes to eat, the food is tasted – even in Corinth.' The tone of his voice implied, unjustly, that Corinth was no safer than Damascus or Castra Regina.

'I smell sorcery,' said the astrologer, still smarting beneath Apollonius' contradiction. 'No matter what the Cappadocian says . . .'

'Utter nonsense,' said the doctor. 'A natural fit. The man had cultivated his pleasures excessively. Long overindulgence in food and wine leads in the end to an exhaustion of the flesh.' He glanced at Apollonius as he said this, obviously expecting approval. The sage said nothing, although Demetrius nodded his head vigorously.

The governor was still looking at Apollonius. 'Is that true, Master Philosopher?' he said. 'Was it the merchant's way of life which determined the manner of his death?'

For the merest instant I thought I saw the ghost of a smile hovering upon the sage's lips. 'I believe you have stated the case exactly, sir,' he said.

The governor bowed his head in acknowledgement of the compliment. 'In the absence of evidence to the contrary,' he said, glancing at his astrologer as he stressed the word *evidence*, 'it seems to me that this is a clear case of death by natural causes. When the son and the wife-to-be have calmed down, I will hear what they have to say – but if they wish to bring forward any accusations that would make this sad affair the business of Rome, they had better have proof, for I will tolerate no baseless slanders.' His gaze flickered back and forth, from the astrologer to the doctor to the steward, then from Apollonius to Demetrius to Calidius, and finally from Damis to me. He knew that what he said would be reported back to Bassus, and what he said was intended to be thus reported. In a quieter voice, speaking to Apollonius alone, the governor added: 'You had better go now, Master Philosopher.'

Apollonius nodded, and allowed Demetrius to lead him away. I followed, with Damis of Nineveh.

Apollonius was not called to give any further testimony in the case. Bassus made no further accusations against Galanthis, nor she against him – but that did not stop the rumours. Whatever barriers there are to enlightenment there are none to vile whispers.

Word flew to the city walls and beyond, saying that Aradus had been murdered by sorcery or poison, and that Bassus had done it to make sure of his inheritance. It transpired that the will of Aradus had not been changed to the disadvantage of Bassus, although the dead man had left behind a letter requesting that Bassus should treat Galanthis generously, and this revelation added fuel to the speculation. The fact that Galanthis accepted the situation was construed as evidence that he had bought her silence and the more ingenious rumour-mongers went so far as to wonder whether the two of them had conspired together to cause the death of Aradus because they were secret lovers impatient to acquire his wealth.

Throughout the next two days I was pestered by people who knew that I had been with Apollonius when he had been summoned to Aradus' bedside. I soon became impatient with them because I had troubles of my own, whose pressure on my heart and mind increased inexorably. My first thought after quitting the company of Demetrius and Apollonius had been to find Nauma and see how she was faring – but she was nowhere to be found. The house of Aradus was in such confusion that it was not easy to pursue my search, and I was eventually persuaded to leave it for the morrow, but when I went back again and still found no trace of her I became very anxious.

Galanthis said that she did not know where Nauma was, and did not seem to care. None of the Phoenician's other servants had seen her go, or knew of anywhere she might have gone. I could not believe that she had left the city without even pausing to say goodbye to me, but there was no trace of her within its walls.

It was a mystery – far more of a mystery, so far as I was concerned, than the death of Aradus. It seemed obvious to me that the two events were connected somehow, and it seemed so to the rumour-mongers too, who quickly began to speculate that Nauma had been the instrument of Bassus and Galanthis, and had been sent away lest she tell what she knew. I was sure that this was untrue, because Bassus swore to me that he had no knowledge whatsoever of the girl's whereabouts, but I was sorely confused as to what the real situation might be.

In the end, I decided to take my problem to Apollonius. I felt, however, that I had to speak to him alone, for I knew Demetrius would certainly be angry with me and I suspected that Damis would laugh at me. While I awaited my opportunity I tried to look at the matter as he would undoubtedly look at it, through the eyes of a philosopher, so that I would not seem too much of a fool when I laid it out before him.

Night had fallen for the second time since the betrothal feast by the time I finally found the chance to be alone with Apollonius. Demetrius and Damis had gone to their beds, and so had everyone else – even Cynics need sleep, but Apollonius, it seemed, had progressed beyond mere Cynicism to some further realm of mental existence.

'I need the benefit of your wisdom,' I told him.

'Perhaps you do,' he agreed. 'Come walk with me, and we shall see what benefit we can derive from careful discussion.'

We walked together in the moonlight, up the hill that stands above the southern quarter of the town. We paused on a ridge, from which we could look back over the rooftops, towards the quays where the merchants' ships loaded and unloaded their goods. While we went I told him everything – not merely that Nauma had disappeared, but *everything*. I told him how I felt about her, and how it had weakened my faith in the doctrines of Demetrius and forced me to take the ideas of Bassus more seriously than before. I told him that I could not see why philosophers could not live like other men rather than in retreat from society, or why they were better not to marry. I told him that I could not see why love was such a threat to the philosophical calmness of mind, although I was beginning to understand that the passions aroused by its loss might blot out the capacity for reason.

'Your reason does not seem to me to have been entirely blotted out,' Apollonius said. 'Tell me, Menippus, what is it that you fear most? Is it the possibility that you may never see your lovely dancer again, or the possibility that she might not have been what you supposed?'

I paused to consider that question carefully, knowing that my answer would determine what he thought of me. In the end, I said: 'What I fear most is that she might have been murdered, to prevent her telling what she knew about the death of Aradus.' I knew it was a risk, but I had carefully thought over what Apollonius had said when he was asked to judge the cause of the merchant's death – and I remembered the ghost of a smile which had haunted his final statement.

'Ah!' he said. 'I doubt that you need fear that. Would you really rather think that she is alive, but does not care about you? Many men, I suspect, would rather think that she had loved them so dearly that only death could keep her from them.'

'I would rather she were alive,' I said. I hope that I was telling the truth. 'I would rather that, even if it meant that she was only amusing herself with me until the time came to do what she had to do.'

'And what do you think she did?' he asked me, although he knew as well as I did.

I was unable to look him in the eye, but I answered him. 'When she kissed Aradus at the conclusion of her dance,' I said, slowly, 'something passed from her mouth to his. He did not open his mouth to cheer, you see, when she had finished, although he pounded the table with all his might. It was one of those sweetmeats, I suppose. The poison was hidden inside a hard sugary coat, unreleased until he had sucked it through.'

Apollonius said nothing in reply to that. He looked out over the city of Corinth as if he were weighing it in the balance – and not merely the city but everything it signified: its history; its commerce; its role in the affairs of empire.

'What kind of poison was it?' I asked him, delicately.

'I had seen the symptoms before,' he said, eventually. 'Always in association with the bite of a snake – usually the Egyptian cobra. In Alexandria they call it Cleopatra's last lover'

'The asp,' I said, to demonstrate that I had knowledge of my own.

'What puzzled me when I attended Aradus,' Apollonius went .on, 'is that the bite of the asp is very rarely fatal, in my experience. Whatever they may say about Cleopatra, I have never seen anyone but a small child die of a cobra bite. In India they have much bigger snakes called hamadryads, whose bite is said to be far more deadly, but I saw snake-charmers in India who had little or no fear of the creatures they employed. It's not easy to know which rumours are to be trusted and which are not, is it, Menippus?'

It did not seem necessary to confirm my agreement with that judgement.

'Surely she cannot have known what she was doing,' I said, 'else she'd never have allowed such a treacherous thing into her mouth. If she was ordered to do it by her mistress, why? If she was paid to do it, by whom? And how was the poison obtained? There is no cobra nearer than Persia or Palestine.'

'I watched the snake-charmers of India most carefully,' Apollonius told me. 'They would not have told me their secret, of course, even if I had not been silent at the time, so I felt that I had to find it out. I made a game of it – I made games of many such quests while I was clinging to my silly vow. At first I thought that they were simply quick enough to avoid the strikes of their playthings – there are creatures call mongooses which kill cobras easily enough by means of their agility. Then I wondered whether the charmers might build up a tolerance to the bites. In the end, I caught one unawares while he was preparing his toys. He was milking its venom into a wooden cup, extracting the creature's entire supply of poison. He had five snakes in all; I imagine that he built up a concentration of venom far greater than any ordinary bite was likely to communicate. He simply threw it away – I thought at the time that it was profligate, that such a commodity might be saleable. Perhaps it can be stored indefinitely in a vial, or preserved in some sticky syrup like the one in the centre of one of those horrible sweetmeats you urged me to try.'

The sweetmeats had not seemed horrible to me while I sucked

them at the feast – but they have always seemed so since I talked
to Apollonius.

'Who gave it to her?' I wanted to know. '*Was* it Galanthis?'

'Galanthis had nothing to gain,' Apollonius said. 'She is
dependent on the generosity of Bassus now – and you know better
than I what that is worth.'

'Bassus, then?' I whispered. 'Can he really have been so
desperate?'

'You know better than I,' Apollonius repeated.

'I don't believe it,' I said. 'In any case, had he been minded to
put his father away he'd never have chosen such a method and he'd
have found a far more convenient time. But who, then?'

'Who is left?' he parried.

I still remembered the ghost of his smile. He had already delivered
his verdict: it was the manner in which Aradus had lived his life that
had determined the manner of his death.

'Marcellus Cato?' I suggested. 'Is it possible that the *governor*
murdered Aradus? Is that why you said nothing when he declared
that no murder had been committed? Did you think he would strike
you down if you denounced him?'

'I think he recognized the hand of his masters, as I did,'
Apollonius said. 'Perhaps he was meant to. There are those in
Rome who reckon that it is always a good idea to remind dissatisfied
exiles that they have not been forgotten. Calidius is a more likely
assassin. It was he who fetched me to see the body, he who studied
me most carefully as I made my replies. I think we understood one
another well enough, Calidius and I. I am an ancient philosopher,
he is an ambitious centurion – we have no reason to quarrel. The
likelihood is that he and the girl were working in collusion. You
must hope so, if you told me the truth. A mere pawn would be
dead by now, but not a skilled executioner whose services would
soon be needed elsewhere.'

I thought about those possibilities for a minute or two before
moving on to the next question. 'Why?' I asked. 'Why should
Rome want Aradus dead?'

'I'm a philosopher,' Apollonius said, 'not an oracle. I can only
guess.'

I did not need to tell him that I rated a philosopher's guesses
far more highly than an oracle's pronouncements. I simply said:
'Go on.'

'We must consider the time and the place,' he said. 'Assassins
usually work by night, brutally and secretly. When they work by
day, it is because they have a point to make. If Cato might have been

expected to find a message in the incident, so might others. This was not merely a murder; it was the interruption of a feast celebrating the betrothal of two people long connected by their business. Did you look closely at any of those coins which the dancer let fall?'

'No,' I admitted.

'I have never used money,' Apollonius said. 'It has always been a point of pride – but perhaps it was also a stubborn refusal to submit to temptation. Money is so fascinating, is it not? Such a wonderful invention. Whatever tales we tell of the military genius of Alexander, the true heart of the Greek empire was coin. Before Athens, all cities grew their own food in their own fields; Athens was the first to obtain its food by trade, putting its artisans to work in the manufacture of goods for the marketplace, and it was *money* which made the marketplace possible. For four centuries after Solon, it is said, the Athenian drachma held its real value: sixty-seven grains of silver before Alexander, sixty-five thereafter – and then came Rome. The *denarius* held its real value while Augustus was emperor, but Tiberius and Claudius began the debasement which Nero completed. Now, the value of a coin is determined by the authority of the emperor whose head is stamped upon it rather than by the value of the metal it contains. Anyone with the skill to make alloys and a crude stamp can increase the supposed value of their metal four- or five-fold by making an image of the emperor. Small wonder that they do – and small wonder that the Romans resent that kind of usurpation. They think of forgery as the rot that might eat away their empire from within, refusing to admit that the *real* rot is the pretence that an emperor's authority can sustain more value in a coin than it would have in ordinary barter.'

I did not know for sure that Aradus had been a forger, or a dealer in false coin, but I knew that it was more than likely. Corinth lay on the trade routes linking Rome to the east, to lands which resented Roman dominion even more than Greece. It was common knowledge that since Nero had debased the coinage so dramatically every metalworker in Asia Minor was seeking to take advantage of the excessive purchasing power of their stock-in-trade. Every merchant at the top table had probably taken a hand in such dealings – and Marcellus Cato too.

'All that glisters is not gold,' I murmured, 'and all that sparkles is not silver.' I did not mean it literally, and Apollonius knew it.

'I dare say that she liked you well enough,' he said, softly. 'You're a handsome youth, after all – but she always knew that you were a philosopher. You *are* a philosopher, Menippus, no matter what Demetrius may think – and there *are* more paths than one to enlightenment, and more ways than one to cross the barriers which block the way. Be a Cynic by all means, but be a realist too. Love if you can; marry if you must – but choose your lovers and your wife with the same care you'd use in choosing a philosophy. There's a good deal of false coin in every marketplace in the world, and I doubt that the world will ever see the end of it now it's begun.'

He was still staring over the rooftops at the distant quays.

'They say that Corinth was a great city,' I reflected, 'before the Romans came . . .' I didn't bother to finish the sentence. All cities had been great before the Romans came, just as all merchants had been honest and all pigs had had wings.

Apollonius said nothing more. He waited for me to move on, and I did. I led the way back down the hill, thinking about murder and justice and love. I didn't ask Apollonius why he hadn't declared that Aradus had been murdered, preferring to let his scrupulously truthful words be misinterpreted and misused. It wasn't that he was scared of retribution; it was because he was a philosopher. Rome was the murderer and false money the motive; Rome was also the law and the falsifier of the money. Apollonius stood aside from all of that; the truth he sought was a higher and finer kind.

'A man does not have to be as self-denying as you are in order to cultivate wisdom,' I told him, defensively. I meant every word, but I was amazed by my own temerity in framing it as a positive statement rather than a cringing question. 'There is room even in a wise man's heart for a little lust and a little comfort.'

'Perhaps there is,' he answered. 'I purged myself so ruthlessly in the fever of my youth that I could not recover any such impulse if I tried, but you might find a better way. At any rate, you must find your *own* way. By all means learn all you can from Demetrius and Bassus, but in the end it is yourself that you must know, yourself that you must make, yourself that you must prove.'

I knew that. I know it still, and I am not dissatisfied with what I am. I would not want to be a magician or a prophet, even in an Age of Miracle-Workers.

'I do love her,' I told him, as we parted. 'I fear that without her love, I'll never be as good a man as I might have been.'

'She might return, in time,' Apollonius said, more kindly than I deserved. 'If she loves you, she'll come back.'

She never did, of course.

[*Author's Note*: The only account of the life of Apollonius of Tyana to have survived into modern times is that written by Philostratus in the 3rd century AD. This was allegedly based on memoirs compiled by Damis of Nineveh, a disciple and companion of Apollonius, although some commentators have suspected that these never existed, Philostratus having invented them to lend weight to his rather fanciful account. The statements and opinions attributed by Menippus to Damis in the story are, of course, all derived from Philostratus.]

A GREEN BOY

Anthony Price

Anthony Price is probably best known for his novels about David Audley of British Intelligence that began with The Labyrinth Makers *(1970). My own favourite is* Our Man in Camelot *(1975), set at an archaeological excavation on a suspected Arthurian site. Price has written a couple of short stories set in Roman Britain, 'The Boudicca Killing' and the following, both featuring the investigations of the battle-weary soldier Gaius Celerius, during the early years of the Roman occupation.*

∾

From Gnaeus Julius Agricola to Marcus Publius Lupus, greeting!

You are absolutely right, of course: this year's campaign has been prosecuted with special vigour because our esteemed general and governor has been thirsting for a great victory of his own in Britain ever since his unfortunate experience long ago at the hands of that frightful woman Boadicea.

You are right, too, about our little scandal, though this did not occur during field operations, but rather while we were settling the army into winter quarters.

To be brief, my dear Lupus, we began to lose valuable corn convoys in ambushes along the northern road network. In view of the late season and the high prices prevailing this loss was serious in itself; but more disturbing was that Marcus Florentius, whom I had promoted to be chief of local intelligence, smelt treachery.

Florentius, as you know, has a nose for such things, yet in this instance was quite unable to substantiate his suspicions with proof.

The convoys had been utterly destroyed, the waggons burnt and the men massacred. Moreover he could produce no motive for any betrayal, since the civilian teamsters are carefully recruited from the tribes' hereditary enemies, and the tribesmen themselves are now far too poor to be able to bribe any of our officers, even supposing they possessed the impudence to attempt it.

In deference to Florentius, however, I agreed to send a senior agent undercover – none other than your old staff quartermaster, Gaius Celer, whose unique knowledge of the area and routes concerned (he sited most of those forts himself) commended him to me.

In fact he had no luck and losses continued to mount, until he received news of an ambush less than a day's journey from our main forward supply depot. As usual it was a corn convoy, but this time a soldier of the escort had escaped.

Celer assumed this would be some addle-pated Batavian, and rode half the night to get to him while the details would be still fresh in his mind; instead, to his astonishment, he found a probationer-officer – one of those babies the governors over the water foist on the legions to do someone (not Caesar!) a good turn, a green boy who –

For one befuddled moment Clodius thought it was morning.

Then his senses began to register conflicting information. Morning in this muddy nowhere was cold and dark, but it was also shouted orders and jangling harness from the Batavian horse-lines nearby, not silence and a single bright flame which hurt his eyes; and certainly not a rougher hand on his shoulder than ever any orderly would have dared to lay.

This was something else, and because he didn't want it to be morning he was grateful for that conclusion for a brief additional moment before reality and the camp-major's parting promises caught up with him.

Better to have died back there with the others: he rubbed his eyes to clear them of sleep and saw in his mind again the rolling bloodshot eye of the draught horse as he grabbed at its mane . . . that had been the instant of choice when he might have saved himself this agony. Except that it had seemed no choice then, but a natural instinct.

'Come on, then – wake up!'

The words were as rough and insistent as the hand, and he was unable to react to either with dignity.

'What is it?' he mumbled thickly, raising himself on an elbow. It wasn't even near morning, he decided, because he was still light-headed from the wine rather than sickened by it.

The man with the too-bright lantern raised it higher, driving the

shadows over the empty cots onto the wall of the hut beyond them.
Now he could see the speaker more clearly, and was surprised and
confused by what he saw. It was not one of the officers of the
camp-major's guard, but just another anonymous quartermaster.
The depot was crawling with them – leathery veterans with
preoccupied faces or self-important fat men with flabby jowls, little
monkey clerks dancing attendance – all persons of little account in
Clodius' estimation.

This was one of the leathery ones, the greyest and most grizzled of
them, habitually wrapped in a long mud-splattered cloak and often
ridiculously astride a tiny bristling pony.

A flash of lantern-light on metal behind the grey man caught his
attention: yet those were not clerks half-shadowed in the doorway, he
realized with sudden fear, but two of the German mounted irregulars
in full battle-order, shaggy giants with blank faces –

He turned back to the quartermaster. It had to be the lost waggons.
Or maybe the drivers and whatever else had been lashed down under
those canvas sheets – the old fool had come to curse him for the lost
convoy!

If it had happened to anyone else it would have been amusing, but
it was happening to him and he felt like bursting into tears again . . .
only it was too late for tears, for the waggons, for the men – and
most of all for himself.

He sat up, brushing ineffectually at the cobwebs of hair on
his face.

'What do you want?'

Silly question: the fellow wanted his burned waggons and dead
drivers back. Or maybe his hundred and eight mules and twelve
draught-horses. No, eleven draught-horses –

'I want you awake first.'

'What for?' It was a sullen obstinacy that now began to wake
inside him. He would be condemned, but he was not condemned
yet, and no superannuated tally-man had the right to persecute him
in the middle of the night, even if it was his last night on earth.

'To answer my questions.' The quartermaster stripped the cloak
off the cot and thrust it at him. 'Wrap that round you, boy. And
get your feet on the ground.'

Clodius clutched the thick folds to his chest, his defiance melting
in the face of undoubted authority. Besides, the German savages
at the door unnerved him; they were at once notoriously obedient
to their orders and oblivious of the niceties of military law. They
would chop him into pieces at a word without a second thought.

He draped the cloak awkwardly round his shoulders and swung

his feet off the cot. For a second the flame of the lantern blurred and danced as the hut lurched around him. Then his vision cleared and he fumbled with his toes for his boots. It was an instinctive movement: in any night emergency on the frontier boots and sword came first, with everything else unimportant. His eyes followed his thought to where his sword hung on its peg, just out of reach.

As suddenly as he had stripped off the cloak from the cot, the quartermaster leaned sideways and hooked the weapon off the wall, offering it to Clodius hilt first.

'If it makes you feel any better –' he nodded and grunted – 'but if I'd come here to murder you – you'd be twitching by now, I can tell you.'

The hilt was ice-cold in Clodius' hand, but the wind of suspicion in his brain was even colder, dissipating the lingering wine fumes there. Quartermasters didn't tramp the depot in the small hours, but slept warm in well-furnished billets. Nor did quartermasters have Germans at their back –

'The convoy was ambushed?'

Clodius stared at him, then nodded mutely.

'Speak when I question you. I like to hear a man's voice.' The grey man spoke softly this time, but the sharp edge of his words was not lost on Clodius. 'So they ambushed the convey, then?'

'Yes.' The word, working its way over the lump in his throat, sounded half-strangled.

'And you survived.'

There seemed no answer to that shameful statement of fact, yet the grey man was still regarding him questioningly. Quite suddenly Clodius knew that an answer was required, but he could think of absolutely nothing to say. He had lost his first command and he had saved his own skin – that was the beginning and end of the story, and of his military career. And of his life.

'The – the gods were with me.'

It sounded hollow now, after what the camp-major had said, a mockery rather than a deliverance. Silence descended on the hut, and with it the dreadful loneliness which had weighed down increasingly on him ever since he had come to Britain. What had once seemed a great adventure under the wide blue skies of home had bogged down in endless nightmare under these eternal grey ones as he had journeyed northwards. It had only been endurable because he could tell himself that it would end once he had reached his legion. But now he would never reach it.

'What's your posting?'

Despair had dulled his wits again: he stared at his tormentor uncomprehendingly.

'What's your posting, boy?'

'The Twentieth.'

'Valeria . . . a good legion. And your regiment?'

The inevitable question.

'The Ninth!'

The grey man would know enough to draw all the obvious conclusions from that: the meagre political influence necessary to set Clodius's foot on the very lowest rung of the ladder was not going to protect him from retribution a thousand miles north, beyond the edge of civilization. It would be months before the municipality of Narbonne learnt of his fate, if they ever did; and then there would be nothing left for them to do except to forget it.

He waited for the equally inevitable snide insult, but the grey man merely nodded at him.

'And how long have you been at this depot?'

'How long?' Clodius repeated nervously, caught by the change in direction of the question. 'Three days – no, f-four days.'

'Four days?' The lantern light glinted on the man's teeth as he clicked them in surprise. 'Four days! Then you begin to become even more remarkable – I'm almost inclined to believe you have divine protection. Do you know why you are remarkable?'

So it was to be sarcasm, not petty insults, thought Clodius bitterly.

'Speak up – do you know why?'

'B-because I ran away.'

'Ran away?' The grey head shook in disagreement. 'Running away isn't remarkable. Think again.'

Clodius closed his aching eyes. The sarcasm was waiting in ambush just ahead somewhere, as unavoidable as the ambush which had destroyed everything.

'Well?'

'I don't know.' The ache beat like a pulse. The whole thing was a pointless cruelty. Why couldn't they go away?

'You're not thinking.'

Not thinking. That was true: he wasn't thinking and he didn't want to think, because every thought came back to the same fearful place. It was why he had drunk the wine to the last dregs – to dull the images of thought. The wine had been the only kindness he had received, and even that had now turned sour.

'Does it matter?' he said wearily. 'I ran away, that's all.'

'Everyone runs away. There was a time our general ran away

back in the Rising. Did you know that, boy? He lost a battlegroup of the Ninth – three full regiments. Did you know that?'

Clodius's mind clouded with bewilderment. He was being told something, but it was beyond his comprehension what it was, just as three whole regiments stretched beyond his ability to imagine. All he could see was the creaking intractable line of his own lost waggons, elongated over miles of trackway when the going was firm and then bunching into a jam of steaming animals and jabbering drivers every time the mud slowed the lead cart no matter how he raved at them.

'You still don't understand?'

'I – I –' Clodius gave up the struggle, staring abjectly at his boots. 'No.'

'Very good.' The grey man sounded as though he had received a full and satisfactory answer at last to a difficult question. 'So now you will tell me just what happened. Take your time and I won't bite you.'

Clodius looked at him stupidly, searching the hard face for a clue – any clue – as to what was happening to him. Somewhere outside in the darkness he heard the night-guard call the second change of watch: it was still four hours short of dawn.

He moistened his lips, swallowed the lump in his throat and tried to gather his wits.

'I was – I mean we were trying to free the cart – the lead cart –'

He stopped as the memory of the trooper's shocked expression came back. They had stared at each other across the tilted, mud-caked wheel. There had been mud on the man's face too, and on his hand as he plucked at the little arrow in his neck just above the iron torque he wore. He hadn't made a sound when it had hit him: he hadn't screamed until his hand had touched it, as though until then he hadn't believed it was there. And then –

'Not the ambush. Start at the beginning.' The grey man's voice interrupted the black memory. 'Just make your report to me as you did to the camp-major, boy.'

The drift of the grey man's questions, confusing though they were, had kindled a tiny flicker of hope inside Clodius. But the mention of the camp-major instantly extinguished the flicker: beside that hideous memory the present seemed unreal, and no mere recounting of the facts would make them any different, or any less disgraceful.

'The – he didn't want to hear from me –' His mouth was dry and his tongue seemed to fill it, '– he said –'

The words wouldn't come out. It was as though saying them out loud would only make them more certain.

'He said? Come on, out with it!'

'He said – he'd have me crucified.'

The grey man frowned. 'For what?'

'For – cowardice . . . for running away.'

'He doesn't have the power.'

'But he said – the General –' Clodius blinked back the tears he could no longer control, '– he said the General never forgives cowardice.'

'Nonsense!'

'But –'

'But nothing. I don't care if you're the biggest coward from here to the Golden Milestone – it doesn't matter that you ran away. It matters that you *got* away. Can't you get that through your thick head?'

Clodius sat rigidly, his sheathed sword clasped to his breast. The pain and dizziness in his head had almost linked up with an increasing uncertainty in his stomach. A wave of nausea warned him that before very long he would be sick, humiliatingly and disgustingly sick. He knew only that he couldn't fight the rising sickness and at the same time take in the contradictory things which were being said to him.

'Look you, boy –' the insistent voice was far off and almost gentle now '– why do you think we have half a legion and seven auxiliary regiments spread over this territory?'

Why? If it was a good question it had never occurred to him to think of it. The army was where it was.

'We have conquered it –' Clodius gulped air, '– so we occupy it.'

'We have conquered nothing and we occupy no more than the ground we stand on. So why do we stand on it? Why do we build our forts?'

Why?

'To – to protect our men . . . so that they can stand siege –'

It was a stupid answer and he knew it.

'Stand siege? These poor barbarians couldn't lay siege to a plate of cold porridge – it is we who besiege them, boy . . . Now listen – listen carefully –'

The dark eyes held him.

'We have beaten them all summer, from the hills to the sea and back. We have killed their young men and plundered their farms and eaten their cattle. But we haven't conquered them because

we haven't broken their spirit. And that is what we are about
to do.'

There was nothing in the world except the eyes and the
voice now.

'They are starving now, but that is not enough. While they starve
they must look down and see us warm and snug and well-fed, sitting
on their best land – and know that we shall sit there this winter and
the next and the next . . . and watching our forts – *smelling* our
forts – that will break their hearts more surely than a dozen lost
battles.

'But to do this our forts must be supplied down to the last measure
of corn and the last pint of oil and the last nail and the last bale
of hay. And do you know how much it takes to feed a soldier of
Rome, boy? Did they teach you that before they promised you your
vine-stick?'

The voice shook – was it with anger or emotion? – as though the
measures of corn and oil were gold and silver.

'But you'll learn – if you live you'll learn!' For once the grey man
wanted no answer. 'One-third of a ton of corn and a cubic yard
of granary space for every man for every year, and three thousand
pints of barley for every horse. And you'll know more about lentils
and hard-tack than the campaigns of the Divine Julius before you're
finished.'

He leant forward until his face was so close that the smell of
sweat and oiled leather and damp cloth enveloped Clodius.

'Four supply convoys we've lost out of this base – yours is the
fifth. And the first snows not six weeks ahead if we're unlucky, and
not half the winter quarters fully provisioned. We don't know how
and we don't know why. But maybe you know, because you are the
first and only survivor we've had. And if it takes a crucifixion stake
on the parade ground to make you remember what you know, then
so be it – the choice is yours, boy.'

Clodius gaped at him, dismayed. 'But I – I don't – I mean, what
if I don't –?'

'I'll be the judge of what you know.' The grey man straightened
up abruptly. 'Who commanded the convoy?'

Clodius looked at him in surprise. It was the last question he
expected. Obviously the man had come straight from – from
somewhere outside the base without speaking to anyone.

'Why – I did.'

'You –?' The grey man's tone was incredulous rather than
insulting. '*You* did?'

'I mean, I was second-in-command, but –' Clodius heard his

own voice hoarse and far off. '– He – the captain had a fever in
the night. He – they said he couldn't ride.'

'They?'

'The camp-major – he said there was no one else.'

Pale, watery dawn, with the mist hanging over the damp ground
beyond the open gateway . . . the line of loaded waggons in the rutted
park beside the gate and the organized chaos of the harnessing-up,
with the drivers twittering in their own sing-song dialect, little dark
men with greasy top-knots who pushed and pulled at the docile,
soundless mules. And the handful of Batavian auxiliaries standing
sullenly by their ponies . . . and the camp-major, with the fat senior
quartermaster well-muffled against the morning chill beside him,
controlling the whole scene simply by his presence, so it had seemed
to Clodius. For which he was abjectly grateful, since no one took
any notice of him and he had no idea what orders to give them
anyway . . .

'Go on!'

'There was no one else – no one to spare.'

'You've said that already. Go on.'

'He – he said to keep them moving, to keep them closed up tight.
No unnecessary halts – just the midday one for the mules.'

'You knew about the other convoys?'

Clodius nodded. 'He said I – the sergeant could bring back the
empty waggons and I – I could go on to my regiment.'

'I mean –' the grey head shook wearily '– the other convoys. Did
you know we'd already lost four convoys on the north road?'

Clodius grappled desperately with the implications of the question. If his only hope lay in being helpful then it would be a blunder
to admit to the extent of his ignorance, even though it wasn't
his fault.

'I knew that – that there'd been trouble,' he compromised
cautiously.

'Did you know about the other convoys?' The repeated question
had an undertone of irritation.

Clodius rocked nervously on the edge of the cot. 'Well not exactly.
I mean, not in detail –' He couldn't bring himself to add that since
none of the officers in the depot had addressed one word to him
outside the line of duty most of what little he knew had been not
heard so much as overheard. But a lame explanation would be worse
than none at all: he had to defend himself somehow.

He stared bitterly at the grey man. It was all the more unbearable because it was so hideously unfair: if he had been Quintus Petillius Cerialis himself he couldn't have saved the damn convoy. Until the ambush he had even made better time than usual if what the Dacian captain had said was true.

'He said to keep them moving and I did – we made good time, as good as anyone could have done. It's a rotten road – the bushes have been cut back, but there's no proper surface on it yet. There's mud –'

'I know the road. I marked it out myself,' said the grey man sharply. 'You made good time – go on!'

'We – well, we didn't see anything suspicious – there wasn't a sign of anything. No smoke signals, no fresh tracks. There was no warning at all – we were almost there –'

'Where?'

'At the fort – we were almost at the fort.'

'Where were you?'

'There's a ford across a stream – the road comes down off the high ground, the engineers have made a cutting – there's a log corduroy and I think the ford's paved – I think it is –'

'I know the place.'

'Well, it was quite near the fort –'

'Five thousand and six hundred paces to be exact. And they hit you as you were crossing?'

'Y-yes – not exactly –'

'How – exactly?'

'How?' Clodius flinched at the memory of the little arrow in the trooper's neck. He had been looking down at the wheel sunk almost to its axle in the mud beyond the edge of the corduroy. They were so close to home that he had shaken off his fear and his mind seethed with useless anger at the driver's incompetence and the stupidity of the men who had been trying to lift the heavily loaded waggon back onto the logs . . . He had opened his mouth, but before he could speak something had flashed past his face soundlessly and the arrow had sprouted in the man's neck, a little reedy thing with bedraggled flights, like a child's toy.

'How – did – they – ambush – you?' The words were evenly spaced, each with the same controlled emphasis.

'I – I was at the rear of the convoy –' Clodius tried to keep his voice steady, '– to keep them moving. One of the escort came back – he said the lead cart had gone off the logs at the edge of the stream. It was – half on them and half off, so the other waggons couldn't get past it.'

'So what did you do?'

'I rode to the front – they were trying to lift the waggon, but I knew they wouldn't be able to – I told them to unharness the horses.' He blinked under the grey man's concentrated stare. 'The two front carts were drawn by horses, not mules –'

'Where was the driver?' cut in the grey man sharply.

'The driver?' All the natives were alike to Clodius, their expressions as inscrutable as their camp-Latin was incomprehensible. 'I don't remember.'

'Then start remembering. Who unharnessed the horses? Was it the driver?'

'Well –' Clodius frowned with the effort of trying to recall the minor details of a confused scene. 'I think – no – there was a trooper holding the horses when I arrived. I didn't see the driver.'

'It didn't occur to you that was suspicious?'

'No –' The contempt in the voice brought up Clodius short. But there was nothing surprising in the driver's taking fright, surely . . . if he had driven the cart off the logway he would naturally have made himself scarce before the convoy commander arrived.

The grey man snorted. 'So – what happened then?'

For the third time the arrow flashed across Clodius' memory.

'They came on us. They were – they were waiting for us, hundreds of them – lying in the bracken on each side. There wasn't any way of stopping them –' His voice faltered. If the man couldn't understand the hopelessness of it – his handful of troopers strung along the trackway, half of them already dismounted, against that howling naked mob.

And the horror of it too, with the animals snorting and rearing, his own pony screaming with the pain of an arrow in its rump and tearing the reins out of his hand as he tried to mount it, all order dissolving instantly into chaos around him. It had been over and finished with them before the savages had even reached them, with no defence possible. It had simply not occurred to him to stand and fight, but only to get away before he was engulfed. He hadn't even drawn his sword.

'So you ran.'

It was the plain fact, the plain statement which betrayed him now, just as it had done before the camp-major. But at the time there had seemed no disgrace, at least no thought of disgrace, because there had seemed no choice. And that was where the cowardice and the disgrace now lay.

'In which direction did you run?'

The question caught him off balance while he was still trying, as

he had tried a few hours before, to justify that plain disgraceful fact
to himself.

'W-what?'

'They came at you from all sides.' The grey man paused. 'How
did you get away, boy?'

How to get away?

The trooper who had been holding the harness behind the
team of draught-horses from the ditched waggon stared at him
open-mouthed, then dropped the harness and vaulted onto the
back of the rearmost of them. But before he could set heels to it
a javelin took him in the chest, pitching him back the way he had
come, over the horse's crupper. Clodius sprang forward, reaching
for the harness, and threw himself onto the same animal. His legs
seemed to have sprouted wings – the leap almost carried him clear
over the broad back and he clasped at the neck with both arms to
keep his seat.

The team plunged and jostled, hooves thudding on the logway.
Then, as though suddenly released, they surged ahead towards
the ford.

The other trooper who had been holding the lead pair appeared
round the flank, reaching as frantically for the harness as he had
done himself. But the forward movement was too much for him;
he missed the strap and clutched instead at Clodius' leg, running
alongside. Clodius kicked out at him, but the man struggled to hold
on and then managed to scramble up behind him just as they entered
the water, wrapping his arms tightly round his officer's waist.

The stream exploded in wild foam as the team hit it, drenching
Clodius's face pressed against the horse's neck. He saw a group
of savages halt in midstream and then scatter before them – one
painted brute, his teeth bared like a wolf's, stabbed ineffectually
at them with his spear before falling away out of sight. Another
great curtain of spray rose, forcing him to shut his eyes against it.
He felt the animals slow down, fighting the deeper water furiously
in their panic. Then they strained forward and he heard the rumble
of their hooves on the logway as they heaved themselves out on the
far side.

As he opened his eyes again the sudden wild hope inside him froze
in despair as he saw another party of savages running along the lip
of the cutting, parallel to him and not ten paces away. They were
carrying short javelins in their hands, and as he watched them one
checked his stride and drew back his right arm, pointing with his
left straight down towards Clodius.

He squeezed his eyes shut again and buried his face into the horse's
mane, his mind cringing away from the javelin. One of the horses
screamed, and the trooper at his back gave a frightful gurgling cry
of agony and clutched at him convulsively –

'– So they hit him and not you?'

Clodius re-focused on the dark eyes, unable to remember what
he had just said.

'And then they didn't pursue you? They let you get away?'

'I – don't know . . .' He shuddered as he remembered the hot
blood the dying Batavian had vomited over his neck and shoulders.
'We went on about two miles before – before he let go of me . . .
and I stopped, but he was dead . . . so I took the lead-horse and
left him.'

The grey man looked at him narrowly. 'You left him? By the
roadside? For the savages to find?'

'For the savages –?' Clodius looked at him. 'But he was dead,
I tell you,' he repeated defensively. 'He was dead.'

'Of course he was dead.' The man gave a derisive snort. 'Dead
and still fighting for you – don't you see?' He paused, and then
shook his head. 'No, of course you don't see. But never mind, boy
– because I know how you got away now. And I know you're an
idiot, but not a traitor.'

'A traitor?' Clodius stared at him incredulously.

Another snort. 'Aye, boy – did it not occur to you that I might
wonder how you did what no one else has done? That I might wonder
why they let you get away?'

'But – they didn't!'

'Of course they didn't. They went after the one who got away
– and they found him dead beside the road, so they thought, and
so they turned back – I'll bet a year's pay on it. An idiot, but not
a traitor – go on, boy, finish your tale.'

Clodius felt his own blood hot under his cheeks. There was no
end to their unfairness: now he was condemned as a fool as well
as a coward – something to be pitied as well as despised.

'I rode to the fort,' he said stiffly. 'There were – there was a
squadron of Dacians there. We rode back to the ford –'

'We?'

'They gave me a horse.' He heard his voice strengthen, hating
the man. 'The savages had burnt the waggons – they'd thrown the
wounded into the fires –'

The smell of burnt flesh . . .

'We followed the tracks to the left – west – where the land

is open, the woods must have been burnt back there in the summer.'

The grey man was sitting up straight, frowning.

'We went about five miles, maybe more – we went until the forest was too thick –'

'You pursued them for five miles?' The question was taut with disbelief.

'At least five miles. We rode fast – the land is open.'

The grey head shook vigorously. 'You rode to the fort, called out the Dacians, rode back to the ford – and then followed the tracks for five miles?'

'Yes.'

'And returned to the fort before nightfall?'

'Yes. The light was just going.'

'Impossible. You had time to get to the ford and back to the fort again, barely. I've ridden every inch of that road – aye, and taken convoys on it too. So don't lie to me.'

'I'm not lying.'

'Up to now you haven't been – now you are.'

'But I'm not.'

'You are. Because time and distance say you are, and they don't lie, boy.'

'I tell you I'm not.' For the very first time Clodius didn't feel unsure of himself, yet strangely his new certainty left him puzzled rather than angry. 'Why should I lie?'

'That's what I'd like to know. It's a little late to show how brave you are.'

The jibe stung cruelly: a coward and a fool, but not a liar. They couldn't prove that!

'It wasn't my idea to go after them, it was the Dacian captain's. He said if they'd loaded the corn on the mules there was a chance we could catch up with them before they reached the forest. It was his idea, not mine.'

Now the grey man's frown was puzzled too. He seemed to be staring at Clodius without actually looking at him.

He scowled. 'Describe the country to me, boy. Five miles from the road – what's it like, then?'

'The country?' Clodius had a vision of endless trees and trackless undergrowth, as featureless and indescribable as the ocean. 'It's – beyond the burnt lands there's oak scrub and bracken. And there's a ridge with a rock outcrop, where we stopped. The forest starts on the other side, and you can see the hills away to the north –'

'You saw the hills from the ridge?'

'A long way off, yes. The captain said –'

'All right!' the grey man held up his hand abruptly to cut him off.

There was a sudden thickening silence in the hut which was somehow more frightening than the fierce questioning had been, like the stillness before the thunderclap.

'I –' Clodius didn't really know what he was about to say, only that he wanted to break the silence. 'I think –'

'Be still! I believe you.' The grey man stared into the darkness behind Clodius, the lantern-light picking out every bristle of the stubble on his face. Then at last he stirred, slowly raising his eyes to the man with the lantern.

'Bassus.'

'Colonel?'

'You will take my Germans, and you will arrest Camp-Major Valerius Gavius and Senior Quartermaster Sullonius Crescens. Put them under close arrest and see they are disarmed – I want no suicides and no injuries. I want them both alive and well. Make sure that they are.'

'Sir!'

Clodius' jaw dropped. The man Bassus was not questioning the grey man's right to treat senior officers like – like felons. *Colonel*?

'And the Batavian captain –' the cold voice went on '– place him under open arrest. Two Germans to his billet, but leave him his sword. Then turn out the night guard – seal off the quartermasters' billet, two men to their records office and two men to every granary and storehouse. A corporal to every gate and no one to leave without my written permission. And you'd better double the parapet sentries – if you need more men you have my authority to call out the garrison. You understand?'

'Yes, colonel.'

'Very good. As of this moment I am assuming command of this depot. I will receive your report in the camp-major's office. Leave the lantern.'

Bassus placed the lantern carefully on the table. Then, straightening up, he gave the grey man a formal salute.

Slowly the dark eyes came back to Clodius.

'A crucifixion, he said, if I remember aright – eh, boy? Do you know how we set about it?'

Clodius looked at him speechlessly.

'No? Well, it's high time you learnt –'

... an old trick, which you will doubtless have guessed by now: the sacks were filled with chaff, not corn, the price of which had

gone straight into the pockets of Gavius and Crescens (both of whom I executed, together with a dozen of their underlings). They used the tribesmen, who were perfectly satisfied with the captured weapons and animals, merely to cover their fraud.

As for the boy, I have sent him to his regiment without a stain on his character; it would clearly be dangerous to tamper with so strong a life-line!

For mark, Lupus, how his luck lay in his invincible stupidity, not only in the ambush but also back at the base. Gavius had promised him a bad death, had filled him with wine – and had carefully left him his sword. Believing what he did, any man of sense would have killed himself – as the Batavian captain promptly and wisely did. But young Clodius didn't know what was expected of him, and consequently survived to meet the one man most likely to grasp the truth.

For Celer knew better than anyone that the supply line forts are sited exactly one day's journey apart for a loaded waggon train. Yet that green, stupid boy had obviously clipped more than a full hour off the best time achieved by experienced officers over the same distance. So because luck is one thing and miracles are another – and corn is heavy – those loaded waggons had to be travelling light.

MOSAIC

Rosemary Aitken

I am sure that in the character of Libertus we are seeing the start of a new type of investigator. Skilled, and clearly with some experience behind him, Libertus is a freedman and craftsman in Roman Britain some years after the conquest. Rosemary Aitken is the author of many highly respected textbooks in the field of language and communication, but has recently returned to her roots with a series of novels set in turn-of-the-century Cornwall exploring the lives of the tin miners. The series began with The Girl from Penvarris *(1995). She currently lives near Gloucester, the Roman Glevum, where this story is set.*

~

'Libertus! Damn the man, where has he got to now?' It was Sergius Maximus, in his customary bad temper.

Libertus the pavement maker struggled to his feet, so that he could ostentatiously bend one knee and drop his head as Sergius blustered into the room. 'I am here. Your servant, master.'

That was not, strictly, true. As his name suggested, Libertus was a freed man, not a slave – a craftsman, given his freedom on the death of his master and now officially 'employed' by Sergius, who wanted a spectacular new mosaic for his new wife. Not that being employed made a great deal of difference. As a freedman Libertus was technically a citizen, and entitled to the protection of the law – but since Roman Law, in this god-forsaken part of the Insula Brittanica, was mostly represented by Sergius himself, the matter was largely academic.

Sergius turned to the young man at his elbow. 'Remarkable work,
you see Marcus. A present for my wife. And for posterity. People
round here won't forget Governor Sergius Maximus in a hurry.'

That was another lie. Sergius was not a governor at all. He had
begun as a centurion in the occupying legion, but when the peace
was enforced and his age permitted he had elected to retire from the
army and take residence in the country. He had acquired an estate,
by the very efficient method of offering the owner a few denarii for
his land and threatening to run him through if he did not accept it.
The land enabled him to set himself up as sort of unofficial local
dignitary – a long way from the nearest Roman outpost, which
was at Glevum, forty leagues away. The Commander at Glevum
troubled him only once a year by sending a messenger with a bundle
of new directives and demands for tax – this year the messenger was
Marcus. Sergius obviously hoped that he would take back reports
of the mosaic with him.

The emissary looked at the pavement politely, but he seemed
more interested in its maker. 'You are Libertus?' he said, heartily.
'I have heard of you. Last year, when my predecessor came – his
guard was murdered and gold stolen. You solved the problem, he
told me. Found the real culprit and saved an innocent man from
stoning. In the nick of time, I hear?'

Libertus flushed. This was dangerous talk. Sergius did not enjoy
it when other people became the centre of attention. He shook his
head, 'A trifling matter, excellence.'

Sergius snorted in agreement. 'As he says – a trifle. Such a fuss over
nothing. Suppose the fellow had been executed? He was a merely a
slave. Probably guilty of something, if the truth were known. You
can't trust these people.' Sergius had acquired household servants
with his 'purchase' as well as having a few dozen slaves taken in
battle. 'Finding the murderer was very clever, no doubt – but it
was mostly chance. Anyone might have done it. But this . . .' he
gestured towards the pavement, 'this requires a real craftsman.
And a master with vision enough to order the work. I shall be the
envy of the Island.'

Certainly Sergius had established for himself a very agreeable
lifestyle – if you discounted the toll it had taken on his appearance.
The swarthy, muscular centurion had become florid and flaccid in
middle age, his battle-scarred face slack with wine and easy living.
He was, Libertus thought dispassionately, quite the ugliest man in the
country. Nevertheless, he bowed again. 'Thank you, excellence.'

Such civilities were wise. Sergius was apt to take lapses very personally. When the vines (which he had introduced at great expense)

failed in the British frost, Sergius had set an example by decimating the estate labourers. (Not, as some ignorant people supposed, simply destroying most of them – but literally 'decimating' them – executing one in ten and leaving their bodies tied to wooden gibbets, one every forty paces on the road to the villa.) It had effectively cowed the others but the vines still perished.

As a free man, and a Roman citizen, Libertus was not likely to be executed or whipped – at least, not very much – without due legal cause, but with Sergius it was always hard to be certain. Libertus had thought of leaving – he was supposedly free to do so, and if he got off the estate Sergius could hardly have him fetched back – but the roads were dangerous with wolves and brigands, and the pittance which Sergius paid him would not have lasted long.

And there was Lavinia. That 'wife' Sergius had spoken of. Or, she would be his wife, tomorrow.

She had stood out against it for a long time. That was why Libertus admired her so. It took courage to stand out against Sergius, when he had set his mind on something. And he had set his mind on her.

She was not really Lavinia, of course. She was Caerlyn, the daughter of the man who had owned the estate, but Sergius preferred a Roman name. He had wanted her, almost as much as the estate, the first time he saw her, but she could not be taken at sword-point, the same way he took everything else.

For one thing she had a 'husband' according to local custom. Sergius didn't mind this, but her father had protested at first. Sergius had to reason with him (privately, in a small black cell at the back of the villa) before he came round. And her two brothers were much the same. But even when the whole family was convinced that this was a wonderful match, Lavinia declined.

Libertus winced for her when he heard it, but she was resolute. She refused to swear a nuptial oath, or put her seal to anything. Rather to everyone's surprise, Sergius did not have her put to death. She did not even have a terrible accident. It proved how much he genuinely liked the girl, and besides, Marcus Septimus had recently arrived. News of a spiteful vendetta would not sound well if it reached the ears of the regional governor.

Sergius tried everything to persuade Lavinia. Flattery, presents, cajolery: nothing worked. Until the young man she called 'husband' was taken into custody and Sergius, very persuasively, offered her the option of marrying at once, 'Or by Mercury, I'll have that young man tied to my chariot wheels and driven to Londinium'.

It had done the trick. Lavinia had consented. And here was the prospective groom – apparently in high good humour and interested in the pavement. Libertus allowed himself to breathe out.

'The border here, you see?' He pointed to the mosaic he had been laying, the patterns traced carefully on the thick bricklike mud beneath, showing him where to place the tiny *tessella* fragments which would make up the final picture. 'And in each corner a picture – the seasons. Spring, see? And here – summer. And autumn.'

Sergius let out a bellow of laughter. 'And winter, look. That scrawny creature in the hooded cloak. 'British cloaks' they call them, Marcus – need them in this benighted province – or half the populace would freeze to death.' He looked at the figure again. 'It reminds me of that crone who comes here, selling berries and fungus. Witch, she's supposed to be. But the fungus is good. There is an orange one –' he kissed his fingers. 'Food for the gods. And the ignorant peasants will not eat it. Pah –' he spat. 'By Mithras, what clods.'

Marcus smiled.

Sergius bellowed with laughter. 'You know what they say about British fungus? Aphrodisiac! Make a man a real man! Well – we shall see tomorrow. You shall try some, Marcus.'

Marcus smiled feebly. 'I don't care for mushrooms. I thought it was red meat that was supposed to warm the blood.'

Sergius slapped his back. 'We shall have that, too. Venison. Suckling pig. Guinea fowl. And snails – good for the juices. I had a cask of edible snails brought down last winter, and that idiot Gerwyn has been tending them, though no Briton believes that they are safe to eat. And then there's fruit and sweet pastry. What a feast it will be, eh, Libertus?'

Libertus knew what that meant. Sergius lying on the couch beside the low table and stuffing himself until his fat frame would hold no more, then sticking a feather in his throat till he vomited himself enough space to eat some more. 'Yes, excellence.'

'There will be wine, Marcus, for you and me,' Sergius said. 'That sickly mead sticks to my gullet, and as for that drink they make with rotting apples . . . The peasants shall drink it. It is all it is fit for – or they either. Libertus, see my wishes are known! And now, come Marcus. I must show you the bath-house. A hypocaust – under-floor heating. The *calidarium* so hot it makes a man feel young again – and the *frigidarium* . . . though one hardly needs a cold pool in this climate . . .'

He led the way out, still boasting about his villa.

Libertus sighed and went back to his work. He did not bother to go to the kitchens. There was not a man or woman on the whole estate who did not know in detail what Sergius intended for the wedding feast. More than that – every peasant on the estate was expected to bring something – berries, apples, mushrooms, as a contribution to the occasion.

Gifts were coming already. He had been watching them through the open arches. A fat labourer brought a bunch of pink roots – boiled they were good to eat. A toothless woman with a basket of eggs, 'for the bride's fertility'. Poor Lavinia. She would be resting now – steeling herself for the ordeal ahead, lying alone in the women's quarters with the shutters drawn, playing the lute, perhaps, or more likely spinning wool on a hand spindle as all well-educated ladies did. Later, when the men had finished, she would go to the bath-house with a slave sent to rub her skin with scented oils and creams. And for what? For that great drunken oaf to paw at.

Libertus sighed, and bent back over his mosaic, considering before he moved a single piece. It was an art, laying mosaics – it took a careful, observant eye to see how each part lay against the next, how each detail fitted together to make the whole. He took one small piece of tile and fitted it expertly into place – and presto, there was a man's arm as certainly as if he had painted it with pigment.

More movement in the courtyard. That crone again, much as he had depicted her, with her basket of forest fungus. How could Sergius eat that stuff! It was decadent, decaying – like the man himself. He watched the bent woman limping in with her offering – the white wispy hair and filthy face half-hidden under the heavy hood, the grubby hands clutching the cloak across the chest, the drab sacking tunic and the clumsy feet bound in rough leather. A kitchen slave came to the door and the woman whispered something. Libertus heard her high cracked laugh, and then she shuffled off again – almost exactly like the picture he had created with his mosaic. Almost.

Sergius came out of the bath-house and Libertus stooped to his work again.

The feast was everything Sergius had promised, and more. Libertus attended, like all the other servants on the estate, just long enough to drink the health of the bride and groom. Sergius drank a jug of wine and insisted that Marcus did the same. The delicacies were brought, one by one, but only Sergius seemed to have any appetite for them. Lavinia was there, looking pale and anguished. She did no more than pick at a mushroom. Marcus seemed to have lost his appetite – and the other guests, being mostly Britons, preferred the more robust fare of venison, beef and pork.

Sergius got up, staggering and went out to vomit. Everyone had been expecting it, and it was quite some time before anyone realized that he was dead.

Marcus took control and called the wise women. Something he had eaten, everyone said. Possibly the snails which he had insisted on. Marcus had Gerwyn flogged, just in case – but his heart wasn't in it. He had eaten one or two of the snails himself and thought they were delicious.

It could have been the fungus, Marcus said, although Lavinia had tasted that too. They would ask the fungus woman. She was sent for, but – suddenly the whole villa was in an uproar – she could not be found. Marcus summoned Libertus, who appeared before him, nervously, in the audience chamber.

Marcus was pacing the room with anxiety, but he got straight to the point. 'Pavement-maker, I have need of your skills. You see how it is. The woman was obviously guilty and has run away. My guards found her hovel empty and her fire cold. I have posted sentries on the roads, but no one has seen her since yesterday. Or so they say.' He spat, expertly, into a pottery bowl placed for the purpose. 'I must find her, Libertus. The people are talking of witchcraft – and we cannot have it said that the Romans are cursed by local magic.'

Libertus looked at the floor. 'You do not believe in sorcery, excellence?'

'Not this time,' Marcus said. 'Do you? There are fifty people on this estate alone who would have poisoned Sergius and been glad to do it. The man was a boor – but he was a Roman citizen, and the law must be observed. Besides, the disappearance proves the guilt. If the crone did not do it for herself, she was paid to do it. By the man who helped her to escape, no doubt. No, Libertus, you shall find her for me. Five denarii to find the murderer and uphold the law of Rome.'

Libertus nodded slowly. 'The money would be welcome, excellence, but there is more than that. I am curious myself. Let me start in the kitchens.'

Marcus shook his head. 'There is nothing to be gained. The hag came with her basket, and gave it to Gerwyn for the feast. After that the fungus was in full view in the kitchen – and there were a dozen eyes to see. They all swear that it was not touched, except to cook and serve it. And why would the crone have disappeared if she were not guilty? Find her, Libertus. She is to be captured, brought before the governor and put to the sword. I will go back to Glevum, tomorrow. You can send to me when she is found.'

There was, indeed, little point in questioning anyone further, but Libertus went through the charade. Marcus was right. People were already talking of witchcraft. The woman seemed to have disappeared. Every building had been searched. Guards had been posted on all the roads for miles but nothing was found. People on the estate knew what to make of that, whatever the Roman said. But no one had any information to give.

He went to see Lavinia – who had gone back to being Caerlyn again. Her husband had been released and she was clearly unwilling to spend time away from him even to speak to Libertus, but when she came she was charming. How she would have been wasted on that odious Sergius. But she had nothing new to tell. 'I am sorry I cannot tell you more,' she said with a helpless smile. 'But I will give you any aid I can.'

Libertus bowed, and took his leave, but at the door he turned back. 'Sergius would have had the cooks flogged,' he suggested. 'To sharpen their memories. Or perhaps the serving-men. Should we, do you think . . .?'

She came over to him, tugging at his arm. 'No! No!' There were tears in her eyes. 'Those poor slaves were questioned half to death by Marcus – there is nothing more they can tell you. Besides, I tasted a mushroom myself. I ask you, Libertus, which of the staff would willingly have poisoned me?' That was true. Everyone in the villa was devoted to Lavinia.

'Then I will search for the fungus-woman.'

She nodded. 'It was the fungus, I swear it. You know where she lives? She has a hovel in the forest, not far from the spring.'

Libertus looked at her thoughtfully. 'Yes, I know the place. Thank you, my lady. You have helped me greatly.' He went out, taking his cloak, and set off into the forest.

He found the place without difficulty – a filthy hovel. Libertus put his head inside and looked around, although the stench was terrible. The fire had died, and the hearthstone was cold. There was nothing in the place but a few rags, a hunk of mouldering bread and a few rotting berries lying on a rough wood platter.

Libertus picked up the bread. It was rank and stinking. He put it down and went swiftly out into the fresh air. The forest seemed green and fresh in the daylight. There was fungus growing nearby – honey-fungus, wild mushrooms. He could see why the fungus-woman had chosen this place for her home – her wares grew all around her. He set off thoughtfully, following the track between the fungus clumps – into the trees and away from the main path.

The track at first was trampled by heavy feet – Marcus' men, no doubt – but a little further on it became a narrow pass slippery with mud and the footprints stopped. Libertus could see why. The track ahead was untrodden – not a single new footprint in the mud – and the last rains had been a week ago. The woman who brought the fungus to the wedding could not have fled this way. No one had been down this track in days. Libertus stopped and thought a moment, and then picked his way carefully onwards. There was another fungus patch ahead.

He went over to it. Suddenly he stopped and bent low. A space of crumpled grass. There was a dark stain on some of the sheltered stalks, but it was dry and flaked at his touch. And beside them, a handful of shrivelled objects. He picked them up – they were mushrooms. Gathered, days ago, now wizened from the sun.

He straightened up and looked around him carefully. There was a small river at the bottom of the rise, and leading down to it, a dried-out ditch. He went over to it, and followed it down its length. There, half-buried under a pile of leaves was what he sought. The fungus-woman – or what was left of her, for the sorry bundle told its own story. The woman had been savaged by a wild animal. No human being had left those bite marks in the neck, nor chewed the flesh from the bones in that dreadful fashion.

Libertus stood for a long moment, considering, then lifted the remains and carried them to the clearing. He went back up the track, scuffling the mud-patch as he went, then into the hovel to scatter the wizened mushrooms onto the platter. Then he set off back to the villa at a run.

Marcus was delighted by the news. It was obvious to everyone what had happened. The old fungus woman had eaten some of her own mushrooms, fallen sick outside the hovel and been set upon by a bear, or wolves. The old fool must have been losing her mind – confusing good fungus with bad. And she had paid the price. It was bad luck on Libertus though. Since Sergius' death was a sort of accident, he could not expect a reward.

Libertus went back to his pavement. Lavinia – or Caerlyn – was there. Her family had repossessed the estate.

'Do you want it finished?' he said.

She smiled at him. She was a beautiful girl. 'Why not? It is a lovely thing. And you have captured the people, so wonderfully.'

'Yes.' He was looking at her, very steadily. 'The woman with the basket now. I am so glad to have done that portrait before she died. Before anyone else took her place.'

Silence. And then a sharp intake of breath. 'You knew?'

He shook his head. 'I guessed. You knew she was dead, didn't you? She must have died some time ago – from the state of the food in the hovel. And that is why there were no footprints on the track – the rain had washed them away – before we ever went looking for her. You must have known. See how you begged me to spare the kitchen staff, but positively enouraged me to hunt for her. I thought you would not bring punishment on a poor old woman, not even to save yourself. Was I right?'

She nodded. 'She died, a week back. Some wild animal had attacked her. We did not know she had been poisoned. My brother found the body.'

Libertus smiled. 'She was not poisoned. She was picking mushrooms. I found the place. And then your brother carried her away and buried her in a ditch? I realized, of course that no animal could have buried her like that.'

She nodded again. 'I told him to. If it was found – well, it could seem like justice. If not – it would seem like guilt. Or witchcraft. She would just have disappeared.'

'And you took her place?'

'With a basket of fungus, yes. There are some – deadly – that look so innocent. And Sergius ate others – inkcaps and puffballs – all sorts of things that local people feared. He swore they . . . made a man lusty.'

Libertus nodded. 'Yes, I heard him say so.'

'I told the boy these were the strongest aphrodisiac. He believed me. No one ever doubted the old woman's word. She knew more about the woods than any man living.'

'You weren't afraid someone else would eat them?'

'It was Sergius' special dish. No one would have dared – except perhaps Marcus and he hated mushrooms. I ate one myself, but I made sure it was a real honey fungus. It was a risk worth taking.'

'You killed Sergius. Deliberately?'

'Yes. I slipped out of the women's quarters and into the disguise. My brother had brought the things – even the mushrooms. The plan came to me as soon as I knew the old woman was dead.' She looked at him. 'So, what will you do?'

He picked up a piece of the mosaic. 'Me? Nothing. Finish this, and ask, perhaps, for a letter if you can find someone to write one. To recommend me as a layer of mosaic pavements. What else should

I tell them? That there was a monster here, who deserved to die? And an old woman, known to be a witch, who came to the feast with a basket of magic mushrooms and then . . . died of her own potion. It was justice, of a kind.'

She shook her head. 'But she did not die of her own potion. You said so. The animals must have killed her, as we thought. You arranged it, didn't you? Moved the mushrooms to her hovel to make it seem that she had eaten some? To make it safer for me?'

'Of course.'

She looked at him intently. 'One thing, Libertus. How did you know? I thought my disguise was perfect – no one could see my face under the hood, and no one ever looks at a crooked old crone.'

He picked up a piece of mosaic. 'Oh, it was good – the smudged, shadowed face, the disguised hands, the clothes that covered you from view – and the white wisps of hair, that was brilliant. Wool, of course, from your spindle? And your eyebrows, too?'

She nodded.

'And you copied her walk, and her laugh brilliantly. But there was one thing you forgot. Your legs. You see, on the mosaic, how I have made her legs? Stumpy, swollen – even though the rest of the woman was thin and wasted. The woman who came into the courtyard that day had slim ankles – and between her leather-bound feet and tattered tunic I could glimpse the legs – the bronzed beautiful legs of a young woman.'

She shook her head. 'You are very observant.'

'I am a pavement maker,' he said. 'A putter-together of unconsidered fragments. Now . . . about this letter . . .'

THE BROTHER IN THE TREE

Keith Heller

Keith Heller has written a number of historical mysteries, the best known being his series about George Man, a London parish watchman, that began with Man's Illegal Life *(1984). He has also written stories featuring the Chinese magistrate Ti Jen-Chieh and William Blake as detectives (though not in the same story!). Here he explores the powers of deduction of the Greek philosopher Epictetus, who lived from around AD 50–120, in one of the most bizarre mysteries I have ever encountered.*

On summer afternoons, when the olive trees and cypresses swayed in a green wind, the students of Epictetus would gather under a spacious colonnade for their lessons. There, sheltered from the sneers of boys and the profiles of girls, the young men would ready themselves for their Master's visit. Some would go over the day's readings. Some would beg others to argue with them or try to tempt them with fantasies of glory or terrors of Caesar. The best pupils would simply sit alone, balancing themselves on mounds of rock between desire and aversion. Their composure amazed even the distant mountains, at least until the bronze sun shifted or a travelling bee roused them off their perches and into the gestures of a frenzied drunkard at a bacchanal. Then their friends knew them again for what they were, nothing but little souls carrying around the corpse of a body, just as the Stoic had always taught them.

The Master was usually late. Since his recent marriage, Epictetus had seemed more and more distracted. Apparently following his idol, Socrates, he had chosen a brooding woman with a tongue shriller than a hound's, a companion to help him save from an early death a sad unwanted child who had been exposed on a hillside to die. The sudden family had filled their modest house with more liveliness than they had ever known. Now, throughout the poor neighbourhood in Nicopolis, the city in Epirus on the northwestern shoulder of Greece where he had been exiled, the philosopher was becoming as famous for his housework as for his principles. He could often be seen hanging out of a window with a rag and a sneeze, or advancing on the vegetable market with a list in one hand and a knitted bag in the other. A lesser man might have thought his reputation diminished by such outrages, but Epictetus was not the most revered philosopher in town for nothing. He bore the weight of such changes manfully and even used the worst of his indignities as lessons in his classes. 'Where is the difference,' he would challenge any scoffer, 'between airing out a room and airing out your own soul?' Of his marketing excursions after fresh produce he said considerably less.

Today, the innermost circle of students was standing at the country end of the colonnade, staring as one out into the forest. Flavius Arrian, the Master's pet and a compulsive recorder, was frowning with worry as he listened to another student finish telling them the latest news. Lesbius, a short man whose constantly sour expression had made his beard grow crooked, had related the morning's warmest gossip as eagerly as a girl, enjoying the evil of others that he had suspected all along. He had assured his listeners that none of this meant anything to him personally. But just so that they would have no doubt on that score, he told them all of it over once again.

'And that's why, Crinus,' he added to the shivering sapling of a man standing next to him, 'the man was left where he is. After a lifetime of imprisonment, where could he go? I suppose our city fathers only want to investigate the crime before anything in the scene becomes disturbed.'

'Who said they thought it was a crime?' All eyes turned to a younger man on a bench who was adjusting the strap on one of his sandals. 'I mean,' Polus went on, 'who can say that the poor fellow wasn't surprised there while he was out hunting or that he didn't fall asleep and get caught in there so tightly that he couldn't struggle free without help? You said yourself that he was found in the loneliest, most dense part of the forest where no one but wild boars ever go. He could have been there for days or weeks, calling for food, and none of us here in town would have heard him. But that doesn't prove that someone deliberately trapped him there in order to murder him.

'I recall getting wedged inside a tree once when I was a boy,' he smiled, 'pretending to be Dryope for some of my friends. We had to wait for a woodsman to come by to cut me out. If we hadn't been near a travelled road, we might never have been able to manage it on our own. I could have been caught there for hours.'

Lesbius scowled down at the handsome young actor on the bench. Polus was talented and already famous, but sometimes he listened to no one's voice but his own. And the uglier Lesbius simply could not bear to be unnoticed.

'I've already told you,' he cried to the growing ring of classmates around him. 'This man had grown old inside the tree! Don't you understand? He must have been forced into a fissure in the tree when both he and it were still very young. He must have been strapped in at first, for they say that the rotted leather fibres still hang on his one exposed arm. But then the tree was allowed to grow up all around him, swallowing him whole, until only his face and his right forearm can be seen. He seems to be struggling outward as if he were sinking into quicksand, only the tree's bole is hard as stone, and its bark swirls around his body as if he were wearing it as a robe. The awful thing is that he could apparently breathe and even eat and drink as well as any of us. But he could not move. He could only grow taller and older in the centre of the tree as the tree grew layer upon layer on top of him. He even had enough room inside to scream,' Lesbius said, for once even his sneering voice shaken. 'But, out there, who could have ever heard him wailing but himself?'

The gathered students shared a moment of private terror, as they each felt that they could not get quite enough air into their lungs. They studied the gay colours of the distant trees and the narrow gaps between them where last night's darkness seemed to have hidden itself. And they had to look away, towards the more spacious, human city, before any of them could catch their breath again or quiet the tingling in their hands.

As Crinus tried to turn away from the story, a larger, more massive student spoke up. His bull's neck, deformed ears, and fleshy nose belonged more in the wrestling ring than in the school of Epictetus. Yet his honest strength and solid good sense often pleased the Master with insights into life and effort that were too simple to be seen by most of the other, cleverer students.

'But what did the dead man look like?' Bato wanted to know. 'Was there nothing left but bones, a bare skeleton, or was there enough of a man remaining to be recognized? If he died from hunger and exposure, was it so long ago that no one in Nicopolis would even know him now?'

'Oh, no,' Lesbius informed them. 'The general thinking is that he died but a few days ago, perhaps during that thunderstorm when whoever had been keeping him alive would not have been able to go out. The body is evidently hardly even cold or hard, and there is still a sweetness in the skin as if the man were only sleeping. Even his eyes are still open, though the rains have left their lashes moistened as if with pathetic teardrops. I'm told that he's still quite the sight and that many townspeople are visiting the area as an attraction. Isn't this what we'd all like?' he asked everyone around him. 'To look on death without actually having to die? Isn't that what we all study here?'

The healthy young men all paused, some sighing, reminded of their worst fears and all the tragedies their own lives might someday contain.

'Do you mean,' tiny Crinus suddenly stammered, 'that someone was cruel enough to keep him alive for twenty or thirty years, locked inside that growing tree? But who would want to do a thing so monstrous? Who was the man, anyway? Does anyone know him? If we knew that, maybe then we'd know who'd want to make someone's whole life into a daily torture. But until then –'

Before anyone could respond, a limping shadow approached the students from the rear as the tardy philosopher came up to join in their discussion. Epictetus, as usual, had heard everything already.

'The dead man,' he began, bobbing his grey beard as his long hair fell across the shoulder left bare by his rough cloak, 'has been identified as the missing son of Aprulla, that old woman at the city gate who raises and trains fighting quail for competitions. She's never made more than a few obols a day, but it's always been enough to keep her and her boys happy. The only sorrow in her life was the loss of the first of her triplets, the silver boy, the one whose grey eyes reminded her, she used to say, so much of her dead husband's. When he disappeared as a boy, she only had the other two. And though that would have been enough for most women – more than enough,' he mused in a weary aside, 'for mine – still, Aprulla mourned for her lost son as if the other twins had never existed. Now, of course, her mourning will never cease . . .'

Everyone around him nodded in sympathy. They had all heard the story before. Not long before her husband's death in a hunting accident, Aprulla had given birth to three of the most handsome baby boys that the town had ever seen. The first one had been named

Felicio, for the joy that she had felt at his full head of hair. The other two were called Kore and Kunos, the first thoughtful as a poet, the second noisier than a volcano. She had kept the triplets secluded in her house through much of their first years, preserving their unity, until that unhappy day when Kunos had hurried in from the forest with a disastrous tale to tell. According to the two brothers, Felicio had gone out with his brothers to explore for coloured rocks when a terrible mishap had occurred. Tempted by an errant butterfly, the lovely boy had hurried ahead, only to tumble into a crevasse in the earth. A scrabbling search had turned up nothing, and the first of the triplets was soon forgotten by the city that had too much living to do to remember. But the mother never forgot, her future days wearing shadows that even her remaining sons could not lighten. Nor did the brothers escape unwounded. Smaller Kore grew inward and melancholy, grey in his eyes and in his dreams. Rougher and more careless, Kunos quickly became the favourite of the town, louder than the loud and never far from wine and women and mistakes that were never his fault. By now, most people had come to accept the twins as polar strangers to each other, never seen in public together, with their mother playing the part of a Medea whose family was being slowly consumed by an unkind fate. But all Nicopolis knew that the last two brothers together would never fill their mother's heart quite as well as the lost son used to do all alone.

Now, with the news of Felicio's being found again poisoned by the imagined dread of his buried life, the town hardly knew what to think or feel. But already many were saying that no one but wild Kunos could have invented such a procrustean destiny for the brother who had every day stolen their mother's brightest smiles away from him.

'Are you telling us,' Arrian asked the Master, 'that the city has already taken Kunos into custody for the torture and killing of his brother? Do they have any evidence for such an action?'

'They haven't touched him yet,' Epictetus said. 'But we all know what a hunter Kunos has always been, how he's forever out alone in the woods, traipsing after game and adventures with a sack of food as his only company. He usually stays out for days at a time and sometimes has little enough to show for his efforts when he does come home. This all looks very suspect now. Add to all this the vicious nature of the man – his animal roughhousing that contrasts so sharply with Kore and his gentleness – and you must see how the situation begins to look.

'I must say I never thought very much of Kunos myself,' the

Stoic added primly. 'No man should ever betray his human reason as madly as that man has done his entire life. It just seems to go against our inner nature.'

He looked up at a frieze of disappointed faces.

'What?' he suddenly demanded of his offended students. 'Do you think that the wide earth holds only teachers and students and wise thoughts? Or do you suppose that a man with a trained eye cannot, like a doctor or a mathematician, spot a tumor or a miscalculation from across a field? Why did I spend so many hours with my own master, Rufus, if not to be able to detect failings and errors in others? You want to take my philosopher's judgements away from me, then, and leave me as only a shell to echo the gibberish of the mob?'

The circle of young men murmured among themselves like dry leaves in woods, until one of the group found enough voice to remind the philosopher of his own words.

'Wasn't it you, Master,' began Maximus, a faded sailor who had come to the practice of reason only late in life, 'who lectured us not to judge even known thieves and robbers too harshly or desire their death, any more than we would that of a blind man or a deaf man? Don't you teach us that the actions of other men are beyond our control, and so none of our affair? Pardon me if I haven't understood you correctly,' the wrinkled man said. 'But does this mean we should suspend your teachings in this one particular case and act just like everyone else?'

Taken aback, Epictetus only grumbled something about how late today's lessons would be and ordered everyone to take out his wax tablet. Then he proceeded to talk at a volume and speed that not even his oldest students had ever heard. He was inspired, and today more than one young man felt his future life change forever at a single turn of phrase. But through it all the philosopher could not help glancing alternately at the outspoken sailor and the waiting forest. And by the close of the session, all his mind was on the woods, listening for a muffled voice that he knew logically must be only the dying wind.

Once the trees closed behind them and obscured the town, the forest grew black as if the morning overhead was connected to some other day. Dead branches hung heavy, and the decay of lifetimes crowded matted around their feet and erased their tracks. Sounds disappeared, or they changed in midair into the weeping of mosses and the panic of insects. Mites and gnats tormented them as the impossible stillness of raw nature overcame them, and from time to time they were forced to stop and hold each other upright by the shoulders. By the time they finally found the stand of trees that was indicated on their makeshift map, they were both so drained that they almost envied the dead brother in the tree his eternal detachment from the world.

Epictetus approached the victim ahead of the old sailor, who had been taught by decades of superstition to be wary. The poplar was larger than most, healthy and alone in a depression of grass and undergrowth. It stood with its back turned towards the distant city as if it were shy with the secret treasure that it had been nurturing for so long. Only as Epictetus rounded the trunk did he begin to see the pale white arm that had grown straight out from a gnarl of bark like a stubborn fungus. The face came later, turned as it was slightly away from the single hand that could never quite reach even raindrops to the eager lips. They had been told in town that the dead man would be released from his life sentence tomorrow when the authorities came to dispose of the body and start their inquiries. Until then, poor Felicio would have to spend one last night, staring out into a darkness that must have looked soft and shining compared to his endless night inside the tree. Not even the sailing moon would have stood still long enough to hear his prayers.

For all the sorrow of his confinement, the dead brother was as well situated as could have been expected. The tree had swept up around him like a second womb, its rough shell protecting him from mice and beasts, but leaving him enough space to breathe and shake his head free from pests. With only his face and right arm exposed, the young man might have only leaned up against the tree in a brown cloak and been magically transformed by contact into a camouflaged wing or a forgotten pelt. His face was fine, though scarred by more than twenty years of exposure, and his arm was as trim as a girl's from lack of work. Up close, he seemed to be at peace, musing silently over a remembered melody that only he could hear. But from a few paces back, he became what he was, a man whose whole life had been a tree's life, lethargic and dull. Seeing him propped up by the wood that had grown all around him, Epictetus did not care to think about the encased legs and abdomen, wilted as tendrils and soiled by years of absolute, incomprehensible misery.

The philosopher could see how it must have been. As a boy, he would have come out here to play. Perhaps he even planted or tended the very tree that was to become his prison. Someone surprised him. Then, as a lark, or out of a black sickness no one could understand, someone bound the boy tightly in the crotch of the young sapling. He would have lifted him through the crease as some country parents ritually passed their naked sons through split trunks before tying the halves back together again. He would have tied the boy at first, ignoring his cries, not seeing the days of wailing and the nights of moaning to come. Later, as the leather straps gave way to chains of bark and weakness, he might have looked upon the growing boy almost as a work of art, a sculpture so alive that it gradually shaped itself through helpless struggles. There would have been something almost holy about the scene – the solitary meadow, the metamorphosis of boy into plant, the frenzy of hopelessness, the devoted watching. Then, through years and years and years, someone would have returned here every day with food and drink, for a talk even, for observations about the city or the weather, for a captive ear to share plans and grievances with as the slow, slow years passed on. There would have been friendship here, one-sided and mad, but comradeship, even love. Over time, it would have become harder to tell the warden from the prisoner as both men declined into an awful parody of a couple, feeding off each other's anguish not unlike a parasite and a host.

It was the irrationality of the act that plagued Epictetus into silence on the long walk back. No one, he had always believed, would sacrifice his own humanity for no reason. There would be nothing to gain from the torture and the murder, nothing to enjoy. Even wild animals would never toy with their prey for so long, until their hunger would have died before their food. Nothing that he knew about in nature would ever indulge itself in such infinite cruelty. Even trees sometimes let their branches twine and grow together towards the same shared sun.

The woman's hut at the city gate was squirming with fowl. Cantankerous quail argued and spat at his legs as he approached her door, and he almost lost his footing on rounded droppings and slick cobbles that sprang to life beneath his sandals. Never very comfortable with open nature in action, Epictetus cowered at the open door, calling out the woman's name as desperately as a suitor. The quail simply would not leave him alone, and he had almost decided to retreat when a vague figure came clucking out of the shadows inside.

'Calm yourself,' Aprulla began, apparently to both the Stoic and the birds. 'Can't a mother be left to grieve for a time on her own?'

'Forgive me,' Epictetus nodded respectfully at her. 'But the death of your missing son has stolen my sleep from me these past few days, and I was wondering if I might not speak to you for a moment about it? I am not connected with the city,' he reassured her. 'My only interest is what I might learn from the incident and what I might help teach others.'

Such a strange request disarmed her, and she welcomed him into the hut for some wine. In the only room, at a table that might have been made out of the twin of her son's tree, they sat in the fluttering light of afternoon and talked like cautious strangers. Aprulla was a worn woman, a body stooped from years of feeding quail and a heart battered by nights of regrets. Her voice came out of the dark as if from a great distance or from the depths of a forest where she had lost her way longer ago than even she could remember. Epictetus had no right to question her about anything. But for his own peace of mind, he knew he had to try to find out why.

'Your son – poor Felicio – went missing at what age exactly?' he began.

'Six? Seven?' she muttered uncertainly. 'Who remembers the past? With other boys, with a life of work and illness, who has the time to count anything but losses?'

'His brothers must have been devastated,' the Stoic assumed. 'After having been together in the womb and then in childhood, it must have been like waking up without a limb.'

The mother only shrugged. 'Who can say? Boys are wolves. Kore, of course, was lonely without his favourite brother. But he's hardly ever happy. And Kunos,' she went on with a frown at her visitor, 'never sees anything that doesn't please him or pay him for his bother. Felicio might have been out on a long journey, for all the notice that his brothers or the town took of him.'

Aprulla spoke with the chronic suspicion and anger of the poor and the defeated. Her eyes in the shadows seemed clouded by tears, or they might have been aged by having seen more than any eyes should have seen in one lifetime. Epictetus hesitated, unsure about going on. But Aprulla encouraged him with her silence. She might have been a tree herself, stolid and unthinking as bark or buried roots.

'Does anyone know,' the Stoic went on, 'who might have wanted to treat an innocent boy so viciously? Are there any families set against yours or your late husband's? Was your husband's death in any way mysterious? Perhaps there was something in it that might help explain this other tragedy.'

Aprulla disagreed. 'Florus went hunting. He took an arrow through the eye. He died. The triplets never missed him. They had each other. They had an uncle. What more did they lack? My quail are satisfied with half as much. And they live and die just like us,' she observed dully. 'Only their fighting is worth a bit more, though hardly to them.'

'And there's no one else?' Epictetus persisted. 'No ugly neighbour or tradesman who has a grudge over a debt? Nothing in your past that might have given rise to a hatred that could have continued for twenty or more years? You understand,' he went on more urgently, 'that I have no direct interest in any of this. It's just that I can't bear to see such unreasonableness running about our countryside like a bandit's orphan. It goes against my soul somehow, until I wonder if what I am trying to teach my students makes any sense at all. If I can't see something like this clearly,' he fumed, 'if I can't comprehend its premises and conclusions, then I might just as well limp on home and turn everything over to my wife. As if I haven't done that already . . .'

The imperturbable mother stared across the table at the greying thinker. He reminded her of those women who spent all their lives studying cooking, but never handled a pot or a ladle. The Stoic was gazing out of the window and down the road that led to the market as if he expected one of her boys to come striding home with an armful of answers, a mouthful of explanations. But she knew better than anyone that life itself was never anything but a question.

'What's to know?' she reasoned in the dark. 'Boys are born. Boys yell. Meanness exists in this world. Boys die. Don't we all? So what are we supposed to do? Tell God that we don't want to go? Isn't all this His party, after all? Isn't He the one who invited us to His festival, who invited us to join in on His holiday dancing and His merrymaking? Wouldn't it be ungrateful of us to hang back when He decides it's time for us to leave? He doesn't want the peevish or the cowardly, one of those guests who idles about all evening and then won't recognize when it's time for him to go to sleep. Why can't we see when we've worn out our welcome? Why can't we give way to others who need our places and our time? Why should we want to crowd the world?'

'But your children?' Epictetus went on, thinking of his adopted son. 'Surely you miss your firstborn son who was kept away from you for so long and who was killed so horribly?'

'He wasn't mine to miss,' Aprulla responded. 'He was God's. Why shouldn't He call him back to Him in His own good time? What else is death but the universe simply rolling along on its own track, replacing one form with another? Oh, it may look like the monster's mask mothers use to frighten their children into minding them. But we grown-ups know better, don't we? I had the triplets. Now I have the twins. Later I'll have one. Then none.' She drained her wine, rattled the cup on the table, and smiled weakly at her confused visitor. 'Then it will be just me and the quail. Then only the quail. But the quail!' she said mysteriously with a glance out the window. 'Oh, the quail will never die.'

Epictetus followed her eyes, but all he could make out was floating dust.

'Still,' the philosopher made one final effort to reach her, 'you do want the city fathers to discover who did this to your son, don't you? You must want justice for what's been taken away from you.'

'What business is it of mine,' she said, 'whose hands God uses to take back what is His? If I'm left with less, I'm left with less. Every morning I clean the birds,' she added reflectively. 'The lice I see and catch I leave behind. But what I miss, I carry away. It's more than enough for me.'

After some more inconsequential conversation, the philosopher turned to go and saw in an obscure corner a small table spread with knickknacks. He noticed at once a pattern to the articles. He saw tridents and three-pronged mattocks, plant and metallic caltrops, toy triremes, treatises on the Athens Thirty and the Thermopylae Three Hundred, stalks of red mullet in tripods, oil vats full of honey and milk and wine, a stuffed buzzard hawk, a miniature of Triton, a three-obol piece in a wrapping of trefoil, and a box containing a preserved anchovy and three hair-eating moths. As his eyes took in the rest of the room, he counted three couches arranged in a triangular design and the makings of the sacrifices slated for the third day after the funeral. Over all spread a crude triglyph that showed a boar, a goat, and a ram all coming together to meet in a common slaughter.

At the door, Epictetus observed sympathetically, 'I take it all these are mementoes of your three sons. I'm only sorry that now their numbers have been so sadly reduced.'

The old quail-woman glanced about the room and waved her hand through the dark air.

'Not for the boys,' she informed him. 'For their father. He was mad about threes. He had to have them everywhere I only thank God that I was able to give him triplets and that his death came before he could feel their subtraction.'

'Yes,' the Stoic said thoughtfully as he stepped back into the pool of birds. 'Superstitions like that are sometimes almost impossible to satisfy.'

'It's not so hard,' Aprulla noted. 'Like actors and their masks, you only have to pretend to be something for a long time in order to become it. Habit can make you believe in anything.'

He hobbled slowly towards his home, haunted and uneasy. The town of Nicopolis greeted him with the usual carnival of humanity that he never failed to find enthralling. Before he reached his house, it greeted him, too, with the news that Kore – the one member of Aprulla's triplets who had always been loved by all – had gone missing and would probably never hear the cries of quail or mother in this world again.

The only one who was not surprised at the appearance of the new student was the Master himself. All the other young men surged forward to see, then recoiled, ashamed of their morbid curiosity. The newcomer was allowed to enter their circle with his harsh features and the anger of a martyr in his knotted shoulders. He was even given the foremost place under the colonnade, Arrian being more than willing to stand aside in the presence of such infamy and suffering. The rest of the class did the same, most of them only staring awkwardly down at the schoolbags that they had not even remembered to open.

When Kunos, the last remaining son of the quail-trainer, was finally settled onto the stone bench, he gazed up at the teacher as if he expected Epictetus to open the discussion. After a long silence passed with no sign of interest from the philosopher, the intruder let out an impatient sigh and looked up at everyone from under weary eyelids.

'I'm told,' he said to the Master, 'that you may be the only man in Nicopolis who might be able to help me.'

'I have helped many,' Epictetus agreed. 'So why not you?'

'As you say,' returned Kunos. 'At any rate, the authorities have it in their heads that these deaths of my brothers –'

'Excuse me,' Masurius, a local jurist, interrupted. 'From what Symphorus and Numenius tell me, poor Kore is as yet only missing, not presumed dead. They hear everything that goes on in the city, and they have never lied to me yet. If I were you,' he cautioned professionally, 'I'd watch my words more closely in the future.'

Nodding, Kunos continued, 'As I say, some think that I might know more about Felicio's death and Kore's disappearance than any loving brother should. Suddenly, everyone is referring to us as Eteocles and Polynices, as if I can't be trusted even in my own family. The next thing I'll be hearing, I suppose, is that I had something to do with my father's death, even though I was only a few months old at the time and only one of three naked babes.'

'I know of no one who has gone to such unreasonable lengths,' Epictetus said to be fair to his fellow townsmen. 'Rumour, of course, is none of your concern. Only say that they who talk of

such matters are ignorant of your other faults, else they would not
have mentioned this alone.'

'Perhaps not,' the brother conceded with a suspicious glower at
the Stoic. 'But it's still an injustice that such accusations may fly
through the streets of Nicopolis without proof. It hurts my mother
and disgraces me, until I begin to wonder if my two brothers weren't
more fortunate than I in the end. At least their honour is forever safe
from harm.

'Which is why,' Kunos hurried on, 'I've come here to your school
today, to your wisdom, Master, and your students. I've come to beg
your help, to tell me what I can do to turn aside the distrust of my
neighbours and help my poor mother to put an end to all this, once
and for all. Why should the unhappy woman be made to suffer for
a third time over a single set of sons?'

Epictetus took a turn around the walkway, lengthening his beard
and glaring at the woods on the horizon. Then he stopped and stood
before both his visitor and his waiting students.

'The most logical course,' he advised, 'would be to find Kore.
In that way, fears about his safety could be answered, and he could
probably vouch for your actions during the past twenty or so years,
when Felicio was out there growing old in his tree. With one stroke,
you could put both mysteries to rest, like the citharoedes who sing
and play their harps at the same time and give such perfect pleasure
to all of us.'

'I don't know about that,' the brother said doubtfully. 'What
with all the robbers working the roads these days, I doubt if we'd
ever be able to find Kore again, much less come up with any new
information about Felicio's long agony. Is this your best thought,
Philosopher?' he added in a critical voice. 'I must say I'd expected
better from the school that's supposed to keep this town's name
alive throughout the centuries to come.'

The wrestler, Bato, brandishing a lethal strigil, was about to come
to his Master's defence, when the Master himself lifted his hands in
temporary defeat.

'Schools change,' Epictetus admitted, 'seven times a day, as
often as the currents between Euboea and Boeotia, if not more.
We do what we can with the time and the materials that we are
offered. But there is no argument that convinces quite as completely
as eyesight. And there are no proofs more telling than those that
come walking back into town with you, safe and sound.

'So, if you want to save yourself from hasty justice,' the Stoic
declared, apparently dismissing the subject from his day's schedule,
'then you should act first to put all the doubting minds to rest. You

should find your brother, dead or alive, and find the steps he took when he disappeared from your mother's home. Only then will you be free to defend yourself like a man, and only then will a final peace come to Aprulla and what remains of her family.'

Under the gossiping vines overhead, the coarse brother softened for a moment as if a rip in a fabric let show a more delicate viscera within. Sitting there in the falling sun, he seemed to teeter between the bullying strength of an unthinking body and the gentler suppleness of a contemplative soul. For a long moment, his better nature won out, and another, less beastly man appeared in his place. Then the veteran hunter shook himself, sharpened himself to a point again, and pushed back the leering students with a threatening glance.

'You may be right,' he murmured to the philosopher. 'Even if we never find Kore again, I should at least make the effort to look for him. It is expected of me, I suppose?'

'I'm sure,' Epictetus nodded, 'that he would do the same for you.'

Aprulla's last son looked up quickly, frowning. But the Stoic was only toying with a leaf.

'But where would we begin searching?' Kunos relented. 'It's a very large world, and who knows where any kidnappers or robbers might have taken him. How would we even know where to start?'

'Oh,' the Master said softly as he turned his head towards the open country, 'I don't think there's any wonder about where he's gone. Where does each of you wind up in the end?'

Rolling up the papyrus rolls of their notes, most of the students prepared to follow the two into the forest. But, explaining that too many eyes sometimes saw more than what was truly there, Epictetus chose to accompany them only Arrian, his notetaker, and Naso, a leatherworker whose dream oracles had led him to philosophy. The rest of the students were dismissed. All they could do was to stand anxiously beneath the colonnade and watch the four men vanish into the forest as if the men had changed their backs and had the backs of birds.

Past the boundary marker of Hermes on a four-cornered pillar, through a patch of fragrant hellebore whose petals were said to dispel insanity, the Master steered his company directly to the central tree from which the body of Felicio had only recently been removed. On the way, he spoke only vaguely of unrelated matters, of the harmony between woods and meadows and of the bonds that existed among men and families. No one, he announced, could contradict himself and still be regarded as a member of the community of thoughtful

adults. No one could wish for and despise the same thing at the same
time. Any man who wanted to be both Socrates and Domitian had
no right to the respect of his fellow citizens. 'A pot and a stone,'
Epictetus insisted as they left behind the nearby city of Cassiope,
'do not go together. Anyone who pretends that they do should
spend the rest of his life on Gyara, the island of exile, and leave
daily life to the rest of us. A man who is tired of being who he is
will never be enough of a man for me. Or for the world.'

As the company walked on, conversing and feeling the summer's
late evening falling upon their shoulders, the quail-woman's last son
seemed to flicker in the dying light like the shadow of a fire. He saw
enemies in every sweeping branch. He overheard conspiracies in the
rattle of mice through the vegetation. He imagined his two brothers
as loose souls in the night, calling to him in barbaric syllables that
only he could hear. In answer, Kunos babbled of a dead father, dead
before he was a father, of a brother who was lost before he could
even become a brother, of little Kore and of his dull goodness that
was never enough to win him either friends or lovers downtown.
As the black-green forest grew up around them like a smothering
sheath, Kunos fractured into pieces of confusion and dread, until he
was barely able to keep his two feet moving straight beneath him.

At one point, Epictetus happened to lead them through a pass
where hunters had strung a line hung with brightly coloured feathers
to frighten deer into their hanging nets. The classmates simply swept
the obstruction away, but Kunos suddenly felt the cord cross his
throat as if it were a noose and flailed backward, clawing at the
empty air in a blind, gulping panic.

'Whose are these hands at me?' he wailed. 'Help! Someone has
killed me here!'

The philosopher stepped towards him and calmly plucked the
line off his chest.

'What, man? Haven't you ever seen a hunter's snare before?
When did you hunt? Only by daylight? No wonder they say you
never caught anything but your own mother's crippled quail.'

The final brother might have argued, but now at last they had
come upon the death tree in its hollow. Turned as it was away from
them, they did not see the obtruding arm until everyone of them had
nearly circled the tree completely. Then they all ground to a halt,
unmanned by the sight of the body that by now was supposed to
have been decently buried.

'What is this?' exclaimed Naso fearfully. 'Do you mean to tell
me that they haven't taken Felicio back to his mother yet? Here's
a new crime.'

'This is intolerable,' Arrian commented, and promised everyone that the city bureaucrats in charge of such matters would hear from him personally in the morning.

Epictetus stepped boldly forward. 'Let's bear him home ourselves. If the city won't do its proper work, then at least its citizens should act their part.'

The students shook their heads, then followed their Master's lead.

'I'm afraid I can't –' Kunos whimpered, starting to retreat.

'Nonsense,' the philosopher said, tugging hard at his arm and pulling him forward.

'Master –' Arrian began.

'What is it?'

'I thought I heard –'

But then, before anyone could speak, the arm before them suddenly shifted in the dark.

'Sweet Zeus above us!' screamed Naso.

'Run!' someone yelled out.

'Where?'

'Anywhere but here!'

The company broke apart like a bush in a gale. The students and the brother all scrambled backward like crabs, but the Stoic peered around the tree for a closer look at the face. He begged everyone to please stay calm.

'It's only Kore, I expect,' he said with relief. 'Someone's gone and imprisoned him here in his brother's tree. I'm afraid this is getting to be something of a family tradition for you,' he added with a light laugh, turning back towards Kunos to lead him up to the tree. 'But he's all right. He's awake now. You can ask him yourself.'

But the brother did not share in the general easing of tension. Instead, he kept reeling back in hysteria, grunting incoherently, convinced that the living arm outside the trunk had to belong to the cadaver of Felicio rather than to the breathing Kore. He screamed and retreated, refusing any aid. In a helpless delirium, Kunos fell to his knees and began tearing at the sod with his nails, frothing about the muzzle and barking inhumanly at the back of his throat. His shoulders hunched, and in the dark he might have been mistaken for any peasant who had angered the gods and been transformed into a snuffling animal or a monster that the world had not yet even named.

Then, as the swaying arm suddenly pointed its middle finger insultingly at him and a voice of wood began echoing his cries, Kunos broke down completely. His heart could take no more.

'For the love of God!' he sobbed. 'Please! Help get me out of this tree!'

As Epictetus motioned the others to stand back and watch, the distracted brother leapt to his feet and attacked the tree. He tore at it until his nails bled, as the brother in the tree continued to moan wordlessly out at him and fend him off with his free hand. In the gloomy forest, the scene soon became a nightmare. The madman danced and beat upon the tree in a mindless ceremony, an ancient pantomime of frustration and awe that frightened everyone who saw it. In a moment, the free brother had become someone else entirely. No longer the swaggering hunter or the roistering street drunkard, he was now only a frightened child who had forgotten who he was. As if he had only now been roused from a long dream, the Kunos outside the tree began imploring the Kunos inside the tree for mercy, telling him of his hidden love for the brother who since birth had always been closer to him than his own breathing. 'If only,' he whispered hoarsely on his knees, 'if only I could have been no one else but me . . .'

Finally, after the Master had seen and heard enough, he led his two students forward, and they pried Kunos away from the tree and bound him with torn grasses. They laid him carefully on a mound where he quietly turned inward like a shrimp and, after repeating a trio of names until he had drained them of all meaning, more or less disappeared from everyone's view.

It was only then that Epictetus, swinging open the slice of bark that had been cut to let out the corpse of Felicio, reached into the heart of the tree and helped out his slave, Manes. The dark tree that had disguised him closed again behind, and the group turned to gather up the brother in a cloak that they carried back into the city as compassionately as if he were a newborn fawn.

'Only think,' the Stoic said as they set out for home, 'how sad it must be for a man to lose his reason as a mere boy and become a beast. Or to watch himself becoming, through all the long years, nothing more than a single dead tree.'

Epictetus never told his wife or his son anything about the new leg that he had a craftsman add to his study table. It was a sculpture in brown marble of a tree with gnarls and swirls of bark. Within the stone knots of the leg, a body seemed to be writhing, and through a pair of holes projected the white face and arm of a fair young man. His features were placid with unhappiness, while his hand hovered peacefully as a band of pale smoke across his captured chest. The colours were pure and deep, and the workmanship was as lifelike as the forest original. But the marble tree did not move.

Neither did the philosopher tell his family of Aprulla's doomed twins. Only to his class did he tell the story of the mother who gave birth to two boys and the father who would not be happy with anything less than triplets. It had been the mother's idea to create an imaginary brother to be added to the twins, a Felicio who had at once become his father's favourite. Little Kore had taken to the game, refining his skills even as a toddler in acting out a dual role for the family and all the neighbourhood. As both the beautiful and the good brother, he had enjoyed the liberties that only more than one life can give. On the same day, he could please his father with Felicio's brilliant talk and satisfy his mother with Kore's quiet poetry. He never had to be the same boy twice. While his brother, Kunos, had squandered his spirit in sports and hunting, Kore had doubled his in fantasies and playacting. Like an actor or a thief, he had put on both the robes that God had given him and the robes that God had withheld. And, before very long, he had begun to wonder if he could ever again be happy with being only and always Kore.

But when their father had died, so did the need for a ghostly third brother. The second loss in the family seemed to have affected Kore strangely. He yearned for the freedom of being two at once, and he began to look upon his real brother, Kunos, with a secret envy. He hungered for the rambling life in the city streets that Kunos had made his own, while his own domestic talents with words and quail-keeping began to feel as hollow as an emptied bowl. Now Kore was an orphan in his own home, and his imaginings soon ran after the hunting and the shouting that only Kunos had been born to do. Eventually, his reason abandoned him, leaving him with only one road to follow. On a bright summer's day, Kore lured his brother out to the tree, dared him to climb up inside the cleft, and crucified him with bands of leather. Then he became both and lived two long lives out in Nicopolis, savouring both the honours due to a good son and the admiration bestowed on the evil. Even his mother had not suspected. Only Kunos, planted and nurtured as a source of inspiration in the woods, knew that Kore was himself and he was not. But Kunos had no one to tell but the tree and the sky. And when a thunderstorm had finally starved him of even his last hope, the dual Kore must have decided to become permanently the Kunos he had always dreamt of being.

Until, that is, Epictetus and his slave had frightened him into madness with a living mirror.

Still, as often as the Master repeated the story under the colonnade, there were among his students many who could not understand how he had guessed the truth. To them, he always made the same reply, while always avoiding a direct look into anyone's doubting eyes.

'What?' Epictetus would answer evenly. 'Do you mean besides the father's obsession with threes and the mother's philosophical imagination? Besides her troubling equanimity, her belief in habit, and her strange remarks about quail lice that weren't there? Or Kore's reference to his twin brothers and himself as Eteocles and Polynices rather than as, perhaps, the three-headed monster of Sparta, Athens, and Thebes or as the Dorians with their three tribes? Weren't all these enough for you? What more did you want? God's own arithmetic to help you add one plus one and come up with two instead of three?

'Remember,' he would say uncertainly and hurry back to his topic. 'All of us have a choice between good and evil, desire and aversion, life and death. God never gives us a third option. Life isn't a syllogism, philosophers. It's a question. It's you who are supposed to be the answers.'

And at the next Saturnalia, when he repaid his slave, Manes, with extra liberties, the Stoic sat at home alone with a cup of wine and his new table leg. He stared at it for hours, remembering a man who had lived out his only life as a tree and probably learned more about what was and what was not within his control than any Master could ever teach. From then on, Epictetus reserved his judgements of others until he got to know them better, until he learned how little he really knew of any other man's daily burdens, of his marble horror and his ivory despair.

THE ASS'S HEAD

Phyllis Ann Karr

Phyllis Ann Karr may be better known for her fantasy novels, which include an Arthurian murder mystery, The Idylls of the King *(1982), but her first professional sales were historical mysteries to* Ellery Queen's Mystery Magazine *in 1974. In the following story she tackles something quite different, and considers how the early Christian religion appeared to the superstitious Romans. Strange though this story may seem, it is based on firm facts cited in* The Christians as the Romans Saw Them *(1984) by Robert L. Wilken.*

∽

THE ASS'S HEAD
by Atramentacio
translated & adapted by Phyllis Ann Karr

Translator's Foreword Very few of Atramentacio's plays have survived, and most of those were discovered less than two decades ago, eighteen hundred years after being written and first produced. Little is known of the author's life. Nevertheless, obscure though he – or, possibly, she – is today, Atramentacio's plays seem to have enjoyed considerable popularity in their own time: the last quarter of the second century CE and some decades following. It has been plausibly argued, largely from internal evidence in the plays themselves, that the pseudonym conceals a woman's hand. A few scholars have suggested some connection between Camolindium, the setting of at least three Atramentacian plays (the other two have reached us only in fragments), and King Arthur's Camelot.

Working against deadline to adapt this play for the modern reader, I confess to having followed the path of least resistance. Rather than choosing one or two viewpoint characters through whose eyes to look (there is no one character who appears in every single scene), refashioning blocks of dialogue into descriptive passages, and multiplying the variety of scenes by turning offstage action into narrative or vice versa, I have simply tried to imagine myself in a front-row seat watching a good production. In Crato and Chloe we see the remnants of the classical Chorus (and also, one might almost be tempted to guess, the seeds of the archetypal old couple of later ballads); their Prologue and Epilogue were probably delivered on the equivalent of bare stage in front of the closed curtain, but the lines themselves indicate that they are to be understood as taking place in Crato's own garden. The one other scene change is indeed in the original play; this may have been an innovation for the times. I have shortened numerous speeches (believe it or not!) and occasionally imagined some tone of voice, bit of stage business, or piece of costuming; but more of such touches than one might expect were suggested by certain lines of dialogue, usually among the ones I omitted. For example, in one such line, Bodicca – surely the playwright had Boudicca (Boadicea) in mind as a model – says: 'Is my left breast not bared for suckling my [own] child by Kynon, even while my right arm remains unencumbered to wield my spear?' This reference could simply echo one ancient belief about the Amazons; but it could also suggest the actual stage costume, which is how I decided to interpret it. In such elements as the portrayal of native Britons, I have attempted to reconstruct, not historical reality as we now know it, but popular contemporary conception as it might have been represented on the theatrical stage in farflung parts of the Roman Empire. In some cases, e.g., the floor plan of Flavian's house, Atramentacio seems more or less reliably informed; in other cases, he (or she) does not. I have tried to reproduce this play 'warts and all.'

DRAMATIS PERSONAE

Cassius Marcellus Flavian, legate of Camolindium in Britain
Gnaius Metellus Lucian, his favorite centurion
Marcus Gordius Octavio, a young decurion, newly transferred from Gaul
Kynon (Roman name: Horatius Marcellus Kynus), a British chieftain, formerly Flavian's son-in-law

Crato, an old philosopher, adoptive uncle to the town
Bucco, a young slave of Flavian's
Dossemus, a tinker
Rufus Sinistris, a traveler
Marcella, Flavian's daughter, formerly married to Kynon
Bodicca, a British warrior-woman, Kynon's present wife
Chloe, Crato's wife, adoptive aunt to the town
Marcellina (also called Kyna), daughter of Marcella and Kynon, formally adopted by her grandfather Flavian, between two and three years of age
Myrtilia, a slave of Flavian, Bucco's mother, formerly Marcella's and presently Marcellina's nurse.
Flavian's adjutant, slaves of Flavian's household, legionaries, British shield-bearers and warriors, townspeople, etc.

The old woman was pacing her courtyard, plucking worms and dropping them to the ground whenever she noticed them menacing her tender green buds. At last the old man rose from his seat in the peristyle and strolled over to join her, still absent-mindedly munching his honey cake. He wore the simple *pallium* of antique Greek philosophers but, in deference to the harsher climate of Britain, under it he had on a soft, well-patched woolen tunic with long sleeves.

'Xanthippe, Xanthippe,' he admonished her, gently shaking his head. 'How is a philosopher to contemplate God's nature in the universe, with his wife stamping about like Flavian's whole legion on the march?'

'Crato, Crato,' she returned, shaking her head back at him wearily but affectionately. 'You may fancy yourself Socrates, but you are not, and no more am I that ancient philosopher's wife. We live in the world's last age, and at earth's farthest end – where you are as good as uncle to all Camolindium and teacher to almost nobody – and your best little scholar should have been here long ago!'

He blinked. 'What? Is it Pytho's day again so soon?'*

'Pytho? You would call Pytho your best scholar? No, no, old man. This is our morning for Flavian's granddaughter, little Marcellina.'

'Little Marcellina. You would call her my scholar?' But Crato's

---

* This suggests some 'in' joke, perhaps concerning an obscure philosophical school, a character in a now-lost play, or even an actor associated with such a character. In any event, after being mentioned in the Prologue, Pytho vanishes completely from *The Ass's Head*.

voice, never truly angry, grew milder yet. 'Little, golden-haired Marcellina, whose baby tongue still sometimes slips and calls herself Kyna, after her British father. Why, she has not yet seen her third summer –'

'But this is her third spring,' his wife reminded him.

'The very turning of the seasons is still a strange wonder to her, and, moreover, she is a girl. How should we call her my scholar?'

'I call her your scholar, husband, for the attention she gives your words – more than they deserve, Pallas Athena knows! – when she climbs into your lap and twines her tiny fingers in your beard.'

'Well, then, call her your scholar as much as mine. If I am Camolindium's uncle, you are Camolindium's aunt, and our small visitor gives you as much attention as me. And yet,' he added dreamily, 'for all that, I am well content that it is she I will see today, and not Pytho.'

'If we see her today. Crato, have you not noticed how high Apollo's chariot is already?'

He glanced up, blinked, and looked down at the half-eaten cake in his hand. 'By all gods and goddesses, heroes and daimons! Only a glutton is still breaking his fast at this hour. Here, great Demeter, accept my offering.' Carefully he crumbled his remaining cake upon a plot of spaded ground. 'To you, and to your fair daughter whose yearly return brings us this fair season of spring – even here at earth's farthest end – and to your birds of the air, I give back this portion of your good gifts to humankind. Now, my Chloe,' he added, calling his wife by her right name as, brushing off his hands, he turned back to her, 'surely no one but a madman would dare molest the granddaughter of our glorious legate Cassius Marcellus Flavian, so let us wait yet a little while longer before scurrying off to him like frightened mice to learn what may have happened to detain her.'

The house of Cassius Marcellus Flavian had been adapted to seize as much as possible of the cold northern sun. Instead of a comfortably private atrium, it had one vast open courtyard, enclosed on three sides by his house – one long row housing *triclinium*, offices, bedrooms, and larder; flanked by two wings, one for kitchen and private baths, the other providing quarters for the family's slaves. The columns of the peristyle separating rooms from courtyard stood spaced widely to allow as much warmth and light as possible into the residence, and also showing off a finely crafted shrine to the household Lares and Penates. On the fourth side of the courtyard was nothing but front wall with its gated doorway.

In such a courtyard, calm ought to have prevailed. But, today, it did not. An aging woman in simple, unadorned *stola* bent to bandage the bleeding head of a young man in his twenties, clad in the tunic of workingman or slave, who lay on one of the benches and tried through moans and groans to render a military-style report to the silver-haired officer towering above him.

This officer, clearly the master of the house and more soldier than senator of Rome, heard the youth out and meanwhile from time to time ordered various slaves on their errands with few and simple words, doing much, by his command and stern example, to stem the tide of panic ... even though his own brows were separated only by a frown so deep an onlooker might have expected blood to drip from it, too – as one of his slaves whispered to another while hurrying off to have wine warmed for the injured man.

The other slave whispered back, 'Gods! Who can blame our unhappy master?'

The first slave halted in her errand long enough to call her friend's attention to a tall young matron, not many years removed from girlhood but bearing herself with sober maturity, who had appeared between two peristyle columns. 'Unhappy young mistress! Ah, Dea Matrona, our poor mistress Marcella!'

The two slaves hurried on, pausing momentarily at the household altar to bow their heads in quick prayer. Marcella, unseen by either legate or injured man, listened with lips compressed and one hand clutching the stone pillar ever more tightly.

'In brief,' said Cassius Marcellus Flavian, 'you have betrayed your charge.'

'Master!' The woman tending the young man's head stared up at the legate with fear in her large eyes. 'You do not ... blame my son Bucco?'

'Was I not struck from behind?' Bucco added with surly respect.

'For whatever reason, you have lost the child entrusted to your safekeeping. A true servant would have laid down his own life in protection of any helpless one given into his charge.'

Bucco darted one angry glance at his master, but immediately bowed his head again beneath his mother's hands.

'Father, no!' Marcella said, coming down from the peristyle.

Flavian turned and saw her. 'Marcella! You overheard?'

'Would you have tried to keep this from me? This knife that cuts into my soul more deeply than into anyone else's?'

'Daughter! Your child is doubly mine. By blood, grandchild. By adoption, daughter and namesake.'

'Father! Man's love for his children may run deep as Neptune's waters – I would never deny this – but mother's love runs deeper still. No man has carried his child within his own bowels, beneath his very heart.'

Bucco's mother bowed her head over his as though to conceal tears.

'But I am your daughter, and Roman,' Marcella went on, visibly holding her emotions in check. 'How well I came to understand this – what it is to be Roman – those months I spent as wife to that British chieftain. Never think it was the rigors of their wild tribal life that brought me home again to you. Am I not a soldier's daughter? No, it was their lack of civilization in all things that shape the soul. Not their lack of drains,' she continued, like one who had turned these thoughts over and over in her mind, 'but the crudity of their brains. Some rough religion they have, but it is not our pious reverence for God and fellow man; some crude honor and coarse affection, but how far it is from Roman honor and Roman love of family. Even though, granted Roman citizenship, my former husband valued his Roman name less than any casual trinket, something to be worn on rare occasions but more often tossed aside. No, do not blame Bucco for trusting that orderly Camolindium would offer no dangers between our home and that of our philosopher friend. Blame Marcellina's father by blood! Summon Kynon here to answer for Marcellina. And, if he will not come, send your legion!'

'Daughter,' said the legate, 'had you been my son, what a soldier you would have made!' Turning to his adjutant, who stood by, he ordered, 'Take this message to Gnaius Metellus Lucian: that he is to go to the British village and bring their chieftain Horatius Marcellus Kynus, whom they may still call Kynon, back here to me at once.'

'Lucian?' Marcella interjected. 'Not Octavio? Father, why not Marcus Gordius Octavio?'

'Gnaius Metellus Lucian,' the legate repeated sternly to his adjutant. 'At once.' As the adjutant hurried away, Flavian turned back to his daughter. 'There are reasons, Marcella, for my wish that you see no more of Marcus Gordius Octavio. Remember my wisdom in opposing your marriage to Kynon, even after making him Horatius Marcellus Kynus, and be content.'

Breathing deeply and rapidly, she stared back unblinking into Flavian's eyes. 'Octavio is not Kynon. Father, do you not think I have learned more wisdom than was mine four years ago?'

'Let us agree that Octavio is not Kynon, nor Kynon's flaws identical with those of Octavio. Would you see our present business imperiled by some quarrel struck as if from tinder when he who had your love once and he who almost has it now come face to face?'

'It is because Octavio cares for my child as much as –' She choked off her own sentence and resumed, dropping her gaze, 'No, you are right. What does any of all this matter, until we have Marcellina safe with us again?'

'Marcellina?' another voice broke in. The old philosopher Crato had arrived, with his wife on his arm.

'I knew it!' Chloe exclaimed before her husband's one-word question could be answered. 'And then, when your messenger all but ran us over at your gate in his hurry, I knew it again!'

'Hush, wife.' Crato stroked her hand soothingly. 'As yet, we know very little. What of the child?' he added anxiously, looking at Flavian.

'All that we ourselves know is soon told,' the legate replied. 'It appears that as my slave of questionable worth was bringing Marcellina to your house this morning, honored friend, some villain or villains struck him from behind and knocked him senseless long enough to make off with my daughter's daughter.'

'Oh, Marcella!' Chloe cried, leaving her husband to fold the young mother in her arms. This sudden show of tenderness broke Marcella's resolve, and her tears flowed freely at last.

The slave Bucco had cast up another fierce look at his master's latest insult, but only his mother noticed it, and she quickly drew his head down again.

Old Crato was pulling his white beard in his apparent effort to ward agitation off with reason. 'Was it not at about this same time last year that another child vanished without trace?'

Everyone else stared at him. Horror was especially plain in the faces of the women – Marcella, Chloe, and she who bent over Bucco.

'They said,' whispered Chloe, 'they said that Christians took him – Oh, God! Can we truly have a coven of Christians here in Camolindium?'

'Hush, wife,' said Crato. 'These Christians are mere harmless fools.'

'I remember that case,' Flavian mused with creased brow. 'A younger child, was it not? An infant boy, less than one year of age . . .'

'Some slave's baby,' Bucco supplied in a tone of respect so studied as almost to constitute insolence. 'Worth only whatever he might have brought on the block. Not to be mentioned in the same sentence with the grandchild of a legate of Rome.'

'My . . . master!' gasped the old slave woman. 'Forgive my son – his wound – he wanders in his wits!'

'Not so far,' said Bucco. 'I remember now. Just before that blow fell, I heard voices. Voices speaking in British. No words that I understood, but one of them might have been "Kyna" or "Kynon."'

Flavian studied his young slave for as long as a bird might need to pull a worm from the ground. At last he said, 'For your sake, Myrtilia, once my daughter's nurse and now my granddaughter's, I will forgive your son. I may never again entrust him with any errand involving another person's safety, but let that be the full extent of his punishment. Now take him to your own quarters, nurse him well, and summon me at once should he find any further details while wandering in his wits.'

Head bandaged, Bucco was able to stagger away with his mother as living crutch. One might have suspected him, indeed, of exaggerating his weakness and giddiness somewhat, no doubt to re-emphasize his blamelessness and prolong his convalescent ease.

Watching them go, Flavian told Marcella, 'Daughter, let us not forget that we have guests.' To Crato he added, 'I have newly received a shipment of books from Rome, among them several that I am sure would interest you. Marcella knows where to find them.'

'Come,' Marcella said, drawing herself into the role of hostess. To a pair of the remaining slaves she added, 'Nathan, Sarah, attend us.'

As the women and slaves started for the house, Flavian muttered in Crato's ear, 'Watch over her, old friend. May your philosophy serve us well in this hour.'

'I have no fear for Marcellina,' the philosopher replied somberly. 'Barbarian though he may be, the child's father can hardly mean her ill. These British love their offspring as much as we love ours. As for Christians, they are mere foolish dabblers in atheism, much maligned, and if they return nothing to the State that nourished them, neither could their contribution greatly enrich society in any case.'

'Nevertheless,' the legate muttered to himself after Crato had followed the others into the house, 'I will leave no stone unturned.' To the last slave left outdoors with him, he said, 'Summon the decurion Marcus Gordius Octavio here to me at once.'

The man hurried across the courtyard, and narrowly missed colliding at the gate with a handsome young officer on his way in.

'Master,' said the slave, stepping back into the courtyard long enough to flourish an extravagant bow, 'the decurion Marcus Gordius Octavio has been summoned here to you at once.'

'I thank you, Dromo,' Flavian said dryly. 'Now go and arrange for Juno to have two lambs in sacrifice for Marcellina's safe return.'

The slave disappeared. The decurion, moving with the disciplined stride of a Roman legionary, approached his superior, halted at a respectful distance, and saluted. One could see the tension in his soul, and the self-mastery with which he held it in check.

'Well, Octavio,' said the legate. 'What god gave you word that I would send for you? Was it Juno, or Venus?'

'Your daughter's daughter has vanished and her attendant been left stunned and witless,' Octavio replied. 'This is no secret in our barracks. Moreover, I was with Metellus Lucian when your order came for him to bring the British chieftain to you. If you would thank any gods for hastening my steps, thank your own household guardians.'

'It remains to be seen whether I will owe thanks to any god for your presence.' Flavian took several paces back and forth, as if in thought, before speaking again. 'Marcus Gordius Octavio, have you seen any Christians here in Camolindium?'

The young man stiffened. 'As you know, sir, I determined to leave that godless sect upon first learning that they would require me to forswear all warfare. The gods fashioned me to serve my country as soldier, and soldier I knew I must remain. It was only on direct order from my commander in Gaul that I pretended still to be one of them long enough for us to catch them at those foul rites by which they would have initiated me fully into their membership.'

Flavian nodded. 'And I alone, in all Camolindium, am aware of all this. It was for obeying Quintus Severan and helping to exterminate that nest of them in Gaul, as well as for your early report to him, accompanied with your own confession and recantation, that you were allowed this second chance, with clean slate, here in Britain.'

'With clean slate, sir,' the decurion repeated, allowing some faint bitterness to tinge his voice. 'Thinking their founder to have been the son of one Panthera, himself a soldier, I had at first supposed their cult akin to that of Mithras. Otherwise, I would never have become their "catechumen," as they call them.'

'I sent for you,' Flavian went on, somewhat impatiently, 'not to rake through old matters, but to learn if you, with your experience of them, have noticed any sign of Christians among us here.'

'I have not looked for them, sir. Nor, until Marcellina's disappearance today, had I seen anything during my half-year in Britain to suggest their presence in or near Camolindium.'

'True. You were still in Gaul last year at this time, when the infant slave disappeared.'

'Mars and Minerva!' the decurion exclaimed. 'Two young children vanished at this season in subsequent years! Sir, that chills my soul.'

'Let us assume the worst. From what you know of them, is my granddaughter likely still to be alive?'

Octavio nodded gravely. 'Until tonight, at least. Possibly longer. They would no more sacrifice a child already dead than we would a calf or piglet.'

'And, if they are among us, would any of them know you? Could this explain why they have kept themselves so well concealed from your initiated eyes?'

'No initiate, sir,' Octavio reminded the legate. 'It stopped just short of that. But, if any Christian here had known me for one of their "apostates" – as they call those of us who awaken to their errors and leave their cult voluntarily – I think they would more likely have sought to assassinate than merely avoid me.'

'Good, good.' The legate paced again, staring at the courtyard beneath his sandals while Octavio stared at him. Neither of them noticed Crato approaching from the house. 'Well,' Flavian resumed at last, 'my chief suspicion still rests on Marcellina's British father. But, if you were to look, would you be able to scent out any local Christians for us?'

'They are cunning, sir. They have learned secrecy well. But, yes, I could find and contact them, if commanded to do so.'

'Then do so at once. I command it.'

'What is this?' the philosopher asked, stepping eagerly forward.

'Crato!' said the legate. 'Old friend, we thought you with my daughter.'

'She has Chloe to comfort her,' Crato explained. 'Nor is Marcella's Sarah any mean help at that skill. And where women comfort one another, men may only be in their way. But have I blundered into some delicate conference?'

'That depends,' Flavian answered carefully, 'on how much you may have overheard.'

'Enough to know that you, like my dear wife, suspect some infestation of Christians in our area, and that this good decurion has some talent for finding those maligned misanthropes.'

'Some talent, yes,' Octavio echoed with noncommital irony.

'Talent born of knowledge,' his commander added slowly and deliberately, frowning at the younger man in a way that went over Crato's head. 'Marcus Gordius Octavio's former legion had experience with a band of them in Gaul.'

'Indeed?' The philosopher turned again to Octavio. 'Is it true that they believe their founder, Jesus ben Panthera, to have had the head of an ass, or is that merely another slander put about by their enemies?'

'Whether they believe it was actually so,' the young soldier replied stiffly, 'I cannot say. It is true, however, that they frequently represent him with an ass's head, mounted on a miniature cross.'

'Ah! This would seem to echo those beast-headed Egyptian gods, in whose land the sorcerer ben Panthera is supposed to have learned his magical arts.'

'Old friend,' the legate remarked with a tolerant smile, 'I see that you know something of these people, yourself.'

'Not enough, not enough.' Crato shook his bald head. 'I would learn more, much more. Few in numbers they may be, but no manner of worshipping any god lacks interest for me, no matter how novel. Indeed, in every novelty I seek that kernel of tradition – that leaven remaining to us from the earliest ages, when God and man were closer – without which no worship can please its deity.'

'If it were not for the danger,' said Flavian, 'I would have sent you to sniff out our local Christians.'

'Danger? What danger? It is their reputation alone that makes such people dangerous. Well, well,' the philosopher concluded regretfully, 'far be it from me to offer myself in place of your soldier going about his duty. But should he find any Christians for you, might I beg the special privilege of meeting them myself?'

Flavian looked at Octavio, who returned his gaze steadily.

'It would increase my stature in their eyes,' Octavio told his commander, 'if I were to bring them another catechumen – as he would seem – and one of Crato's standing in the community. I think, however, that I should begin by reconnoitering alone.'

'Go, then. Our friend can await your report here with me.'

Octavio saluted and took his departure. The legate summoned slaves and had them arrange chairs and a midday repast for him and his guest just within the peristyle, where the spring sun could warm them as they ate.

Crato, arguing that philosophy demanded maintaining one's strength, nibbled away more conscientiously than the legate; but neither man showed much appetite for the plovers' eggs, mussels, and barley bread brought out to them. Flavian emptied a full goblet of the local honey-wine he had set (saving his better vintages for Marcellina's safe return), but he drank it well watered. In truth, their *prandium* consisted less of food than of conversation, and even that was desultory at best, and soon cut short by the arrival of Gnaius Metellus Lucian with Marcellina's father by blood.

Striding in on the heels of his Roman escort, the young British chieftain made a striking – even magnificent – spectacle. He came only in leather breeches and a short bearskin cloak thrown over one shoulder and held together, by its own paws, beneath his other arm, leaving his chest open to display his widest expanse of woad tattooing. Blue whorls covered his arms as well; indeed, every inch of visible skin, even his cheeks and forehead. A rich golden torque, its twin ends tipped with lions' heads of fine if barbaric workmanship, adorned his neck, while rough fur buskins covered his feet to the calf. Beside him walked a tall British woman, as sun-brown and woad-blue as himself, and similarly costumed, except that a band from waist to right shoulder, while leaving her left breast bare, modestly covered her right. The British couple carried nothing, but young tribesmen, still only partially tattooed, followed them bearing their spears and shields.

'Rome!' the chieftain cried, with neither preamble nor salute. 'What is this? You have let my daughter be stolen?'

Flavian, who had risen to his feet at the chieftain's entrance, shot back, 'Horatius Marcellus Kynus of the British people! Or Kynon, if you so prefer to be called! If you have taken her yourself, do not attempt to hide your guilt from the eye of Roman Jupiter.'

'We?' exclaimed the woman at Kynon's side. 'Why should we take the child? We foolishly believed her safe beneath the eagle wings of your vaunted Rome!'

'Who is this woman?' the legate demanded to know.

'Did you think I would keep Marcella's place empty in my bed forever?' Kynon queried back by way of reply. 'Bodicca is my wife now.'

'Now and for all our years to come,' the woman added, laying one hand proudly on Kynon's shoulder. 'This time he has a wife forever, now that Bodicca has finally found a man worthy of her.'

'So you have taken a second wife,' Flavian answered icily. 'What better reason to steal back your child, for this second wife to rear?'

'Roman,' Bodicca demanded with cold fire, 'do you suppose me incapable of bearing Kynon sons and daughters finer than any your own pallid offshoot could give him?'

'Questions heaped on questions,' Crato interposed, stepping forward and spreading his hands pacifically. 'With all respect to my own gods, might this old philosopher suggest that there is a time and place for direct and simple answers?'

'Well said, honored friend,' Flavian approved.

'Here, then, is my direct and simple answer,' Kynon told them. 'Neither I nor any of my people have taken or laid hand on my daughter Kyna, whom you call Marcellina, even though it would have been no more than my right to reclaim her. I left our dear child with Marcella, in memory of the love we once shared, for however brief a season. Now give me direct and simple answers to my questions: How did you, with your boasts of Roman might and Roman peace and Roman laws, allow this thing to happen? Did you not love your granddaughter enough to see to her protection? And how, after allowing it to happen, did you dare summon me here to accuse me of the outrage, rather than to beg a father's help in saving his stolen child?'

'I make allowance for your natural feelings,' the legate replied. 'From no other man alive would I permit any suggestion that this thing happened through failure of love on my part or my daughter's. As for your other questions, when a child is seized with violence from her guardian within our very city walls, who else should we suspect of violating Roman peace, if not those who hold Roman laws in open contempt?'

'We have accepted your standards among us,' Kynon returned angrily. 'We have lived in peace with you for generations. On what grounds do you charge us with contempt? Simply because we do not grovel?'

'Husband,' said Bodicca, sounding less like wife than co-commander, 'this helps no one recover your child.'

Crato sighed. 'Your lady shows wisdom. Let us lay aside all arguments of larger rights and wrongs until little Marcellina is safely home again.'

'I am willing,' Flavian agreed.

'Well!' said Kynon. 'So am I, for the present. Let us begin by looking at how it happened. You said that she had a guardian, from whom she was seized within your very walls?'

'One of Marcellus Flavian's slaves was bringing her to my home for such lessons as her small and feminine mind is ready to digest,' Crato explained.

'One . . . of . . . your . . . slaves?' Kynon repeated disbelievingly, staring at the legate. 'This comes of your Roman habit of entrusting the work befitting free men and women to slaves instead!'

Flavian met the Briton's gaze without blinking. 'The man was struck senseless, and that from behind. Before he lost consciousness, he heard British voices speaking your name, or that of Kyna, and other words in your British tongue – another reason for my initial suspicion of you.'

'But not the first reason, was it?' Kynon said shrewdly, adding, 'A true guardian would have given his life in defense of his charge, not merely lent the gods his poor wits for a few moments and then come back to them babbling nonsense. Where is this slave who made such poor work of protecting a helpless child?'

'His head was broken and bloodied,' said Flavian. 'His mother is nursing him in his own quarters.'

'His mother is nursing him!' cried Kynon. 'While the gods know who is nursing the child entrusted to him, and with what sort of care? Bring him out and let us question him!'

'He is my slave, and I have questioned him to my satisfaction.'

'I do not trust the questioning of a man who coddles incompetence at sight of a little blood.'

'I tell you,' said the legate, 'we know where and when it happened. I coddle no one. I demand as much of my slaves, according to their capacities, as of my soldiers. But I am satisfied there is nothing more to be learned from . . . Well? Let me hear your report!' he interrupted himself, looking across his courtyard.

Octavio had returned, and was standing at attention waiting his chance to be recognized. On his commander's order he stepped forward and saluted. 'Hail, legate of Caesar. There are indeed Christians here in Camolindium, as I have proved by making contact with certain members of their sect.' He stopped speaking, as if done with his report.

After a few heartbeats, Flavian said, 'Particulars?'

Octavio glanced at the pair of Britons with their legionary escort. 'Particulars, sir, you might prefer to hear alone.'

'Does this touch on the disappearance of my child by your commander's daughter?' Kynon demanded.

The legate looked at Octavio, who replied.

'I cannot yet be sure, but I think that it may concern Marcellina.'

'Then it touches me as well,' said Kynon, 'and I will hear it.'

'And I with my husband,' said Bodicca.

The Britons stood as if rooted in the ground as immovably as the trees they worshipped. After studying them for a moment, Flavian said in no uncertain terms, 'Then let my centurion Lucian show your shieldbearers the hospitality of our barracks.'

'We will allow him to buy them one cup apiece, well watered, in Bibulo's wineshop, that stands hard by your house,' Kynon answered with resolve to match Flavian's. 'Let them leave our weapons here.'

The two commanders stared at each other. Without dropping his gaze, Flavian ordered, 'Be it so!'

Gnaius Metellus Lucian saluted, the young Britons laid their leaders' spears and shields neatly upon the ground, and all of them departed together.

When they were gone, Flavian told his decurion, 'Whatever you have to say, it can be spoken for their ears as well as mine. Being Marcellina's father by blood, Kynon has the right to hear it, as has she who now shares his bed.' Nobody mentioned old Crato, who also stood by listening with interest. Had he not already volunteered to play Octavio's catechumen?

'I lingered in the marketplace,' Octavio continued his report, 'furtively using my toe to draw their fish sigil in the dust. At length someone noticed it and replied by scratching her sigil beside mine. That woman . . .' Again he hesitated, but, filling his lungs deeply, resumed unprompted, 'That woman, sir, was your own slave, Myrtilia.'

Flavian's shock was audible by his sharp intake of breath. Crato exclaimed softly, 'So close to home!'

'I had thought Myrtilia in her own part of my house, nursing her son,' said the legate.

'She left him long enough to buy some few ingredients for her nursing – salve, herbs to season broth . . .' Octavio shrugged. 'Learning my own pretended membership in their cult, she delivered me to their chief *flamen*, who proves to be none other than Dossemus, the one-eyed hunchback and mender of pots.'

'Dossemus?' said Crato. 'I would have pointed to him in example of how little is actually needed to remain alive.'

'I would have pointed to him,' said Flavian, 'as living example of filth, squalor, and idleness. Next thing to a beggar, that creature mends two or three pots only when he can no longer dodge the absolute necessity for some few small coins to rub together, briefly. Well? What did you learn from Dossemus?'

'They meet this evening at nightfall,' Octavio replied. 'I won enough trust to learn when, but not where. When I seal the proof of my faith by returning with my new catechumen, they will take us both there.'

'I will set spies to follow you and bring word back to me and our legion,' said Flavian.

Octavio's answer was filled with doubt. 'Dossemus and his

fellows have had reason and opportunity to learn every one of our faces by sight – regular legionaries, auxiliaries, and scouts, and all your slaves as well. Give them any suspicion whatever that they are being followed, and Marcellina is lost. Nor would I guarantee our honored Crato's safety in such case.'

'Is she still alive even now?' Kynon cut in. 'Cernunnos! How long you Romans take getting to the heart of a matter!'

'She will be safe until deep into their ceremony,' Octavio assured him. 'They will not even bring her forth until after they have sent their catechumens away.'

'What?' Crato blinked. 'Ah! Of course. This alleged abominable sacrament of theirs is for full initiates only. Well, then, we have no problem. As soon as sent away, I will return and lead you back.'

Octavio objected, 'These Christians are slow to trust even one another. Had demonstrating the orthodoxy of my supposed beliefs and ritualistic knowledge as learned in Gaul been enough to satisfy Dossemus in full, he would have named the place and left me to find my own path there. Since he did not, no doubt they will blindfold both me and my catechumen before leading us to the site.'

'I should recognize it once they unbandage my eyes,' Crato said with quiet confidence.

Octavio looked at him admiringly. 'Honored philosopher, it is fortunate I had you to name as my neophyte. All my own supposed orthodoxy might not have been enough, but they are eager indeed to number such citizens as you among them. May God, Who sent you to play this role, enable you to slip away from all other catechumens who may be present, and return here in time.'

'But you yourself will remain for their most secret ceremonies?' said Flavian. 'How did you persuade them that you were fully initiate, and yet remaining a soldier of Rome?'

'By pointing out the excellency of it as cover, for now, and explaining my supposed determination to remain soldier only in time of peace, and desert before obeying any order to go to war.'

The British chieftainess spoke. 'With all these great suspicions of theirs, will they not have set someone to watch you, decurion? What will they have concluded upon seeing you come into the legate's courtyard?'

'Nothing, I hope. They know that a soldier must sometimes go about his commander's business, and I took care to explain that another matter entirely – some little trouble in the barracks – was bringing me here today. They also know that Crato visits our legate not infrequently, nor did I see any reason to hide his present concern for Marcella's daughter.' He turned to the old philosopher. 'Nevertheless, it will be best to avoid any chance of being seen leaving this house together. We are to meet Dossemus in the shop of Marcus the butcher. They will begin your instruction as soon as you arrive, even without me. But let me warn you, sir, to put your mind on guard. They will not let you see any sign that they have the child, nor hear any hint of what is to come after you are sent away. Their words to their catechumens are entirely fair, sweet, and in some specious way even noble.'

'I will go at once,' Crato said eagerly, 'before my wife happens to come out. It would only worry her. Be sure to give her my fondest regards and tell her . . . tell her . . .'

'That you have returned home to search out some scroll of philosophy most appropriate to comfort us in this hour,' Flavian finished for him, laying one hand on his shoulder. 'Go, old friend, with my thanks and those my daughter would add if she knew anything of this.'

It was only after Crato's departure that Flavian sat, for the first time seeming to let his years weigh upon him. 'Myrtilia!' he mourned. 'My late wife grew up beside her, almost more like sister and sister than mistress and slave. She nursed our daughter from the cradle. Of all women in Camolindium, Myrtilia was the one, after Marcella herself and Crato's good wife, with whom I would most have trusted Marcellina.'

Bodicca, who had never ceased eyeing Octavio, stepped forward and seized the young soldier by one wrist. 'Show me,' she demanded, 'how to make this fish sigil!'

Pulling his arm free of her grip, Octavio looked to his commander. At Flavian's nod, the decurion knelt and with his finger traced two curves in the earth, their tips meeting at one end while parting tail-like at the other.

Bodicca copied it twice, nodded, and said to the legate, 'Now, direct me to this slave's quarters.'

Almost wearily, Flavian gestured at the left-hand wing of his house. As Bodicca disappeared into it, he went on as if to himself, 'And this is my reward for being so lenient a master as to allow my slaves their own outer door, for locking it only at night. Too long have I been gentler with my slaves than with my soldiers!'

Octavio cocked one brow, as if silently questioning Cassius Marcellus Flavian's leniency toward his soldiers, but kept silent.

'Will you confront this woman with her accuser?' Kynon asked, drawing Flavian from his sad reverie.

The commander shook his head. 'No, I think it is not yet time for that. God! How many of my slaves may be involved? Well, Octavio, return to barracks awhile on whatever errand you invented for the Christian *flamen*'s ears, and from there seek Dossemus out again when you judge the time ripe.'

'Should I bid men prepare to march this evening, sir?'

Flavian shook his head. 'Metellus Lucian will see to that. Do not try to heap his duties upon your own.'

Octavio came to attention, snapped his salute, and departed. Watching him go, Kynon muttered to the legate, 'Bodicca does not entirely trust that man.'

'You consulted with your new wife concerning him, did you?'

'I sensed her feelings. They are mine.'

'Based upon anything in particular?' Flavian inquired coldly. 'Or do you mistrust Octavio simply because he is Roman, and my man?' Standing up, the legate went on, 'Let us understand each other, Briton. You have disliked me from the day we first met, and I you from the day you began to seduce my daughter. But for the sake of your people as well as mine, these personal enmities must be ignored.'

'It is you who have first mentioned them today, Roman. Today, when a common cause requires us to join forces. For the present, I allow your soldier to pass unchallenged, for my suspicion is even sharper on that slave who let the child be taken from his care.'

'Bucco?' Flavian spoke slowly, meditatively. 'He did not lose her without having his own head bloodied. Yet he is also Myrtilia's son . . .'

As Flavian spoke, Bodicca returned, dragging the old nurse by one arm, two more slaves trailing at a timid distance.

'She is one of them, indeed!' the warrioress exclaimed, thrusting Myrtilia to the ground in front of the legate.

The unfortunate slave clawed the ground at Flavian's sandals and wailed, 'Mercy! Mercy, master! Mercy!'

'Ask mercy of the gods!' Flavian replied, staring down at her in distaste. To Kynon, he said, 'Summon your shieldbearers, and kindly relay to Gnaius Metellus Lucian that I wish him present.'

'What of this woman's son?' said Kynon.

'In due time, Bucco shall stand before us as well.' Keeping one eye upon the as yet uninvolved slaves, who did not move, Flavian added, 'And that time will be soon. But it is not yet.'

'I go, Roman, because it is my own free choice to accept your direction in this for now.' Kynon strode across the courtyard to the gate.

The legate turned his attention back to his moaning slave woman. 'Myrtilia, Myrtilia! Is it true that you are Christian?'

'Master, mercy!'

'I tell you,' Bodicca declared, 'it is true. And, for a moment, she mistook me, also, for one of their breed!' The warrioress rubbed her forefinger as though it needed rough purification after tracing the unholy sigil.

Flavian said, 'I cannot do otherwise than believe you. Were it false, she would deny your accusation, not simply grovel at my feet for mercy.'

Kynon returned with Lucian and the British youths. The legionary saluted his legate and awaited orders.

'Take these lads – with their chieftain's permission –' Flavian told his centurion, 'secure the outer door to my slaves' quarters, and leave the Britons to guard it until you can bring men from the barracks to relieve them. It must be guarded well. Allow no one to pass in or out. Detail men to find any of my slaves who may already be abroad for any reason, and discreetly bring them back, by way of my gate. Then return to me yourself.'

The British shieldbearers looked at Kynon, who nodded and waved them on. Saluting again, Lucian led them from the courtyard.

Bodicca said, 'But we must know the place of the Christian meeting! We should post watchers to follow any slave who slips out, not alert them –'

'Have you not already alerted them, dragging Myrtilia out like this?' Flavian jerked his head toward the silent slaves. 'Will anyone who may slip out of this house lead us to their meeting, or will they give them warning not to hold it, and to dispose of their victim before she can be found to incriminate them? Besides,' he added, in tones equally stern but less angry, 'Myrtilia will tell us where they meet tonight.'

'Oh, Holy Spirit!' the old nurse moaned, 'now put Your words into my mouth!'

'I will not ask you to name any of your fellow Christians, Myrtilia,' the legate continued, almost gently. 'Not even among my own slaves. Let them prove their own guilt or innocence. I ask you to tell us only where they gather this night.'

Myrtilia rose to her knees, straightened her back, and replied, her voice ringing as if inspired, 'You will not ask me to betray my brothers and sisters by name, but "only" to betray them to you all together at their most sacred worship! Never! Draw me apart with horses – feed my poor flesh to wild beasts – I will never betray my brothers in Christ Jesus!'

Flavian momentarily allowed his anger free rein. 'Have you not already betrayed master, family, and your own nurselings

– yes, Marcella and Marcellina both – who trusted you like a mother?'

Still appearing transfixed, even ecstatic, Myrtilia cried, 'Every fleshly bond must be set aside and despised for sake of God's kingdom.'

'Do not blaspheme!' snapped Flavian. 'Spare yourself that sin, at least.' Trembling very slightly, he sat again. 'To apply torture at once smacks of illegality –'

' "Illegality"?' cried Bodicca. 'By the Horned God, Roman, what choice is there between your "legality" and your own grandchild?'

The legate frowned at her. 'I might with equal justice ask why you interest yourself so fiercely in this matter. My daughter's child is no kin to you.'

No Roman matron, Bodicca continued to speak for herself, while Kynon looked on proudly. 'There is this tie: her father is my husband. There is also the bond of motherhood, that unites all women, those who have already borne their children, those like myself who have yet to bear, and even those who, through no fault save fate and the will of the gods, may never bear, but only share in spirit with their fellow women. All,' she added, digging one toe into Myrtilia's ribs, 'except such unnatural mothers as this.'

'Without faith, without truth, without Christ Jesus,' the slave woman shrilled back, 'what can such as you know of spiritual bonds?'

Turning scornfully, Bodicca seized each of the onlooking slaves by one arm and marched them back toward their own quarters. So purposeful was her stride that Flavian permitted her boldness without comment, merely returning his attention to her husband, who had begun to speak.

'I can hardly fault your hesitation to apply torture, Roman,' said Kynon, 'knowing as I know how our British children laugh as they try your leaden balls and arm-squeezing cord on one another in sport.'

'If they laugh,' Flavian replied, 'they do not know what they are doing.'

'It is plain, Roman, that you have never watched our British children at play.' Kynon seized Myrtilia's arm, dragging her roughly to her feet. Flavian stood with a sharp exclamation, but Kynon went on over his protest: 'If you love your daughter's child as much as you claim, Roman, you will let a British father do what must be done to get her back alive and safe.'

'May I remind you,' Flavian answered, his voice low but

menacing, 'that you are in my city and my house? You have until my centurion returns. Not one moment longer.'

'Enough.' Throwing his luckless captive half to the ground, so that she hung clamped between his knees unable to regain her balance, the chieftain drew the long knife he wore at his belt and slowly, almost delicately, forced its tip beneath her right thumbnail.

Her shrieks brought Marcella back to the courtyard, with Crato's wife on her heels and her personal slaves following close behind. At almost the same time, Bodicca and her two forcibly enlisted attendants returned, hauling Bucco out with his head still bandaged.

'Father! What –' Marcella began, and broke off as she saw more clearly what was happening. 'Myrtilia! Oh, Myrtilia, what is this?'

'She is your old nurse no longer, my daughter,' the legate replied. 'She has disowned all such fleshly bonds. She is Christian.'

'Christian!' Stifling her scream, Marcella held one fist to her mouth as she stared at the scene before her.

'Christian!' Kynon spat out. 'Marcella, they have our child. Tonight they sacrifice our little Kyna, if we fail to learn their meeting-place.' Prying up Myrtilia's first finger, he slid his knife's tip beneath that nail in turn.

'No!' sobbed Myrtilia. 'Oh, Jesus, Jesus –'

'Stand firm!' Bucco bawled at her. 'Mother, stand firm in our holy faith!'

'So, then!' Flavian exclaimed. 'You are also one of them! Hold him fast!'

'Don't worry, Roman,' Bodicca said grimly.

'What did I tell you?' Kynon added, beginning on his victim's middle finger. 'That blow to his head was meant only to blind you to the truth.'

'Truth!' Myrtilia panted between her shrieks. 'Truth shall set us free!'

'Stand firm, mother!'

Flavian looked from Myrtilia to Bucco. 'You do not despise this particular fleshly bond, I see.'

'Master,' Bucco answered, sneering, 'we are no longer merely mother and son according to the flesh. We have become lovers in that spirit of which flesh is only symbol and seal, in that kingdom where there is neither slave nor master, but all are free and equal in Christ Jesus our crucified lord.'

Myrtilia continued to scream and sob. Tears trembled in

Marcella's eyes. Breast heaving, she bowed her head over her
fist, while the philosopher's wife put one arm around her shoulders
and hugged tight.

'Marcellina . . .' the young mother gasped out. 'Myrtilia? Oh,
Marcellina, my darling little Marcellina! Oh, Juno, Marcellina!'

The legate turned to her and spoke as if to one of his soldiers.
'Daughter. We must know how far this contagion has infected
our household. Gather the rest of our slaves and see to it that
each of them in turn prays and burns incense to our own Lares
for Marcellina's safe return. Test them further by asking each of
them to join you in cursing this executed magician or evil god
'Christ.' Nathan and Sarah,' he added, glancing at Marcella's
personal slaves, 'may follow their ancient custom and sacrifice
only to their own god. Jealous as Yahweh is of his own people,
he is hardly likely to share them with Christ Jesus.'

Before their eyes, Marcella pulled herself together. 'I will curse
that evil name myself with joy each and every time I administer the
test. Have no fear of me, Father.'

With her attendants and Chloe, the young matron took her way
to the slaves' quarters. Soon, the line of Cassius Marcellus Flavian's
slaves could be seen filing solemnly across the courtyard from their
wing to the household shrine, there to burn pinches of incense and
offer pious prayers for Marcellina's safe return, even while Myrtilia's
ordeal continued. When the British shieldbearers returned, signaling
that they had been relieved by Flavian's legionaries, Bodicca set
them to holding Bucco and shooed her borrowed slaves away to
take their turns in proving their devotion to both the gods of their
own household and people, and that one high God who sat above
all other deities and belonged to all peoples and nations.

Constantly encouraged by her son, the old woman held firm until
blood dripped from all ten fingertips. Then Kynon let her fall limply
to the earth, and it was Bucco's turn to shriek.

'My son! My son!' Myrtilia screamed with him, more piteously
even that under her own torture. 'Oh! My son in flesh and more
than flesh!'

'Remember – mother – remember . . . the promise and glory!'
Bucco grunted back at her in the midst of his cries of agony.
'Remember – Maria at her son's cross! Remember – pray for –
body and blood!'

The legate sat and watched with both fists tightly clenched and
lips compressed in a hard, thin line. Two slaves carrying market
baskets half filled with food came unobtrusively through the gate,
accompanied by a legionary. They stared in shock at what was

happening to Bucco, and quietly joined their fellows in prayerful procession to Flavian's household shrine.

'Speak! Speak, curse you!' Kynon shouted, growing desperate as he ran out of fingernails to torture. 'A child! Would you murder an innocent child?' Half frenzied, he drove his fist into Bucco's stomach, doubling him over stunned and choking.

'Bucco! My son, my son!' wept Myrtilia. 'Christ Jesus! Oh, Christ, welcome my son Bucco – he dies Your holy martyr!'

' "Holy"!' Kynon panted, recollecting himself and hauling Bucco's head up to make sure he still breathed, was still conscious. 'Behold a "holy" man who murders and eats little children! We have a name for such, and it is "ogre." "Ogre," do you understand me, Christian slave? "Ogre" – "monster" – "devil"!' Seizing Bucco's arm, he twisted ferociously enough to dislocate the shoulder.

Barely in time to forestall the breakage of bones, Gnaius Metellus Lucian returned to report his legate's orders carried out.

'Your time is up, Briton,' Flavian said, rising from his chair. 'I regret as keenly as you that these child-murderers will not reveal their secret and thus in some measure redeem themselves, but your British ways of questioning appear no more useful than our Roman methods. They gain us nothing.'

'They gain you nothing,' Bucco groaned weakly, 'but they gain us heaven. Come, finish your work!'

Myrtilia only sobbed, exhausted.

With military discipline, Lucian ignored angry Britons and bleeding victims alike. 'Sir,' he told his commander, 'we found none of your slaves abroad save Dromo and Geta, who were at market shopping for food. We delivered them back as you ordered. I have four men still searching.'

'They will find no one,' Marcella said, returning to her father. 'All our slaves are here, and I have tested each of them. Every one was eager to offer incense and prayer to the Lares and Penates of our house for Marcellina's return – save only Nathan and Sarah, who prayed with equal fervor to the god of their own people. Most of them, indeed, had prayed and sacrificed already, either to our household gods or to their own personal patrons – for everyone in our house loves Marcellina – but they happily added new prayers to their former ones. Some few there were who hesitated to curse Christ Jesus. I have noted their names, but, for myself, I feel assured that their hesitation was due, not to secret reverence, but to superstitious fear of any deity of such fearful name and reputation.'

'Cassius Marcellus Flavian!' Bucco cried, recovering sufficiently from his pain to sound boastful. 'I and my mother alone of all your household are to be numbered among God's elect!'

'Take them away!' Flavian commanded. 'See to their injuries, but shackle them well.'

Marcella said softly, 'First let me speak a little with this woman who was once my nurse.'

Flavian nodded and turned away. As Kynon and Bodicca, for once accepting Lucian's supervision, dragged Bucco from the courtyard still spewing his mixture of cant and curses, Marcella came down, Chloe still at her shoulder, and knelt beside Myrtilia.

'Oh, Nurse, Nurse!' the young woman mourned. 'Nurse, who was almost more to me than my own dear mother, who died so young! Oh, Myrtilia, how could you, of all our people, betray us?'

Feebly, Myrtilia rolled onto her back, Chloe assisting when she saw the injured woman's intention. The old nurse groped for Marcella, who, taking only enough notice of bloody fingers to avoid hurting them further, took the slave's hand into her own and clasped it gently.

'I have loved my son ... with love beyond that of parent and child,' Myrtilia whispered. 'Was I for that an unnatural mother?'

Chloe whispered, 'Oh, Hera!'

Horror flashed across Marcella's face, but she hid it at once and answered only, 'How, Myrtilia, dearest nurse? How, of all women, could they have so corrupted you?'

'There,' Myrtilia protested with what little strength was still within her, 'there will be no more distinction of rank or wealth, riches or power, slave or master. There, it will be perpetual Juvenalia, and all shall be equal forever in God's own light!'

'A pretty state of anarchy,' Chloe muttered under her breath.

'But Marcellina! Our darling Marcellina!' Marcella went on, tears flowing down her face. 'Did you not love her as you had loved me before her? Did you not love her for her own sweet sake as well as for mine? Oh, Myrtilia, did you never love us at all? Has your whole life been one long lie?'

'Marcellina,' the old nurse murmured sorrowfully. 'Little Marcellina ... my little, loved one ... No! I never meant – I would never have agreed – I never knew of this until after ...' Her voice rose with some tremble of anger. 'Christ Jesus, do you demand even this? No! They meet – they meet tonight in the Cave of the Twin Lindens.'

For one moment, as she fell back panting, an expression of blessed peace filled her face. Before Marcella could breathe thanks, however, Myrtilia's brief respite shattered – her eyes flew open, staring terrified at something beyond Marcella's shoulder – she cried, 'No! Lord Jesus, forgive –' and then, with one long scream ending in the rattle of death, she fell back, eyes already glazing over.

Her final moments had drawn the attention of everyone in the courtyard. Flavian was first to speak. 'The Twin Lindens,' he said slowly. 'Yes, I know that place.'

'God!' whispered the philosopher's wife, closing Myrtilia's eyes. 'Who would choose to worship any deity so vengeful and merciless as this Christ Jesus?'

Marcella relinquished her nurse's hand, carefully crossing it with its companion arm across the dead woman's chest. 'Myrtilia, Myrtilia,' she murmured. 'May God grant you mercy at last. May I meet you again, cured of this superstitious madness, in Elysian fields.' Looking up at her father, she added, 'Let us always remember, if we get Marcellina back safely, it is because this woman recovered her senses at the end, and braved the wrath of her cruel deity.'

'She will have honorable burial,' Flavian agreed. 'Let us hope your would-be suitor plays his part as well.'

Night had fallen – imperceptibly, inside the Cave of the Twin Lindens, lit now by one lamp on a bronze lampstand. Its light no more than partially illuminated an altar, neatly draped in pure white cloth, near the back of which rested a mound the height of a man's arm, shrouded over with separate cloth. Beside this altar a huge old wolfhound lay chained to the lampstand, his shaggy large head resting on his front paws, quiescent save for occasional little whines.

Some dozen red-robed Christians and three in white, all with faces deeply hooded, were grouped before the altar, where their *flamen* Dossemus and a tall man with silvering red hair stood facing them. The tall man had just finished reading aloud, in Gaulish accent, from a scroll he bore reverentially in his hands. As he rolled it up, kissed it, and laid it on one end of the altar, Dossemus led the assemblage in chanting.

Their hymn was slow and stately, yet at its words Octavio, who stood cloaked in red as far from the altar as he could stand without raising suspicion, shuddered. Only white-cloaked Crato, standing next to him, noticed. Bending closer, Crato murmured, 'I find nothing vile in any of this. Silly and unphilosophical, but hardly heinous.'

' "His body and his blood," ' Octavio muttered back. 'Did you not hear those words? There! Again! "We will share his body and his blood." '

'I can cite you eight or nine Creation allegories making Earth herself and her fruits some god's body, with water or wine for blood. Moreover, they sang, "his." Not "her." '

'To them, it makes no difference. Whoever their victim, he – or she – is thought to become their Christ Jesus of the ass's head.'

'And you have seen their sacrifice with your own eyes?' Crato inquired skeptically.

Octavio either misheard or chose to skirt his companion's question, for he answered, 'No, you will not see it. They send their catechumens away while all is still innocent enough. Only the initiates feast and, after feasting, tease their hound into upsetting the lampstand, when they use darkness to couple promiscuously.'

'So say many who have never actually witnessed such things,' Crato argued.

'Shhh!' Octavio told him. 'The catechumens' ritual is ending.' As if he had simply been answering such questions as the Christians might expect any true catechumen of theirs to ask, the decurion turned from Crato and joined in a chant they would clearly expect him to know:

> *'Holy, holy, holy, God one and only!*
> *Thou alone art holy, Thou alone art Lord.*
> *Heaven and earth quake at Thy glory.*
> *All glory forever to God, the sole Lord!'*

'Somewhat presumptuous,' Crato nodded to himself, 'yet not, I think, beyond divine forgiveness.'

'The most sacred mysteries are about to commence,' droned the dwarfish *flamen*, and the red-haired giant added in his foreign accent, 'Let all catechumens depart.'

As Crato turned to obey, his companion caught his sleeve and muttered one thing further in his ear: 'If anything happens, tell Flavian – that visiting "apostle" is Rufus Sinistris, who may remember me from Gaul.'

Crato and the other two in white filed from the cavern. Once they had disappeared, Rufus Sinistris turned to face the altar, stood several moments with face and arms uplifted in silent prayer, and then, reaching forth his left hand, flicked the white cloth from the arm-high mound.

Revealing an ass's head, smeared with blood and impaled on a T-shaped cross cut to its size.

Hiding his reluctance, Octavio joined everyone present in prostrating himself before this grisly idol.

The two presiding *flamens* rose first, passing together behind the altar. Rufus Sinistris returned bearing a silver chalice and a long, thin-bladed dagger. Dossemus brought a brazier filled with glowing coals and a small grill, which he arranged beside the altar, at the end opposite the lamp.

Again Dossemus went behind the altar, and this time returned carrying a large platter on which rested what at first appeared in the weak light to be one huge lump of kneaded dough.

It was the child Marcellina, curled up and heavily dusted with white flour.

She appeared almost too heavy for small, hunchbacked Dossemus, and Rufus Sinistris soon relieved him, lifting the tray with its dormant burden and placing it on the altar before the crucified parody of a god. Octavio raised his head high enough to watch them closely. In her obviously drugged slumber – how little it would take to drug one so young! a single cup of unwatered wine would more than suffice – Marcellina's tiny chest moved shallowly up and down.

But for how long? Already Dossemus was turning her upon her back, stretching her small limbs out in miniature cruciform.

Rufus Sinistris lifted his dagger and held it with both hands, high above Marcellina, its blade pointing downward. He chanted, 'This is the most sacred body of Christ Jesus Our Lord, which will send up fragrant incense to God as it roasts. This is the vessel of Christ Jesus' most sacred blood, soon to fill our chalice and cement our spiritual fellowship one with another. Let us eat and drink and be glad!'

Octavio could wait no longer. Springing up with all his military training, he lunged across the cave and caught the giant from behind, catching his dagger even as it began its descent, jerking it to one side and immediately striking it across the floor. The hound pricked its ears up and barked once.

Dossemus caught Octavio in turn from behind. Still grappling with Rufus Sinistris, the soldier dislodged Dossemus with one kick. The hound barked again, and this time went on barking.

Rufus Sinistris gave Octavio far more trouble than did Dossemus, nor was it any longer merely two against one. By now the other cultists were on their feet, thronging in upon Octavio, whose only advantage was that his opponents kept getting in one another's way.

'You!' shouted Rufus Sinistris, twisting round to see his

attacker's face in full lamplight. 'Brothers! Sisters! This is the apostate who betrayed our people in Gaul, that time I escaped only with Our Lord's help, who wanted me to labor yet awhile in His fields! Behold the betrayer! Let us drink his blood before the child's!'

Sinistris' words brought still louder howls of rage from his fellow Christians – but now the old hound was on his feet, too, mingling his barks and howls with theirs, dashing back and forth on his short chain. The lampstand jerked, trembled, wavered, and went crashing over, plunging the cavern into deep darkness.

For several moments, all was black confusion of blows, grunts, shouts, and curses, the hound's barking, and – suddenly – a child's high-pitched cry wailing over all. The din of combat had broken even Marcellina's drugged sleep.

Another sound rose above the turmoil – the sound of soldiers arriving. Soon their torchlight began to penetrate the cavern, casting upon its far wall the shadows of the twin trees which lent it its name.

One by one, the Christians took notice and left off fighting. Some cowered in awe, some tried in vain to crawl away and escape or hide, some seemed to ponder their chances of changing sides. As the army came ever closer, two women bent over Octavio and dabbed at his bloody injuries with their garments, as if preparing to pretend that they had wanted to help him. The hound gradually subsided, but Marcellina continued to wail. Dossemus huddled behind the altar. Rufus Sinistris stood proud, clutched the ass's head with both hands as if intent on saving a sacred thing from desecration, and began to chant a hymn. First one and then another Christian joined him. No more than those two.

Flavian, Kynon, and Bodicca burst into the cavern, heading their combined force of Roman legionaries and British tribesmen. After one glance around, the warrior woman strode to the altar, stepping lightly over Octavio on her way, and gathered floury little Marcellina into the safety of her arms.

'Does he live?' Flavian asked, indicating Octavio.

'He does,' the wounded decurion answered for himself, struggling weakly into a sitting position.

'As does your granddaughter,' Bodicca added, turning toward Flavian. 'And she, I think you will find, is whole and uninjured.'

'Thank God!' cried Marcella, pushing forward through the ranks of warriors to accept her child from the smiling British woman's arms. 'Oh, thank Juno and Vesta and all our Lares! All praise to the Great God of all!'

'Well, daughter,' said Flavian, 'if it proves that Octavio has served us this night as nobly as he appears, by what I see here, to have done, I think I may judge his way clear to your hand.'

'Never mind that,' Kynon growled, adding to his tribesmen, 'Seize these rascals. Let none of them escape!'

'Bind them over to Roman jailers,' Flavian amended, motioning for his own men to join Kynon's in arresting the cultists. 'They must have Roman justice.'

'As you will, Roman. They are, after all, your own criminals.' Smiling grimly, Kynon half knelt and fondled the hound between its ears. 'But not this fine fellow, whom I claim for my only prisoner and prize. He, I think, is guilty of no more than bad companions, and they not, perhaps, of his own choosing. It should prove easy enough to redeem him, at least, to live out the rest of his nights at my feet.'

The hound craned his neck and licked Kynon's hand.

'Perhaps it is as well,' Crato sighed on learning about Myrtilia and Bucco, the first dead and the second secured with his fellow criminals. 'Had Flavian depended on my old feet, his legionaries could never have come in time.' The philosopher sighed again. 'Ah, Xanthippe, Xanthippe, I sought to believe good of all men. It seems that God has shown me my error.'

'It was blessed error, born from nobility of mind, like Pallas from the brainpan of Zeus.' Chloe kissed her husband's bald head. 'But, husband, once again I remind you, you are not Socrates, and I am not Xanthippe!'

[Translator's Afterword: In the original, Crato has a fifty-line Epilogue pointing the moral that there are indeed evil creeds abroad in the world (not merely isolated individuals misinterpreting basically innocent creeds), and that it is a grave mistake to seek excuses for such creeds. From my own vantage point, safe in twentieth-century America and post-Vatican II Catholicism, I draw another moral entirely from Atramentacio's work: Before we modern Christians succumb to the temptation of portraying any unpopular minority as a criminal cult – whether we are inspired by misinformed zeal or by the seductive charm of a ready-to-hand Evil Conspiracy – it might be wholesome to remember there was a time when *we* were the tiny, misunderstood, and dreaded minority; when the word 'Christian' must have fallen upon ordinary, honest, God-fearing ears very much as the word 'Satanist' falls upon ours; when real people suffered real hate crimes thanks to the promotion of such misunderstanding; when everyone who killed us truly and sincerely thought he or she was offering homage to God.

Notice how carefully Atramentacio dissociates the Hebrew characters from any suggestion of guilt. The playwright appears to have been a liberal and fair-minded worshiper of the one high God conceived to be over all nations and people (and Whom Christian apologists were to identify with the Father preached by Jesus), as well as of more localized Roman deities; and to have worked from accounts as speciously reliable as much of the anti-Wiccan, anti-New Age religion, etc., material currently used in our own Sunday schools and law enforcement agencies.

Among the most sobering reflections of all is provided by the evidence, found in the writings of Church Fathers, that the Christians themselves of those first few centuries were perfectly willing to believe such outrages as found in *The Ass's Head* – always about other, 'heretical' Christian groups, of course. Never about their own.

It will have become obvious why Atramentacio's work was lost for so long. The wonder is that any copy of *The Ass's Head* survived at all for rediscovery in our own day.

One change I made in the action. It is, I hope, a change that might have been made by even the most conscientious director of a staged production. In the original, Myrtilia's death is accompanied by a rather fearsome divine (or, if you prefer, diabolical) apparition, which all the other characters see with her. This is certainly in keeping with the dramatic conventions of the classical stage, but it strikes me as inconsistent with Octavio's personal history, with the action in the cave, and with the general tone of the play. It could also make the cave action seem anticlimactic, and I despaired of trying to convey, in a few words, the mindset that would have allowed the ancient Romans to witness such an apparition and continue to call the Christian belief 'superstitious' – in their sense of the word, which differed somewhat from our sense of it. For all these reasons, I limited the vision to Myrtilia's eyes alone, thus moving her death more into line with such examples, drawn from early Christian literature, as the deaths of Ananias, Sapphira, and Nichomachus, and trying at the same time to render it susceptible to medical explanation. I have made no other essential changes in the play.]

THE NEST OF EVIL

Wallace Nichols

It would be difficult to imagine this anthology without one of the Slave Detective stories by Wallace Nichols. Throughout the 1950s and well into the 1960s Nichols produced a regular stream of stories about Sollius, the slave of senator Titius Sabinus, whose detective skills are known throughout Rome. The stories appeared exclusively in the London Mystery Magazine *and have not been collected in book form. In* The Mammoth Book of Historical Whodunnits *and* The Mammoth Book of Historical Detectives, *I reprinted the earliest Sollius stories, which take place in the final years of reign of the Emperor Marcus Aurelius. The following is one of the later stories from the series, set in the reign of Septimius Severus, but the years have not dulled the detective powers of Sollius one jot.*

～

One morning in the late Roman spring Sollius the slave, returning from an errand for his master, Titius Sabinus the Senator, heard hurrying footsteps behind him. Continuing on his way, the Slave Detective – for so ran his fame in Rome – slightly slackened his pace to let the other overtake him. But he kept taut and wary: many among the dregs of the City wished him ill.

'Sollius, Sollius . . .' came in a panting voice.

The Slave Detective glanced over his shoulder. An elderly man, a fellow slave, as could be seen from his base attire, gestured to him to stop.

'What is it?' Sollius asked as soon as the other came up.

'Will you come in and speak with my mistress, Dacia, the wife of Marcus Albinus the architect?'

Sollius recognized the name as that of an architect of repute in Rome.

'There is great trouble in our house,' went on the old slave beseechingly.

'That house – where is it?'

'You've just passed it,' and he pointed to a small mansion on the Palatine, clearly the residence of a rich man.

Sollius nodded, and followed the other into the atrium.

Dacia, obviously agitated, was a still-handsome woman in latish middle age. She greeted him breathlessly.

'Only you, Sollius, can help me. I saw you pass by – and so to see you was a grace of the Gods.'

'What is your problem?' he asked.

'My son has been arrested by Licinius the Prefect.'

'For what crime, lady?'

'Murder,' she answered, a sob behind her voice. 'Get him released,' she went on hysterically. 'I will pay you anything you ask.'

'I can only serve you, lady, with the permission of my master.'

'I will get it – but at least hear me now.'

'As you will,' he answered, and humbly composed himself to listen.

'We are a strange household,' she began, wringing her hands. 'Marcus Albinus is my second husband, and Agenor is my son by my first husband, a gentleman of Greek origin. I have a daughter, Nanno, by Albinus. Recently my husband adopted the daughter and only child of his greatest friend who died three years ago, leaving her destitute. She is a girl of the same age as Nanno, seventeen, and she is – O Gods, was! – named Melissa. She was found stabbed yesterday. The Prefect has arrested Agenor. But he is – he must be – innocent. Save him, Sollius!'

'Ask permission from Titius Sabinus, lady, and I will look into the case. Meanwhile it will do no harm to ask the City Prefect what evidence he has against your son.'

'I will see the noble Sabinus at once – and oh, Sollius, hasten to the Prefect!'

The Slave Detective changed his steps to the barracks of the Urban Cohorts, and there broke in upon Licinius, whom he saw to be frowning.

'The very man I most desired to see and for whom I was about to send!' cried the Prefect, leaping up. 'I can keep order in the Emperor's City, but I'm a poor hand at solving mysteries.'

'You have one?' innocently inquired Sollius.

'A murder,' replied Licinius grimly. 'On what seems overwhelming evidence I have arrested a man – yet, against its showing, I half believe him not guilty. You must help me, Sollius.'

'That means two I must help,' smiled Sollius, 'you and Agenor's mother.'

'You know about the case already?' cried the Prefect, open-mouthed. 'Is this magic?'

'Neither magic nor knowledge. Only a mother's anguish. So tell me.'

'It seemed such a simple case,' sighed Licinius. 'There was bad blood between the young man Agenor and the girl Melissa. He had tried to seduce her – though his mother won't believe it – and she had repulsed him, as a slave witnessed, with a biting mockery at his deformity, for he is slightly humpbacked, a scowling fellow, as you will see. I have little liking for him, but justice is justice, and I am unhappy: still, the evidence is against him.'

'What is it?'

'He was found standing over her, the knife that had killed her in his hand. He swears he had found her dead, and had taken the weapon – which was a hunting-knife of his own – out of her body from hatred to see it there. She was a very beautiful girl, with Greek looks from a Greek mother. Moreover, he had taken his repulse, which was only a day or so before the murder, and as the same slave has sworn, with evil looks, words and threats.'

'Threats?'

'That beauty, when scornful, deserved a brand, burnt in!'

Unaccountably, Sollius shivered.

'What was the stepfather's part in this?'

'He has never approved of his stepson, and kept him without money. I should have believed Agenor more surely guilty had it been Albinus who had been stabbed. However angered the young man may have been at the girl's treatment, he loved her.'

'Love so easily turns to hate,' sighed Sollius. 'May I see him?'

Agenor was not a prepossessing youth, but his fear had subdued his native sullenness, and he saw in the Slave Detective a possible saviour.

'I will tell you all you ask – all,' he cried vehemently.

'How was it that you were the first to find her?'

'I had just come in from the Baths. She was lying near the threshold of my bedroom. Her killer could not have long left her, for she was still warm, but dead, quite dead.'

If that were true, thought Sollius, it meant that the murderer, if not Agenor, was most likely another member of the household.

'It was daylight?'

'In the middle afternoon. On my way in I saw no one running from the house.'

'Was Melissa liked in the house?'

'Except for my stepfather, by no one – by neither the family nor the slaves. My stepfather spoilt her abominably, even at the expense of his own daughter.'

'That would not make for peace between the two girls,' murmured Sollius.

'Nor between Melissa and my mother,' added Agenor. 'Have you questioned Silvius?'

'Who is Silvius?'

'The head slave. He hated her,' he added venomously. 'She had enticed him – and then haughtily mocked him when he became familiar. She was not a good girl.'

He began to sob, and put his head into his hands.

'But I loved her – by all the gods, I loved her . . .'

Before taking any further steps in the case the Slave Detective had to return to his master's great mansion on the Esquiline to receive the necessary permission. He found that Dacia had already visited Sabinus and obtained it. Taking the younger slave Lucius, his usual assistant, with him, he limped back to the house on the Palatine.

'Tear the heart out of the head slave,' he instructed him. 'His name is Silvius. I shall first interrogate Marcus Albinus.'

The architect received him in his working-room, dismissing a young slave who had been busy at a drawing board. He was a gross man between fifty and sixty, with an intelligent but sensual face. He was very grave in his manner as he greeted Sollius.

'This is a terrible thing,' he said heavily. 'It has been a very great shock to me. I was in here, working at my drawing board alone, when I heard the commotion in the house. I rushed out – to see my adopted daughter in the state you know, and my stepson being held by my head slave. I have really nothing else I can tell you. It is terrible, terrible . . .' he kept repeating.

'Do you believe your stepson guilty?'

'How else? He was found on the spot – and the girl was but then dead. I myself – this room is quite near – heard them quarrelling, and then silence. And hasn't the City Prefect arrested him? The Prefects of Rome do not make many mistakes, and Licinius is a good Prefect.'

'You dislike Agenor?'

'A most unsatisfactory fellow! His mother – my second wife – indulges him beyond all reason.'

'Then you would not favour his love for your adopted daughter,' said Sollius softly.

'By no means, slave! I was glad that she had rejected him, though I fear now that it was the cause of this tragedy.'

'May I speak now to your own daughter?'

'If you must,' conceded Albinus. He clapped his hands for a slave and gave directions that Nanno should meet the Slave Detective in the atrium.

Sollius waited for her by a stilled fountain. Presently she came, a girl without charm or beauty. Dacia came with her.

'This is Nanno,' said her mother, and Sollius bowed meekly.

'Do you know,' he asked, 'where you were when Melissa was stabbed?'

'I was here in the atrium, arranging flowers. I heard cries, and a slave told me what had happened.'

'You did not go to see? You were not far away here.'

'I was very busy with the flowers. I took the commotion to be yet another drunken scene with Agenor.'

'You must not be so foolishly bitter with your half-brother,' snapped her mother angrily.

'You did not get on with Agenor?' Sollius asked.

Nanno shook her head.

'It has always been a great grief to me,' said Dacia.

'Let us leave Agenor. What were your relations with Melissa?' pursued Sollius, his eyes suddenly keen.

'None of us, save my husband,' interposed Dacia, 'found Melissa anything but false, secret and intolerable. She must have left a trail of hate wherever she went. Some broken lover will have got into the house by stealth, and taken his revenge.'

'Your son, lady, fits that supposition.'

She looked at him angrily.

'I am hiring you to defend my son!'

'I am but showing you, lady, how difficult that is!' he retorted, then turned again to Nanno, and asked, with a deep glance: 'What young man did she steal from you? I can soon find out who it was. Tell me!'

'The only man I shall ever love!' she cried, and ran blindly out of the atrium.

'This house is a cauldron of hate,' he said. 'Where were you yourself, lady, when the girl was killed?'

'In the garden, instructing the gardener. We both rushed in at the cries. He will tell you so.'

'I shall ask him,' replied Sollius gravely.

'Do you always work *against* your clients?' she asked haughtily.

'I work for truth and justice. I have no other clients,' he answered, his gaze level and by no means that of a slave, and he saw her grow pale. With a deeper anger – or a new fear? He had no guess, nor, for once, a speaking intuition.

'Truth and justice,' she rejoined with spirit, 'commit you to defend my son.'

'It seems,' he replied quietly, 'that no one grieves for the dead girl.'

'Except my husband,' she flashed back. 'He valued her above his own daughter. The adopted daughter of his old friend went in silk, his born daughter in the mere Roman wool. You will not find the murderer in the house, O Sollius. He will be one of Melissa's tormented lovers, slipping in stealthily. Have you looked for such a one?'

'The City Prefect is covering that,' Sollius answered, and broke off the interview.

Leaving the atrium, he saw Lucius emerging from the slaves' quarters. He called to him, took his arm, and led him into the gardens.

'I have a question to ask the gardener,' he said.

He found him so exceedingly deaf that it was difficult to make him understand the question when it was asked.

'I heered nothin,' he growled at last. 'The mistress just tugged at me and rushed me indoors – and there we found . . . what we found.'

'How long had she been with you?'

'Long? Why, she'd but just come!'

'You saw young Agenor by the body?'

'Ay, and the mistress gave a great shriek, she did. Oh, yes, I heered that!'

Sollius was silent for a moment, then he nodded, and turned away. As he and Lucius passed out through the atrium they saw Dacia comforting her sobbing daughter. None of them spoke. The Slave Detective and Lucius walked to the barracks of the Urban Cohorts.

'What did you learn from Silvius?' inquired Sollius as he limped along.

'He hated the girl; that is sure. And he saw Agenor by the body and holding the knife – and, so he says, Dacia ran in almost at the same moment. He could just have had time to slip in and do the killing, slip out again, and then, hearing Agenor unexpectedly entering, have run in on the clever impulse of accusing him of the murder. Silvius is a sly man. I can tell you that.'

'Everybody, except Albinus, seems to have hated the girl. The house is a nest of evil,' sighed Sollius. 'Each and all seem to have had motive and opportunity in equal degree. None of them was sufficiently away from the spot where Melissa was killed, not even her adoptive father. Licinius, indeed, can justify his arrest of Agenor. He could be justified in the arrest of any of them.'

'One of whom,' commented Lucius dryly, 'we are hired to prove innocent.'

The Slave Detective made no response, and was unwontedly frowning. He seemed to walk with more pain than ever from the old wolf-trap injury.

'You make me suspect each of them in turn,' laughed Lucius.

'As I do myself!' almost snarled Sollius, and then they reached the barracks, entered and sought the Prefect.

They found him irritable and dispirited.

'Is the case solved?' he asked, a sudden gleam of hope in his eyes.

'What,' asked Sollius without answering the question, 'did your cohort men discover about intruders to Albinus' house?'

'They asked diligently but there seemed to be none, neither fishsellers nor beggars,' Licinius replied heavily.

'You confirm me,' nodded Sollius. 'It is an inside case – of that I am sure. Each in the house had proximity, opportunity and motive, but one is guilty. That one must be tricked into full sight of us. If anything there are too many clues.'

'Has your intuition not spoken?' asked the Prefect with a touch of slyness in his tone.

'It has spoken,' answered Sollius seriously, 'but, though I trust it, no paramount clue is evident. I am not always right, Prefect. Do not release Agenor because I may suspect someone else. There is more evidence against *him* than against any other. You may still,' the Slave Detective sighed, 'have the right man,' and he sat for a long moment twiddling his thumbs. Then he went on: 'The one hope is that one in that house of hate does love another.'

Again he sat twiddling his thumbs. The Prefect and Lucius glanced at each other, and waited. At last his edict came.

'Send a centurion, and arrest them all – Agenor's mother,

half-sister and stepfather, and also the slave named Silvius. We will interrogate them together. Send at once.'

The water-clock had but registered little when the Centurion brought in his gaggle of protesting prisoners.

'This is monstrous!' burst out Albinus. 'I shall complain to the Emperor – by whom I am known personally.'

'Severus is in Britain,' answered the Prefect curtly. 'Meanwhile it is a matter of murder. You will answer our questions.'

Further protest was silenced by an uplifted hand, and then Licinius turned to Sollius.

'Let the play begin,' he said.

The Centurion had lined them up to face the Prefect and Sollius with military precision, using his marching stick to level them off. He and the Prefect stood in full uniform, bronze-girt and helmeted. In his drab tunic and bare legs Sollius showed very unimportantly between them – except for his stance and his eyes. The Prefect's office was lofty and oblong, and in its furnishing was more in the grave taste of the old Republic than in the gilding of the long-confirmed Empire.

'Let Agenor be added to them, Prefect,' said Sollius, and Licinius gave the order to a soldier standing guard at the door.

Presently Agenor was brought in, and the Centurion ranged him at the end of the line, stationing him, as it happened, next to his half-sister, Nanno. Every eye was fixed, most uncomfortably, rather upon the slave than upon the Prefect.

'The girl, Melissa,' Sollius began, 'gave cause for all of you to hate her.'

'Not me!' pronounced Albinus haughtily.

'She caused dissension in your house,' Sollius asserted.

'I, at least, loved her,' cried Agenor.

'And she laughed at you!'

'I always treated her as a daughter,' said Dacia.

'And she repaid you with ingratitude. She put discord in a harmonious circle. All of you had opportunity. I have worked it out, and it is so.'

None of them could raise a voice in denial. Each had been at rest or at work near by at the time of the murder. Sollius levelled his glance keenly upon them in turn from one end of the line to the other. He had one doubt in his mind: which, of two, was the one that another loved? Whose eyes fastened most frequently upon another's? Was that, however, in a knowledge of guilt, or in a desire to protect? One person's eyes thus flickered – and at two faces. The face of that person was grey. The Slave Detective knew that he would have to make his choice – and at once, for the silence was growing painful and the Prefect was looking at him in puzzled disbelief in his intuitional efficiency.

'Licinius,' he snapped suddenly, 'arrest Dacia!'

A cry of anguish went up, but it was not hers.

'Fool, O Slave Detective – it was not she, but I!'

Out from the line broke Albinus, striding menacingly up to Sollius. The Centurion plucked him back.

'Melissa was a goddess' – he spoke with a slight foam at the corners of his lips – 'how sweet at first, and then how evil! But I loved her – beyond my peace I loved her, so deeply that I became unclean to myself. I saw the devastation she had caused in the house and in my own heart. It came to the pass that I must either take her, or destroy her. All our lives had become shadowed as from the Furies' wings! I chose to destroy the pest!'

He broke into a wild sob, and would have fallen had the Centurion not supported him.

'Take him!' ordered the Prefect. 'And release the others.'

Sollius grinned at him when they were alone together.

'I had in the end to guess at the lever of his affections – his wife or his daughter. I had to accuse one of the two. As it was, I guessed rightly. That is all there is to it, Prefect!' he added in mock modesty, and limped out.

IN THIS SIGN, CONQUER

Gail-Nina Anderson and Simon Clark

Simon Clark has established himself as a writer of effective supernatural horror with his novels Nailed By the Heart (1995) and Blood
Crazy (1996). His interests are wide and varied, and in the following
story he teams up with art historian and writer, Gail-Nina Anderson,
to explore a locked-room mystery set in the library at Alexandria
during the reign of the Emperor Constantine.

～

Upon taking the city of Alexandria on Egypt's Mediterranean coast
in the year 642, the Arab General Amr sent a rather prosaic message
to the Caliph reporting: 'I have taken a city of which I can only
say that it contains 4,000 palaces, 4,000 baths, 400 theatres, 1,200
greengrocers and 40,000 Jews.' Little here illuminates any of the
splendours of Alexandria, burial place of Alexander the Great,
capital of the Pharaohs under the Ptolemy dynasty, the site of one
of the Seven Wonders of the World, the fabled Pharos lighthouse,
and home to one of the greatest libraries of the ancient world.

ALEXANDRIA, EGYPT – AD 331
A LETTER WRITTEN BY
THEOCRITAS AMUN-ARTEN, PHYSICIAN

I am frightened.
Tonight, the statues of old Egypt have come alive and climb the

walls to leap from roof to roof across this great city. A man lies
dead in the next room. If his murderer is not identified, and more
importantly the map not found, by the time the sun rises in six hours
time we are to have our throats cut on the library steps.

You are the focus of my love, dear one. I thank all gods of
all faiths that chance brought us together. Now my feelings flash
from anger to sorrow to despair. Because, in this life, we are to
be parted. At this moment I feel rage for I'll never again see your
throat suddenly flush as pink as a rose, nor take a Sybarite's delight
at the drip of the oil from your fingertips.

I do not know if you will be permitted to claim my body for burial.
The best I can do is write you this letter in the hope it will somehow
find you. I write because I know how I felt when my father died in
Rome. I became obsessed with the nature of his illness and those
hours of suffering he must have endured so far from his family here
in Alexandria.

I want you to know that I am surrounded by my friends who
have, like me, made this lovely library their second home. There is
young Marcus, who you know well enough by now; the beautiful
Marcus, you tease, with the eyelashes fit for a girl. He'll turn heads
in the marketplace no longer.

He has begun to grow a beard but it's as red as copper. His hair,
as you know, is black so he's completely perplexed. Earlier he said
to me, 'Theo, you're a physician. Have you any explanation why
although my hair is black my whiskers are red?' I laughed and told
him I don't know everything. He smiled and said, 'One day you
will, Theo, one day you will.'

Seated beside me, eating olives, and spitting the stones into a cup
is Chrysippus, a court scribe. You've met him at the festival; a big
bald man, forever eating or forever wondering where his next meal
is coming from. He waddles like a tipsy elephant. He is also the most
generous man I've ever met. These, and my other companions sitting
on the benches opposite me, are not great men but I will be proud to
die with them in the morning.

There . . . I have described my friends. How, I wonder, would
they describe me? I recall Chrysippus did so once in a letter to his
brother. *My good friend, Theocritas Amun-Arten is a physician*,
[Chrysippus wrote]. *He is a kindly man with oh-so weary eyes and
the face of our favourite uncle. He walks with his eyes hard down
to the street stones, always preoccupied with some new medical case
he must treat.*

*If we dine out, Theo has a great, nay, insurmountable, fondness
for duck roasted in a pot with honey, beer and apricots. His main*

passion is also his vice which has the power to leave him exhausted and sorrowful. Theocritas Amun-Arten is a man who, one can so readily believe, has been commanded by the gods to find a cure for every disease known to man. So he drives himself too hard. And yet he has worked so many, many miracle cures. But still this gentle, softly spoken man will blame himself, curse and beat his chest until bruised if he loses so much as a single patient – no matter of which caste, creed or race.

Now, as I write this beneath the reading lamps, hanging by their long cords from the ceiling spars, Marcus is saying we shouldn't sit here and meekly wait to have our throats stuck like goats, but we should find the murderer and the map that General Romulus believes is so important. Chrysippus spits olive stones as he speaks: 'Find the murderer . . . impossible . . . the man was murdered in a locked room . . . he was alone . . . there is no murder weapon . . . it's as if a ghost walked through the walls . . . killed him . . . then disappeared with this miserable little map that's more valuable than all our lives.'

'So, you're just going to sit there and wait for the blade?'

'No, I'm going to sit here . . . eat olives . . . drink Librarian's wine. There is nothing in the room or on the body to tell us who the murderer is, or where the map has gone.'

Marcus looks at me, his young doe eyes show more regret at losing life, than actual fear. He has a wife and baby; they will starve.

He speaks to me. 'Theo. You are an intelligent man. Is there no way of learning who killed the scribe and stole the map?'

'All I can say is, I imagine an unsolved murder is like an illness that still has no diagnosis. You must carefully examine the patient and look for the individual symptoms, no matter how minor, or seemingly unimportant, then you must collect them together and arrange them into some order that will help you identify the illness.'

'You mean,' began Chrysippus in his slow, elephantine way, 'that if we list . . . everything that is in the room with the victim . . . it will somehow, magically, tell us who the murderer is?'

I smiled regretfully. 'Not exactly, Chrysippus. But we could begin by noting certain peculiarities.'

'Such as?'

'The colour of the soles of the man's feet.'

'Why should that be important?'

'Those who arrived here barefoot look at your soles. They're the colour of chalk, because Alexandria's streets are covered in a chalky white dust. The murder victim's feet are smeared black.'

'And that means?'

'And that means . . .' I shrugged. 'Even though the victim never appeared to leave the room in which he was locked, he must actually have walked across an area of ground that was covered with some rich black material.'

Marcus added, 'Then there were the dried lotus blossoms on the floor. They weren't there when the man was locked into the room.'

'Theo, would these clues tell us who murdered the scribe and where the map is hidden?'

I shrugged helplessly. 'I can't say. What it does tell us, is that though everyone in the library believes that the scribe was locked into the room, that he never left the room, then was found murdered, in actual fact he had, during that time, been somewhere else.'

Around me are the faces of my friends. They are looking at me. And I see expressions that trouble me more than the fear I saw before.

They are looking at me and they are seeing hope. A hope that I can find the murderer – and the map – before sunrise, and so spare them the executioner's blade.

You, my love, might be curious to know what circumstances pitched me into this evil circumstance. I had been attending to Praxicles – you will recall he's the carpenter who lives in the same street as your mother. I did intend to come straight home; however, I'd had word from Librarian that he'd recovered documents relating to some medicinal remedies I'd been rather anxious to obtain.

As I hurried along Canopic Street toward the library, I saw the statues come to life and begin to stream across the rooftops, and, with a shiver, I knew there'd be blood on the streets by dawn.

The statues of ancient Egypt come to life?

It sounds fantastic doesn't it? And our old saying can actually strike fear into the hearts of visitors to our city. The truth is much more mundane. Whenever there is a threat of civil unrest the monkeys that nest amongst the ancient statues flee for their safe haven. The old temple of Amun. I hurried there too, for different reasons though. Because the temple was a place of worship no longer. For two centuries it had been one of the finest library museums you could find.

As I climbed the library steps the light from the great lighthouse on Pharos had already begun to burn out across the sea, with the fiery magnitude of a sun. High above my head I saw the flitting shapes of the monkeys leaping onto the library roof, until they covered it completely like a seething, living thatch.

Surprisingly, the library's iron doors were locked and it was only by dint of hammering and shouting that I managed to summon one of the library servants. It was an omen I should have heeded.

'Why are the doors locked so early?' I asked.

The servant made a bored gesture to the rooftops. 'They've come alive again, so Librarian ordered the doors locked to keep out the mob.' The man clicked his tongue in disgust as more monkeys scrambled, chattering and screaming, onto the roof. 'One day those filthy apes will be the death of someone in here. I've told Librarian a hundred times that the filthy brutes will bring the roof down on –'

'Mosse, if you please . . . I need to copy some documents.'

The servant gave a careless shrug. 'Go right in, Theo . . . it's a circus in there anyway.'

'Why?'

'Some stupid Roman's got himself locked in one of the reading rooms. Librarian and the rest of you book-flies are trying to open the door.'

I hurried into the body of the building anxious to make my copies and return home but cynical Mosse thought I was curious to see what was happening in the reading room and called after me, 'It's the Isis reading room, Theo, you can't miss it, all the book-flies are clamouring round the door and cackling like geese. I ask you, have they no homes to go to? Don't they have friends they can get drunk with, rather than swarming round here? Leave the place to the filthy apes to roost in I say, but no they . . .'

His voice faded behind me as I hurried through this fabulous maze of shelving piled high with the cream of books from around the world. Above me, the monkeys had climbed in through the windows to cling to the top of the columns or sit on the shoulders of stone gods. They chattered restlessly, their gemstone eyes glinting down at me in the lamplight.

I intended to hurry by the dozen men clustered around the Isis door but Marcus saw me.

'Hey, Theo. Guess what? Some –'

'Some Roman has got himself locked in the Isis room. Yes, Mosse told me. He'll dine out on that for a week. Why he despises all Romans so passionately God only knows.'

'I am ordering you to break down the door,' demanded a stranger, his face as red as raw meat. 'My assistant is inside there with a document that . . . that men would die for.'

Librarian, tall, calm, dignified, tried to soothe him. But this red-faced man, who despite the heat wore a woollen cloak, speckled brown and white like the breast of a thrush, would not be placated. 'Break down the door – break it down, I tell you! I order it in the name of General Romulus.'

The babble stopped dead. Even the monkey hordes high above our heads seemed to fall silent at the sound of that dreadful name.

Librarian's face turned white. 'You did say, General Romulus?'

'You heard correctly.'

Librarian nodded grimly. 'Break down the door.'

Romulus's reputation was as fierce as it was terrible. Wherever there was rebellion and civil unrest Emperor Constantine knew who would quell it: ruthlessly, completely, utterly. When the citizens of Rome herself rioted because of famine, Romulus turned the streets into freshets of blood that foamed and swirled and gushed in Babylonian flood. Survivors whisper that Romulus then bared his chest, drenched his hands in the blood and painted his breast, throat and face, until he looked like the son of the barbarian he is.

So, Librarian argued no longer.

We broke down the door.

There, in the centre of the room, lying face down, was the body of a grey-haired man of about forty. His name, we later learnt, was Diomedes, he was Roman, an assistant to the red-faced man, and most clearly, he'd been beaten around the head until his soul had eagerly fled its body.

What terrified the red-faced man was the loss of some precious map that had just been located within the library. Face redder than ever, he searched the room for the map. It wasn't a long search because apart from a table, a rope and a pair of broken stools the room was quite bare. Then he tugged at his dead servant's clothes like a man skinning a goat, in the hope the map would be concealed in there.

It wasn't.

Clutching his head as if Athene herself threatened to burst from his forehead, he crouched on the floor and whimpered. When Librarian tried to console him the man shook his head. 'You don't understand. I had the map in my hand. A map drawn on a rabbit skin. I remember the colour of the inks, the tear in the top right-hand corner. Now I've lost it.'

'But it's only a map, my friend.'

'Only a map . . . *only a map*! General Romulus has had me

searching for the filthy thing for five years. And now I've sent word to his headquarters that I have it in my hands.'

Even as he spoke we heard the sound of feet on the marble floor. This wasn't the hesitant, self-absorbed step of the book-fly. This was the muscular rhythm of the soldier.

With a moan the red-faced man gritted his teeth and stood up as General Romulus entered the reading room. He was dressed as if ready for battle, complete with shining breastplate and scarlet-plumed helmet (however, incongruously, his teeth were polished a brilliant white, like those of a rich man's wife). He was accompanied by his German bodyguards; a ferocious body of men with huge blond beards, blue eyes and legs like tree trunks. Their armour was scarred and dented from years of hand-to-hand combat.

We quickly left for the main body of the library, leaving Librarian and the red-faced man with the general.

I will, my love, spare you a detailed description of the general's rage at the theft of the map. How he screamed at the two men. How he slapped them, and even kicked at the unfortunate corpse of Diomedes.

Then out he marched to where we nervously stood.

His upper lip glistened with sweat; his ferocious eyes stabbed at us. 'You know what's happened. One of my servants has been murdered. And a map, a very, very valuable map, has been stolen. Therefore, I have decided to execute you all, so I shall be certain of punishing the murderer, the thief, and any tight-lipped witnesses who aren't being so helpful as they might.'

I saw the hands of the bodyguard go to their swords.

'But,' continued the general, 'I need that map, and as you were the only ones in the library when the murder took place, one of you must know where it is. So, this is my promise to you. If, when I return in six hours' time, the map has been found you will be free to go to your homes. If it remains missing, I shall suspect an Alexandrian insurrection is brewing. I need no reason, but what better reason could there be for taking you out onto the library steps and personally cutting each and every one of your skinny throats? Understand? Find the map . . . you live. No map: you die.'

After leaving a number of his bodyguard to ensure we didn't escape he marched away into the night.

You can, my love, imagine our fear, and the wild plans that we made and then discarded. 'Escape from the library,' Marcus suggested.

'How? There are no windows at ground level, the doors are locked; the place is as secure as a prison.'

'Overpower the bodyguards?'

'What a stroke of genius,' grunted Chrysippus. 'After all they are only gigantic Germans armed with swords and axes. Theo, you terrorize them with a roll of papyrus while I knock them out with a couple of Virgil's odes. My God, Marcus, those men could shake us to death with one hand; don't you . . .' He stopped and sighed. 'I'm sorry Marcus. I didn't mean to be so rude . . . forgive me. It's just . . . why is it so difficult to admit that I'm afraid of dying?'

I said nothing. I watched our German guards. They were fascinated by the monkeys scurrying to-and-fro in the massive vault of the roof. At first they roared with laughter at their gymnastics. Then they brought out bows and arrows, thinking what sport it would be to shoot them. They managed to bring down one slow-moving female, shot through the heart, with her baby, which died in the long fall to the marble slabs.

The monkeys' fury erupted. Fragments of statues lying in niches, birds nests, scraps of papyrus rained down on our heads. The guards in turn swore back in their guttural subterranean language. They fired more arrows, which did not find any new victim. All the book-flies retired to the peace of the Isis room and left the beasts to battle it out.

'Well, Theo,' said Marcus, gazing down at the body of the scribe, looking even more dishevelled after its post mortem abuse, 'you believed there might be a way to learn who murdered the man and perhaps even find the map.'

I shrugged. 'Theoretically I believe it may be possible, but I don't know if I am the man to do it.' I looked up from the body. Librarian, Marcus, Chrysippus and the rest watched me hopefully. Even the red-faced man looked eager for me to continue.

I was their only hope, my love. If I failed there would be no harm done. After all, we would be leaving this world in the morning. Yet still I felt reluctant to shoulder that burden, the responsibility of their flickering hope.

I sighed. 'I'll do my best.' I looked at each of the men in turn. 'Do you all consent to my examination of you all, and do you pledge to answer all my questions truthfully?'

They all nodded vigorously, clutching at me as the slimmest chance for survival.

'Thank you.' I nodded. 'Now, I understand everyone in this room was in the library at the time of the murder?'

'All except, my assistant, Mosse,' said Librarian. 'He's working in my office.'

'I will have to speak to him,' I said. 'He's a suspect, too.'

'Surely not Mosse? He can't bring himself to squash a spider.'

'Understand clearly that he and everyone else here must all be suspects until we find the murderer. And the thief who stole the map.'

Marcus scratched his curly head. 'Surely they must be one and the same?'

'Not necessarily.'

Chrysippus blew out his cheeks. 'Where will we begin to solve this riddle?'

'By taking one very small step at a time.' I tried to sound confident, but I was far from certain I could achieve anything in the five or so hours before General Romulus returned expecting to find one map and one murderer. 'As I have said, I intend to approach this as if I am treating a patient. As I'd need to know all the patient's symptoms, so I need to examine every detail surrounding the murder; it doesn't matter how unimportant, how trivial they seem. I must know everything.'

Firstly, I made a list of all who were present in the library at the time of the murder. Excluding the late Diomedes, there were nine in all:

Librarian
Young Marcus
Elephantine Chrysippus
Servant Mosse
Benjamin (an elderly Jew, copying Hebrew texts)
Silanus (a teacher of mathematics from Sicily)
Ha'radaa (some kind of cleric from the East; he could only speak a few words of Roman)
Staki (a local rogue, probably only in the library to steal books in the hope of selling them back again)
Gabinius (the red-faced scribe employed by General Romulus)

First I took Gabinius to one side and asked him why he and the late Diomedes had come to the library.

'General Romulus commissioned me five years ago to find a map.'

'And tonight you found it?'

'Yes. The search took us from Athens to Rome, through Spain, and finally here to Alexandria. It was a map drawn by the captain of a merchant ship during the reign of Tiberius.'

'Why is it so important?'

'I have been ordered by the General not to tell a soul about the map.'

'You're afraid the General will have you killed if you breathe a word about the map to me? I don't think that's an important consideration now, do you?'

'Listen to me. I'm as good as dead now. What I don't want to do is anger Romulus so much that he orders the execution of my family, because, believe me, Amun-Arten, that's exactly what will happen if I tell you about the map.'

'I can't force you, but it might help.'

'I'm sorry. I won't discuss the map.'

'Tell me what happened tonight then.'

'The door was locked, as you know, when we broke in we –'

'No. Tell me everything from you leaving your lodgings.'

'That was this morning. Diomedes and I walked to the library together from the house I've been renting. It's the first house in Hadrian's Square.'

'No one followed you here?'

'Not that I'm aware of.'

'Nothing unusual had happened recently?'

'Such as?'

'No thieves had stolen any of your belongings, no strangers calling at your house?'

'No. But wait a minute . . . there was something . . .' His eyes flashed with triumph as if he'd solved the riddle. 'I believe I know who was responsible.' He beckoned to me so he could whisper in my ear. 'The old man, sitting on the floor there.'

'You mean Benjamin?'

'Yes. I would often see him standing near the house. He must have been watching us.'

'You saw him every morning?'

'Yes.'

'Good, I'm pleased to hear it.'

'Good heavens, why?'

'Because he is obeying my instructions.'

The man's face turned dangerously red. 'What's this? There's a plot?'

'Calm down, Gabinius. You say you live in the first house in the Square of Hadrian?'

'Yes.'

'Next door to you is a man who keeps a herd of goats.'

'I don't understand what you –'

'Benjamin, like most inhabitants of Egypt, has teeth worn down to the pulp. The millstone grit in our bread makes no distinction between creed or race. Three years ago Benjamin came to me so undernourished because he couldn't bear to chew any food that his wife feared he would die. Abscesses in the gums, you see. So, I pulled his teeth and drained the abscesses with a hollow reed. I also recommended he drink a cup of milk every morning to supplement his diet. I'm heartened that he still heeds my advice.'

'But he's a Jew,' added Gabinius more loudly as if seeing a way out of all this.

'I see, and we should blame Benjamin, *the Jew*, for the theft?'

'Yes . . . yes of course!'

I sighed heavily. 'Benjamin is an Alexandrian who happens to be a Jew. Librarian is Gnostic. Marcus belongs to a Hermetic order. Chrysippus divides his worship between Apollo in the temple across the square and Bacchus in the tavern down by the harbour.'

'But surely –'

'But surely not even General Romulus could seriously suspect such an elderly gentleman as Benjamin to be physically capable of so determined a piece of violence? Moreover, Romulus will want his map. Does Benjamin have it?'

'I imagine not.' The red-faced man shook his head, defeated.

'Now tell me what happened when you arrived at the library.'

Gabinius told me that they began sifting through the documents in search of the map. When they found it their screams of joy brought Mosse running, thinking Librarian was being murdered. At the same time the monkeys began arriving – a clear indication that there would be riots that night in the city. Librarian ordered that the library doors be locked in case the mob decided to rush the building. Regrettably the mob has lately seen books as a symbol of imperial authority. So if they can't burn the Emperor they burn his books.

After the initial elation of finding the map had worn off, Gabinius realized he had a problem. With the map of such vital importance in his grasp, his first impulse was simply to run to the General's quarters straight away to deliver it in person; with the mob threatening to take to the street, however, that was too hazardous. So he decided to send a messenger and await the arrival of armed guards to escort them and the map safely to the General. As always men's egos can overcome logic. He decided he wanted to greet Romulus on the steps with the good news and so bask in the General's congratulations, and no doubt promises of financial reward. Still fearing some harm might come to the precious map, he chose to lock both it and his assistant, Diomedes, into the Isis Room. The door was reinforced with iron strips and carried hefty bolts on both sides, so it could be locked on the outside by Gabinius and on the inside by Diomedes. Librarian, Mosse and Gabinius could all attest to seeing Diomedes alive and well – the map securely in his hand – as the door was locked; Gabinius even took the precaution of sitting on a stool right outside the door, a warder of his own good luck and, no doubt, a terrible temptation to Fate. He intended to wait there until the moment came to greet the General at the library entrance. A message was sent. Then almost half an hour later there came the sound of a commotion from inside the room. There were shouts, a series of heavy banging sounds, then complete silence.

Quite naturally alarmed by what must be happening inside the room Gabinius unbolted his side of the door, only to find it still bolted on the other side. Within moments all the book-flies and Librarian were there trying to rouse the man inside the room. That was around the time I arrived at the library. Then, of course, the door was forced and we found the unfortunate man dead. It took little of my skill to determine that his head injuries, caused by heavy blows, were the cause of death. He had, however, suffered bruising and grazing to other parts of his body; and his fists were badly bruised as if he'd punched his assailant. I noticed the man had a set of exceptionally fine teeth with no sign of decay, or indeed any of the kind of excessive dental erosion that is common in a man of his years. I clicked my tongue at the waste of such good teeth in a dead mouth.

Marcus had noticed the injured fists and said hopefully, 'If we find bruises on the body of one of us then surely we have the murderer.'

'Gentlemen,' I said, 'if you will all submit to an examination.'

All those present had no recent injuries. Except, that is, the Eastern cleric by the name of Ha'radaa, a tiny dark-skinned man with oriental eyes, dressed in a simple saffron-yellow robe. He had recent bruising to one cheek bone and his upper chest. Interrogating him wasn't easy; he spoke only a few tourist phrases of Roman. He seemed very suspicious of us all and despite remaining softly spoken and constantly smiling I detected an agitated mind.

'So, we have our murderer?' Marcus allowed himself a smile. 'He was bruised in the fight with the scribe, before killing him.'

'And the map?' I asked.

'He's hidden it somewhere amongst the books so he can collect it later.'

Again I gave a helpless shrug. A habit I'd developed in the last two hours. 'Possible. Very possible. But those bruises may be anything up to a day old. And how on earth did he walk through that locked door, kill the scribe and steal the map? Librarian, do you know anything about this Eastern gentleman?'

'Very little. He first came into the library three days ago. What was he interested in? Ah, yes. He's been copying the ancient Egyptian papyri. I thought it a little odd because, as you know, no one knows how to read the ancient Egyptian hieroglyphic script – and few would care to.'

I tried speaking with Ha'radaa again, but he could only answer 'yes' and 'no', and the look of confusion on his face was painful to see.

An idea occurred to me. The temple walls were covered with those impenetrable hieroglyphics. I pointed at an inscription ringed by a cartouche. The man's eyes brightened, the smile broadened. 'Imhotep,' he said happily. I pointed to another. Without hesitation he said, 'Rameses.' Then slowly I ran my finger along a line of glyphs and he read them in a form of archaic Egyptian that was alien to me.

'Thank you,' I bowed my head to acknowledge his wisdom, then I turned to Marcus. 'He does seem to be here to genuinely study the ancient texts, but because of the bruising we must place him at the top of our suspects list.'

'Are you going to question everyone here? Staki's a known criminal.'

'True.' I nodded. 'And if he knew the map was of great value he might be tempted to steal it. But he's a petty pickpocket, an opportunist thief who'll steal a tunic from a washing line, or a book from one of these shelves; not a murderer.'

'Where's he sloped off to anyway?'

'He's sitting facing the corner. Obviously he's hoping no one will notice him.'

Then a surprising thing happened.

The man to take most notice of him was little Ha'radaa. Immediately the man began shouting in his strange sing-song language, then launched himself at Staki. Staki bellowed and used big theatrical gestures that spoke in any language, 'Come near me and I'll punch your head in.'

Ha'radaa slapped his chest and his forehead while pouring out a torrent of words that no man there could understand.

At last we parted them.

'What was all that about, Theo?' asked Marcus.

'Goodness knows. My guess though, is it's a personal matter between them. And if it doesn't have any bearing helping us find the map and the murderer I think it best if we ignore it. Time is running out, my friend.'

Marcus swallowed and lightly rubbed his throat, no doubt

imagining the press of iron there in a few short hours. 'I'm afraid, Theo. My wife is pregnant again. Who will look after her when –'

'Hush, friend, hush,' I said softly, then smiled. 'Congratulations on the happy event anyway. You must bring Kiya to my house tomorrow evening, so I can satisfy myself everything is going according to nature's plan.'

'But –'

'But nothing, Marcus. This is where we roll up our sleeves and solve the mystery.'

'Are you going to question the others?'

'A waste of time . . . a waste of very precious time. No, the only man who can tell us what happened in here is that man there.'

Marcus looked incredulous. 'Diomedes? He can tell us nothing. The man is cold.'

'Correction, young Marcus, that corpse can tell us everything. And the physician who cannot question the dead is scarcely worth his salt, my friend.'

I then took the precaution of clearing everyone out of the room apart from Librarian, Marcus and Gabinius. Chrysippus was charged with keeping Ha'radaa and Staki apart. They all took refuge in the adjoining reading room because the monkeys were still raining pieces of statue down onto the guards. The latter, not learning from experience, went on firing their arrows upward, hitting nothing but stone; their angry voices echoed from the walls.

I pushed the door of Isis room shut. 'Gentlemen, do you remember if the room is still as you found it when we forced the door?'

Librarian said, 'More or less, but the body has been – ahm – somewhat disturbed since the discovery. Friend Gabinius searched it for the map, and, ahm, General Romulus abused it in his anger.'

'Do you agree, Gabinius and Marcus?'

Both nodded. 'Right,' I said. 'Allow me to talk this through with you. I acknowledge I'm all too human, therefore all too fallible. So please correct me if I miss anything. We have a room lit by three large oil lamps that hang by long cords from the ceiling. This is a reading room so they are suspended at a little over head-height.'

'Is this relevant?' interrupted Gabinius, face redder than ever.

'It is relevant. In fact I believe it is vital. So, please, let me have your cooperation. Now, where was I? Ah, yes. The room itself is very tall. I imagine eight men could stand on each other's shoulders before the one on top could reach the ceiling. The room itself must have once served as some kind of antechamber to the main temple. We have bas-relief carvings of animals on the walls, carved hieroglyphics. Only at the very top of the walls do we have any apertures that admit daylight.' I looked up and could just make out, reflected from the limestone walls, the soft peach glow of the lighthouse burning out there on the Pharos, guiding ships safely through the night. (How I wished, there and then, I could walk with you down to the shore, hold your hand, and watch the waves whispering, like the song of Arion, across the sand in the moonlight.)

I took a deep breath and continued: 'The floor consists of rectangular stone slabs. It is scrupulously swept clean of litter and dust. And you'll agree, gentleman, it is clean of any marks apart from a little of the deceased's blood. There are a few dried lotus petals and a length of stout cord. Good. Now, on to the furnishings. In the centre of the room is one oblong stone table. It is bare. And there are two stools. Both of which have been broken.'

'They must have been used in the fight,' said Marcus.

'At the moment, I feel we should confine ourselves to describing what we actually do see. Not speculating how the stools became broken. If we jump to conclusions about the stools we may jump to the wrong conclusion about what happened in here.'

'But we heard the crash of stools being used as clubs.'

'Yes, that's correct,' said Gabinius, clearly irritated by my slowness, and hesitancy. 'The assailant or assailants used the stools to beat my assistant to death.'

'Marcus,' I said. 'Take this stool, it's the more intact of the two. That's it. Hold the legs with both hands. Yes, that's right.'

'But what do you want me to do with it, Theo?'

'Why . . . hit me with it of course.'

'You're joking, Theo.'

'There's no time for jokes. Just use the stool as if it were a club and hit me with it. Go on, Marcus. Quickly.'

Although baffled he did as he was told, lifted the stool like a club and –

– *clunk* –

– the stool hit one of the low hanging lamps. It swung sending shadows dancing madly around the room.

Startled, Marcus lowered the stool. Librarian steadied the lamp.

'Is it broken?' I asked.

'He's knocked the bottom out of it. Careful you don't step on the oil. You'd slip and crack your skull.'

I skirted the pool of oil on the stone slabs. 'Let's examine the other two lamps. See? They're intact.'

'So,' Marcus said, his eyes bright. 'You realized that if the murderer and victim had fought with stools they would have smashed one or more of the lamps when they raised the stools.'

'So, how did the stools get broken?' Gabinius sounded even more irritable. 'How did someone get into this locked room and kill my assistant and steal the map? Did they have wings and fly in from one of those windows up there?'

I looked up. 'I don't know about you gentlemen, but I don't believe in witchcraft. Whoever killed this man was mortal.'

Puzzled, Marcus ran his fingers through his tight curls. 'Could anyone have entered through the window up there?'

I shrugged. 'Possibly. But somehow he would have had to scale the outer wall of the library (the height of eight men remember) and then climb down here into the room, without the victim noticing; then returning the way he came – the murderer would have had to have been as agile as a monkey.'

'Earlier you mentioned the state of the soles of the dead man's feet. That they are coated with a black substance when they should be grey with street dust.'

'Well remembered, Marcus. Yes, I think they hold a powerful clue to what happened in here. I think the dried lotus petals are significant, too. Oh? Please, you mustn't allow me to miss any details. The cord . . . how did that cord come to be in the room?'

'Ah, there is no mystery there,' Librarian said. 'It's simply cord of the type we use to suspend the lamps from the ceiling spars. Mosse left it here after replacing one of the lamp cords last week. I intended reminding him about it.'

Marcus shook his head. 'You must have one heck of a long ladder to reach the beams.'

'No, years ago we perfected the technique of tying a light line to a weight and throwing it over the beam, then we haul the heavier cord over so it's looped over the beam then tie both ends to the lamp hooks.'

'Ingenious,' I said, 'but was Mosse so untidy as to leave the cord on the floor?'

'No, it was hanging from one of the iron pegs on the wall. In the commotion it must have been knocked to the floor.'

'So, we have stout cord, maybe thirty paces in length. It is uncoiled.'

'No mystery.' Gabinius now sounded bored. 'With all the people milling about in here, they uncoiled it with their feet.'

'Perhaps.'

'Look,' hissed Gabinius. 'We have a suspect. The foreigner, Ha'dar –'

'Ha'radaa.'

'Okay, whatever the devil's name is. He has fresh bruising. Why don't we simply beat the truth out of him. The guards would be happy, *more than happy*, to help there.'

'You can beat most men into confessing to a crime they might or might not have committed, but I don't think even those animals out there could beat Roman out of a man who clearly can't speak the language.'

'But all this talk of looking! Looking for clues! Looking at the feet of the corpse! Looking at the filthy lotus petals! Looking! Looking! Where the hell is it getting you?'

'Look around you, Gabinius, what *don't* you see now?'

'What *don't* I see? You're talking in riddles, Amun-Arten.'

'Look, by your feet. What was once there, and is there no longer?'

'You're talking nonsense, man.'

'The pool of oil,' said Marcus his eyes widening. 'It's drained away.'

'There's nothing so extraordinary about that!' said Gabinius, hotly. 'It's simply drained between the cracks in the stonework.'

'But,' I held up a finger, 'it's a reminder of what lies beneath our feet. Look, the walls are solid, the door was locked from both the inside and the outside, the windows are too high to admit anyone. The only possible entrance is through the floor.'

Gabinius snorted. 'So the murderer burrowed in here like a mole.'

I shook my head. 'Beneath Alexandria is a labyrinth of ancient catacombs; a vast necropolis occupied by a million dead. The catacombs can even be accessed through the cellars of some of the houses in the very street that runs outside. Chrysippus once showed me one that can be reached through the stable in his back yard. We walked for a mile beneath the city streets. And in the ancient tombs there were thousands of coffins, and on the coffins were these.' I picked up a dried petal. 'Garlands of lotus blossom, dried crisp as ashes.'

'Those lotus blossom leaves weren't in here before Diomedes was locked in the room with the map,' Marcus said eagerly. 'Somehow the murderer brought them in here, perhaps stuck to his clothes.'

Librarian nodded sagely. 'A murderer who gained access to this reading room via a subterranean tunnel, which has an entrance through this very floor.'

Even Gabinius' hopes were renewed. 'And for some reason poor Diomedes ventured down into the catacomb where the floor is covered in black dirt.'

'What now, Theo?'

'Bring an iron bar and we'll begin levering up the stone slabs until we find the entrance.'

Librarian ordered Mosse to bring the iron bar, and we began. Marcus, Gabinius, and even Librarian, shouted excited instructions to each other as we began lifting the stone floor slabs. How we chose the slabs to lift was made easy for us. Most had been cemented down, so we discounted those. With every slab we lifted we expected the characteristic gush of tomb air, heavy with the scent of ancient spices that had been used to pack the bodies; then steps leading down into a well of shadow.

But the time passed; each lifted slab exposed only the compacted sand of the building's foundations. Perspiration poured off the three men. Hope and excitement began to turn to disappointment. Then despair.

We'd lifted every loose slab. Nothing but sand. At last I sat with my back to the wall, the corpse with his blackened feet still lying mute in the middle of the floor, and I held one of those dried lotus petals in my hand and cursed and cursed my arrogance and my stupidity. You, love, have said time and time again that I am obsessed with being able to treat and to cure every disease I encounter. And time and time again, love, you have rightly told me it is not my fault when a patient of mine dies. But still I will pace our rooms, whispering curses and slapping my forehead in frustration at my ignorance.

I knew now this case had no diagnosis. I'd merely been playing games to while away the time before I felt the blade bite my throat. Then I'd watch my life flow away into the gutter, and I knew I would cling, as a drowning sailor clings to a broken spar, to the memory of your beautiful eyes when they open in the dawn, and your trusting smile, and I'd feel so humble, yet so proud, that you made the decision to spend your life with me.

We have stopped searching now. The iron bar lies discarded against the wall. The monkeys still throw stones down onto the guards.

Now I am using what time I have left before General Romulus returns to finish my letter to you. Don't grieve long for me, my love. Begin a new life. Part of me will be the desert winds that seem to call your name. And part of me will be the desert sands that forever fall from blue skies to speckle your bare shoulders like freckles. When you brush them from your skin, brush gently, my love. For somewhere I will feel the brush of your fingertips against my cheek.

Theocritas Amun-Arten

THE CLERK'S TESTIMONY

My name is Chrysippus. I am a court clerk of twenty years. My profession is to record verbatim speech of the litigants and the judicial decisions. Theocritas Amun-Arten, a good friend since boyhood, has asked me to complete this letter to you on his behalf.

Theo asked me into the Isis reading room to record the testament of the murdered scribe's master, one Gabinius Larentia.

Gabinius spoke plainly. A condemned man's statement to be committed to history: 'My name is Gabinius Larentia. I make this testament freely knowing I will be dead within the hour. I was commissioned five years ago to locate a map drawn by the captain of a merchant ship in the time of Tiberius. There are stories handed down from ancient Phoenician sailors of a vast unknown continent. Legends say it is reached by sailing due west beyond the Pillars of Hercules and far out across the Atlantic. The captain of the merchant ship went in search of this land in the West and returned a year to the day later with the map I located today in this very library. On the reverse of the map is recorded information about the land. Its climate is Mediterranean, the rivers are swollen with fish, bison roam the flatlands in herds so vast no human eye can comprehend them. And there are men there with skins as red as copper.'

Theo asked, 'What did General Romulus plan?'

'He planned to create a new and greater Rome. You see Romulus is a pagan Roman. He despises the Emperor Constantine's conversion to Christianity, and the removal of the seat of the Empire's power from Rome eastwards to Constantinople. The General's plan was to make a pact with the barbarians in the North, to simply let them walk into Rome and occupy it, while he intended to turn Spain into his fortress state. While Constantine battled to oust the barbarians from Rome, Romulus would execute a three-year plan that would see the exodus of the cream of Roman citizenship via Spain, westward across the ocean to the new and forever pagan Rome. He envisaged fleets of ships more than a thousand strong, carrying Roman families and gold. The ships would be beached on the new world beyond the Atlantic and broken up, their timber to be used in the construction of the city.'

'What would the result of this exodus be?'

'The Empire would be destroyed. Firstly, because Romulus would bankrupt the Western half in the building of the enormous fleet of ships and by denuding it of its craftsmen, armies and its finest citizens; and secondly because Constantine would never be able to defeat a barbarian army that has barricaded itself inside Rome's city walls. Ultimately, the barbarian would take Constantinople herself and the Empire would be lost forever.'

'But if all that is needed is to sail due west why does Romulus need the map?'

'He dreamt that the gods visited him, offering him the map as a token of success. But they warned if he failed to find it, and so failed to restore the old gods to Rome, then they would smite him down from above.'

'So Romulus is superstitious?'

'Extremely superstitious. He was actually afraid to leave his headquarters after dark because he heard that the gods of old Egypt came alive tonight.'

Theo gave a grim laugh. 'He's obviously not aware of Alexandrian folklore.'

Wearily, Gabinius smiled. 'I was alarmed too, until I learnt you were referring to your apes.'

Theo began to pace the floor of the room looking thoughtfully at the body of the scribe. 'Gabinius, you have faith in the General's plan.'

'He doesn't pay me to have faith in him. He paid me to find the map. Which I lost tonight.'

'You're a pagan?'

'I show my face at the temple of Jupiter from time to time.'

'So you wouldn't be unduly worried at the loss of Constantine and the destruction of Christianity?'

'Christianity's a fad. It just happens to be fashionable with the upper classes at the moment because the Emperor's family are Christian.'

'I see.' Theo rubbed his jaw. 'You hate Christians?'

'Hardly. I employed one.' Gabinius pointed at the dead man on the floor.

'Diomedes was a Christian?' Theo looked up in surprise. 'Are you sure?'

'Absolutely.'

Then there came the march of feet with military precision. The six hours were up. General Romulus had returned for his map.

Theo said urgently, 'Listen, did Diomedes have a family? It's important. You must tell me.'

'At this moment nothing's important,' said Gabinius, his red face at last turning grey. 'We are all ghosts now.'

'Gabinius. Listen to me. Did that man have a family?'

The sound of footsteps grew louder. The chattering of the monkeys stopped at the arrival of more soldiers. I saw Theo look up. The grey light that precedes the dawn had touched the top of the stonework. As Gabinius, resigned to his death, started to leave the room, Theo caught him by the arm.

'Gabinius! Did the murdered man have a family?'

'Theo, friend Theo, if I can call you that now. We can continue this conversation at our leisure in the next world.'

'Wouldn't you like to stop in this one a little longer?'

Gabinius stopped and frowned. 'Why? What do you know?'

'Does the dead man have a family? It's vital that I know.'

Romulus entered the room. Gabinius closed his mouth tight. Theo looked at me despairingly. Then almost as if the words had sprung from his lips unbidden, Gabinius turned to Theo and said. 'Yes. A wife and four young children.'

Theo nodded with gratitude and let out a sigh as if a sack of bricks had been lifted from his shoulders.

Romulus spoke like a man who had anticipated a certain outcome and realized he wasn't going to be disappointed. 'Gabinius, I understand the map hasn't been found?'

Gabinius nodded, his face even more grey.

General Romulus' expression was sour. 'Then I will honour my promise to you all. You will each be taken outside and your throats will be opened.'

Under his breath, Theo said to me, 'Chrysippus. Keep writing down all that you see and hear. Don't stop writing. Even if I'm killed here where I stand, keep writing . . . *keep writing.*'

I was puzzled and, believe me, very frightened. I was to die too, but the very force of feeling in his voice kept my pen moving.

I write now what I see in front of me. Just as it happens.

Standing before me, as I inscribe the sheets of papyrus clipped to my scribe's board, is General Romulus, three of the German bodyguard, young Marcus, Gabinius and Librarian. The body still lies on the floor; the lamps still burn.

What mystifies me, even alarms me, is the transformation of Theocritas Amun-Arten. Even General Romulus is taken aback. It's as if Theo has undergone some mystical transfiguration. He looks suddenly larger than life, animated, as if some great spirit has filled him, infusing and enthusing him. His eyes shine, he moves from side to side; his hands sweep outward in priestly gestures as he speaks: 'General Romulus. I am offering myself as the first of our number to be executed.'

'A Christian?' Romulus snorted. 'Always eager for self-sacrifice aren't you?'

'My offer has a number of conditions that I should like you to agree to.'

'You're a strange specimen of a man. Conditions? You want to negotiate a contract, just moments before your death?'

'Yes, I promise I will lie as still as stone on the library steps and guide the executioner's blade myself if I prove unable to explain fully and clearly what happened to this poor man – and the map. Also I must have your promise that you will not order any harm to be done to the family of anyone in this library.'

'That won't be necessary, funny little man. I already know what happened.'

This time Theo looked surprised. 'You do?'

'I owe my present status to more than sheer brute force. I thrive on information. My German bodyguard aren't ignorant men. One of them stood outside this doorway and carefully listened to every word said.'

'If you know who the murderer is why haven't you got the map?'

'You really do have bad manners. I thought my status carried with it at least a modicum of respect.'

'Being obsequious won't save my throat now.'

'True.' He signalled to one of his guards in the doorway. 'My men have arrested the murderer. We'll merely have to look a little further afield for the map.'

Theo's eyes widened as the man was brought into the room. 'Ha'radaa?'

'Of course,' said Romulus, pleased. 'You identified him yourself. The dead scribe has bruised fists. This oriental's chest and arms are bruised from the blows.'

'But how did Ha'radaa enter and leave a room via a door that is locked on both sides?'

'The man is small, appears agile. He will have scaled the outside of the building, which the monkeys seem to have no trouble in doing.'

'You're suggesting that like a monkey he can –'

'Once through the window at the top of the wall,' Romulus continued, 'he climbed down inside the room, using those iron pegs set in the wall.'

'But those iron pegs only reach as far as the stone ledge, which is only half way up the wall, he would have needed –'

'A rope? Probably. So here is our criminal.'

'I believe, General Romulus, you have made a mistake.'

'Oh, so our little Egyptian says I am mistaken.'

'With respect, General, I can show you what happened in this room. First, though, I think I should dismiss this gentleman as a suspect . . . Marcus, please ask Staki to step inside.'

When Staki arrived, he stood nervously shifting his weight from one foot to the other.

'Can I have a look at your hands, please, Staki . . . no, palms downward please. Thank you. Your left fist is bruised. The right fist has a cut, which has become infected. If you'd take my advice, Staki, you should treat a suppurating wound with a little honey. You've been in a fight, Staki?'

'A few days ago. I . . . I . . .'

'Who were you fighting?'

Staki stared glassily in front of him. 'Sailors in the harbour tavern. They were . . .'

'You are lying,' said Romulus incisively.

Theo glanced at Ha'radaa. 'Why did this gentleman become so angry with you earlier this evening?'

'I . . . well . . . he obviously mistook me . . .'

Theo shook his head. 'If we had the time to go into this further, Staki, I think the truth of the matter is, that you and probably your thug friends happened across this visitor to Alexandria here, beat him up and robbed him?'

Staki's heavy lips trembled and he looked as if he was going to protest his innocence until his eyes met the hawk eyes of the General. His head dropped. 'Yes. We followed him from Caeser's Square and jumped him in the alley way that runs at the back of the temple.'

General Romulus gave a dry smile. 'Punishment for petty robbery and assault is flogging. But there would be little point in flogging a dead man would there?'

The guard escorted Staki and Ha'radaa out of the room.

'So,' said Romulus. 'You've now lost your prime suspect. You know, you had a chance to save your skins there by simply pinning the blame on the oriental.'

'But that would have been unfair.'

'So you're more concerned about fairness and justice than your survival?'

'Aren't those the foundation stones of our civilization?'

'Well . . . you must be the first Egyptian I've met who's far too honest and honourable for his own good. But I'm afraid your principles are more impressive than your good sense. What's your name?'

'Theocritas Amun-Arten. I'm a physician.'

'Right, Amun-Arten, give me your account of events in this room tonight. You've got the time it takes the executioner to sharpen his knife on the stone.'

Theo nodded, accepting the challenge. 'First, I'll admit my mistake. I believed there was an entrance through the floor to the catacombs that honeycomb the rock beneath the city. The assailant had entered the room via that passageway, so I wrongly postulated, killed Diomedes and made off with the map. As I've described before the Egyptians place garlands of lotus blossom on the coffins of their dead. My belief was that the assailant had inadvertently carried a few of the petals into the room with him.'

'There are lotus petals in the room?'

'Yes. If you give me enough time I'll be able to explain how they came to be here. And no, General, there is no secret passageway into the room, we lifted all the slabs that are loose. There is only sand beneath them.' Theo thoughtfully placed a finger against his nose. 'Until moments ago one mystery I couldn't explain away was the state of the dead man's feet. His soles are covered with a rich black substance.'

'So?'

'You'll see, General, that the floor of the room is kept scrupulously clean. Now, if you'll allow me to conduct one small experiment. Chrysippus, please hand me a clean sheet of papyrus. Thank you. Now, I beg you to watch carefully.'

Theo crouched down beside the body, took hold of one of the dead man's feet in one hand, and pressed the sheet of papyrus against the bare sole of the foot with the other.

'See, gentlemen?'

There on the sheet of papyrus was one distinct black footprint as if stamped there in ink. Theo continued: 'By rights there should be black footprints covering the floor. Where are they? Or was the black substance applied to his feet after death? Or did the deceased visit a place where the floor was covered with the black dirt, and then, for some reason, on his return his feet no longer had reason to touch the floor?'

'He was carried here?' ventured Marcus.

General Romulus shook his head. 'Or do you suggest that after he muddied his feet he magically flew back into the room to die?'

'I think, General, you are close to the truth.'

'And I know, Amun-Arten, you're blasted close to the blade.'

'You want the map?'

Romulus nodded grimly. 'So, who killed the scribe?'

'Why, General . . . you're looking at the killer.'

Everyone followed the direction of the General's gaze. Gabinius' jaw opened as if the muscles of his face had ceased to work.

'Amun-Arten, what in the name of the blasted gods are you saying?'

'I'm saying, General Romulus, that Diomedes murdered himself.'

'Suicide?'

'Yes. But he went to extraordinary lengths to make it look like murder.'

'But what on earth for?'

'I'll explain the *why* later. But first the *how*.' Moving his arms in those great priestly gestures, Theocritas Amun-Arten paced the floor as he explained. 'Diomedes chose, quite calmly and rationally, to kill himself. He chose also to make it look like murder. He's in a locked room. He has no knife. That limits the means of suicide quite severely, and even more so if it must be disguised as murder. There is the lamp cord hanging from the iron peg. But he could only hang himself with that, and that would clearly look like suicide. Murderers in a hurry don't hang their victims. He also chose to make us assume, particularly you General, that he'd bravely fought his attacker before being bludgeoned to death. Quite simply he punched the walls until his fists were bruised. I'd guess he cleverly wrapped his hand in some article of clothing first to make it look as if he'd punched at flesh rather than solid stone. It must have taken a will of iron that even you, General, might admire.'

'But there was a fight. The stools are broken. His head smashed.'

'I demonstrated earlier that one or more of the overhead lamps would have been broken if there had been a fight in here using the stools as clubs.'

'One is.'

'Ah, I sacrificed that one in an experiment earlier this evening.'

'Continue, Amun-Arten, I'm curious to know how the man contrived to beat himself to death.'

'Quite simple. He employed a force of nature. Please, come here. See, the iron pegs set in the walls. He used these to climb the wall as far as the stone ledge. It is perhaps the height of four grown men standing on each others shoulders. You can imagine him standing there, he's frightened, he's praying to his God, but he believes the self-sacrifice is vital. Then, carefully assessing what he must do, he bends at the waist, then falls forward, allowing that force of nature to rush him downward head first onto the stone floor below. Death would be instantaneous.'

'And I'm supposed to swallow that fantastic idea? Witnesses heard a struggle first, then a loud pounding.'

'Those were made by Diomedes. He needed to make the people outside that door believe there was a furious fight taking place in here. So, he tied that length of cord to the stools, climbed up here to the ledge, carrying one end of the cord with him. He then hauled the stools up after him, beat them against the wall, breaking them, shouting all the time, before throwing the stools down to the ground; then himself.'

'Reasonably plausible, Amun-Arten, but you've no proof. And where did the dried lotus petals come from?'

'Marcus,' said Theo, 'it's quite a hazardous favour I'm asking, but would you climb the wall, using those pegs, to the stone ledge? Then I want you sweep your hand along the surface as if you're sweeping crumbs from a table.'

With difficulty Marcus scaled the wall using the iron pegs. Reaching the ledge, with his head just a little above it, he swept his arm across the stone work. Light objects like scraps of paper fluttered down. One fell onto the General's shoulder. Briskly he brushed it off. 'Dried lotus petals. Who put them there?'

'The ancient Egyptians, when this was still a temple. Statues probably stood on the ledge. They've been toppled now, but some of the lotus garlands remain from their festivals. They've probably been there for a thousand years or more. Now ...' He called up to Marcus, 'Marcus, please show the General your hand and arm. Good ...' Theo smiled. 'You see. It is covered with the same greasy black as Diomedes' feet. It's a mixture of soot and the greasy dust lifted into the air by the heat from the lamps. If you'd like to send one of your men up there they'll find, I believe, the whole of the ledge is thick with a layer of that black dirt. They'll also find footprints that will match with those of the deceased. Naturally, when Diomedes stood on the ledge prior to his fall he did not notice his feet had become blackened.'

The General nodded slowly. 'Very well, Amun-Arten, I accept your explanation. In the face of the weight of evidence I can do no other. But why did Diomedes kill himself?'

'You knew he was Christian?'

'No, is that important?'

Gabinius let out an involuntary moan. His eyes locked hard onto Theo in terror.

General Romulus understood perfectly the reason for the man's fear. 'What don't you want Amun-Arten to tell me, Gabinius?'

Theo answered for the man. 'To reach the truth I persuaded Gabinius to tell me why the map was so important to you.'

'Well, after tonight I'm confident you'll all keep my secrets safe.'

Theo obviously registered the General's threat but didn't stop speaking, 'Diomedes was Christian. He knew of your plan to move the Empire westward to a new land across the Atlantic. He knew this new Empire would be strictly pagan, and that the results of this vast exodus would destroy the old Empire and Christianity would be wiped out beneath a flood of invaders with their own barbaric gods. I don't believe for a moment Diomedes, nor even Gabinius, thought they would ever find the map, pointing the way to this mythical new world across the sea. When it did appear it caught Diomedes by surprise. He was locked into a room knowing full well that in probably less than an hour you'd walk through that door, you'd have the map in your hands, and that Christianity would be as good as dead.'

'But why all the elaborate play-acting, then killing himself in such a bizarre fashion?'

'Naturally he could have simply destroyed the map,' said Theo, 'and he knew you would have executed him anyway. No, he wasn't afraid to sacrifice himself to safeguard his faith, but he was a family man. And he knew you would have exacted retribution on his wife and children. He balked at sacrificing them, too. So in the heat of the moment he concocted his plan to make it look like murder.'

'And the map?' The General's expression was stony. 'Presumably he burnt it.'

'It wouldn't have burnt easily; it was drawn on a rabbit skin.'

'Then where is it?'

Theo knelt beside the body and gently opened the mouth and, with his fingers, reached inside. 'Here, it is. Or at least a fragment of it.' Theo held a scrap of parchment between finger and thumb. 'We can imagine Diomedes frantically tearing at the map with his teeth, and he has exceptionally good teeth, too, unlike we poor Egyptians. No doubt half choking in the process he swallowed the map – a difficult task, then also with great difficulty he will have climbed up the wall using those iron pegs. Undoubtedly, his love for his God empowered him. Post-mortem convulsions after he hit the floor will have caused the partial regurgitation of the shreds of skin into the back of his throat.'

'Perhaps the map can be pieced together,' said Gabinius, kneading his hands together hopefully.

Theo shook his head. 'There are powerful acids in the stomach. The pigments on the map will have been utterly destroyed.'

General Romulus picked up his helmet from the table and sighed. 'Diomedes was either a fool or ruthlessly ambitious. He should have known that if Christians will gladly sacrifice themselves for their God then their faith is indestructible anyway. Is it possible that the old gods have led me astray and that this puling, humbling Christ in whose name even the Roman Emperor now fights is fated to prevail?'

Theo raised an eyebrow. 'Ruthlessly ambitious? You think Diomedes sought sainthood through martyrdom?'

'Quite. This religion of self-sacrifice apparently carries its own rewards. Let us hope that he enjoys them now in Heaven, for his family will most certainly get little more enjoyment during their brief time they have left on Earth. Although this wretch is beyond punishment for his treachery, his family certainly are not.'

'But you promised that –'

'Amun-Arten. You are too trusting. Why should a senior Roman General be bound by his oath to a funny little Egyptian with no history worth speaking of and certainly no future worth mentioning? The moment is too bitter for mercy. Goodbye.'

As soon as General Romulus, his helmet under one arm, had left the room Gabinius, wild eyed, turned on Theo. 'You heard that, Amun-Arten? Even after all this, he's going to kill us anyway. Probably this very moment, out there on the library steps. Don't you –'

He was silenced by the arrival of one of the lieutenants who barked, '*Physician. Come with me. Now!*'

I, Theocritas Amun-Arten take up the pen once more. I am tired; the end, at last, has come.

On being summoned by the General's lieutenant, I followed him from the Isis room into the main body of the library. He marched quickly and I had to run to keep up with him. I had no doubt he was eager to cut my throat.

Then I saw a bizarre and incredible sight. Some of the body-guard were pointing towards the distant ceiling, and while I watched in amazement, dried lotus petals fell gently from the vault of the roof. I've heard descriptions of snow from travellers. Surely this must be how it looks, fluttering palely from a dark sky. I followed the lieutenant to my death through this softly falling cloud of petals that misted the air white. Perhaps the monkeys had run out of stones to throw and had found the dried lotus flowers that must clutter every niche and ledge.

Through the mist of gently falling petals I made out figures. They were gathered about another figure that lay face down on the floor.

It was General Romulus. He had gone forward to meet his ancestors.

I asked what happened.

'The General was walking towards me,' said the lieutenant, 'and appeared to be about to deliver his orders, when he was hit by a piece of stone thrown by one of the apes.'

I looked up through the swirl of petals cast by the now silent monkeys. Sitting in one of the niches that had once contained one of the gods of Egypt, was a huge specimen, the father of his tribe. He looked steadily back at me, the serene wisdom of Thoth in those ebony eyes.

'The General is dead?' asked the lieutenant.

I answered softly, 'Oh yes, quite dead.'

After the guards had carried away the body Marcus picked up the lethal piece of stone and handed it to me.

Librarian appeared. 'I saw Romulus fall as if he'd been hit by a thunderbolt.'

The piece of stone in my hands was a granite fist, twice the size of mine.

Librarian looked at the blood on the floor. 'What killed him?'

'The hand of god.' I held up the granite fist. 'Which god?' I shrugged. 'A god. Any god. It doesn't really matter at all.'

The rising sun is bringing a pink blush to the houses and temples and churches of this wonderful city. The streets are peaceful; the air still. In a little while, I'll put down my pen and follow the monkeys as they stream homeward to their nesting places.

After the events of this turbulent night I feel both a satisfaction, and the warmth of a serenity that touches upon the divine. And now that warmth becomes a glow of anticipation. Because I know in just a few short moments I will open the door of our house, be greeted by the scents of home: sandalwood and musk and thyme, mingling with freshly baked bread, and as I climb the stairs, my heart will feel the fire of love, because, I know, at last, that's where I will find you.

LAST THINGS

Darrell Schweitzer

Darrell Schweitzer is an American editor, reviewer and author. His work is primarily in the fantasy field, in which he scored a marked success with his novel The Mask of the Sorcerer *(1995), but he has also written several stories with a Roman background. In 'Last Things', his first serious murder mystery, Schweitzer explores the rule of law at the very moment that the Roman Empire collapsed in the West in* AD 476.

❧

I can't tell you how immensely pleased I was, though not really surprised, to see that the house of Plautia Marcella stood as it always had, nestled among trees on a ledge above a stream and a narrow valley, in the foothills of the Alps. Throughout my journey I had noted the general impoverishment of the countryside; the very few, stick-thin tenants still laboring in the fields; the burnt villages; the tracts of waste; but here, as my carriage inched across the ancient stone bridge and I gazed up through the dusk at the welcoming villa, time seemed never to have passed. Here was a place immune to the ravages and follies of men and the death-throes of empires. The sight was more comforting than I can put into words.

I had been a guest here many times in my youth, in the old days, when the third Valentinian wore the purple and Roman political fictions went on as they always had, like a stately dance of shadows. Here there was light. Here were solid things. The great lady Marcella's husband had grown greater still in the imperial service, leaving her richer than dreams of avarice – and I think she had few of those, desiring only to live in the old way, without hindrance.

So, in her house, you might think that Trajan still ruled. Some *genius* hovered above the place, a guardian spirit who insured that the life of Plautia Marcella remained like the unrippled water in a tranquil pool.

She would survive, I used to believe, until the end of time, until the deaths of the gods.

But aren't the gods already dead? Ah, I digress.

Suffice it to say that inside this house, strict decorum was always observed. A gentleman wore a toga, never daring to appear in the actually more practical Germanic trousers the twit Valentinian once tried to outlaw. ('A few more attempts like that, and I shall actually believe he is alive, not a stuffed dummy,' Lady Plautia once said, but softly, because in those days the emperor's mother, the Christian gorgon Galla Placidia, was still among us, and everything was said softly.)

There one spoke perfect, classical Latin, rife with allusions. The eunuch-chamberlain Gregorius greeted one at the door. He was a dark, frail little thing, an Armenian with a whispering voice, whose beardless condition made him seem forever a child. It was his task to exchange initial pleasantries and small gifts to and from his mistress, then conduct the guests to the baths, where we would linger in sumptuous luxury, often accompanied by music, sometimes Gregorius himself on a lyre or pipe. And at last, at the appointed hour, one followed Gregorius and the other servants in stately procession into the *triclinium*, the dining hall, where Plautia Marcella held her court and the games (of wit and eloquence) were about to begin.

In those days, when I was fourteen or fifteen, I was the best friend of her favorite nephew Sabellianus. For all that I felt smothered in such company and had been more interested, as Sabellianus was, in hunting or riding, I genuinely liked her. The very artificiality of her condition appealed to my already ripening cynicism. Here was a lady who had *style*.

I was a would-be poet then, spinning vast tapestries of word-play and rhetoric, and if, sometimes, I lost all sense of what I was trying to say in the process, Plautia Marcella always praised my compositions. She too was a cynic, not in any strict philosophical sense, but someone who accepted mere surfaces and did not peer underneath, because she already knew there was nothing there.

Laughter, I associate with her, and very faint mockery, like the wind under the eaves. I could mock Virgil merely by not being Virgil. She could mock Galla Placidia by not being empress.

We became confidants. She was of a far higher social rank than I, which removed any sense of competition. There was no danger

I would ever be asked to marry her daughter, Plautilla, who had the potential of becoming another gorgon. So she told me things she told no one else, particularly after my boyhood friendship with Sabellianus had ended, and he had gone off to become a priest and convert the heathen who were arriving across the Rhine in inexhaustible waves. I still visited. We two, together, had our little jokes and our secrets. But there was no possibility of scandal between us. She did not lust after me. She called me one of her puppies.

Once, when only Gregorius was present, she said to me, 'I have seen the goddess Hecate, walking in my garden with her two black hounds.'

That startled me. I said nothing. She waited for my response, but when I did not laugh, or ask if the hounds had left muddy prints or worse on the garden path, she smiled mysteriously, and the three of us rose and went out into the garden, which spread over a series of terraces behind the house. There Gregorius unearthed a small stone altar and the three of us, just for the fun of it I think, committed a capital crime. We sacrificed, just pouring a little wine over the stone. It was evening, dark very suddenly and the wind blew through the trees. Lady Plautia spoke of spirits, of *daemones*, which haunt every fold of the earth, whether the established ·Church likes it or not. She conversed with invisible gods as if they were her dinner guests. I could almost see them. The wind blew. The moon was covered with a cloud, and Hecate, goddess of the dead and of witchcraft walked nearby.

I did not even suggest to myself that the lady was mad. No, this was a performance, for my sake. I found it thrilling.

Later that night, in my chamber, I actually wrote a good poem.

Now that I am old and tell this story, I still wonder what, actually, Plautia Marcella believed. Certainly she worshipped Christ and even endowed a little church once, professing, as everyone did, that in the crucified Nazarene, Rome had found a powerful new ally. After all, she pointed out, the cross on which He died was now on the money, or else the christogram, the *chi-rho*, depicted on many imperial reverses as being inscribed by a winged victory – which already the vulgar called an angel – onto a shield. So if the penniless carpenter, who did not even own the robe He wore, now found His way onto the golden *solidus* of Rome and those *solidi* found their way into the purses of silken-robed churchmen, then clearly even God was moving up in the world.

But what did she believe? Did she, as I strove to, achieve the placidity of a still, secret pool by believing in nothing at all?

*   *   *

She believed in enough to write to me, without any elegant flourishes, *Come at once. I need you.*

It had begun to rain by the time my carriage reached the house. I ran to the door and knocked. There was no answer, but the door was unbarred, so in breach of all etiquette, I let myself in and stood dripping in the semi-darkness of the familiar atrium. A single lamp hung flickering from a stand. The room was filled with huge shadows. I could see, though, that the niches in the walls for the household gods were filled, as always, with flowerpots, though the flowers seemed to be dead.

The floor at my feet was muddy and wet. It would never have been so in the old days.

How long had it been? Twenty years? In the meantime Attila and his Huns had come and gone. The savior of Rome, the supreme commander Aetius, died at the actual hand of Valentinian, who no longer had his gorgon mother around to prevent such a rash deed. Lady Plautia's husband, who had been a partisan of Aetius, perished soon thereafter, as did Valentinian and several of his successors, set up and knocked down like chess-pieces by the barbarian who had taken Aetius' place, the formidable Count Ricimer. Rome was sacked twice more. Even Ricimer could not save it. The government cowered in Ravenna. People said the world was coming to an end. But the house of Plautia Marcella was still here, eternal, although the floor was dirty.

Somehow I began to find less comfort in mere survival.

I started at a sound. Another light flickered and drew near, and I saw that it was the lady's chief servant Gregorius, who had grown white-haired and wizened, his head bobbing atop his thin neck like autumn's last leaf clinging to a twig.

His dark eyes, however, sparkled as before.

'Ah, welcome young master Titus.'

No mention of my own long list of pompous political titles. Here I was still Young Master Titus. I bowed.

'Greetings to you and your lady.'

The eunuch jerked his head back, like a startled peacock, and his half-smile vanished. 'Yes, from my lady.' Then he did something which puzzled me. He crossed himself.

I hadn't time to ponder what it meant. I took care of the preliminaries, making sure that my horses and my own servants were cared for. Two other servants I didn't know, both of them elderly, shuffled off to carry out Gregorius' instructions. Then we proceeded. There was no ritual bath. I wiped my wet face and hair with a towel. Gregorius offered me a fresh toga, fussing over me to make me presentable, as if I were still a child.

Then, without further ado, he ushered me into the dining room where the Lady Plautia Marcella waited like the timeless Sphinx among her pillows, her powdered face framed by the towering curls of an archaic wig, her eyes still alive behind it all as if she were peering out through a mask of stone.

Her brocaded gown rustled as she shifted herself slightly. Then, another surprise. She fingered a golden cross she wore around her neck. She seemed, I thought, distracted and even afraid.

I bowed and she nodded.

'So you dropped everything and came. I am deeply touched.'

I did not trouble her with the news that all discipline was breaking down in the City, crimes went unprosecuted, the law courts too often addressed empty air, and if one of the assistants to the urban prefect disappeared for a few weeks, no one would much notice.

'I wish I had the time to keep up a proper correspondence.'

She clutched her cross and made a bony, spotted fist. Her wrist shook, and her face twitched slightly, uncontrollably, reminding me that for all her façade, she was truly ancient, possibly as old as eighty.

She jerked her head and seemed to be trying to remember something, then said suddenly, 'And what about your poetry? Dear boy, you were going to conquer the world with poetry, once upon a time.'

I shook my head sadly, both amused and melancholy that I was still her Dear Boy past the age of forty.

'No?' she said. Did I detect a genuine regret?

'Alas, I must leave the poetry to Sidonius Apollinaris. Have you heard of him? I've attended a few of his readings. His work is the perfection of eloquence, and doesn't threaten to mean anything at all.'

The lady's face flickered, and for just an instant she seemed her old self. But there was no witty epigram, no wrenching parody of Sidonius' latest, merely a sigh.

'I've always enjoyed you, Titus. I really have.'

'And I you, Lady. Truly.'

I bowed again. She held out a trembling hand for me to kiss her ring.

Then I took my place on the couch adjoining hers. Two elderly servants came and laid out a simple meal. I observed that they set three places. I raised an eyebrow.

Plautia cleared her throat.

Now I received my third surprise of the evening, more alarming than the other two.

Someone else bellowed in a hoarse voice. 'So he's finally here? This isn't a social call you know, just some stupid police business.'

Another lady raised herself up on her elbow. She had been lying on the third couch, out of sight. She was red-faced and visibly drunk. She held up her wine-cup for a refill, and one of the servants reached for a pitcher, but Plautia shook her head and he put it down again.

'Mother, you treat me like a child!'

It took me quite a while to convince myself that this really was the once-beautiful, if terrible-tempered Plautilla, daughter of my hostess, half-sister to the now martyred Sabellianus. She had grown stout in middle age. Her beauty was utterly gone. She had been married, I knew, to a certain Valerius Aper, about whom, I knew in my police capacity, no one had ever had anything good to say, save that he was rich. Nor was anything good said about how he spent his money or the way he licked Ricimer's boot-heels until the barbarian finally tired of him and my men found Aper face-down in a sewer with his throat cut.

So here was Plautilla, a widow, living in the house of the widow of a much more honorable man. She had never had patience for anything other than her own whims. She surely felt buried alive.

To me she virtually spat, 'You managed to tear yourself away from your pet menagerie of informers and slaves. How very good of you to come.'

'Child!' exclaimed Plautia Marcella.

'I *said*, Mother, that I am *not* a child!'

'You are what I say you are. Now greet our guest politely.'

Plautilla rose to her feet and waved the cup in an exaggerated salute. 'Greetings, oh greetings and more greetings, to the illustrious Titus Vibius Balbinus Pompous Tedious Preposterous whatever-the-hell-the-rest-of-your-names-are, favorite of the gods, lackey of the Caesars ever since you served as one of Tiberius' little fishies –'

Her mother gasped, genuinely shocked at this reference to an obscenity of four hundred years ago. I was startled that Plautilla was that well-read.

'And now, I think,' said the daughter, 'I shall take my leave, so you two can chew over old times and rot.'

She lurched from the room, first grabbing one of the servants and pointing back at the table. The servant fetched Plautilla's plate of food after her.

When she was gone, and the noise of her voice faded, Lady Plautia sighed and said, 'Good riddance. Do you think I could get rid of her by marrying her off to the king of the Vandals? It might put some fear of Rome in him.'

I said softly, 'King Gaiseric is already married, I believe.'

'Too bad. How about the king of the Goths?'

'Him too.'

She smiled. That was, I think, the very last flicker of her old self that I saw.

Her manner became grave. She dismissed the two servants. Gregorius came in and sat down in Plautilla's place. She offered him a few morsels from her own plate, a sign of great honor to a servant.

Gregorius watched me, expectantly.

'The actual reason I have summoned you here, Titus,' the lady said, 'is that I feel death very near. Now wait, before you start reciting clichés about what a wonderful life I've led or how death is but the twin of sleep, or the usual poeticisms, or even a remonstrance that someone my age should at least get used to the idea of my own demise, let me explain what I am afraid of. *I am bewitched*, Titus. Someone is trying to murder me by witchcraft. Demons whisper at my window. There are apparitions, portents. It's very clear –'

'But –' I couldn't believe I was hearing this. Not from her. Witchcraft and the gods had been toys for her, one more subtle joke. Did she actually want me to believe that Hecate walked in the garden? I concluded, with great sorrow, that Plautia's mind had gone soft. For her, senility would be far worse than death, because she would lose her dignity.

Yet she continued, forcefully and coherently, and I deferred judgment.

'I am not afraid to die, of course, if death means that I can rest, but you know perfectly well that the victim of witchcraft does *not* rest. Of that, I am truly afraid. I would be condemned to haunt this place, until the time of the deaths of the gods.'

Aren't the gods already dead? I wanted to ask, reverting likewise for the very last time to my own former self. Instead I said, 'How can you be certain?'

She seemed very tired all of a sudden, almost unable to speak. She nodded to Gregorius. 'Tell him.'

The eunuch's head bobbed more precariously than ever. 'I found them. The signs.'

'Tell him what signs.'

'The head of a rat nailed to the door. A bundle of bloody feathers in the Mistress's bedclothes. A mirror with a nail driven through it. And, most recently, her name written in secret places inside her private chambers, each day appearing with one letter removed, diminishing.'

'Today there was just the "P". I know I shall die very soon.'

'And the apparitions?' I asked.

'Yes,' said Gregorius. 'I have seen them.'

I wanted to ask more, but events moved too swiftly. The Lady Plautia felt suddenly ill and Gregorius hurried her off to bed. It was only half an hour later that he came to me in my room, tearfully and in secret, and whispered that his mistress was dead.

So she was. I followed him at once to her room and beheld her sprawled across the bed. She had tried to get up and had fallen back, and lay staring at the ceiling with an expression the vulgar might take for abject terror. But of course her eyes were merely open, and glassy, rolled up so that only the whites showed. I closed them with her hand. Her mouth hung open, slack, of course, because the facial muscles of a dead person lack the energy to hold any expression.

I didn't think she had died of terror, though by the terrified manner of Gregorius, he obviously did. More likely, poison. I didn't have time to worry about how much I might have consumed myself at supper. Most likely it had been cumulative, administered on many occasions.

To Gregorius, I said, 'Does anyone else know of this?'

'Not yet – not yet, Sir. Not yet.'

So I was no longer Young Master Titus. All things must pass, in time.

'Then – can you do what I require of you?'

He nodded his head so eagerly I thought it might fall off. Now his manner was that of a child again, a scared child, but, I hoped, an obedient one.

'Good. Give out to the servants that the mistress is ill, but very much alive ... Say that she is delirious, both cursing her daughter and demanding to see her. Say that she commands her daughter's attendance, and that Plautilla must come alone. Then keep everyone in their rooms and away from the corridor outside. Can you do this?'

'Yes, Sir, I can. My poor lady!' He crossed himself.

'Do it for her.'

Then he was gone and I knew what I had to do.

Now in my old age, as I tell you this story, I tell you also that it is total disbelief which opens the eyes. The scales fall away. The ugly, unpoetic truth is revealed, all mysteries are unravelled, and even the secrets of the dead and of the gods fail to deceive.

If you believe in nothing, all is light.

I lifted the lady's corpse out of the bed and concealed it, unceremoniously, in a chest half-filled with gowns. She weighed almost nothing. She felt like a bundle of sticks. Then I wrapped one of her gowns about myself and put on her wig, not the towering one she'd worn at dinner, but a smaller one she'd worn to bed. Plautia Marcella was that vain, even in private, even as she'd come to her room in distress. That my hairline had receded past my ears cannot cause much surprise, because I am a man, but she was balding too, and the effect was undeniably hideous. It was something she could not allow. Her whole life had been a matter of things she had not allowed: time passing, decay, the loss of beauty, death by witchcraft. At the very end she had commanded, and the Fates and Furies did not obey. These were her last things.

I merely disguised myself thus, extinguished the lights, and lay beneath the covers, waiting.

I did not have to wait long. When I heard shuffling footsteps outside in the corridor, I rolled over to face the door, so I could watch what followed through half-opened eyes.

When the door opened, I deliberately rustled the bedclothes and let out what I hoped was a convincingly soft moan, so that whoever stood in the doorway and peered into the darkened room would know that the occupant was indeed and perhaps unexpectedly still alive.

I beheld an apparition. A glowing face, wild in its aspect, with eyebrows raised to silvery points floated into the room. The eyes were heavily shadowed, outlined in black. The thing wore a golden tiara in piled, dark hair, to suggest the crescent moon rising in the night sky. (But wait a minute, I thought, isn't that supposed to be Diana who wears the moon, not Hecate?) I discerned, too, a flickering lamp held in one outstretched hand. In the other, a bronze dagger gleamed faintly.

The thick, rustling form swayed around the bed, performing what was perhaps supposed to be a dance, chanting in what might have been bad Greek, or the unknowable language of Olympus, or even the secret speech of the underworld, which is heard only by the shades or by those about to die, and spoken by the dark Goddess of Death.

This goddess was somewhat heavier than those depicted in classical statuary, and reeked of wine.

When the dagger drew near enough, I reached up and seized the wrist of the hand that held it.

The would-be divinity shrieked as I leapt out of the bed. The moon-tiara clanged to the floor. I lost the wig I was wearing. Though my opponent was considerably heavier than I was, I easily wrestled her out of the room and into the corridor, where there were lamps lit in some of the alcoves and I could see what I was doing.

I snatched Plautilla's own lantern from her and set it down on a table.

'Look at you!' I said. 'What did you think you were doing?'

She rolled her eyes and laughed. 'Look at *you!* Dressed up in Mama's clothes. I knew you were like that all along.'

I let the mistress's nightgown slide from my shoulders, onto the floor.

Plautilla howled and spoke some more of the language of the gods. She wrestled with me, still holding the dagger.

'Fear me!' she said, reverting to ordinary Latin. 'Titus, be afraid. I am possessed by the spirit of Hecate!'

I twisted the dagger out of her grasp and slapped her across the face with the back of my hand.

'I think the Goddess would find a more suitable vehicle to ride in.'

Plautilla's resistance ceased. She sobbed. 'But you *believe* in these things! Mother certainly did. You should have seen her shiver and shake. She even started saying her prayers like a good, pious Christian. I had to laugh. *But the old mummy wouldn't die.* I couldn't wait for ever.'

'You thought you would inherit her fortune.'

'Who else? What else could the bitch do with it?'

Still holding her by the wrist, I pulled her face close to mine, and said in as vicious a tone as I could manage, 'Maybe she was going to endow a home for retired gladiators.' I don't think she appreciated my joke, that the gladiators would have to be very old indeed, and very few, since there had been no such performances in Rome in about seventy years.

She spat in my face.

'No goddess would behave thus,' I said. 'And once it is clear that there is no goddess . . . you have made no attempt to conceal anything, have you?'

Indeed, there was no labyrinth of clues, no puzzle. Everything was as clear as writing on the walls, the letters diminishing to a single, final truth.

She had concealed nothing. With utter contempt she showed me where she had left more chicken feet bundled above the door, and yet more places where she had traced mysterious sigils and curses on the walls with charcoal. And there were other masks she had worn, to provide other apparitions. There were even two black dogs kept tied up in a shed behind the garden. The poor creatures seemed starving. I unleashed them and let them run.

At the very last, Plautilla showed me the place in the cellars where she had set the skull of a child on an altar and traced signs on it in blood with her finger.

This alone had not been designed for her mother to discover. This alone, she had done in private. I wondered if Plautilla might not be the credulous one, even slightly mad. *What did she believe?*

'So, what are you going to do?' she said. 'If this is all rubbish and doesn't have any effect, then how are you going to prove that I murdered my mother? I just did a little show and dance for her. She always wished we could have theatrical entertainments again, like in the old days. So I am innocent of any crime. Let me go. And get out. This is my house now.'

I let go of her and picked up the skull. It felt fresh, boiled to make it bare, rather than one from which, over time, the flesh has naturally decayed. Plautilla almost had a point. I could not prove poison. There was a case here for criminal witchcraft, but if Plautilla argued that she did *not* believe in these things, that they were only evidence of a much lesser crime, a sort of fraud, and no heathen gods or demons had been seriously invoked, she might win. She had enough money now to bribe any judge I had ever encountered.

What then?

The skull. It was fresh, the one thing she had too-brazenly flaunted. She had at the very least desecrated a recent grave, or, more likely, murdered some unknown child, perhaps because she truly believed, or merely to make her own performance more convincing.

These matters become so simple when one detail is enough, and you don't have to prove anything more.

But now that the world is coming to an end, there are signs and portents everywhere, and we who do not believe still see them, just like everyone else.

In the morning I conducted Plautilla to my carriage, bound. As I was now serving in my official capacity, I put on the uniform of my office, which included a military helmet and a mailed cuirass. I wore a sword, which clinked and clattered as I walked. I looked up at the house one last time, certain I would never see it again. I wondered if the ghost of its mistress would haunt the place.

In the course of our journey, Plautilla cursed me, sometimes speaking in her supposed supernatural speech, still trying, I think, to awaken some superstitious fear in me. Sometimes she spoke of old times, pretending we had been friends once. It was all I could do not to strike her.

We came to a main road, then to an imperial posting station. In my official capacity, I could draw on supplies here, have my horses looked after, or even get fresh horses if I were in that much of a hurry.

But the German lout in charge laughed when I showed him the badge of my office.

'Haven't you heard?'

Several of his barbarian companions gathered around, snickering.

'Heard what?'

'Your little Augustus has been booted out.' The German sashayed, as if to indicate a little girl. 'The army in Ravenna killed Orestes the patrician, and his little baby emperor is gone . . . away.' The Germans laughed. Some of them drew their fingers across their throats.

Actually the emperor Romulus was about sixteen at the time, and I later found out that he was not killed, merely sent to live near Naples, but he was indeed the last.

'What's more,' the German said, 'our general Odoacer decided to make himself king. So there isn't any Roman Empire anymore, and there's no Roman law, and we don't have to obey you.'

Again the Germans laughed.

'I think I know what you will obey,' I said. I flipped a golden *solidus* onto the counter. It fell reverse side up, with the cross showing.

Later, I unbound Plautilla and let her eat dinner across from me, seated at a table in the German manner. I hoped she found this an unbearable hardship.

'You have to let me go,' she said. 'You heard what the man said. There's no law anymore. At least none that you represent.'

'I ought to kill you then, and it wouldn't be murder.'

She almost laughed, but her laughter froze in her throat.

Yet I did not kill her, if only because by doing so my hands would be indelibly soiled.

So I left her there. I gave the Germans a couple more coins and implied that they should do with Plautilla whatever they felt appropriate.

Never mind law and conscience. Thus we are compromised.

Can a soul be damned which does not believe in souls or damnation? A puzzle. A labyrinth. I am without a clue and deduce nothing.

Jesus Christ have mercy.

BEAUTY MORE STEALTHY

Mary Reed and Eric Mayer

It is easy to imagine that after the fall of the Roman Empire, barbarian hoards overran Rome, civilization collapsed and the world entered the Dark Ages. It wasn't really like that, and these last two stories prove that point. For a start, the Emperor Constantine had moved his imperial capital away from Rome to Byzantium, which was renamed Constantinople in AD 330. After the death of Theodosius I in AD 395 the Empire was split between the West, centred on Rome, and the East, in Constantinople. Even after the Empire in the West fell in AD 476, the Empire in the East continued for another thousand years. In the first few centuries the traditions of the Roman Empire remained, though it became increasingly influenced by Near Eastern tradition. The following story is the third by Mary Reed and Eric Mayer about John the Eunuch, Lord Chamberlain to the Byzantine Emperor Justinian, who ruled from AD 527–65.

᠊᠊᠊᠊᠊᠊

Because Theodore was a meticulous man, a virtue in his former profession as a barber, every member of his household, save one, was able to mark the hour at which his wife Anna was found dead in her bedroom. To insure that he would never be late for anything, and that nothing would ever be late for him, Theodore had placed clocks everywhere in the elegant city home which had formed a part of his wife's dowry.

So Peter, who was stirring the dates he was stewing in honey when a high-pitched cry startled him, was able to see the time by checking the height to which the measuring stick had floated in the urn beside the kitchen brazier.

And when the wailing began next door to the guest room in Lady Anna's apartments, where Lady Sophia was just removing her veil and shaking the dust of the street from her cloak, she immediately shot an annoyed glare at the water clock on the dressing table and noted the level to which the cross-shaped float had descended in its silver bowl.

Even Hypatia, who was in the garden shoveling the last spadeful of dirt on to the spot in the flowering herbs where she'd buried her mistress's cat, when she heard screams coming from the house, had only to turn her dark-maned head towards the sundial which had not yet been reached by the shadows cast by the surrounding walls.

Only Euthymius, Anna's attendant, did not note the time, because when he announced himself with a soft knock, tiptoed delicately into his mistress's room and nearly tripped over her body, the elaborate mechanical *clypsedra* there had been knocked out of its wall niche onto the floor.

Now John the Eunuch, Lord Chamberlain to the Emperor Justinian, knelt beside the remnants of the clypsedra. The bent tubes and bits of decorative metalwork were scattered across the tiles. The thin, sunburnt Greek carefully picked up the engraved face of the clock. Its rod and flotation device hung limply from the pointer which the ascent of the water in the clock's vessel had pushed to the ninth hour on the dial. It was now the eleventh hour.

John tested the pointer with his finger. It was set firmly enough, he supposed, to have resisted the impact when it hit the floor. He applied more force until it slipped backwards along the dial. If only time could really be reversed.

'As Christ is my witness, it was the tenth hour when I heard Euthymius cry out,' said Peter. The wizened cook's eyes were red, as if he'd been crying.

'I too was disturbed at that time,' agreed Sophia. She dabbed at her eyes with a silk handkerchief.

Hypatia, the young gardener, looked on mutely, dark eyes wide. She had only just stopped crying for the poor cat. She was not ready to cry for its owner. Finally John reassured her in Egyptian and she answered quietly in her native tongue.

Euthymius, whose shrill cries had alerted the rest of the household, now stood by silently, tears streaming down his pudgy face. John felt an irrational revulsion toward the eunuch attendant.

In the cramped room, the fragrance of perfume mingled with the smell of death. All was in preparation for evening. Anna's finest robes had been laid out across the yellow and white coverlet of the nuptial bed, a pair of white gloves lay on the dressing table, alongside her jeweled combs and brooches, and white rose petals were strewn across the floor, bed and furniture.

'She must have died an hour before Euthymius discovered her,' mused John. 'She must have fallen against the clock and knocked it to the floor. The dial stopped when it hit. Is there anyone in the house other than those present? Was anybody else in the house earlier?'

'No one today.' Sophia was firm. 'Except for your friend Anatolius. But you know that, because he is the one who brought this dreadful news back to the palace. It was to be a special day, after all,' she added, bringing the handkerchief to her dry eyes again.

None of the others disagreed. 'I want no one to leave the house, then,' John announced. He had no power under law to give such an order but who in this modestly wealthy household would contradict the Lord Chamberlain? Aside, perhaps, from Anna's husband, a man of modest origins who had never accepted his place. John was afraid Theodore might insist upon the authorities being brought in at once.

But the horror of his wife's shocking death had at least temporarily humbled even the former tonsor. A handsome man with a carefully clipped beard, he had placed his back to the far wall as if to remain as far as possible from the body of his wife. He did not try to contradict the Lord Chamberlain but simply nodded towards the two *excubitors* (watchmen) John had recruited to accompany his small party to Theodore's house.

'See the entrances are guarded.' The tone of command used by the master of the house came easily for he had ordered more than one great man to lower his head, the better to shave the back of his neck. 'You,' he indicated the larger of the two, 'station yourself at the tradesmen's entrance. Euthymius, show the guard where he is to take up his post.'

The watery-eyed attendant composed himself with a visible effort and led the excubitor away.

'The tradesmen's entrance opens on the alley,' Theodore explained to John. 'If anyone tried to force his way in, he would probably choose that door.'

'I'm more concerned with anyone who might try to leave,' John softly replied.

'Well, I can assure you we will all remain here, for the night at least. But, when the sun rises . . .' Theodore's voice cracked and John saw his eyes move toward the body of his wife. '. . . When the sun rises, I must . . . begin making arrangements. I –'

'I understand. In the meantime, you may move her to a more suitable spot, Theodore. But, please, touch nothing else in the room.'

Theodore nodded, but remained silent. His face was nearly as ashen as his wife's.

'What killed her?' John asked the physician.

Gaius made a frown, as if he were just considering the question, although he had examined the body for some time while John stood by. He was stout and had the bulbous red nose of one who worshipped Bacchus too freely and too often. He was not pleased, being dragged at a moment's notice to a consultation. And even less pleased because he'd not been sought out for his expertise but merely because his place of business was on the way to the house. 'There was evidence of vomiting,' he said at last. 'That would implicate the digestive faculty, some imbalance in the upper part of the stomach, not the lower. Notice the yellow bile – please forgive my drawing attention, Theodore – on the front of the tunic – honey produces yellow bile. A tainted sweet, perhaps?'

John looked down into Anna's face. Her skin, beneath white chalk, was tinged with blue. John had talked to her at more than one formal dinner at the palace. Her features had been plain, her mind a rich embroidery. Now only the unremarkable features remained, incongruously painted, thin lips ochered, narrow eyes surrounded with kohl, stubby fingernails reddened, her hair braided with beads. How humiliated she would have been to be seen like this by others than her husband.

'A tainted sweet,' John mused. 'Do you mean one turned bad, or poisoned?'

Gaius hesitated. As a physician at the Byzantine court he had seen even more poisonings than John and had learned discretion. 'Ah, as to that, I cannot be sure. I fear a physician serves not the dead but the living.'

'Among whom you count yourself,' snapped John.

Gaius reddened.

'And what about the blue around the lips, Gaius? I am not a physician, but I have seen poisonings.'

'An imbalance of the humours may be brought about by means both natural and unnatural, Lord Chamberlain. If only I had been summoned sooner . . .'

John laid a thin brown hand on Anna's pale, upturned palm and bid her a silent farewell. He had been fond of her. Like John, she had been forced to be more a creature of intellect than she might have desired.

John climbed to his feet. Bringing him closer to Gaius' flushed face. He smelled wine on the man's breath. The physician had been drinking when Anatolius pounded frantically at his door to summon him.

'Yes, I'm sure you would have balanced the humours by letting the blood. Well, our friend's humours have found their ultimate equilibrium without your help.' John's words displayed a glibness he did not feel.

John faced Anatolius across the scarred wooden table in the kitchen. The air was still redolent of honey, leeks, mussels, and the rest of the special dinner Anna had ordered but would never consume.

'I want to speak to you first, my friend. You know the grounds well, don't you? Especially the gardens?'

'Yes. I've been here . . . often . . . lately'

Despite the renowned beauty of the grounds of the Imperial Palace, Anatolius, personal secretary to Justinian, had never before been one for gardens, unless perhaps to dally with his love of the hour, among the fragrant blossoms of the yellow garden or, if he was fortunate, the darker groves where light would be the last thing lovers would wish. John's young friend was, it seemed, cursed with a sensitivity to plants. His eyes and nose tended to stream in their proximity. He was prostrated as easily by a flower as by a woman.

It had, therefore, been a source of puzzlement to John that lately Anatolius never turned down an invitation to dine at the house of Anna and Theodore. For Anna was as famous for her devotion to her garden as Theodore was for his devotion to his wife.

Now, John was faced with another, more somber puzzle.

'You haven't asked me why I didn't call in the authorities.' John was blunt.

'Nor have you asked me why I alerted you rather than the prefect.'

John smiled thinly. 'I speak a little Egyptian, from my years in Alexandria. The new servant – Hypatia – I see she is a lovely young thing. From Egypt. Named after the philosopher, no doubt. It is something to do with her, I imagine.'

'So why didn't you call in the authorities?'

John paused, choosing his words. 'The authorities are very clumsy. They are used to dealing with clumsy criminals, who slit throats in dark alleys. There is something – delicate – about this murder.'

'You don't believe it was tainted food, do you?'

'The lady retired to her room, when?'

'The seventh hour or maybe the eighth, according to what Theodore told me.'

'And before then she had been perfectly well.'

'Theodore said she'd had a bit to drink. To calm her nerves. She was agitated at times.'

'But she wasn't sick before she retired to her apartments. And she wasn't there more than an hour or two. Tainted food doesn't work so fast. She must have been overcome quickly. No one seems to have heard her call for assistance.'

'You think she was poisoned in her room?'

John ignored the question. 'I intend to speak to everyone before I come to any conclusions. This Egyptian girl, with the dark hair and the high cheekbones. The gardener. You've taken an interest in her?'

Anatolius was taken by surprise. 'She is not only beautiful but extremely knowledgeable about plants, especially flowers and herbs.'

'And what do they say at the court about poor, plain Anna, that there would always be dirt under her nails, if she didn't keep them perpetually ragged with her gardening. So a slave with such knowledge was especially valuable to her.'

'A slave? Yes. You're right, John. But I can't think of her as a slave. Catullus wrote about a flower that grows concealed in an enclosed garden. Unknown to the cattle, not bruised by any plough. Breezes caress it. The sun makes it strong.'

'Many long for it.' John finished the verse.

A breeze from the open window overlooking the gardens in the inner courtyard caused Anatolius to blink and sniff.

John smiled wanly. 'Yes, my friend. I understand. And I understand why you would ask me here, because who is more skilled at poisoning than one who knows herbs?'

In the courtyard, long evening shadows had moved across the face of the marble sundial, so that time could no longer be read from its lines of inlaid bronze. It was necessary therefore to tell time in the manner of the older empire, when the citizens of Rome had measured their days by the position of the sun over familiar columns, statues and walls. And although John was not so familiar with the house of Theodore as was Anatolius, who though by his side was deep in thought, it was easy enough to calculate that if the rays of the summer sun no longer reached over a three-story house, then the last measured hour of the day must have arrived, even if dusk had not completely fallen.

'I fear that when the dawn arrives, Theodore will not be persuaded from calling the prefects,' John commented, as much to himself as to Anatolius. 'And who knows where they will point.'

'Why? Some new edict of the Emperor?'

'No. People are more reasonable in the daylight.'

'You have twelve hours then.'

'If only they were the longer hours of a winter night.'

'Do you really think fingers will be pointed at Hypatia?'

'I can't say.' John did not voice his conclusion, which was that Hypatia, an herbalist and a foreigner, newly arrived in the city, would be the obvious suspect if not presumed automatically to be the culprit. Nor did he tell his young friend that she might well be responsible. If that were so, he would have to prove it beyond question. As if even an incontrovertible truth would save their friendship under such circumstances. John was not one to flinch from the unpleasant, but he truly wished he could be somewhere else this night.

He tried to turn his thoughts toward the facts. What did he know of Lady Anna, except that she had been an intelligent and pleasing conversationalist? At even her best, she had been a plain woman – a dusty hen in a court of peacocks – but her father was a senator and she had carried with her a good dowry. Even so her marriage to the handsome Theodore had caused a seven-day wonder at the court. Several prominent matrons' tongues had been viperish at the prospect of the union lasting, although John, noting all had unwed daughters, rather suspected their tattle was fueled by thwarted maternal ambition. Yet several years had passed and the marriage, though sadly childless, had flowered and flourished as had the gardens Anna loved so much. And, after all, Theodore may have been a most well-proportioned man, and had made himself comfortable as the court's most sought-after tonsor – still there was a limit to how high a barber could elevate himself socially and how much wealth one could clip from the beards of the rich. And to say that the marriage was of mutual convenience was not to imply that it could not be much more as well.

They found a bench artfully concealed in a miniature copse near the back of the gardens. The air was heavy, as the gathering darkness drew up and held the scent of flowers and herbs. Occasionally the sounds of the street, the clatter of cart wheels on cobblestones, the shout of an itinerant merchant, penetrated the sheltering walls, only faintly.

'Country in the town,' John said suddenly.

'Martial,' Anatolius identified the author of the epigram.

John nodded. 'Very apt. Tell me what happened today, Anatolius.'

The young man sat down beside John. The Lord Chamberlain wondered if his friend had shared this artfully secluded seat with a more suitable companion.

'It seems unbelievable,' Anatolius began. 'I was here only last week, and Anna and Theodore were planning a celebration for the anniversary of their union. Theodore said he would dress her hair. Of course, he knew about such things, being a barber. He'd color her nails, patch her blemishes, as he'd done for his customers. And now she's gone.' His eyes welled, whether because he was recalling Anna or due to the effect of the flower-perfumed air on his allergy, John could not say.

The Lord Chamberlain remembered the unkind remarks the wags at court had made when Anna and Theodore had first married – that she'd taken him for a lady's maid – and later, that maybe Theodore should trade duties with his wife's attendant Euthymius, because the eunuch might have as much chance fathering heirs as her husband had.

'But how did you come to be here, today, Anatolius?'

'I ran into Theodore at the market beside the Mese this afternoon. He'd been looking for plantings for Anna's garden. The yellow one, he said. She had devised a little conceit. Apparently her favorite color is – was – yellow and so half the flowers were to be yellow. And the other half were to be white, which she also loved.' He made a snuffling noise, as if even the thought of so many flowers disturbed his faculties.

'I remember Lady Sophia once claimed Theodore had purchased all the white roses in the city to give to his wife on the feast of Venus,' John mused. 'She seemed put out. I think she wished someone would bestow such attention on her. They are lovely flowers.'

'Yes, Anna planned to plant white roses, he told me and apple trees – white blossoms, you see. Also pears, I believe. Sacred to Athena, they say. Yellow flowers had been more difficult to find but I understand she had already established a few. Hypatia pointed them out to me the other evening. She is really quite wise in these matters. She was telling me some of the uses of plantings.'

'Lord Chamberlain, so this is where you've been hiding.'

John was startled because in the shadows the figure which had appeared suddenly on the path between the shrubberies appeared ghostlike. But only for a moment would anyone mistake the Lady Sophia for some flimsy wraith.

'Sophia, I'm sorry to see you again –'

'Under such sorrowful circumstances. Yes, I know. And also very inconvenient circumstances. My chair is arriving in an hour. My attendants will already be on their way.'

John, feeling at a disadvantage, stood. 'I'm afraid they will have to return in the morning,' He was glad her expression was half-concealed by the shadows.

'Surely you don't intend to detain me also?'

Detain someone who, due to the predatory tax collecting of her late husband, was one of Constantinople's richest women and thus entitled to a life free of petty inconvenience, was what she meant, John thought. But he confined himself to pointing out that he would need to ask the lady a few questions, later on.

'Without my dear Anna's company I have no wish to spend the night in this house. Attended by Euthymius. Poor Anna, she had no taste in servants.'

'It is maddening, isn't it?' put in Anatolius, bounding to his feet. 'Come, Sophia, Theodore has a magnificent stock of wines. The air's getting cold. Maybe we can find something to ward off the chill.'

Taking her by the hand he pulled her politely away, all the while prattling brightly. John thanked his friend silently.

The old cook, Peter, had reclaimed his kitchen. He was very slowly sweeping up the freshening sawdust he had spread over its floor, singing some lugubrious Christian hymn to himself, tunelessly but loudly, when John entered the room. John, being a Mithran did not recognize the hymn. He hoped it was not one of the Emperor's own compositions, any or all of which he feared he might one day be asked to incorporate into an imperial ceremony.

'Peter, may I talk to you for a moment?'

'Lord Chamberlain, I would be honored. I am flattered you know my name.'

John's perfect memory for names was the least of his talents. More remarkable was his grasp of the relative locations of each person so named in the palace hierarchy.

'Tell me, John, what were you preparing for this evening?'

The old cook hobbled over to a cupboard, using his twig broom as a support, and pulled out a scrap of parchment. He squinted hard and began to read, haltingly. 'Sea mussels with leeks, oysters, melons cooked with mint, a pear soufflé in honey and wine sauce, cooked apricots –'

'It sounds like a feast.'

'A private celebration, for my master and mistress.'

'Private. Yes, I see. Might some of those recipes inflame the passions?'

Peter's walnut-wrinkled face darkened. 'It wasn't the pleasures of the flesh that were wanted, your excellency, but only that a holy union be fruitful in the eyes of Our Lord.'

'Of course.' John refrained from pointing out that Theodore and Anna did not worship Peter's Lord but the older gods. 'Was the food fresh, Peter?'

The old cook straightened his back, outraged. 'I learned my trade in the camps.'

'Yes, we used to say a careless cook could put a legion on the run faster than a troop of mounted Persians.'

'As you say.'

'Who has access to your kitchen?'

'When I am cooking? No one.'

'Are you sure no one was in here while you were preparing the meal?'

'There was no chance for anyone to slip anything into the food,' said Peter, stiffly. 'After I left the military I worked for a time at the palace. I keep my eyes open. Besides, the lady ate nothing this morning. Not so much as a piece of fruit. She was too nervous.'

'Is that why she was drunk?'

'Drunk? Hardly. She took a little wine, I believe.'

'And what are these?' John indicated a basket set on the stone floor by the brazier.

'Just some sweets.'

John bent and plucked one of the sticky confections from the basket.

'I was cooking them when I heard Euthymius cry out. I finished preparing them. I didn't realize, until later –'

'Dates. Stuffed, I see. What's in them?'

'Ground nuts. I sprinkle them with salt and stew them in honey,' Peter explained with pride. 'A little specialty of mine.'

John popped the date into his mouth and chewed. 'Very good,' he remarked.

John left the kitchen and wandered thoughtfully through the house. The air was hushed. He could hear the oil lamps sputtering. He found himself in Anna's apartments. The rooms were deserted. The unseemly invasion by men who would never have dared enter while the lady was alive had ended. John felt he was trespassing in this woman's place, although, he realized uneasily, by custom eunuchs were also allowed access to such apartments.

A low groan drew his attention and, following his ears, he came to the bedroom where Anna had died. Her body had been removed from the room, which had been left otherwise undisturbed, according to John's instructions, except that someone, perhaps the overly well-organized Theodore, had not been able to resist placing the broken clypsedra back into its niche.

Or perhaps it had not been Theodore who had replaced the clock, but Euthymius, who stood in the middle of the room, moaning softly, tears streaming down his cheeks, worrying a fingernail – for all the world like a small, distraught child.

John stepped quietly through the doorway. A few white rose petals floated on the puddle of water left by the clock. A mercenary in his youth, the Lord Chamberlain was inured to a different sort of death, where the end of one's span was measured by the flow of blood from the veins.

'Euthymius.'

Anna's attendant turned. He wiped brimming eyes. 'I'm sorry I – but, then, you – you understand, of course.' Euthymius' sentence ended in a hiccoughing sob.

John fought back revulsion. 'No,' he said, too loudly. 'No, I don't understand. What do you mean when you say I understand?'

Euthymius looked confused.

The Lord Chamberlain was a thin, hard man. He had served as a soldier for years before his – wounding. He had killed men and loved women. Euthymius, on the other hand, had been castrated as an infant. He was the typical eunuch. Surely no one would mistake John for fat and ungainly Euthymius? His whimpering disgusted John.

'No one was to enter this room,' John said curtly. 'You'll have to leave.'

'The master asked me to fetch a coverlet for her, and yellow was her favorite.'

'She has no favorites now.'

'Yes, Lord Chamberlain.' Euthymius began to sob uncontrollably. 'They moved her. It was my job to do that. They moved my poor mistress and didn't even tell me. They had no right.'

John concealed his surprise. A slave – even a distraught slave – did not speak of the 'rights' of his master.

Euthymius managed to regain some control. 'If you want to speak to me about –'

He took a step toward John who stepped aside. The overpowering pomade on the eunuch's curled hair buried the room's gentle scent of rose petals, but did not quite mask a more offensive odor.

'If I need to speak to you, I will summon you.'

John waited until the attendant had left. Then he turned his gaze on the room. He was sure the answer lay here. Anna had been poisoned here. Regardless of what had been said, it was almost certain someone had brought something into the room to her. A lady did not retire, in perfect health, to her private chambers only to be found dead a scant two hours later.

But John wanted to speak to the household before he examined the room. In his own way, he was as methodical as Theodore. Although, John realized, a more genuinely scientific mind than his would have wished to find a physical cause before peering into the human souls which could have set that cause into motion. Yet while there were opportunities to commit crime at every turn, it was the motivation that was usually lacking.

A thought struck him. Had Euthymius moved anything other than the clock?

He was distracted by raised voices from the next room, the guest room. Theodore stormed past Anna's door. John opened his mouth to speak but Theodore made a dismissive gesture.

'Not now. I have a long list, Lord Chamberlain. Certain things must be done.' Evidently realizing then the imprudence of being rude to one so high at the court, he abruptly shifted to a conciliatory tone. 'I'm just distraught, John. And Sophia, she was Anna's best friend. Practically lived here. She is stricken. Please excuse me.'

He pivoted and hurried off, his footsteps echoing on the marble. John looked into the room his reluctant host had so lately left.

'Forgive him, Lord Chamberlain. We all have our own ways of dealing with grief.'

The Lady Sophia's way was to lounge on a couch, a goblet of wine at hand, and color her fingernails.

John did not judge her harshly. He was familiar with the patrician class. It was not uncommon for those of rank to disdain a vulgar display of emotions in front of those they considered not their equals.

'I am taking your friend's suggestion, you see.' Sophia paused long enough to bring the goblet to her mouth. 'Theodore does have a splendid stock.'

Her face was flushed with wine. Perhaps it was that, coupled with the way the flickering light from the single lamp on the dressing table softened her features, or maybe just the artfully applied make-up, that made John realize, abruptly and for the first time, that she was young as Anna had been, and that one might almost consider her lovely – a term he would not previously have associated with the widowed Lady Sophia.

Sophia, her senses honed as sharply by court life as John's, noticed he was appraising her.

'Don't tell Gaius I'm drinking. He claims I drink too much. Not that he has any right to talk. He'd insist I drink nothing but barley water.'

'You've seen the physician professionally? Is he reliable?'

'I see him as seldom as possible. He hasn't treated me for poisoning, so I can't vouch for his expertise there, if that's what you mean.'

John paced over to the dressing table. The cross in the clock's silver bowl had already sunk toward the ring marking the second hour of night, as the water escaped through a small aperture in the bowl's bottom into a holding vessel. The lamp beside the clock flared, illuminating a make-up box whose lid hung open revealing compartments for jars of unguents, rouge, kohl, ochre and a dozen other artifices. Most of its jars were jumbled on the table next to Sophia.

'I understand this was to be a special day for Anna and Theodore?'

'Indeed. And the matter being so private – why was I here?'

John nodded.

'I had agreed to come over to hold her hand, if things didn't go right. Anna was overwrought. She'd confided her plans to me, of course. We were very close. She sometimes lent me her jewelry, since she didn't wear it too often. Too cumbersome, she said. She gave me some of the new creams and potions and such that that new servant of hers concocted. A clever girl, that young Egyptian. But too clever for a servant, if you ask me.'

John enquired when had Sophia arrived at the house.

'I was just taking off my cloak when I heard Euthymius cry out. I'm here often, of course. I have no one at home, any more.'

'Anna's father, he was a supporter of your late husband, wasn't he?'

'Yes. He spoke out for Victor in the Senate, when the . . . troubles came.'

When the taxpayers demanded his head, thought John. And they'd been given it too, in the end. Literally. But not the deceased's money. That had been left to Sophia.

'But how did a senator's daughter come to be betrothed to a barber?'

Sophia looked irritated. 'The senator likes the way his beard is trimmed. He gives away his daughter. What do you think, John? Why do people fall in love? But, then, you wouldn't understand that – men and women – any more than poor fat Euthymius.'

John bit back his thoughts. 'But, financially, it must have benefited Theodore?'

'Theodore wasn't just an ordinary tonsor, John. He had raised himself up. He employed assistants. He was a man of substance. Quite a charming man. Not all are born to their rightful place in society. Some must make their own fortunes.'

'Nevertheless, Anna's dowry –'

'Would pass to her children. Not to Theodore.'

'But there were no children.'

Sophia glared up at John in a manner that made him forget any impression of loveliness. 'They didn't know that was going to happen, did they? Certainly they tried hard enough. Theodore was – not able to father children.'

'You know that?'

'As I told you, I was her friend.'

The faint light from the sickle moon illuminating the bronze bands of the garden sundial could not reveal that the second hour of the night had passed.

'Thank you for helping to ward off the chill, earlier, Anatolius. Lady Sophia seemed much calmer when I finally spoke to her. What of the others?'

'Theodore is with Anna. In the main reception hall. Euthymius has been wandering about in an agitated state. He says he needs to talk to you.'

'Later. I doubt the attendant has much of value to say. Too flighty. What about Gaius?'

'Ah . . . our reluctant recruit . . . he has taken up residence in one of the sitting rooms and has granted an audience to a selection of Theodore's wines.'

'Taking up where we forced him to leave off, in other words. I'm surprised the man has such a good practice at the court.'

As John's eyes grew accustomed to the soft darkness he could distinguish the pale glow of Anna's white and yellow flowers against the black masses of their leaves.

'You asked Hypatia to meet us here?'

'Yes.' Anatolius gave a sudden oath. 'A thorn,' he explained, putting his wounded hand to his mouth.

'You should learn to curse in Egyptian, as I do.' John smiled thinly. 'You run less risk of offending.'

Anatolius plucked a white rose from the bush. 'It is a mystery, isn't it, that beauty can hurt so? If only I were a poet!'

'You don't need to be a poet to appreciate beauty – or to see irony.'

'Look, here is a beauty more stealthy than the rose.' Anatolius indicated a tall plant with pale delicate flowers. 'This is one of Anna's yellow plants. I have heard it called Hecate's flower. Hypatia's name for it I can scarcely pronounce. Its root can produce a deadly poison. Is it something like that you suspect?'

John touched one of the leaves. 'Such things are certainly no secret to anyone who gardens.'

'But I understand in smaller quantities it is effective against fevers and relieves the toothache. And I am told it can even be used in aphrodisiacs.'

'Yes. In Egypt it is sometimes added to what they call *manzoul*.'

'You know of such things?'

John laughed, softly. 'Ah, my friend when I was in Alexandria there was a girl, Cornelia. I had no need of manzoul then.' John's tone was matter of fact. He had long since come to terms with his affliction. 'Hypatia would be able to tell you how to make it, I'm sure. It's a mixture of oils with spices and honey added to sweeten it. They swear by it in Alexandria. In fact madams quite often keep a supply on hand in case certain of their clientele need its assistance. Of course, they also charge double for such cases, or so it is rumored.'

'Besides that, thieves use it to render chickens unconscious, the easier to make off with them.' It was Hypatia, who had been listening in the shadows. She spoke in Egyptian. 'You know the customs of my country, Lord Chamberlain.'

'I hope the information I have been giving Anatolius was correct.' John replied in the same tongue. He noted wryly that this was the second time he had been surprised in the thickly-grown garden Anna had so diligently cultivated.

'Indeed. And you speak my language passably.'

In the dim moonlight Hypatia's tawny skin appeared much paler than it had inside the house. Her large eyes were black wells. John could understand why Anatolius had been attracted to the girl.

'I am sorry to have to question you at this hour.'

'No one will sleep tonight.'

'It must have been a shock, the Lady Anna's death.'

'Don't think badly of me. I haven't been able to cry for her. I know it makes no sense, but I can't seem to stop crying for her poor Nefertiti. That was what she called her cat.'

'You'll cry for your mistress soon enough. How long have you been here?'

'Four months. I am new to your country.'

'You arrived in time to help with the spring plantings.'

'She loved her gardens. A day never went by when she didn't pull on her gloves and work the earth.'

'But you assisted in other ways?'

'That is so. I helped her with her toilette.'

'I see you helped her dress for tonight?'

'Oh, the master told you?' The question was without guile.

'Her hair is dressed after the Egyptian manner or as it was, as I recall, when I lived there. But wasn't that Euthymius' job?'

'That is true. But my lady Anna liked to talk with me. We shared interests.'

'You were friends?'

'She was my mistress,' Hypatia was almost curt. 'Anyway, the master sometimes helped out in that line too. I had other tasks also. I made perfumes and unguents for her hands, cosmetics, things like that. Sometimes, I would brew potions if she had ailments of the throat or – ' she hesitated for a second, '– feminine problems such as ladies sometimes have.'

'I have heard that there was tension between man and mistress?'

Hypatia looked at the starry sky and John saw a fleeting reflection of the sickle moon in the depths of her eyes.

'The master adored her. Anything she wanted, he would ensure it was hers. He waited on her like a handmaid. This very morning, since it was their special day, he did her toilette himself. He was an expert, of course. My lady told me that the court dandies expect their tonsor to stick as many patches to their faces as any woman would wear. But my lady had lovely skin.'

John wondered if the departed gentlewoman had also told her beautiful young servant that the ladies of the court joked that none of them would have taken as a lover a man as homely as she? 'I know about his devotion,' he said, 'but, between husband and wife, there should be more.'

'My mistress loved him with all her heart. She was sad that there were no children to bear the family name, if that's what you mean.'

'Had the master grown cold to her?'

'Sometimes, after awhile, those who cannot are afraid to try.'

'I noted many of the banquet tidbits were those which the superstitious believe will inflame a man.'

Again the girl nodded. 'She had prayed to Venus that she would be fruitful, and then she dreamed –' the husky voice faltered and the dark wells of her eyes brimmed salt.

John nodded, 'Yes, I do understand. And tell me, did you brew anything to assist her? Peter had cooked a meal for passion, and Venus' flowers were all over the bedroom. It would seem –'

'Yes. She asked me if I could make something. To encourage him.'

'It was manzoul? Perhaps you erred in measuring the ingredients?'

'I am not so careless. Besides, the manzoul was never finished. I brewed the potion yesterday, in my room. I knew there wouldn't be time this morning. There was the kneading of the sweetmeats, in which the potion was to be placed. But when I went to the kitchen to make them, there wasn't enough honey left.'

'Peter had stewed dates in honey. Wasn't there more in the house?'

'I don't think so. Lady Anna instructed Euthymius to buy some. He always spends an hour or two at the market in the afternoon. The mistress preferred that I help finish her toilette. The master had been assisting earlier, but she was so nervous, she went out to the gardens and pulled weeds. Her hair came undone and I had to dress it all over again. The mistress was pleased. It was a new style for her. She even gave me a goblet of her wine. And afterwards I went out for a walk in the garden and – I found poor Nefertiti.'

'Where was this?' John asked gently.

'Just over there, in the corner, by the statue of Eros. It was like some terrible omen. It must have been an omen. I had no idea that – that –'

Hypatia could hold back tears no longer. She bowed her head, John placed his arm around her shoulders and felt her shaking. Now, he suspected she was crying for her mistress. Tears, John thought, not the water in Theodore's clocks, were the truest measure of this day.

Nearly a third of the summer night's short hours had passed by the time John's interview with Hypatia ended. As he passed through the colonnades and re-entered the house with its guttering lamps and dripping clocks, his mind refused to settle but fluttered and drifted, a butterfly in a windswept garden. It was his way. He did not find his way step by step, but leaped, sometimes blindly, often to the wrong places. His leaps sometimes took him places plodders could never reach. In the course of his official duties as Lord Chamberlain he clung to the rigid details of court ceremony, while his mind wandered freely.

Now he wished he had the night-time hours of winter, longer than those of the summer, for the Romans insisted on twelve equal hours of night and day. It was an amazing audacity, that man would try to fit to a procrustean bed, time, which could not be seen, or heard or felt.

On his way out of the garden, where he had left Hypatia and Anatolius, he had passed the patch of freshly spaded earth where the cat had been buried. Had it been an omen, that the cat was found dead at the base of the statue of Eros?

Or a warning?

The perfume of roses met John when he entered the reception hall. Theodore had had Anna's body placed on a couch between two pillars near the back of the room, away from the lamplight. An enormous bunch of roses sat in a vase atop a nearby table. A few petals had fallen on to the inlaid tabletop. John picked up a petal, its sweet silkiness sliding through his fingers.

'They say all roses were white, until your goddess of love walked on them, a thorn pierced her foot and her blood dyed the blossoms scarlet. Isn't that the legend, Theodore?'

Theodore was lingering near the center of the hall, facing the couch where his wife lay. It was as if he were afraid to approach her, stranger that she had become.

'You call it a legend,' he said finally. 'You're like Peter, you worship a newer god.'

'Not Peter's God.'

'Jupiter, Jesus, Mithra . . . the gods change, the world doesn't.'

'Do you have any idea who might have done this, Theodore?'

'You really believe Anna was . . . no, I can't imagine. This is a small household. Surely it might have been an accident? Something tainted?'

'She had eaten nothing. So the servants tell me.'

'I've written down all necessary arrangements. In case I cannot carry on tomorrow.'

'I will see to everything if it should become necessary to do so.'

'Thank you, John. You were a good friend to Anna.'

'She had a great spirit, Theodore. I regret I must ask, however, before you retire, can you tell me anything more about today?'

Theodore continued to direct his gaze toward his wife. 'What do you wish to know? I was away from the house most of the day. I met Anatolius in the market.'

'Earlier?'

'Anna had planned something special. She was secretive. I helped her with her toilette. Rouged her cheeks, colored her nails and did her hair, that kind of thing. We were in the kitchen so I would have good light to work by. The sun comes in there in the morning. I know many laugh. But, it was my profession to assist all to look their best, and it has served me well. I was most familiar, you understand, with her imperfections and so knew what had to be done. I was better at it than her attendant. Better than her little friend the Egyptian, for that matter. Though Anna seemed much taken with her. Not that I assisted Anna often in that way. It wouldn't be a manly thing.'

'No,' agreed John, 'I can see that.'

John climbed to the servants' quarters on the third floor on the opposite side of the house from Anna's apartments. The old cook, alerted by the creaking stairs, opened his door when John reached it. The Lord Chamberlain wedged himself into Peter's living quarters, finding standing room between the mattress, whose straw stuffing erupted from one corner, and a rough wooden chest. He placed his feet carefully to avoid an earthenware chamber pot.

'Yes,' admitted Peter, 'the master attended to the mistress's toilette in the kitchen. When I said no one comes into my kitchen when I'm cooking, I didn't mean the master and the mistress. Who am I to order them about? Besides, I hadn't started cooking. I was cleaning and chopping.'

'How was the mistress?'

'She seemed as well as I've ever seen her. There was no need to paint her like that.'

'And her spirits?'

'More than one of your pagan poets was quoted. I tried not to listen, Lord Chamberlain. It was private.'

A flickering candle on the small chest revealed no decorations apart from a large wooden cross hanging over the worn mattress. Although Peter had embraced cold Christianity in his old age, John guessed the former legion cook had drawn warmer and less demanding mistresses to him in his youth. 'You don't approve of the old gods.' His curiosity was piqued.

'There are no old gods, if you'll pardon my saying so, excellency. Even though some will worship anything – lightning, a tree, a bull or a cat, the sun and moon or the sea.'

'I understand that you would not eavesdrop, Peter, but surely you could not help seeing? What, exactly, were these preparations that you mention?'

'Exactly? If I'd watched that closely I'd have dumped some of my fingers into the pot with the melons I was chopping. You've seen the painted ladies at court, Lord Chamberlain? Well, after she was rouged and such she looked like that. Then she was off straight out to her garden. She thought it would calm her down. She liked to have her hands in the earth. She'll be part of it now herself, God rest her soul.'

John changed the direction of his questioning. 'Is this part of the house used much?'

'Only by the servants. The other rooms were to be for the children. The master had them closed up, finally. The master and mistress haven't set foot on the stairs for a year or more. Now she never will.'

The old man made a mystical sign that the pagan John recognized as Christian.

Anna's room had grown cold. John had found a candle in a hall cupboard and discovered it was notched – another clock. He felt it was wrong somehow to start the hours again in this room where the disarmed clypsedra stood guard. Better for it to remain timeless.

Nevertheless, he needed light, so he moved around the small space, lighting lamps on the dressing table and in the twin wall niche opposite the clypsedra. Oil hissed and flared up, spilling an orange glow across the tiles and on to plain plaster walls.

Anna's apartments were directly opposite her husband's suite. Looking out of the open second-story window, across the gardens, John could see the black rectangle of Theodore's window. Ironically, he could just make out the glimmering statue of Eros below it.

John sighed. It was quite usual for married couples to maintain separate rooms and was as likely to signify a show of wealth as any lack of affection. The poor, in the crowded tenements of Constantinople, had no choice but to share their verminous straw.

He turned back to the room which looked as plain as its owner. A low wooden bed with turned legs hugged one wall. Anna's robes still lay across the yellow counterpane draped over the bed. A chest, with an inlaid top, and next to it a simple wooden chair, completed the furnishings.

Not only had Anna died here, but it was here she had ingested the poison that had killed her so quickly. Of that, John was certain. And yet, she had retired to this room and not emerged. Nor had anyone entered.

Who had said so?

John could believe Anna would have retired to her private apartments to await her husband's return. Theodore had definitely been away from the house. Anatolius' meeting with him in the market attested to it. Yet Anna had been dying even as Theodore spoke to Anatolius. Euthymius had also been to the market, as usual. And Sophia had not yet arrived. Peter was in the house, cooking, and hadn't left the kitchen, or so he said. Not that Anna would have accepted anything from him in her room, since, aside from a husband, men were not allowed within a lady's apartments. Which left Hypatia. Who had been with Anna earlier, who had become a great favorite with her and spent more time with her lately than even Anna's attendant Euthymius, or so it seemed.

John wished he could examine the room in daylight. It seemed empty of any clue to what had occurred. The top of the chest was barren. What had he expected? A crumb, from a secreted sweet? A telltale ring from a wet goblet? The floor was bare, save for the mat beside the bed. Anna's clothes lay undisturbed. John noticed the pair of gloves draped across the bed's headboard were rough work gloves, soiled with earth. Her gardening gloves.

John directed candlelight into the corners. Something glinted. He bent and picked up a pearl-worked brooch.

He got on his knees to shine the light under the bed. Something near the wall cast an elongated shadow. Flame licked back along the shortening taper, burning his hand. He bit back an oath. The candle hit the floor and went out.

John put his shoulder to the tiles, reaching under the bed. His fingers slid across grit. There. His fingertips touched something more substantial, pushed it away. He shifted his body, until his ear was against the cold floor, stretching further, straining, until he had whatever it was under his fingers.

He pulled it out. In the fitful light from the lamps he examined his prize. Embedded in a clump of hair, dust, fingernail parings and dried insect husks, was an apricot pit.

John smelled pomade over the more subtle, pleasing scents of damp earth and slumbering flowers before he saw Euthymius looming between the columns at the edge of the garden. The Lord Chamberlain had retreated to the steps of Theodore's private bath house, to be alone, to think, before the night fled entirely. It was more than half gone now, according to Theodore's accursed clocks. The lady's chambers might be reserved to the women and the third floor to the servants, but clocks were everywhere, and so was Euthymius, it seemed.

'Lord Chamberlain. I have to speak with you.'

To John's discomfiture the big eunuch dropped down on to the marble step beside him.

'You've spoken to the others, already, haven't you?' Euthymius sounded plaintive.

'Yes,' John admitted. He probably should have spoken to the attendant earlier, although he doubted Euthymius could add anything to what he had already ascertained.

'It was terrible, finding her like that.' The attendant's voice was piercing. John reminded himself that it was not Euthymius' fault, the eunuch had not chosen to be what he was. Still, John found himself sliding away.

'I thought she'd fainted,' Euthymius was saying. 'Then I bent over and touched her cheek and she was cold. Cold.' The big body shuddered.

'She seemed well in the morning?'

'She was wonderfully well. The master helped with her toilette. Usually that is my job. Oh, she loved the way I did her hair. We talk, you know, about everything. She tells me all about court, about the fine ladies, who aren't so fine in private. She confided in me, did my lady.'

'Did she confide in you about any troubles she and her husband may have been having?'

'There were no troubles between them. Who told you there were troubles? Was it that Egyptian girl?'

'No. It seems to be common knowledge.'

'Common is the word. Not everyone was in my lady's confidence as I was. It was all tittle-tattle. That Egyptian girl. She has her big eyes on the master. I have seen the looks she gives him. She doesn't know, but I see things.'

Euthymius' whine grated against John's ears. What he said did not ring true. Or was that only John's prejudices?

Who in the household, when it came down to it, except for Hypatia, could have concocted a quick-acting poison? She had, in fact, by her own admission, done so in her room. And only she and Peter had been in the house when the murder occurred. The solution was so obvious, aside from the actual administration of the poison, that it was really surprising no one had reached the same conclusion.

And why had John avoided it? Because of his friendship with Anatolius. No matter that in the normal course of things that youth would have forgotten Hypatia in a month. At the moment she was the light of his life. And if John were to state what appeared to be a simple truth, that she had killed her mistress in hopes of seducing the master, his passionate young friend would never forgive him for extinguishing that light.

People would do many things in the name of friendship. Yet how could John allow a murderer to go free? If only he could determine exactly how it had been accomplished. If the method could be demonstrated beyond doubt, perhaps Anatolius would have to admit her guilt – if she were the guilty one – and would forgive John any necessary actions.

'Euthymius, tell me, did you bring anything into Anna's room for her to eat? Did you see her with anything?'

'Nothing. She was too agitated to think about food.'

John glanced around as he cogitated further, deciding on his next question. The path leading away from the bath house was a lightless tunnel. At its end loomed an indistinct shape, imperceptibly lighter than the inky mounds of surrounding vegetation. John identified it as the statue of Eros. This put a thought into his mind.

'The cat,' he asked. 'do you know anything about it? Hypatia said she found it beside Eros.'

'Found?'

'It was dead.'

'Dead? I didn't know. The Egyptian doted on that cat. I cannot say I'm surprised. It was like her, the nasty thing. Devious.' The eunuch did not sound distressed. He added, 'I saw her carting it up to her room more than once.'

'They say the amount of poison in the root of Hecate's flower varies, according to the soil and the climate,' John mused. 'Hypatia was a foreigner. She may have mixed what would have been an appropriate amount of root for Egypt into the manzoul. But perhaps a root grown here would be more poisonous. There may have been too much added to the mixture.'

Anatolius looked stunned. 'But even such an accident, involving a foreign servant and a lady –'

He didn't have to complete the thought. Such an event would prove as lethal to the servant as the mistress.

'Here. This must be it.' John took a small porphyry jar from the windowsill of the girl's small room. The jar was half-filled with a gummy concoction that stung his nostrils.

Hypatia was not there. John wasn't surprised. The cramped

quarters would have felt like a prison. He suspected she was somewhere in the shadowed garden below.

'How can you be sure it is the . . . potion?'

'I'll have to turn this over to the prefect. They will probably test in on some poor creature or other. You will swear I found it here?'

'If I must.'

A glint of illumination caught his eye. Across the narrow hall, old Peter had cracked open his door, allowing a hint of candlelight to escape. As John turned, the door closed discreetly. 'Those creaking stairs might as well be an alarm bell,' he remarked.

'What about Peter?' Anatolius suggested. 'He was preparing food, after all. He was also in the house at the time Lady Anna seems to have died.'

John shook his head. 'The prefects look for the physical method. Yet, if the inclination exists, there are innumerable methods. I prefer to look for the inclination. What reason would old Peter have to kill his mistress?'

'She was a pagan.'

John balanced the porphyry jar in his hand, feeling its weight. 'Religious zealots have done worse, it is true.'

And infatuated young men grasped at straws.

Gaius the physician had drunk the third toast to Zeus hours before, and hadn't stopped there. When John and Anatolius reached the reception hall, Gaius was roaring and staggering in circles like a wounded bear at the games.

The noise had brought the entire household to its source. Even the excubitors had abandoned their posts. They lurked in the back of the room, uncertain with how to deal with one of the party they had accompanied the previous day.

Although Gaius' tone was unmistakable, the sense of what the physician was trying to say in his slurred rage was harder to fathom.

'Not worth it to you? You think I won't tell what I know? I'll give it out for free and take my pleasure in seeing you both rot in the dungeons.'

Theodore and Sophia had arrived before John and Anatolius. Theodore had placed himself protectively in front of the couch where the body of his wife lay. Sophia stood on the other side of the room, fists clenched. John moved quickly to her side.

'He's crazed with drink,' Sophia mumbled. Her own eyes were glassy. She swayed slightly.

'So the great Lord Chamberlain has arrived to represent our

mighty emperor,' growled Gaius. 'And your fellow creature, too, I see.'

John looked towards the door where Gaius directed his gaze. Euthymius was approaching, timidly and ponderously.

Gaius made a sweeping, theatrical motion of greeting with his hands, bending low, nearly falling forward. 'Come in. Everyone come in. Ah, there you are, Peter. Old, yet more a man than most of those present. And our little beauty, the clever gardener. All here, now, are we? What do you say now, Sophia, your great ladyship? And you, Theodore, beard trimmer. Is the price still too steep? When the rats in the dungeons chew your ankles, you'll wish you were sticking patches to gentlemen's pimples again. You'll wish they'd hire me to sew you up.'

'Be quiet,' Sophia shrieked. 'Stinking drunk! Liar!'

Gaius laughed. 'Too late, I'm afraid. The offer is withdrawn.'

'Make him keep silent, John.' Sophia's speech was nearly as slurred as the physician's. 'Can't he at least respect the dead, if not the living?'

'This is intolerable, Lord Chamberlain,' Theodore broke in, outraged. 'I must call for the prefects.'

'Gaius, what is this about?' John's voice was firm, but with no hint of anger. He knew men could say terrible things when drunk.

'Haven't you deciphered it yet? All night you've had, too. It's nearly dawn, the water's run out of all the clocks.' Gaius whirled about and leapt toward Anna's couch. Theodore, who had until now seemed reluctant to approach too near to his dead wife, put his back to the couch, blocking the crazed man's path.

'So warm to her in death, so cold in life,' sneered Gaius. 'I delivered more than one of your bastards, Theodore. You think patients don't talk? But that is court life, is it not? And if a man wishes to keep his interest in his wife's dowry, rather than father heirs who will claim it from him, well, we are men of the world. But murder, Theodore. That is something else. That was worth something to conceal. Or so I thought. Until the Lady Sophia told me otherwise.'

Sophia took a step forward but John grabbed her shoulder. 'Filth! You are filth!' The spittle she directed at her tormentor dribbled down her chin. She was, after all, a lady and not versed in such skills.

Gaius laughed again. 'Don't you know a woman with child should be more careful of her health? This is my medical advice to you, my lady. You don't want Theodore's bastard born dead.'

Sophia shook her head. 'No,' she said. 'No . . .'

'You both wanted Lady Anna dead, didn't –'

Gaius' oration came to an abrupt end as Theodore, moving swiftly, grabbed a gesticulating arm, yanked it up behind Gaius' back and flung him headfirst onto the tiles. His head hit the floor with the hollow thump of a dropped melon. Luckily for the physician, a melon that fails to break. He lay still, but his chest still moved.

In the ensuing silence John's voice sounded loud, although he spoke softly.

'Theodore, is what he said true?'

'Of course not. Anna was my wife. I loved her.'

'Liar! Beast! How dare you say such a thing!' Sophia escaped John's grasp and leapt across the room. She lashed out at Theodore, her sharp talons drawing blood from his cheek. At a nod from John, the excubitors moved forward, and restrained her.

Theodore looked stunned. Red pearls of blood welled up on his smooth cheek.

'You're drunk,' he said to Sophia, as if only just realizing this fact. 'I was only saying what –'

'You didn't have the courage, after all,' whispered Sophia. 'She was right. You aren't a man.'

'It was the Egyptian, not the master,' came the quavering voice of Euthymius. The eunuch had stopped tearing in nervous exasperation at his fingernails. 'The girl wanted to take her place. She took my place. The mistress chose her. She chose her.'

'John,' Anatolius began, 'please, don't –'

But John did not hear him. There was, for a moment, a strange look in his eyes, almost confusion. Because his unruly mind had caught a glimpse of the truth and leapt into the void, and now, he looked around, amazed at where he found himself.

The Lord Chamberlain walked over to where Anna lay.

'Thank you, Euthymius. You have been very helpful.' He spoke to Theodore. 'I was puzzled by the cat. The girl says she found it by the statue of Eros in the garden. That is beneath your window.'

Sophia laughed harpy-like. 'I should have known. You promised you'd do it but you had to test the poison first, of course. So meticulous. Everything planned. Except this child in my belly. I knew you wouldn't have the courage. Did the cat cry out in pain?'

'It was the Egyptian who killed the cat,' shrieked Euthymius, 'not the master. She dropped it out of her window. Her room is on the third floor. Right over the Eros. I wondered why she was taking the cat away.'

'No, I never would.' It was Hypatia. 'The cat is sacred.'

In her panic, the girl had shouted out her protest in Egyptian.

'The cat is sacred to Egyptians,' John translated, for the others in the hall. 'She would never have killed a cat. It represents one of their gods.'

Peter gave a loud sniff of disapproval.

'And you never saw Hypatia take the cat up the stairs, Euthymius,' John added. 'You think Peter wouldn't have noticed and mentioned such a thing when I spoke to him? It was, after all, the mistress's cat.'

John saw that Anatolius had managed to move over toward Hypatia. She had accepted his comforting arm around her shoulder.

'I know what goes on upstairs,' confirmed Peter. 'I would have seen anything unusual.'

'Including the master, had he mounted the stairs and gone looking for the poison in Hypatia's room.'

John paused, waiting for the room to fall quiet. A bird chirped, outside in the garden, signaling the as yet unglimpsed dawn more accurately than any of Theodore's clocks. Gaius, prostrate on the floor, groaned as he began to wake.

'I was puzzled by the manner of the poisoning,' John confessed. 'I jumped to the obvious conclusion that it was the potion made from Hecate's flower that was used. And I was right. But it seemed to me that Anna must have ingested the poison when she was alone in her apartments. Unless someone was lying.'

Theodore glared at him. He was beginning to look very tired.

'When I searched Anna's room I found nothing. That was not suprising. There was nothing to find, except this.' The Lord Chamberlain produced the apricot pit he had pulled from beneath the bed. 'This pit suggested poisoned fruit. But Anna had not eaten all day. And the pit, you can see is an old one, dried out. What should have attracted my attention, but what I never thought about until Euthymius reminded me by his own habit, was the bit of fingernail with all the other debris from the floor. Anna bit her nails, didn't she?'

'The nail color,' Theodore looked amazed.

'Yes. Her nails weren't perpetually ragged from the gardening, as they joked at court. Anna wore gloves to garden. Her nails were ragged because she bit them when she was nervous. And when would she be more nervous than on this important anniversary? You painted her nails, Theodore. The slightest amount of the potion is fatal. I was convinced that what killed Anna was in her room. And, indeed it was, until I allowed you to have her body removed.'

'I didn't do it,' denied Theodore. 'You heard Peter. I never go up to the servants' quarters.'

'I know,' John agreed. 'I said you painted her nails, not that you put the poison into the color. That would have directed attention to you. Oh, you intended to kill her – you and Sophia planned it. But you had some idea of administering the poison later, in private. You knew you would be in private today, of all days.'

'You can say what you like, but I warn you . . .'

'So the murderer did not have to be in the room with Anna, or even in the house, when the poison was ingested.' John continued. 'That was when she bit her polished nails. And even better, from the murderer's point of view, as soon as you finished painting her nails, she pulled on her gloves and went out to garden. Maybe the poisoner suspected she'd do that. So an hour or more had passed before the gloves came off and the poisoning actually occurred.'

'You have no proof that I intended to poison her. And the cat might have been found under my window, but as Euthymius says, it must have been Hypatia's doing – no matter what the girl says about her odd religious views.'

'Yes,' agreed John. 'You are innocent of Nefertiti's death also. The cat, having attested to the potency of the poison, was dropped, in a deliberate manner, from Hypatia's window. Peter would have noticed you moving about upstairs, Theodore, but not Euthymius. He was a servant too, and they were servants' quarters.

'And Euthymius took care of Anna's unguents and cosmetics. Not only could he move about freely upstairs, but he had access to the apartments where the cosmetics were stored.

'Euthymius was unhinged by jealous rage because, as he saw it, his mistress had forsaken him and preferred the company of the new Egyptian servant. He intended to take his revenge on both, by killing her and pointing the finger at the only person in the house who could have done it.'

The eunuch said nothing, but began to sob. John motioned the excubitors toward him.

John turned to Anna, placing his thin hand gently along the side of her head.

'It reminds me of the verse you recited, Anatolius, about a flower growing concealed in an enclosed garden. This lovely flower was concealed by its own plain features. And, as the poet said, many may long for that which grows concealed.'

Theodore laughed.

'You are amused at your wife's death?' John's tone was sorrowful rather than sharp.

'Isn't it humorous how the Fates arrange our dispositions?'

'You think that what you set out to accomplish has been achieved, don't you?' John's voice was gentle.

'I don't know what you mean, Lord Chamberlain. Can't you see, I am bereaved? It wasn't I who poisoned poor Anna.' A grin was spreading over Theodore's handsome face.

'You wished her death though, and even planned it.'

'Did I? Surely I didn't say that?'

The first tendrils of daylight crept in from the garden beyond the window, illuminating in starker detail the group in the reception hall.

'You would have killed her,' Anatolius stalked over towards Theodore. 'This is what you wanted. It isn't right.'

'We cannot be prosecuted for our wishes or plans, can we?' Theodore sneered.

'Fate can be kind to some and unkind to others,' said John. 'But it is not always unjust.'

Theodore laughed louder. 'Well, Lord Chamberlain, I'm sure Sophia and I will have many happy years to reflect on that. Now, I must ask you all to leave. Suddenly this long night has caught up with me and I feel my hospitality waning.'

He extended his hand toward Sophia. She looked up at him numbly. Her anger was gone. In her eyes there was some other emotion, pity perhaps. Gently she touched the cheek she'd scratched, wiping away the blood.

'I'm sorry, Theodore,' she whispered.

Theodore took her hand impatiently. 'Come away, now,' he said. He pulled her after him.

John drew his hand gently across Anna's forehead, brushing aside an errant strand of hair. He was aware of Anatolius at his side.

'Such a nimble mind, she had, Anatolius. She would appreciate this, I know. You see, after Theodore finished coloring her nails, the make-up box was left on the dressing table in the guest room. Anna's good friend Sophia often helped herself to the rouge, and the kohl – and the nail color. Yes, the master's lover was coloring her nails when I spoke to her last night.'

John bent toward Anna. 'Your husband will be joining you presently,' he whispered. 'I would like to hear that conversation.'

The Lord Chamberlain kissed Lady Anna's cold forehead.

THE POISONED CHALICE

Peter Tremayne

*With this story we conclude our journey through the ancient world.
Peter Tremayne has already written four novels and a dozen or more
short stories featuring his Irish investigator, Sister Fidelma. The first
novel was* Absolution By Murder *(1994). The events of the following
story take place just before the time of the second novel,* Shroud
for an Archbishop *(1995). Tremayne shows that law and order
continued in Rome after the fall of the Empire. By the time of the
setting of this story, in the year* AD 664, *Italy had come under the
power of the Lombard kings who held an uneasy alliance with the
rising power of the Papacy. As one empire fell, so another rose.*

~

The last thing Sister Fidelma of Kildare had expected, during her
pilgrimage to the Eternal City of Rome, was to see murder committed
in front of her eyes in a quiet little backstreet church.

As any citizen of Rome would have expected, Sister Fidelma,
like every discerning *barbarus* on their first visit, was duly
impressed by the immensity of the city. As neither a Hellene
nor a Roman, the term 'barbarian' was, however, a pedantry
when it applied to the young Irish religieuse. Her Latin was
more polished than most of Rome's citizens' and her literary
knowledge was certainly more extensive than many scholars'. She
was the product of Ireland's distinguished colleges, which were so
renowned throughout Europe that in Durrow alone there were to
be found the sons and daughters of kings and princelings from no
less than eighteen different countries. An education in Ireland was

a distinction that even the scions of the Anglo-Saxon kings would boast of.

Fidelma had come to Rome to present the *Regula coenabialis Cill Dara*, the Rule of the House of St Brigid, in Kildare, to be approved and blessed by the Holy Father at the Lateran Palace. She had been waiting to see an official of the Papal household for several days now. To while away the time, she, like the many thousands of other pilgrims who poured into the city, spent her time in touring the ancient monuments and tombs of the city.

From the *xenodochia*, the small hostel for foreign pilgrims close by the oratory of the Blessed Prassede, where she was lodging, she would walk down the hill to the Lateran Palace each morning to see whether she was to be received that day. She was becoming irritated as the days passed by without word. But there were so many people, from so many different countries – some she had not known existed – crowding into the palace to beg audience that she stoically controlled her frustration. Each day she would leave the palace in resignation to set off in search of some new point of interest in the city.

That morning she had chosen to visit the small *ecclesia* dedicated to the Blessed Hippolytus, which lay only a short walk from her hostel. Her purpose was for no other reason than the fact that it held the tomb of Hippolytus. She knew that her mentor, Abbot Laisran of Durrow, was an admirer of the work of the early Church Father and she had once struggled through the text of *Philosophoumena*, to debate with Laisran on this refutation of the Gnostic teachings. She knew that Laisran would be impressed if she could boast a visit to the very tomb of Hippolytus.

A mass was being celebrated as she took her place at the back of the tiny *ecclesia*, a small place which could hold no more than two or three dozen people. Even so, there were only half-a-dozen people scattered about with bowed heads, hearing the priest intoning the solemn words of the ritual.

Fidelma examined her co-religionists with interest. The sights and sounds of Rome were still new and intriguing to her. She was attracted by a young girl in the forefront of the worshippers. Fidelma could see only her profile emerging from a hood which respectfully hid the rest of her obviously well-shaped head. It was a delicate, finely chiselled, attractive face. Fidelma could appreciate its discreet beauty. Next to her was a young man in the robes of a religieux. Even though Fidelma could not see his face fully, she saw that he was good-looking and seemed to reflect something of the girl's features. Next to him stood a lean, weather-tanned young man, dressed in the clothes of a seaman but in the manner she had often seen adopted by sailors from Gaul. This young man did not look at all content with life. He was scowling; his expression fixed. Behind these three stood a short, stocky man in the rich robes of a senior religieux. Fidelma had seen enough of the abbots and bishops of Rome to guess that he was of such rank. In another corner was a nervous-looking, swarthy man, corpulent and richly attired and looking every inch a prosperous merchant. At the back of the church, stood the final member of the congregation, a young man attired in the uniform of the *custodes* of Rome, the guardians of law and order in the city. He was darkly handsome, with a somewhat arrogant manner, as, perhaps, befitted his soldierly calling.

The deacon, assisting in the offering, rang a small bell and the officiating priest raised the chalice of wine and intoned: 'The blood of Christ!' before moving forward to join the deacon, who had now taken up a silver plate on which the consecrated Host lay.

The small congregation moved forward to take their places in line before the priest. It was the handsome young religieux who took the first position, receiving the Host, placing it in his mouth and moving forward to receive the wine from the chalice held in the hands of the priest. As he turned away, his young female companion moved forward, being the next in line, to receive the sacrament.

Even as the religieux turned back to the congregation, his face suddenly distorted, he began to choke, his mouth gaping open, his tongue thrusting obscenely forward. A hand raised to his throat as the colour of his agonized features went from red to blue. The eyes were wide and staring. Sounds came from him that reminded Fidelma of the squealing of a pig about to be slaughtered.

Before the horrified gaze of the rest of the congregation, the young man fell to the floor, his body writhing and threshing for several moments. Then it was suddenly still and quiet.

There was no sound for a moment or two. Everyone stood immobile with shock.

A moment later, the shriek of the young woman rent the air. She threw herself forward onto the body. She was on her knees crying and screaming in a strange language made incomprehensible by her distress.

As no one seemed capable of moving, Sister Fidelma came quickly forward.

'Do not touch the wine nor the bread,' she instructed the priest, who was still holding the chalice in his hands. 'This man has been poisoned.'

She felt, rather than saw, the heads of the people turn to stare at her. She glanced round observing expressions ranging from bewilderment to surprise.

'Who are you to give orders, sister?' snapped a rough voice. It was the arrogant young *custos* pushing forward.

Fidelma raised her glinting green eyes to meet his dark suspicious ones.

'I hold no authority here, if that is what you mean. I am a stranger in this city. But in my own country I am a *dálaigh*, an advocate of the law courts, and know the effects of virulent poison when I see it.'

'As you say, you hold no authority here,' snapped the *custos*, clearly a young man who felt the honour of his rank and nationality. 'And I . . .'

'The sister is right, nevertheless, *custos*.'

The voice that interrupted was quiet, modulated but authoritative. It was the short, stocky man who spoke.

The young guard looked disconcerted at this opposition.

'I *do* hold authority here,' continued the short man, turning to Fidelma. 'I am the Abbot Miseno and this *ecclesia* is part of my jurisdiction.'

Without waiting for the guard's response, Abbot Miseno glanced at the officiating priest and deacon. 'Do as the sister says, Father Cornelius. Put down the wine and bread and ensure no one else touches it.'

Automatically, the priest obeyed, accompanied by the deacon, who placed his tray of bread carefully on the altar.

Abbot Miseno glanced down to the sobbing girl.

'Who was this man, daughter?' he demanded gently, bending down to place a hand on her shoulder.

The girl raised tear-stained eyes to him.

'Is he . . .?'

Miseno bent further to place his fingers against the pulse in the man's neck. The action was really unnecessary. One look at the twisted, frozen features would have been enough to confirm that the young religieux was beyond all human aid. Nevertheless, the action was probably designed as a reassurance for the girl. The abbot shook his head.

'He is dead, daughter,' he confirmed. 'Who was he?'

The girl began sobbing uncontrollably again and could not answer.

'His name was Docco. He was from Pouancé in Gaul.'

It was the young Gaulish seaman, who had been standing with the religieux and the girl, who answered him.

'And you are?' asked Abbot Miseno.

'My name is Enodoc. I was a friend of Docco's and also from Gaul. The girl is Egeria, Docco's sister.'

The Abbot Miseno stood for a moment, his head bowed in thought. Then he glanced up and surveyed Sister Fidelma with some speculation in his eyes.

'Would you come with me a moment, sister?'

He turned and led the way into a corner of the church, out of earshot of the others. Fidelma followed him in curiosity.

In the corner the abbot turned, keeping his voice low.

'I studied at Bobbio, which was founded fifty years ago by Columban and his Irish clerics. I learnt much about your country there. I have heard about the function of your law system and how a *dálaigh* works. Are you truly such a one?'

'I am a qualified advocate of the law courts of my country,' replied Fidelma simply, without any false pride, wondering what the abbot was driving at.

'And your Latin is fluent,' observed Miseno absently.

Fidelma waited patiently.

'It is clear that this monk, Docco, was poisoned,' went on Miseno after a moment's pause. 'Was this an accident or was there some deliberate plot to kill him? I think it behoves us to find out as soon as possible. If this story went abroad I shudder to think what interpretation would be given to it. Why, it might even stop people coming forward to receive the blessed sacrament. I would be grateful, sister, if you would use your knowledge to discover the truth of this matter before we have to report this to higher authorities.'

'That will not please the young *custos*,' Fidelma pointed out, with a slight gesture towards the impatient young guard. 'He clearly thinks that he is better suited for this task.'

'He has no authority here. I have. What do you say?'

'I will make inquiries, abbot, but I cannot guarantee any result,' Fidelma replied.

The abbot looked woeful for a moment and spread his hands in a helpless gesture.

'The culprit must be one of this company. You are trained in such detection. If you could do your best . . .?'

'Very well. But I am also one of this company. How can you be sure that I am not responsible?'

Abbot Miseno looked startled for a moment. Then he smiled broadly.

'You entered the *ecclesia* towards the end of the service and stood at the back. How could you have placed the poison in the bread or wine while it was on the altar before the eyes of us all?'

'True enough. But what of the others? Were they all here throughout the service?'

'Oh yes. I think so.'

'Including yourself?'

The rotund abbot smiled wryly.

'You may also count me among your suspects until you have gained knowledge to the contrary.'

Fidelma inclined her head.

'Firstly, then, I need to check how this poison was administered.'

'I will inform the impatient young *custos* that he must be respectful to you and obey your judgements.'

They returned to the group standing awkwardly around the body of the dead Gaul, whose head was still being cradled in the arms of his sobbing sister.

The abbot cleared his throat.

'I have asked the sister to conduct an inquiry into the cause of this death,' he began without preamble. 'She is eminently qualified to do so. I trust you will all,' he paused slightly, and let his eyes dwell on the arrogant young *custos*, 'cooperate with her in this matter for it has my blessing and ecclesiastical authority.'

There was a silence. Some glances of bemusement were cast towards her.

Fidelma stepped forward.

'I would like you all to return to the positions you were occupying before this happened.' She smiled gently down at the girl. 'You do not have to, if you wish, but there is nothing that you can do for your brother except truthfully answer the questions that I shall ask you.'

The Gaul, Enodoc, bent forward to raise the young girl to her feet, coaxing her away from the body of her brother, then gently guided her back to her place. There was a reluctant shuffling as the rest of the congregation complied.

Fidelma moved forward to the altar. She bent to the silver plate with its pieces of bread, the Host, and taking a piece sniffed at it suspiciously. She cautiously examined the rest of the bread. There was nothing apparently amiss with it. She turned to the chalice still full of the Eucharist wine and sniffed. She could not quite place the odour. However, it was bitter and even its smell caught at the back of her throat, making her gasp and cough sharply.

'It is as I thought,' she announced, 'the wine has been poisoned. I do not know what poison it is but the fumes are self-evident. It is highly dangerous and you have all seen its instant effect so I should not have to warn you further.'

She turned and sought out the young guard.

'Bring two stools and place them . . .' she turned and sought out an isolated corner of the *ecclesia*, 'place them over there. Then go and stand by the door and prevent anyone entering or leaving until I call for you.'

The young warrior looked outraged and glanced towards the abbot. Abbot Miseno merely gestured with a quick motion of his hand for the young man to comply.

'I will speak with you first, deacon,' Fidelma said, turning towards the spot where the guard had placed the chairs.

Once seated Fidelma examined the deacon. He was not more than twenty years old. A youth with dark hair and a rather ugly face, the eyes seeming too close together and the brows heavy. His heavy jowl was blue with badly shaved stubble.

'What is your name?'

'I am Tullius.'

'How long have you served here?'

'Six months.'

'As deacon, it would be your job to prepare the wine and bread for the blessing. Is this so?'

'Yes.'

'And did you do so today?'

'Yes.'

'Tell me about the wine.'

The deacon seemed disconcerted.

'In what way?'

'Tell me about the wine in the chalice. Where did it come from, how was it poured and whether it was left unguarded at any time?'

'The wine is bought locally. We keep several *amphorae* below the *ecclesia*, in the vaults, where it is stored. This morning I went down into the vaults and filled a jug. Then, when I observed the numbers attending the service, I poured the wine into the chalice for the blessing. This is the usual custom. The same procedure is made for the bread. Once the wine and bread are blessed and the transubstantiation occurs then no piece of the Host nor of the blood of Christ must be discarded. It must all be consumed.'

Among the Irish churches, the taking of the bread and wine was regarded merely as a symbolic gesture in remembrance of the Christ. Rome, however, had started to maintain that the blessing actually changed the substances into the literal flesh and blood of Christ. Fidelma's sceptical smile was not derogatory to the new doctrine but a reflection as to how the poisoned wine could possibly be regarded as the physical blood of the Saviour. And who, she wondered, would now volunteer to consume it?

'So, Tullius, you poured the wine from the jug into the chalice once you had ascertained how many people were attending the service?'

'That is so.'

'Where is this jug?'

'In the sacristy.'

'Take me there and show me.'

The young deacon rose and led the way to a door behind the altar. This was an apartment of the *ecclesia* where the sacred utensils and vestments of the priest were kept.

Fidelma peered around the small room. It was no larger than six feet wide and twelve feet in length. A second doorway, leading to a flight of stone steps descending into the gloom of the vaults, stood almost behind the door which gave ingress into the *ecclesia* itself. At the far end of the sacristy stood a third door, with a small diamond-shaped window in its centre, which, she could see, led to the outside of the building. Clothes were hung on pegs and there were icons and some books on shelves. There was also a bench with some loaves of bread and a wine jug on it. Fidelma bent over the jug and sniffed. There was no bitter odour. Cautiously, she reached down into the jug with her forefinger and dipped it in the wine. Withdrawing it, she sniffed again and then placed it between her lips. There was no bitter taste. Clearly, then, the wine had been poisoned only after it had been poured into the chalice.

'Tell me, Tullius, the chalice, which was used today, is it the same chalice that is used at every service?'

The deacon nodded.

'And the chalice was standing here, in the sacristy, when you brought up the jug of wine from the vaults?'

'Yes. I had purchased the bread on my way to the *ecclesia*, as I usually do. I came in here and placed the loaves ready to cut into small pieces. Then I went down to the vault and poured the jug of wine and brought it up here. I placed it by the chalice. Then Abbot Miseno entered and, as I recall, passed directly through the sacristy to join the congregation. When I judged it was a small attendance, I poured the wine accordingly.'

Fidelma frowned thoughtfully.

'So Abbot Miseno had already passed into the *ecclesia* before you poured the wine into the chalice?'

'He had.'

'And are you saying that at no time did you leave this sacristy after you had brought up the jug of wine and poured it into the chalice?'

'I judged the attendance while standing at the door. While I was doing this Father Cornelius came in. In fact, he did so not long after the abbot.'

'Father Cornelius being the priest who officiated?'

'Yes. He changed his vestments for the service while I poured the wine into the chalice. I then returned to check if anyone else had joined the congregation.'

'Then, at that point, your back was towards the chalice? It was not in your field of vision the whole time?'

'But there was no one in the sacristy with me except . . .'

'Except Father Cornelius?'

The deacon's mouth had snapped shut and he nodded glumly.

'Let me get this picture clear. Father Cornelius changed his vestments as you were standing at the door examining those entering the *ecclesia*?'

'Yes. I remember warning him that Abbot Miseno had already entered.'

'*Warning* him?' Fidelma was quick to spot the word.

'The abbot is in charge of this *ecclesia* as well as several others in the vicinity. However, he and Father Cornelius were . . . how can I say it? . . . Their views did not coincide. Abbot Miseno has been trying to remove Father Cornelius from this church. That is no secret.'

'Do you know why?'

'It is not for me to say. You may address that question to Abbot Miseno and Father Cornelius.'

'Very well. What then?'

'Father Cornelius was annoyed. If fact, I think he was in an evil temper when he arrived. Anyway, he pushed by me and went straight to Abbot Miseno. I saw them speaking together. I would say that the conversation was not friendly. The appointed hour for the service came and I rang the bell as usual. Father Cornelius then went to the altar to start the service.'

Fidelma leant forward.

'Let me clarify this point: you say that you poured the wine into the chalice while Father Cornelius was changing his vestments; that you then went to stand by the door, turning your back on the chalice?'

'Yes. I think so.'

'Think? You are not sure?'

'Well . . .' the deacon shrugged, 'I would not take oath on it. Perhaps I poured it just after he left the sacristy.'

'Not before he left?'

'I cannot be sure now. This matter has been a shock and I am a little confused as to the order of events.'

'Can you be sure whether there was anything else in the chalice when you poured the wine?'

'The chalice was clean.' The deacon's voice was decisive on this point.

'There was no coating on the chalice, no clear liquid which you might have missed at the bottom?' pressed Fidelma.

'Absolutely not. The chalice was clean and dry.'

'How can you be so sure when you admit to confusion over events?'

'The ritual, which all deacons in this office fulfil, is that before the wine is poured, a small piece of white linen is taken and the inside of the chalice is polished. Only then is the wine poured.'

Fidelma felt frustrated.

The wine had been poisoned. It had been poisoned while it was in the chalice and not before. Yet the only time that the chalice was out of sight for a moment, according to the deacon, was when Father Cornelius had entered the sacristy. That had been the only opportunity to introduce poison into the chalice. But the deacon was not sure whether the priest had left before or after he poured the wine.

'What happened then?' she prompted Tullius, the deacon.

'The service was ready to start. I took the tray of bread and carried it to the altar. Then I returned for the chalice . . .'

Fidelma's eyes sparkled with renewed interest.

'So the chalice stood here on its own while you carried the bread to the altar?'

The deacon was defensive.

'It was here only for a few seconds and I had left the door open between the sacristy and altar.'

'Nevertheless, it stood unobserved for a short while. During that period anyone might have entered the outer door and poisoned the wine, leaving before you noticed them.'

'It is possible, I suppose,' acceded the deacon. 'But they would have had to have been quick to do so.'

'What then?'

'You carried the wine to the altar? Yes. Then the service commenced. The chalice stood in full view of everyone during the service until the moment Father Cornelius blessed it and the Gaulish religieux came forward to receive communion.'

'Very well.'

Fidelma led the way back to where the small congregation were still sitting in silence. She felt their eyes upon her, suspicious and hostile. She dismissed the deacon and motioned for the priest, Father Cornelius, to join her.

'You are Father Cornelius, I believe?'

'I am.' The priest looked tired and was clearly distressed.

'How long have you been priest here?'

'For three years.'

'Do you have any idea how poison was introduced into the Eucharist wine?'

'None. It is an impossible thing.'

'Impossible?'

'Impossible that anyone would dare to perform such a sacrilege with the Eucharist.'

Fidelma sniffed slightly.

'Yet it is obvious that someone did. If people are out to murder, then a matter of sacrilege becomes insignificant compared with the breaking of one of God's commandments,' she observed dryly. 'When Tullius, the deacon, brought the wine from the sacristy, was it placed on the altar?'

'It was.'

'It stood there in full sight of everyone and no one went near it until you blessed it and raised the chalice, turning to administer the sacrament to the first communicant?'

'No one went near it,' affirmed the priest.

'Did you know who would be the first communicant?'

Father Cornelius frowned.

'I am not a prophet. People come to receive the sacrament as and when they will. There is no order in their coming.'

'What was the cause of your differences with Abbot Miseno?'

Father Cornelius blinked.

'What do you mean?' There was a sudden tone of anxiety in his voice.

'I think my Latin is clear enough,' Fidelma replied phlegmatically.

Father Cornelius hesitated a moment and then gave a shrug.

'Abbot Miseno would prefer to appoint someone else to my office.'

'Why?'

'I disagree with the teachings of Augustine of Hippo, that everything is preordained, which is now a doctrine of our church. I believe that men and women can take the initial and fundamental steps towards their salvation, using their own efforts. If men and women are not responsible for their own good or evil deeds, then there is nothing to restrain them from an indulgence in sin. To argue, as Augustine has, that no matter what we do in life, God has already preordained everything so that it is already decided if our reward is heaven or hell, is to imperil the entire moral law. For my heresy, Abbot Miseno wishes to have me removed.'

Fidelma felt the harsh passion in the man's voice.

'So? You would describe yourself as a follower of Pelagius?'

Father Cornelius drew himself up.

'Pelagius taught a moral truth. I believe men and women have the choice to become good or evil. Nothing is preordained. How we live our lives determines whether we are rewarded by heaven or hell.'

'But Pope Innocent declared Pelagius to be a heretic,' Fidelma pointed out.

'And Pope Zosimus declared him innocent.'

'Later to renounce that decision,' smiled Fidelma thinly. 'Yet it matters not to me. Pelagius has a special place in the philosophy of the church in my country for he was of our blood and faith. Sufficient to say, Abbot Miseno holds to the teachings of Augustine of Hippo?'

'He does. And he would have me removed from here because I do not.'

'Yet Abbot Miseno has the authority to appoint whomsoever he likes as priest of this *ecclesia*?'

'He has.'

'Then surely he has the authority to dismiss you without argument?'

'Not without good cause. He must justify his actions to the bishop.'

'Ah yes. In Rome bishops have more authority than abbots. Those is not so in Ireland. Yet, on the matter of Pelagius, surely heresy, even a just heresy, is cause enough?'

'But I do not openly preach the teachings of Pelagius nor those of Augustine. They are a subject for my conscience. I perform my duties to my congregation without complaint from them.'

'So you have shown the abbot no good cause to dismiss you?'

'None.'

'But Abbot Miseno has suggested that you resign from this church?'

'He has.'

'And you have refused.'

'I have.'

'Did you know the Gaul who died?'

Again Cornelius blinked at the sudden change of subject of her questioning.

'I have seen him several times before.'

'Several times?'

'Himself and his sister. I believe that they are pilgrims staying in a nearby *xenodochia*. They have attended the mass here each day.'

'And the other Gaul, who seems so friendly with the girl?'

'I have seen him only once, yesterday. I think he has only recently arrived in Rome.'

'I see.'

'Sister, this is a great mystery to me. Why should anyone attempt to poison the wine and cause the death of all the communicants in the church today?'

Fidelma gazed thoughtfully at him.

'Do you think that the wine was meant to be taken by all the communicants?'

'What else? Everyone would come to take the bread and wine. It is the custom.'

'But not everyone did. The poison was so quick in its action that undoubtedly only the first person who took it would die and his death would have served as a warning to the others not to drink. That is precisely what happened.'

'Then if the wine were meant only for the Gaul, how could the person who poisoned the wine know that he would be the first to come forward to take it?'

'A good point. During the time that the Gaul attended the services here, did he take communion?'

'Yes.'

'Was he always in the same place in the church?'

'Yes, I believe so.'

'And at what point did he usually come forward to take the wine and bread?'

Cornelius' eyes widened slightly as he reflected on the question.

'He was always the first,' he admitted. 'His sister was second. For they were both in the same position before the altar.'

'I see. Tell me, did you enter the church via the sacristy?'

'Yes.'

'Was the deacon, Tullius, already there?'

'Yes. Standing by the door trying to estimate the numbers attending the service.'

'Had he poured the wine into the chalice?'

'I do not know,' confessed Father Cornelius. 'Tullius told me that Miseno had arrived and I went to see him. I think Tullius had the jug in hand as I left the sacristy.'

Fidelma rubbed her chin thoughtfully.

'That is all, Father. Send Abbot Miseno across to me.'

The abbot came forward smiling and seated himself.

'What news? Are you near a resolution?'

Fidelma did not return his smile.

'I understand that you wished to remove Father Cornelius?'

Abbot Miseno pulled a face. A curious, protective gesture.

'I have that authority,' he said defensively. 'What has that to do with this matter?'

'Has Father Cornelius failed in his duties?' Fidelma ignored his question.

'I am not satisfied with them.'

'I see. Then the reason you wish him removed has nothing to do with Father Cornelius' personal beliefs?'

Abbot Miseno's eyes narrowed.

'You are clearly a clever investigator, Fidelma of Kildare. How do you come to know so much?'

'You said that you knew the manner in which a *dálaigh*, an advocate of the laws of my country, acted. It is, as you know, my job to ask questions and from the answers to make deductions. I say again, has the removal of Cornelius anything to do with the fact of his beliefs?'

'In truth, I am liberal about these matters,' replied Abbot Miseno. 'However, Cornelius will tell you otherwise.'

'Why, then, do you wish him removed?'

'Cornelius has been here three years. I do not believe that he has fulfilled his functions properly. There are stories that he keeps a mistress. That he flouts more than one doctrine of our church. His deacon, a worthy soul, keeps this flock together in spite of Father Cornelius. And now Christ Himself has demonstrated clearly that Cornelius is unworthy of the priesthood.'

'How so?' Fidelma was intrigued at the Abbot Miseno's logic.

'The matter of the poisoned Eucharist wine.'

'Do you accuse Father Cornelius of being the poisoner?' Fidelma was astonished at the apparent directness of the accusation.

'No. But if he had been a true priest, then the transubstantiation would have taken place and the wine would not have been poisoned. It would have become the blood of Christ even though it contained poison, for the blessing would have purified it.'

Fidelma was nonplused at this reasoning.

'Then it would, indeed, have been a miracle.'

Abbot Miseno looked annoyed.

'Is not the fact of transubstantiation a miracle, sister, one that is performed every day in all churches of Christendom?'

'I am no theologian. I was taught that the matter was a symbolism and not a reality.'

'Then you have been taught badly. The bread and wine, when blessed by a true and pure priest, truly turns into the blood and flesh of Our Saviour.'

'A matter of opinion,' observed Fidelma distantly. She indicated the corpulent and richly attired man who sat apart from everyone else. 'Tell that man to come to me.'

Abbot Miseno hesitated.

'Is that all?'

'All for the moment.'

With a sniff of annoyance at being so summarily dismissed, the abbot rose and made his way to the corpulent man and spoke to him. The man rose and came hesitantly forward.

'This matter is nothing to do with me,' he began defensively.

'No?' Fidelma looked at the man's pouting features. 'And you are . . . ?'

'My name is Talos. I am a merchant and have been a member of this congregation for many years.'

'Then you are just the person to answer my questions,' affirmed Fidelma.

'Why so?'

'Have you known Father Cornelius for some time?'

'Yes. I was attending this congregation before he became priest here.'

'Is he a good priest?'

The Greek merchant looked puzzled.

'I thought this questioning was to be about the poisoning of the wine?'

'Indulge me,' Fidelma smiled. 'Is he a good priest?'

'Yes.'

'Are you aware of any complaints about him? Any conduct that would not become his office?'

Talos looked awkwardly at his feet. Fidelma's eyes glinted.

'I am personally not aware of anything.'

'But you have heard some story?' she pressed.

'Tullius has told me that there have been complaints, but not from me. I have found Father Cornelius to be a conscientious priest.'

'Yet Tullius said that there were complaints? Was Tullius one of the complainants?'

'Not that I am aware. Yet I suppose that it would be his job to pass on the complaints to the abbot. He must also be conscientious in his job. Indeed, he would have cause to be.'

'I do not understand.'

Talos grimaced.

'Tullius has been studying for the priesthood and will be ordained on the day after tomorrow. He is a local boy. His family were not of the best but he had ambition enough to overcome that. Sadly, the gods of love have played him an evil trick.'

'What do you mean by that?'

Talos looked surprised and then he smiled complacently.

'We are people of the world,' he said condescendingly.

'You mean that he prefers the company of his own sex?'

'Exactly so.' She saw the Greek's eyes glance disapprovingly across the *ecclesia* and, without turning her head, followed the direction of the look to the young *custos*.

Fidelma sniffed. There were no laws against homosexuality under the auspices of the Brehons.

'So when he is ordained,' she went on, 'he will move on to his own church?'

'That I would not know. I would presume so. This church cannot support two priests. As you see, it boasts only a small congregation, most of whom are well known to each other.'

'Yet the Gauls are strangers here.'

'That is true. But the dead religieux and his sister were staying in a hostel across the street and had been attending here during the week. The other, he had been here once. There was only one other complete stranger here today – you.'

'You have been most helpful, Talos. As you return to your place, would you ask Enodoc, the Gaul, to come here?'

Talos rose and left hastily, performing his task perfunctorily on the way back to his position.

The Gaul had been comforting the girl. Fidelma watched as the young man leant forward and squeezed the arm of the girl, whose head hung on her breast, as if she were asleep. She had ceased her sobbing.

'I know all about the advocates of the Brehon laws,' remarked the young man pleasantly, as he seated himself. 'We, in Gaul, share a common ancestry with you of Ireland as well as a common law.'

'Tell me about yourself,' Fidelma invited distantly, ignoring the friendly overture.

'My name is . . .'

'Yes, that I know. I also know from whence you come. Tell me what is your reason for visiting Rome.'

The young man still smiled pleasantly.

'I am the captain of a merchant ship sailing out of the city of the Veneti in Armorica. It is as a trader that I am in Rome.'

'And you knew the monk named Docco?'

'We came from the same village.'

'Ah. And you are betrothed to the girl, Egeria?'

The young man started with a frown.

'What makes you ask this?'

'The way you behave to her is that of a concerned lover not a stranger nor that of a mere friend.'

'You have a perceptive eye, sister.'

'Is it so?'

'I want to marry her.'

'Then who prevents you?'

Again Enodoc frowned.

'Why do you presume that anyone prevents me?'

'Because of the way you defensively construct your sentence.'

'Ah, I see. It is true that I have wanted to marry Egeria. It is true that Docco, who is the head of his family, did not want her to marry me. We grew up in the same village but there is enmity between us.'

'And yet here you are in Rome standing together with Docco and his sister before the same altar,' observed Fidelma.

'I did not know Docco and Egeria were in Rome. I met them by chance a few days ago and so I made up my mind to argue my case further with Docco before I rejoined my ship to sail back to Gaul.'

'And was that what you were doing here?'

Enodoc shrugged.

'In a way. I was staying nearby.'

'Forgive me, but the port of Ostia, the nearest port of Rome, is a long way from here. Are you telling me that you, the captain of your ship, came to Ostia and then, hearing by chance that Docco and Egeria were in Rome, made this long journey here to find them?'

'No. I had business to transact in Rome and left my ship at Ostia. I needed to negotiate with a merchant for a cargo. Yet it is true that I found Egeria and Docco simply by chance.'

'I am told that you have been to this *ecclesia* before.'

'Yes; but only once. That was yesterday when I first encountered Egeria and Docco in the street and followed them to this place.'

'It was a strange coincidence.'

'Coincidences happen more often than we give them credit. I attended the service with them yesterday.'

'And was your plaint successful?'

Enodoc hesitated.

'No, Docco was as firmly against my marriage to Egeria as ever he had been.'

'Yet you joined them again today?'

'I was leaving for Ostia today. I wanted one more chance to plead my case with Docco. I love Egeria.'

'And does she love you?'

Enodoc thrust out his chin.

'You will have to ask her that yourself.'

'I intend to do so. Where did you meet them this morning? Did you come to the *ecclesia* together, or separately?'

'I had some business first and then went to their lodgings. They had already left for the church and so I followed.'

'At what time did you get here?'

'A moment or so before the service started.'

'And you came straight in and joined them?'

'Yes.'

'Very well. Ask Egeria to come and sit with me.'

Clearly despondent, Enodoc rose to his feet and went back to the girl. He spoke to her but seemed to get no response. Fidelma noticed that he put his hand under her arm, drew her to her feet and guided her to where Fidelma was sitting. She came unprotestingly but was apparently still in a stupefied state.

'Thank you,' Fidelma said, and reached forward to take the girl's hand. 'This is a great shock for you, I know. But I need to ask some questions. Be seated now.' She turned and gazed up at Enodoc. 'You may leave us.'

Reluctantly the Gaulish seaman departed.

The girl had slumped on the stool before Fidelma, head bowed.

'Your name is Egeria, I believe?'

The girl simply nodded.

'I am Fidelma. I need to ask some questions,' she repeated again. 'We need to discover who is responsible for this terrible deed.'

The girl raised her tear-stained eyes to Fidelma. A moment or two passed before she seemed to focus clearly.

'It cannot bring back Docco. But I will answer, if I can.'

'You were very fond of your brother, I take it?'

'He was all I had. We were orphans together.'

'He was protective of you?'

'I am . . . *was* younger than he and he raised me when our

parents were killed during a Frankish raid. He became the head
of my family.'

'What made you come to Rome?'

'It was a pilgrimage that we had long talked about.'

'Did you expect Enodoc to be here?'

The girl shook her head.

'Do you love Enodoc?'

Egeria look at her without answering for a moment or two and
then shook her head slowly.

'Enodoc came from our village. He used to be our friend when
we were children. I liked him as a friend but no more than that.
Then he went to sea. He is captain of a merchant ship. I hardly
see him. But whenever we meet, he seems to think he has a claim
on me.'

'Indeed; he thinks that he is in love with you.'

'Yes. He has said so on several occasions.'

'But you are not in love with him?'

'No.'

'Have you told him so? Have you told him clearly?'

'Several times. He is a stubborn man and convinced himself that
it was Docco who stood against him. That Docco had the ability to
make up my mind for me.'

'I see. Are you telling me that he thought that it was only Docco
that was an obstacle to marriage with you?'

The girl nodded and then her eyes widened a fraction.

'Are you saying . . .?'

'I am merely asking questions, Egeria. When did you meet Enodoc
today?'

'When he arrived for the service.'

'You and your brother were already in the *ecclesia*, I take it?'

She nodded.

'You had taken up your position at the front?'

'Yes.'

'Did your brother normally take that position?'

Egeria sniffed a little and wiped a tear from her eye.

'Docco always liked to be the first to take the ritual of the
Eucharist and so he liked to place himself near the priest. It was
a habit of his, even at home.'

'I see. At what stage did Enodoc join you?'

'A few moments before the service began. I thought that
he had finally accepted the situation but then he appeared,
breathless and flustered as if he were in a hurry. I thought that
the priest, Father Cornelius, was going to admonish him because

he had halted the opening of the service while Enodoc took his place.'

Fidelma frowned.

'Why so? I came very late into the service yet Father Cornelius did not halt the service for me.'

'It was because Enodoc entered at the back of the altar and crossed in front of the priest to take his position with us.'

Fidelma could not speak with surprise for a moment.

'Are you saying that Enodoc entered the *ecclesia* through the sacristy?'

Egeria shrugged.

'I do not know. He entered through that door.' She turned and pointed to the door of the sacristy.

Fidelma was silent for a while.

'Return to your place, Egeria. I will not be long now. Please ask Enodoc to come back to me.'

Enodoc was as pleasant as before.

'You have been selective with your truths, Enodoc,' Fidelma opened.

The young man frowned.

'How so?'

'Docco was not the only person to stand in your way to marriage with Egeria.'

'Who else did so?' demanded the Gaul.

'Egeria herself.'

'She told you that?' The young man flushed.

'Yes.'

'She does not really mean it. She may say so but it was merely Docco speaking. Things will be different now.'

'You think so?'

'She is distraught. When her mind clears, she will know the truth.' He was confident.

'Perhaps. You did not mention that you entered this *ecclesia* through the sacristy.'

'You did not ask me. Is it important?'

'Why did you choose that unorthodox way of entering?'

'No mystery to that. I told you that I had to see a merchant this morning. I finished my business and came hurrying to the church. I found myself on the far side of the building and heard the bell toll for the opening of the service. It would have taken me some time to walk around the building, for there is a wall which is a barrier along the road. To come from the back of the church to the main doors takes a while, and I saw the door to the sacristy so I entered it.'

'Yet you had only been in this *ecclesia* once before. You must have a good memory.'

'It does not take much memory to recall something from the previous day, which was when I was here.'

'Who was in the sacristy when you entered?'

'No one.'

'And what did you do?'

'I came straight through into the *ecclesia*.'

'Did you see the chalice there?'

Enodoc shook his head. Then his eyes widened as he saw the meaning to her questions. For a moment, he was silent, his mouth set in a tight line. His tanned features reddened but he overcame his obvious indignation.

'I am sure that the chalice was already on the altar because as I entered the priest was starting the service.'

Fidelma met his gaze and held it for a moment.

'You may return to your place.'

Fidelma sat thinking for some moments and then she rose and walked towards the doors where the young *custos* stood. The young man watched her with narrow-eyed suspicion.

'What is your name?' she asked as she came to face him.

'Terentius.'

'Do you usually attend the services in this *ecclesia*?'

'My house is but a short walk away and my position as a member of the *custodes* is to ensure that law and order prevail in this area.'

'How long have you performed that duty?'

'Two years now.'

'So you have known Father Cornelius since you have been here?'

'Of course.'

'What is your opinion of Father Cornelius?'

The guard shrugged.

'As a priest, he has his faults. Why do you ask?'

'And your opinion of Tullius? Do you know him?'

She saw the young man flush.

'I know him well. He was born here in this district. He is conscientious in his duties. He is about to be ordained.'

She detected a slight tone of pride.

'I am told Tullius is from a poor family. To be honest, I am given to believe that his is a family known to the *custodes*.'

'Tullius has long sought to dissociate himself from them. Abbot Miseno knows that.'

'Had the service started, when you arrived here?

'It had just begun. I was the last to arrive ... apart from yourself.'

'The Gaulish seaman ... had he already entered the church?' Fidelma asked.

The guard frowned.

'No. As a matter of fact, he came in just after I did but through the sacristy.'

'You came in through the main doors, then?'

'Of course.'

'How soon after everyone else did you enter the church?'

'Not very long. As I was approaching along the street, I saw Abbot Miseno outside the building. I saw him arguing with Father Cornelius. They were standing near the sacristy door as I passed. The abbot turned in, then, after he had stood a moment or two, Father Cornelius followed.'

'Do you know what they were arguing about?'

The young soldier shook his head.

'Then you came into the *ecclesia*? What of the Gaul?'

'A moment or so later. Father Cornelius was about to start the service, when he came in. We were halfway through the service when you yourself entered.'

'That will be all for the moment.'

Fidelma turned in deep thought and made her way to Abbot Miseno.

The abbot watched her approach with impatience.

'We cannot afford to take long on this matter, Sister Fidelma. I had heard that you advocates of the Brehon Courts were quick at getting to the truth of the matter. If you cannot demonstrate who killed this foreign religieux, then it will reflect badly on that reputation.'

Fidelma smiled thinly.

'Perhaps it was in hope of that event that you so quickly suggested my involvement in this matter?'

Abbot Miseno flushed in annoyance.

'Do you suggest ... ?'

Fidelma made a dismissive gesture with her hand.

'Let us not waste time in rhetoric. Why were you arguing with Father Cornelius outside the sacristy?'

Miseno's jaw clamped tightly.

'I had demanded his resignation from this office.'

'He refused to resign?'

'Yes.'

'And you came into the church through the sacristy? Did Father Cornelius follow you?'

'Yes. He had changed his vestments and suddenly came out of the sacristy, straight to me and tried to renew the argument. Luckily, Tullius rang the bell for the service to start. I had just told him that I would do everything in my power to see him relieved of his position.'

'Everything?'

Miseno's eyes narrowed.

'What do you imply?'

'How far would you go to have him removed?'

'I will not deign to answer that.'

'Silence often speaks as loudly as words. Why do you dislike Father Cornelius so much?'

'A priest who betrays the guiding principles of . . .'

'Cornelius says that you disapprove of him because he holds to the teachings of Pelagius. Many of us do. But you claim that it is not that but more personal matters that make him fit not to be priest here.'

'Why are you concentrating on Father Cornelius?' demanded Miseno. 'Your task was to find out who poisoned the Gaulish religieux. Surely you should be looking at the motives for his killing?'

'Answer my question, Abbot Miseno. There must have been a point when you approved Cornelius in this office.'

Miseno shrugged.

'Yes. Three years ago I thought he was appropriate to the task and a conscientious priest. I do not mind admitting that. It has been during the last six months that I have had disturbing reports.'

Fidelma tugged thoughtfully at her lower lip.

'And where do these reports emanate from?'

Abbot Miseno frowned.

'I cannot tell you that. That would be a breach of confidence.'

'Did they come from a single source?'

Miseno's expression was enough to confirm the thought.

Fidelma smiled without humour.

'I suspect the reports came from the deacon, Tullius.'

Abbot Miseno stirred uncomfortably. But he said nothing.

'Very well. I take the fact that you do not deny that as an affirmative.'

'All very well. So it was Tullius. As deacon it was his duty to inform me if anything was amiss.'

'And your task to verify that Tullius was giving you accurate information,' observed Fidelma. 'Did you do so?'

Abbot Miseno raised an eyebrow.

'Verify the reports?'

'I presume that you did not simply take Tullius at his word?'

'Why would I doubt him? Tullius is in the process of taking holy orders, under my supervision. I can trust the word of Tullius.'

'The word of someone currently seeking ordination, you mean? Such a person would not lie?'

'That's right. Absolutely not. Of course they would not lie.'

'But a priest, already ordained, would lie? Therefore, you could not take Cornelius' word? Surely there is a contradictory philosophy in this?'

'Of course I don't mean that!' snapped Abbot Miseno.

'But that is what appears to be happening. You took Tullius' word over that of Cornelius.'

'The accusation was that Cornelius had dishonoured the priest-hood by taking a mistress.'

'Talos suggests that Tullius takes male lovers. You indicate that you know of this. The conclusion therefore is that not only did you take the word of a deacon against a priest, but you preferred to condemn a man on the grounds that he had a female lover or mistress while supporting a young man who is said to have a male lover. Why is one to be condemned and the other to be accepted in your eyes?'

Abbot Miseno set his jaw firmly.

'I am not Tullius' lover, if that is what you are implying. Tullius is under my patronage. He is my protégé.'

'Are you retracting your claim that Tullius had a male lover?'

'You have spoken to the young *custos*.' It was a statement rather than a question.

'Do you admit you are prejudiced in your judgement?'

'Are you saying that Tullius lied to me? If so, what proof do you have?'

'As much proof as you have to say that he told the truth.'

'Why should he lie to me?'

'You are about to ordain him. I suspect that you now intend him to replace Cornelius here?'

Abbot Miseno's face showed that her guess was right.

'But what has this to do with the death of the Gaul?'

'Everything,' Fidelma assured him. 'I think I am now ready to explain what happened.'

She turned and called everyone to come forward to the place before the altar.

'I can tell you why Docco, a visitor to this country and this city, died and by whose hand.' Her voice was cold and precise.

They appeared to surge forward, edging near to her with expectant expressions.

'Sister Fidelma!' It was Egeria who spoke. 'We know there was only one person who wanted my brother dead. Everyone else here was a stranger to him.'

Enodoc's face was white.

'This is not true. I would never harm anyone . . .'

'I don't believe you!' cried Egeria. 'Only you had reason to kill him.'

'What if Docco was killed simply because he was the first to take the sacrament?' interrupted Fidelma.

There was a tense silence.

'Go on,' urged Abbot Miseno in an icy tone.

'Docco was not singled out as a victim. Any of us might have been the victim. The intention was to discredit Father Cornelius.'

There was an angry glint in Abbot Miseno's eyes and they narrowed on Fidelma.

'You will have to answer for these accusations . . .'

'I am prepared to do so. It was something that the abbot said that gave me an idea of the true motive of this terrible deed. He said that if Father Cornelius had been a true priest, then once the wine was blessed and the transubstantiation occurred, the poison would have been rendered harmless when the wine became the Blood of Christ. The motive of this crime was to demonstrate that Father Cornelius was unworthy to hold office.'

Father Cornelius stood gazing at her in awe.

Fidelma went on.

'For some time the deacon, Tullius, had been feeding stories to Abbot Miseno about the misconduct of Cornelius, stories which Cornelius categorically denies. But Abbot Miseno was convinced. Tullius was his protégé and could do no wrong in the abbot's eyes. Furthermore, Miseno was about to ordain Tullius and, as a priest, he would need his own *ecclesia*. What better than to give him this church . . . once Cornelius had been removed. But Cornelius was not going without a fight. Any accusations of misconduct would have to be argued before the local bishop.'

'Who are you accusing?' demanded Cornelius, intervening. 'Miseno or Tullius?'

'Neither.'

Her answer was met with blank looks.

'Then whom?'

'Terentius of the *custodes*!'

The young man took a step backwards and drew his short ceremonial sword.

'This has gone far enough, barbarian!' he cried in anger. 'I am a Roman. No one will believe you.'

But Tullius was moving forward.

'What have you done, Terentius?' he cried in a high-pitched voice. 'I loved you more than life, and you have ruined everything.'

He ran as if to embrace Terentius and then seemed to freeze in mid-stride. It was clearly not meant to happen but the young deacon had inadvertently run forward onto the sword which the *custos* had been holding defensively in front of him. Tullius gave a gurgling cry, blood gushed from his mouth and he fell forward.

Enodoc reached forward and snatched the sword from the guard's hand. There was no struggle. The *custos* stood frozen in shock staring down at the body of his friend.

'But I did it for you, Tullius!' he wailed, suddenly sinking to his knees and reaching for the hand of the corpse. 'I did it for you.'

A short time later Fidelma sat with Father Cornelius and Abbot Miseno.

'I was not sure whether Tullius and Terentius had planned this together, or even whether you might be part of the plan yourself, Abbot Miseno,' she said.

Miseno looked pained.

'I might be a fool, one of ill judgement, but I am not a murderer, sister.'

'How did you realize that Terentius was the murderer?' demanded Father Cornelius. 'I cannot understand this.'

'Firstly, the motive. It was easy to eliminate the fact that Docco was an intended victim. There were too many improbables, too many coincidences had to happen to ensure that the Gaul was the first and only victim. So I had to look for another motive. That motive was not so obscure and, as I said, it was Abbot Miseno's interpretation of the fact of transubstantiation which gave me a clue. The motive was to discredit you, Father Cornelius. Who would benefit from that? Obviously Tullius the deacon.'

'So why did you think Tullius was innocent?'

'Because if he had been involved, then he would have given himself a better alibi for, it appeared at first, only he had the opportunity to poison the wine. Then I learnt that Tullius had a male lover. It became clear that it was Terentius, the *custos*.'

'Yes, but what made you so sure he was the murderer?'

'He was the only other person with opportunity. And, most importantly, he lied. He said that he had entered the church by the main doors just before the Gaulish seaman. He also told me that he had been coming along the street and saw you both quarrelling on the path to the sacristy.'

'Well that was no lie, we were arguing,' Miseno confirmed.

'Surely, you were. But the sacristy, where that argument took place, as Enodoc told me, is entered by a path on the other side of this church. You have to walk a long way round to enter the main doors. Enodoc didn't have time to do so, so blundered through the sacristy into the church.'

'I do not follow.'

'If Terentius had seen you both arguing then he was on the path outside the sacristy and therefore he was on the far side of the building. What was he doing there? Why did he not come through the sacristy, like Enodoc, knowing the service was about to start? He had been there enough times with Tullius. No, he came in through the main doors.

'He had seen your quarrel and gone to the sacristy door. Watching through the window, he waited until he saw Tullius take the bread into the *ecclesia*; then he slipped in and poisoned the wine and left, hurrying round the church to come in by the main doors and thus giving himself an alibi.'

'And he did this terrible deed purely in order to help Tullius become priest here?' asked Miseno, amazed.

'Yes. He had reasoned out that it did not matter who was killed by the poison, the end result was that you would believe that Cornelius was not fit to be a priest because the transubstantiation had not happened. That would ensure Tullius became priest here. That plan nearly succeeded. Love makes people do insane things, Miseno. Doesn't Publilius Syrus say: *amare et sapere vix deo conceditur*? Even a god finds it hard to love and be wise at the same time.'

Miseno nodded. '*Amantes sunt amentes*,' he agreed. 'Lovers are not sane.'

Fidelma shook her head sorrowfully.

'It was a sad and unnecessary death. More importantly, Abbot Miseno, it is, to my mind, a warning of the dangers of believing that what was meant as symbolism is, in fact, a reality.'

'There we will have to differ on our theology, Fidelma,' sighed Miseno. 'But our Faith is broad enough to encompass differences. If it is not – then it will surely perish.'

'*Sol lucet omnibus*,' Fidelma replied softly, with just a touch of cynicism. 'The sun shines for everyone.'

SOURCES AND ACKNOWLEDGEMENTS

Acknowledgements are accorded to the following for the rights to publish the stories in this anthology. Every effort has been made to trace copyright holders. The Editor would be pleased to hear from anyone if they believe there has been an inadvertent transgression of copyright.

'Mosaic', © 1996 by Rosemary Aitken. First printing, original to this anthology. Published by permission of the author and the author's agent, Dorian Literary Agency.

'Murderer, Farewell', © 1996 by Ron Burns. First printing, original to this anthology. Published by permission of the author and the author's agent, the Mitchell J. Hamilburg Agency.

'In This Sign, Conquer', © 1996 by Simon Clark and Gail-Nina Anderson. First printing, original to this anthology. Published by permission of the authors and the authors' agent, London International Scripts, Ltd.

'Investigating the Silvius Boys', © 1995 by Lindsey Davis. First published in *No Alibi*, edited by Maxim Jakubowski (London: Ringpull, 1995). Reprinted by permission of the author's agent, Heather Jeeves Literary Agency.

'A Pomegranate for Pluto', © 1996 by Claire Griffen. First printing, original to this anthology. Published by permission of the author.

'The Brother in the Tree', © 1996 by Keith Heller. First printing, original to this anthology. Published by permission of the author.

'The Things That are Caesar's', © 1996 by Edward D. Hoch. First printing, original to this anthology. Published by permission of the author.

'The Gateway to Death', © 1955 by Brèni James. First published in *Ellery Queen's Mystery Magazine*, February 1955, as 'Socrates Solves Another Murder'. Unable to trace the author or the author's representative.

'The Ass's Head', © 1996 by Phyllis Ann Karr. First printing, original to this anthology. Published by permission of the author.

'Death of the King', © 1959 by Theodore Mathieson. First published in *Ellery Queen's Mystery Magazine*, September 1959 as 'Alexander the Great, Detective'. Reprinted by permission of the author.

'Aphrodite's Trojan Horse', © 1996 by Amy Myers. First printing, original to this anthology. Published by permission of the author, and the author's agent Dorian Literary Agency.

'The Nest of Evil', © 1965 by Wallace Nichols. First published in *London Mystery Selection* 64, March 1965, as 'The Case of the Nest of Evil'. Unable to trace the author or the author's representative.

'A Green Boy', © 1973 by Anthony Price. First published in *Winter's Crimes 5*, edited by Virginia Whitaker (London: Macmillan, 1973). Reprinted by permission of the author.

'Beauty More Stealthy', © 1996 by Mary Reed and Eric Mayer. First printing, original to this anthology. Published by permission of the authors.

'The Statuette of Rhodes', © 1996 by John Maddox Roberts. First printing, original to this anthology. Published by permission of the author.

Preface: 'A Murder, Now and Then . . .' and 'The White Fawn', © 1996 by Steven Saylor. First printing, original to this anthology. Published by permission of the author.

'Last Things', © 1996 by Darrell Schweitzer. First printing, original to this anthology. Published by permission of the author, and the author's agent Dorian Literary Agency.

'The Gardens of Tantalus', © 1996 by Brian Stableford. First printing, original to this anthology. Published by permission of the author.

'The Favour of a Tyrant', © 1996 by Keith Taylor. First printing, original to this anthology. Published by permission of the author.

'The Poisoned Chalice', © 1996 by Peter Tremayne. First printing, original to this anthology. Published by permission of the author, and the author's agent, A.M. Heath & Co. Ltd.